TAINTED LOVE

D0532573

TAINTED LOVE

A novel by
Anna Chilvers

Bluemoose

Copyright © Anna Chilvers 2016

First published in 2016 by
Bluemoose Books Ltd
25 Sackville Street
Hebden Bridge
West Yorkshire
HX7 7DJ

www.bluemoosebooks.com

British Library Cataloguing-in-Publication data
A catalogue record for this book is available from the British Library

Paperback ISBN 978-1-910422-16-8

Printed and bound in the UK by Short Run Press

For Poppy and Izzy

Prologue

It was the end of the summer, a hot spell when the days burned up the grass on the hillside and the nights had us sweating in our stone houses as though they were stacks of glass boxes. I turned and turned, unable to sleep, and the cotton sheets stuck to my body and bound my legs. I thought of Peter sleeping in the open, of him and his dad night-running under the stars, creating coolness in their wake, a coolness that would have dissipated by the time the coffee was on and the bus passed the end of our street taking folk to work.

I wished I could run like Peter.

I closed my eyes and fell into an uneasy sleep.

In my sleep I was visited by a man and a boy. The boy was tall and good-looking, about my age or older. He sat on the end of my bed and looked at me, but said nothing.

The man roamed about the room. Neither seemed aware of the presence of the other. The man had brown trousers fastened with a belt and a short sleeved check shirt which only just stretched across his belly and left a triangle of exposed flesh. He seemed agitated.

I lay in bed and looked from one to the other.

'Who are you?' I said.

The boy still said nothing. His eyes were dark and glinted with reflections of the street light outside my window.

The man stopped next to my bed and stood over me. He said 'I just want you to know, it's not what I wanted. I didn't choose this.'

'What?' I was alarmed and struggled in to a sitting position. 'What are you talking about?'

'I'm your mother's nightmare. But it's not my choice or hers. If we could, we would separate. She would come back to you.'

'My mother?' I was fully awake now. 'What have you got to do with my mother? Why are you here?'

'She sends a message,' said the man. 'She wants you to know that she loves you.'

I leaped out of bed and flew at him, beating against his chest with my fists.

'Get out! Get out of my room. Get out of this house and don't ever come back.'

His chest was huge and solid and I felt like a child.

'I'm sorry,' he said. 'Truly.'

He turned and walked out of the room.

The boy hadn't moved.

'Well?' I said.

He smiled and I felt pain rush through me. I ran to the window and threw it open wide. In the garden the night stocks were trembling and the hawthorn tree whispered a warning.

I looked back and he had gone.

Part One

THE RETURN

1. Lauren

When I got home on the first day of term, Mr Lion was in the kitchen stuffing a chicken with chilli and apricots, and listening to Jackie Wilson. He'd dyed his mane black and straightened it, and strands kept falling across his face. The table was littered with bottles and jars – olive oil, tabasco, coriander seeds, black pepper, ginger, nutmegs, lemons and limes. When Mr Lion cooked, the dinner was never short on flavour. He had a mound of vegetables on the chair next to him. The mortar and pestle were stained red with juice from the chillies.

'Did you borrow my straighteners again?'

'Hi Lauren, good day at college?'

'You really should get your own, you know. Your mane is too wiry for mine. You'll burn them out.'

Mr Lion tossed his head and the silky hair fell black, heavy and long over his shoulder. He did look pretty cool. Jackie was singing *The Who Who Song*.

'What you cooking?'

'Roast chicken and vegetable stew. You want some?'

'Maybe. I'm going up to see Peter. Can I bring him back for dinner?'

Mr Lion snorted. 'If you can drag him down off those hills. I haven't seen him in town for months.'

'I know, he's getting worse. He's hardly been into town all summer. He was in college today, but he came in the back way from the woods. And he's started wearing a hat.'

'Poor lad. Yes, bring him down and we'll put a bit of fire in his belly. He can't hide in the woods forever.'

Hiding in the woods is what Peter does. I looked in the fridge and found a bowl of tuna and pepper salad.

'Can I eat this?'

'I don't know, it's Andy's not mine.'

'Dad won't mind.'

There were no clean forks in the cutlery drawer. I looked in the drainer on the sink.

'What time will dinner be?

I shovelled in a mouthful of tuna, pepper and mayonnaise. It was too cold, it could have done with half an hour out of the fridge first. But I really wanted to get up to Peter, so I ate it anyway. I'd kind of got used to the shoes he'd had made, although I didn't like them, but the hat was really bothering me.

'Seven thirty. If you're not here, we won't wait.'

'Don't worry. I'll be here, and so will Peter.'

Even though it was a hot day, it was cool in the woods. The trees littered their shadows across the path and the air danced with coins of sunlight. The woods here hang onto the sides of a steep valley, the trees holding tight with woody fingers to the constantly eroding soil. I followed the path which winds in halfway up the slope. In places it's crumbling and at one point a tiny stream crosses it, drawing at the edges and washing them down the hill. A couple of boulders pin the path down and make it possible to pass in winter when the stream has grown after rainfall. Today the stream was just a layer of shimmering sweat darkening the mud.

The path widens when you reach the old millpond. The water was still and the trees were silent, thick-leaved, keeping out the sunlight. There's a tiny path heading off to the left, barely noticeable, especially when the brambles have been growing. Like someone's drawn a stick through, and it hasn't quite closed back on itself yet. The sort of path animals make. This is Peter's path.

I first met Peter here in the woods when I was six years old. My dad and Mr Lion had decided to take me walking up on the tops and I didn't want to go. I was lagging behind, making a nuisance of myself in the hope that if we got off to a bad start they'd call it off. But they were used to my tactics. They strode ahead, knowing that as soon as they went out of sight and left me alone amongst the towering trees I'd run to catch up. This time, though, just as the panic grasped me, I heard something moving in the brambles and stopped to look.

Whatever it was stopped too. I stared at the thicket, peering between the leaves into the dark spaces underneath. Dad and Mr Lion were nowhere to be seen and the wood was full of a quiet stillness which teemed with non-human life. I could hear sap pushing against cell walls, leaves and stalks thrusting out from trees, from the ground, the hum of flowers turning to the sun. Insects swarmed in pools of sunlight. There were damp scurryings in the undergrowth. I felt very small.

'Is someone there?'

Speaking felt better – a normal, human sound. A question no one would answer because no one was there. I rocked back a little on my heels, ready to run off and find the grown ups.

But then someone did answer.

'Hello.'

I couldn't see anyone. There was no movement.

'Who's that?'

'Peter.'

'Who's Peter?'

'I am. Who are you?'

'I can't see you.'

'I'm hiding.'

'I'm Lauren. Come out here.'

There was a rustling, a sound which moved beneath the brambles. I tried to follow it with my eyes, but the leaves on the surface didn't move. Then suddenly he popped out on the path beside me.

We stared at each other. Then he touched my hair.

'Yellow,' he said.

'Why aren't you wearing any clothes?'

He looked down at himself as if he hadn't thought about it before.

'I don't need any.'

Just then my dad came walking back up the path, wondering why I was taking so long, and when he saw Peter he stopped. Slowly a smile spread across his face.

'Where's the old goat been hiding you then?' he said to Peter.

'This is Peter. Can he come with us, Dad? Please.'

'If he wants to.'

So Peter came with us on our walk, and I had more fun than I'd ever had. Peter knew where to find toads and beetles, the best places to cross the rushing streams, which trees were easy to climb, and how to hide even where nothing was growing. After that I played with him whenever I could. He didn't go to school back then and, same as me, he didn't have a mother. My Dad trusted me with Peter because he and his dad knew the woods and the hills better than anyone alive.

Above the bramble thickets at the top of the woods, the path ends where the stream comes out from under a big stone. I put my fingers in my mouth and blew three short blasts.

Then I sat on the stone and waited. The sun shone through a gap in the trees and I dangled my feet above the stream. The trees were singing quietly and the brambles were silent. Peter would come. Even if he was far away he would hear my whistle, and before long he would come. That's the way it always was.

Sometimes he liked to creep up on me, appearing suddenly at my side before I'd heard a thing. Today he came bounding down the hillside, his hooves barely touching the rocks and the grass, and flung himself down beside me. He wasn't wearing the hat now, nor shoes or trousers.

'Lauren!' he said in an outrush of breath.

And we kissed. The sun warmed our cheeks and I breathed his animal smell. The woods smelled of honeysuckle and wet stones.

'Why didn't you speak to me at college today?' I asked him when we stopped for breath.

He shifted his bum and looked down.

'I dunno. You were hanging around with that crowd. They're idiots.'

'They're not idiots. They're my friends.'

'Joel Wetherby wants to go out with you.'

'That doesn't make him an idiot, just because he likes me.' I shot a glance at him, but he was still looking at the floor. 'Maybe I will go out with him.'

'He calls me Goat Boy.'

I put my hands on Peter's head and smoothed back his hair. I could feel the bumps, the nub of them hard against my palms. When I parted his hair I could see the skin stretched tight. It wouldn't be long before they burst through.

'You're going to have to get used to it.'

'I am used to it. But why do I have to go to the stupid place anyway? Why can't I just stay here in the woods?'

I shook my head and kissed him on the nose. 'Mr Lion's cooking. Will you come back with me?'

Peter shrugged.

'Roast chicken. The kitchen smells amazing.'

'Maybe later, when it's dark.'

'No. Come back with me now and be a proper guest. Mr Lion's invited you.'

Peter put his hand on the back of my neck, wrapped my hair around his fingers and tugged gently. I could feel the tingles going through my body into my hands and feet. I stretched my palms.

'Soft as thistledown,' he said, 'and sunshine.'

'Say yes. Say you'll come.'

He put his other hand on my knee and started to slide it upwards. I pushed it back down.

'Peter! Say you'll come to eat with us.'

He put his lips right up close to my ear.

'Ok,' he whispered. 'I'll come.' I turned my head so my lips met his. 'But first come with me, there's something I want to show you.'

He took me up to Hough Dean. I hadn't been there in ages. When we were little we used to go and play in the deserted farm yard and dare each other to go inside the house. The door was nailed shut and most of the windows were boarded up, but there was a little one at the back which had been missed and the glass was broken. If you were careful you could get your hand in and lift the latch. Once the window was open there was room for a small person to squeeze through.

I'd got my body halfway in once but, just as I was about to wriggle my legs through, the smell hit me. It was thick and strong, like something rotting, and I gagged. You couldn't see anything in the dark, but there was no way I could breathe that air for even a minute. I pushed back out and nearly knocked Peter over.

Peter said it was probably bats. I wasn't going back in to check, and Peter didn't much like houses at the best of times.

The easiest way to get there is to take the mile-long track up from the Craggs car park, but that way you approach the farm straight on. Peter wanted to watch without being seen, so we went along the valley and climbed over the hill behind the farmhouse.

There was a van parked in the yard, and a black Porsche. The boards had been removed from the windows and the doors were open. There were a couple of men up ladders painting the newly stripped window frames, and the noise of a drill coming from inside.

'Someone's moving in?'

Just then a woman walked out of the house. She was wearing a red mini dress, black high heels and shades. Her hair was blonde and very expensive. She crossed the yard to the Porsche, opened the door and bent in, looking for something.

'Is that the new owner?

Peter nodded.

'Why would someone like that buy Hough Dean?'

'I dunno. They started work about a week ago. They're working really fast.'

The woman straightened up, a mobile in her hand. She dialled a number and leaned back against the hot black metal of the car, the phone to her ear.

'There's a boy too,' Peter said.

'What, a little boy?' It was hard to tell what age the woman might be from this distance.

'No. About our age. Maybe eighteen or twenty.'

'Anyone else?'

'No. I've only seen the two of them.

The lane up to the farm is full of potholes. I wondered how the Porsche managed it. The woman would have to get the track repaired.

'Another thing,' he said. 'I don't think she bought it. My dad always told me that the owners of this place had gone away, but that they'd return one day. I think she's the owner. I think she's come back.'

The woman finished her phone call and walked back across the yard into the house.

'Come on,' Peter nudged me. 'Let's go and have some of Mr Lion's chicken.'

As we got near to town Peter became quiet. When we reached the top of the stream, he asked me to wait while he fetched his clothes. He was gone for ten minutes and returned wearing a pair of jeans, a t-shirt and some trainers. I didn't say anything.

We walked down the hill holding hands, but Peter let go when we got to the square.

Joel Wetherby was there with a gang of his friends. He called out as we walked past. 'How do you keep those trainers on, Goat Boy, when you've got no feet?'

Peter didn't respond. He kept on walking.

I called back over my shoulder, 'Don't be a dick, Joel.'

They all started laughing, and I heard one of them say, 'You're in there, mate.'

We were just in time. Mr Lion was serving up the chicken and it smelled fantastic. Dad was home from work and we all sat around the kitchen table together to eat. Peter hadn't said anything about the lads in the square, and I didn't feel like bringing it up. I wish he would stand up for himself and answer back sometimes.

Mr Lion is a DJ. He plays Northern Soul nights at clubs all over the north of England and he has thousands of records. He's also a brilliant cook. He could be a chef in a really swanky restaurant, probably have his own TV show and everything. But most of the time he can't be bothered, so when he decides to make something it's just us that get to eat it. Me and my dad and anyone else who happens to be visiting. Today he'd excelled himself. You'd think a roast chicken was just a roast chicken, but Mr Lion can create magic. It was so good that we all forgot to talk and just concentrated on eating.

After, when the dishes were cleared away, Dad got a bottle of wine out and poured us all a glass. Mr Lion lit a fag and his little white dog, Beauty, curled up in his lap.

I said, 'We went up to Hough Dean. There's someone moving in.'

Dad and Mr Lion both seemed to freeze. Then Mr Lion lowered his arm and tapped his ash in the ash tray. Dad took a sip from his wine glass like he was trying to look normal, but his arm and his face were as stiff as a puppet's.

'Are you sure?' asked Mr Lion.

'Yes. A blonde woman with a Porsche. Looks like she's loaded.'

'Meg,' said Dad. His wine glass wobbled and he put it on the table.

'Who's Meg?' I said

Mr Lion took another drag on his cigarette. 'How old did she look, this woman?'

I shrugged. 'Thirty maybe. Forty. We weren't very near.'

'Well, probably best to leave her be. She won't want kids hanging around bothering her.'

'We weren't hanging about. We were up the hill. She couldn't see us.'

Dad said, 'Just keep away.'

'What was that all about?' I said to Peter when we were up in my room. .

'They were pretty freaked.'

'Maybe she's an evil witch who used to catch children and roast them in the oven.'

'Or turn them into toads.'

I turned the computer on.

'I've got homework. Can you believe on the first day back they've given us homework?'

'Maybe she's your mother.'

I laughed and typed in my password. 'My mum's called Cassie.'

Peter sat behind me rubbing my back.

'Peter.'

'Yes.'

'Will you walk home from school with me tomorrow?'

His hands stilled for a moment and I could hear him breathing. Then they started moving again, and he said, 'Ok.' His voice was light as though it was of little consequence. 'I've got physics last thing, so let's meet in the normal place.'

The normal place was where we used to meet after school every day back when we were in Year Seven and Eight. Before Peter started getting embarrassed in front of other kids and sloping off on his own every afternoon. It was just down the lane from the sixth form college, where the path starts up through the woods over the hillside. I was there on time, but Peter wasn't. On one side of the path there were trees and mossy boulders, and on the other, the sewage plant with its round concrete pits silently stinking in the sunshine. At the spot where Peter should have been waiting there was somebody else. He was wearing a black trenchcoat, despite the September warmth.

He turned and I saw who he was – recognised the sunglasses he'd been wearing earlier.

'Hi,' I said when I got near enough.

'Hello.'

He stepped back to let me past, but I stopped and leaned against the tree.

'I'm meeting somebody here,' I said.

'Oh, right.'

Not being able to see his eyes, I couldn't tell if he was put out by this. The glasses were very dark.

'You were in the library,' he said. His accent was odd. A bit posh, slightly foreign maybe, but I thought I could detect a hint of Yorkshire in there too.

'I'm Lauren.'

'Richard.'

He held out his hand and I shook it, grinning. Was he for real? He was wearing black fingerless gloves.

'Who are you meeting?' he asked.

'My boyfriend.'

'Oh.'

The sun was full on the path at this time of day and I leaned my head against the trunk of the tree, which was humming softly in the warmth. I half closed my eyes, and watched him.

He shifted from foot to foot, looking about. I wondered if he was waiting for someone too.

'Where does this lead to?' he asked, nodding towards the path into the woods.

'Up to the tops. If you walk across the fields up there you get to Heath. From there you can drop down into Hawden. It's a nice walk.'

'I'm just trying to get my bearings. It's all changed since I was here.'

'Did you live here before?'

He frowned and half turned away. It was a moment before he answered. 'When I was younger.'

I waited, but he didn't say any more. I'd already thought he might be the boy from Hough Dean, but now I was certain. His stance didn't invite questions.

'What's with the shades?'

He turned and looked at me. 'What about them?'

'You were wearing them in the library at college. How come Miss Watts didn't tell you to take them off?'

'It's an eye condition.' I couldn't see his eyes through the dark glass, only my own reflection repeated in each lens, the trees behind me. 'My eyes are sensitive to light. These glasses react to light conditions: they get darker as the light gets brighter.'

'Right. So that's why they're so dark right now. Because of the sunshine.'

'Yes.'

He turned away again, stared into the woods.

'Are you waiting for someone?' I asked him.

'No.'

He shoved his hands into his pockets and walked a few steps up the path, hesitated, then came back again.

'Are you going that way? When your boyfriend gets here.'

'Yes.'

'Will you show me the way?'

My phone went off just then. It was a text from Peter, saying he was staying behind to finish off a physics experiment and he'd catch up with me later. I stared at the message wondering what to say. I could make an excuse, say Peter had changed the plans and I was meeting him somewhere else. But what the hell? If Peter couldn't make the effort... and Richard didn't know anyone here. It couldn't hurt to be friendly.

'It looks like Peter's not coming. I can show you the way if you like, though it's not difficult. There's only one path.'

He smiled for the first time. I wished I could see his eyes.

He was a fast walker. For some reason this surprised me. Something about his clothes, his voice, and also his nervousness about the path, had made him a city boy in my eyes. I didn't imagine he was used to walking through woods, up hillsides. I thought I would have to slow my pace to his. But it was the other way round. By the time we reached the top of the tree line I was sweating and breathless.

He stopped next to a big rock at the side of the path.

'God, it's the Milkmaid,' he said. 'She has a different view these days.'

I looked at the stone then back at him.

'What are you talking about?'

'This rock, the Milkmaid. Don't you know the story?'

I shook my head.

'There was a milkmaid and her lover cheated on her, so she turned herself into stone. She stood here watching the valley, watching her lover and his new girl. He could never do a thing for the rest of his life without feeling her gaze upon him, her judgement. In the end he went mad and drowned himself in the mill pond. When he was gone, she turned her attention to other cheating lovers. If anyone in the village is ever unfaithful, they can expect to feel the eyes of the milkmaid watching their every move.'

I wondered if he had made it up on the spot. I'd never heard that story before and I'd lived here all my life. I walked around the stone. I guess if you used your imagination, squinted a bit, you could just about make it into the shape of a girl carrying a pail in each hand. A solid, lumpen girl with no features.

'Where did you get that from?'

He shrugged and seemed to lose interest. 'I dunno. Someone told it to me when I was a kid I expect.'

He started off along the path again. The bracken whispered as we passed, but I didn't listen. I was almost jogging to keep up. When we reached the place where the stream crosses, he didn't bother with the stepping stones but leapt over in one jump. I thought he must be really fit. I tried to imagine him in shorts and a t-shirt, running shoes, but my imagination failed me.

At the top of the hill he stopped again and took a packet of fags from his coat pocket. He offered me one but I shook my head.

'Aren't you hot in that coat?'

'I'm used to it,' was all he said. Which seemed like a ridiculous answer to me. Why be used to being uncomfortable?

He lit his fag with a match and took a deep drag. The sky reflected in his sunglasses, made them blue.

'The land doesn't change,' he said. 'The shape of it. It's been the same for hundreds of years.'

'How old were you when you left?' I asked.

'I was very young.'

Which is what he said before, but how young? Did he used to come up here on his own? If so, he can't have been that tiny. But if he'd been old enough to go to school I would surely have met him. I wondered if he was being deliberately enigmatic. I hadn't really got the patience for that. If he wanted to impress some girl by being mysterious then he'd picked the wrong one.

He finished his fag and crushed it out under his boot.

'I'm going down the hill from here,' I said. 'The quickest way to Hough Dean is if you carry on along the top and drop down when you get to the other end of Heath.'

He raised an eyebrow, and I realised he'd never said he was from Hough Dean.

'Thanks,' he said. 'I remember the way from here. Sure you don't want a fag?'

It was his way of saying thank you, but I don't smoke, so I shook my head again.

'You're alright. Thanks.'

On the way down the hill I looked up a couple of times to see if I could spot him striding along the top, but I never did.

2. Peter

When they were kids, the woods, the moors and the sky were everything they wanted. If they found a crop of blackberries or St. George's mushrooms or wild garlic, they felt like they'd struck gold. Now those things weren't enough. Peter didn't know what she wanted any more.

He adjusted the polariser to nought degrees and took the first power reading.

She was interested in books and history. When he looked at the block of words on the page he saw tiny black stitches fastening his soul to the earth. He wanted to rear and snort. Run like a goat. She talked to him about people who used to live and breathe but were now just names, stories, dust. Most of them got things wrong. All through history people had been making mistakes and hurting each other.

He felt safe here in the lab. This made sense. He turned the dial to ten degrees, twenty, noting the power reading at each stage. At ninety degrees the light disappeared. He loved that. He could use Malus's formula to predict the polarisation and then watch it happen. He'd shown her sunlight shining through a prism, dividing into the seven colours of the rainbow, told her how the spectrum continued beyond those things we can see.

'Our eyes are only tuned to certain frequencies, but there's more, much more in the world if only we knew how to look.'

She smiled at him. The colours lay across her pale skin, her golden hair, turning her red, indigo and violet.

'You're such a geek, Peter,' she said.

3. Ali

I couldn't believe the bloody view out of the window. Stone bridge, river, ducks, a green hill rising behind the town, tended flower beds. There were cobbled streets for fuck's sake. Even the people were bearded, be-hatted and grizzled in their wellies and flowered skirts. I shouldn't have come here. I was a city girl and this picture-book England made me sick. There was probably even a shop called the Olde Worlde Something Shoppe. It's the sort of place you'd want to come to with a machine gun. And so tiny. I'd only been there two hours and I'd probably walked every street. How could you get lost in a place like that? How could you hide?

The coffee was all right though. Fuck, I needed it. I hadn't slept for over thirty-two hours, and then it wasn't for long. I'd gone to bed around midnight, and it was just after two when the police came banging on the door downstairs and I had to grab my stuff and get out the back window as quickly as I could. There's a jump from the first floor window down to the old garage roof, which is none too steady, but it was that or a night in the cells. 'Cos, even though it's not me they want, they'd throw us all in the slammer for the night. They think we're all addicts and it's really cool to keep us away from our stuff, stress us out for a while. I'm not an addict. I've tried most stuff, and sometimes a white-out is what the doctor ordered. But I can take it or leave it. Not like some of the others.

It was Smith they were after. Last night he and Jeannie were out the window and gone before I'd even worked out what the noise was. Some of the others were doped up and took a bit longer, but they were all away before the police decided to break the door down. The way it works, everyone lays low for a few days, then we start creeping back to the squat one by one. If the police have caught Smith by then, they leave us alone. But if he comes back so do they, every night until they catch him or give up. They never keep him for long.

I went down to the arches. There were always a few people hanging around there. New kids who'd arrived in Leeds with a sleeping bag and couldn't think of anywhere better to curl up than fifty yards from the station they'd come in at. And some nutters too, who no one would have living in a squat with them. Someone would have a bottle of vodka I could share, or something else to keep me awake through the night. The next morning I'd go up to the square and find someone who'd let me have a corner for a night or two until it was safe to go back to the squat.

That was the plan. I was on my way down there, quite pleased with myself for getting out so quickly, carrying all my stuff in my back pack. I don't own much – a spare pair of jeans and a couple of t-shirts, a toothbrush. Usually a book that I've picked up somewhere. And my gran's ring which I wear on a piece of leather around my neck, under my clothes so no one can see. Walking down to the arches, I put my hand into the neck of my shirt and I realised it was gone. That's when the shit kicked off.

Now I was sitting in this cosy fucking café in Cutesville, West Yorkshire, with a cup of rocket-strength coffee and no idea what to do next. I couldn't see the locals letting people sleep under bridges round here. Anyway, there was only fucking water under all the bridges I'd seen. I may have slept in some unsavoury places in my time, but I didn't fancy a raging river.

There wouldn't be any squats. Probably no homeless people at all. Here everyone would be accounted for and wrapped up soundly in their beds by ten thirty. Maybe I could sleep in the park, in one of those flowerbeds covered with bark chippings; it might be quite cosy if it doesn't rain.

Two women were sitting by the window gossiping about people going by in the street. They knew all their names. It reminded me of when I was a kid. When we went out shopping my mum knew everyone she saw, stopped and chatted on street corners. That's what I love about cities, no one knows you. Often as not, no one even sees you.

These two were shameless.

'Look, there's Sally Lumb. I haven't seen her in ages.'

'That's because you're never out this early. I often see her when I drop the kids off at school.'

'I don't know how she manages, living up there on her own. It must be so lonely. I'd be scared stiff. There's no streetlights or anything. It must be pitch black at night.'

'I don't think Sally is the nervous type. Not about things like that. She'd be much more bothered by neighbours dropping in. I think she just wants to be left alone.'

'I walked past Old Barn a couple of weeks ago. We'd been for a walk up on the tops. All those outbuildings as well as the enormous house, just for her! It's the sort of place a family should live in.'

Nosy cows. I looked out of the window and saw a woman leaving the butchers. She stopped outside, took her pack off her back and opened it to put in the parcel she'd just bought. She was wearing denim dungarees, a dirty anorak and a red cap which looked like it came from a Dickens film.

'I don't know why she doesn't get a bike. It's a long slog up to Old Barn carrying your shopping.'

'At least she doesn't drive everywhere, like you.'

The woman slung the pack onto her back and walked off down the street. My coffee was just about gone. I slipped out of my seat and down the stairs and when I got outside the woman was just turning right into the main street.

She was easy to follow. I left a distance, but her red hat stood out. When she went into the health food shop I stopped and looked in the window of the bookshop. It was tiny. I couldn't see it being very easy to nick books in there. I'd have to find the library and see if that was any better.

The woman's back pack looked heavy when she came out. She'd finished shopping and she headed out of town, crossed at some lights and walked up a hill past a church. The road was steep and she walked fast. Even though I wasn't carrying the weight she was, it was hard to keep up.

At the top of the hill the road bent to the left and there was no sign of her. There were rows of stone terraces on both sides, with pots of flowers by the doors and no gardens. She could have gone into one of them, but I didn't think so, not from what those women in the café said. There was a track on the right, potholed and full of puddles, leading off into some woods. I hurried up it. After a few minutes I could see her red hat up ahead, appearing every now and then through the branches of the trees.

We kept going up. On the right there was a drop down to the river in the valley bottom, and it got steeper and steeper. I wondered what would happen if you slipped and fell down there, if the roots and shrubs would save you or if they would scratch and gouge at you as you fell to your death.

We passed a couple of houses with 4x4s parked outside, and a dog rushed out barking. I like dogs, but I didn't stop to talk to it as Sally Lumb was speeding ahead. The trees were thick further up and I couldn't see her any more.

Then the track split. One fork went down to the river, over a bridge where there were a couple more houses. The other went up through the trees. I thought I'd be able to see her if she'd gone down to the river, so I kept going up.

After about ten minutes I came out above the woods onto open hillside. I could see her ahead. She'd left the track and was heading across a field towards a farmhouse. I sat down by the wall and waited. I was breathing hard. That was a steep fucking climb.

The sun was shining and it was quite warm. I got my book out of my bag and read for a bit. Now I knew where the house was there was no rush. Best to wait 'til dark and she was tucked up inside her house, then I'd go and have a good explore, find a cosy spot in a barn. If anyone came to Hawden looking for me, they weren't going to find me up here.

I'd read about ten pages when I looked up and she was standing there in front of me.

'Hi,' she said.

'Hi.'

She was wearing muddy walking boots and she'd taken off her anorak.

'I'm making some lunch. Do you want to come in?'

I stared at her.

'I know you've followed me up here. I don't know if you want to steal from me, or what you're after. But it's a steep walk and you must be hungry. Come in and have some food and we can talk about it.'

She was smiling. She didn't look scared. And for some reason I didn't think she was about to phone the police. What harm could it do?

I smiled back at her and it felt weird.

'Ok,' I said.

She'd made soup and it had some sort of meat in it, and other bits too. I poked at them with my spoon.

'It's mutton broth, with barley and lentils.'

I took a spoonful and it tasted fantastic. My gran used to cook – I mean really cook, from things she chopped up and did stuff to. Not like my mum. My mum's idea of cooking was to open the packet and put the contents in the oven. The only soup we ever had came out of tins.

They gave me a sandwich at the police station, but that's all I'd eaten since leaving the squat. I hadn't had time to think about food. Though with the money I had, I could have had a slap-up meal. Could have had breakfast at that café. I didn't think of that. I finished the bowl of soup and she ladled some more in, giving me bread and butter to go with it.

'My name's Sally,' she said.

'Ali,' I said through a mouthful of bread.

She laughed. 'We rhyme.'

'I wasn't going to steal from you.'

She didn't answer. Just looked at me as she ate her soup.

'I need somewhere to stay. I was going to sleep in your barn.'

Still nothing. But she didn't take her eyes off me. I wondered how she did that, eat soup without looking at it. I'm sure I'd spill it or miss the bowl or something.

'I suppose I might have stolen some food. But only what I need. Not money or anything.'

'Have you run away from home?'

This time I laughed. 'Home! No, I haven't got a home. I left that years ago.'

'But you want somewhere to hide.'

'Yes. I guess I do.' She probably thought I was on the run from the police. I almost wished I was.

We both finished our soup and I waited. I didn't want to tell her any more. She stacked the bowls and took them over to the sink, put the bread back in the bread bin, the butter in the fridge. Then she lit the stove and put the kettle on, took cups out of the cupboard.

When the tea was made she put a mug in front of me and sat back down at the table.

'Ok,' she said. 'You can stay here. But there's no need to sleep in the barn, there are lots of spare bedrooms.'

The house was enormous – there were five bedrooms including hers. They all had beds in, carpets and curtains, furniture. More people must have lived here once. She let me choose my own room and I chose one at the front of the house with a window facing out onto the valley. You could see the track, and you'd see anyone coming as soon as they left the cover of the trees.

I'd landed on my feet. How good was this? Maybe she'd want me to earn my keep – do some work about the place or something. But I didn't mind that. It was so out of the way, no one was going to find me here.

It was when I went to the bathroom that that things started to seem a bit weird. I asked her where the loo was and she sent me upstairs.

There was a piece of string tied up above the bath, like a little washing line. And tied to it a whole row of tampons, tied on by their string. About twenty or so, and they'd all been used. The first ones hadn't got much blood on, only patches. But they got darker and bloodier along the line, until those in the middle were fat and bloated and had blood right up the string. Then they got lighter again, and more brown. The bathroom smelled of old seaweed.

When I went downstairs she didn't say anything about them and neither did I.

I remembered taking the ring off. I sleep on my front and the stone was digging into me. If I've had a lot to drink or I'm stoned I don't always bother, but that night I was sober and straight and I put the ring on the floor at the side of my mattress before I went to sleep. You might think when the police came knocking on the door downstairs I was in such a hurry I just forgot. But that's not the case. Gran's ring is the first thing I put on when I wake up. The reason I didn't this time is because someone had taken it. And the only people to come through my room and out the window before I got out myself were Smith and Jeannie.

Down at the arches I sat with a group of winos and had a swig from the bottle they were handing round. When there was a police raid there were unspoken rules. We kept apart and said nothing, even if the police caught us. We left it a few days before we returned to the squat. Most of all, we denied all knowledge of Smith – not just his business, but his very existence. And if shit kicked off for us, we could expect Smith to do the same.

But this was different. This was something outside of squatters' rules. I used to go and see Gran every day after school until she died when I was twelve. She gave me this ring herself. She probably knew that if she put it in her will then mum would never let me keep it. It was her engagement ring and it had real diamonds and sapphires in it. It was worth money. It was also beautiful. I couldn't see Smith taking it. I think Jeannie saw it as they dashed past and found it irresistible.

There was this straight guy Smith knew from when he was at school. Worked in an office, had a car and a girlfriend. Every now and then he and Smith met up and got drunk together. I saw them once, when Smith was hiding out. He was scrubbed up, wearing the other guy's jeans and a jumper he'd never normally be seen dead in. He could have walked right past the police and they'd've not looked twice. He was hiding out in full daylight.

The guy had a place out near the university.

It got light pretty early although summer was nearly over. It was the best time in the city, when everyone was still asleep: no one about, just the street cleaners with their trucks. You could walk in the middle of the road, even the main roads. The few cars were going north, south, hoping to reach their destinations by breakfast time. This city was just part of their early morning dream. Later on, they'd look back at it, barely remember passing through, wonder if the ring road bypassed the city completely.

I walked up through the streets to the area around the university. Watched the day as it began to wake up. First a few joggers and dog walkers. Then people started to leave for work, just a few to begin with. No students yet. They would appear later, in a mad scramble to get to lectures on time with clothes askew, bags dangling, books, pens and coffee.

Smith's friend wasn't a student.

I knew where he lived. When I saw him with Smith that time, I followed them. You never know when that sort of information might be useful. There was a boy delivering papers and he shoved a copy of *The Guardian* through the guy's letterbox. A few minutes later someone pulled it through.

I hung about for a bit, wondering what to do, but decided that upfront was the best way. When the paper boy had left the street I went up and knocked on the front door.

A woman answered, dressed ready for work in smart grey trousers, shiny black shoes, navy jumper. She was Asian, with long straight black hair and a stud in her nose. Really beautiful.

'Hiya, are Smith and Jeannie here? I need to talk to them.'

There were tell-tale smudges under her eyes, suggesting a night of lost sleep, but she was good at hiding it. Didn't flicker.

'I'm sorry, I think you've got the wrong address.'

The straight guy appeared behind her in the hallway, a piece of half-eaten toast in his hand.

'Is there a problem?'

'This girl, she's looking for someone...'

'Smith and Jeannie. I know they're here. I just need to talk to them for a minute. Only a minute, then I'll go away. Promise.'

The man shook his head. 'I don't know what you're talking about.'

'Come on, man. I know they're here. I'm not the police. I only need a moment.'

The woman spoke again. 'Look, we're very sorry. Your friends aren't here. There must be a mistake. We don't know anyone like...' She looked me up and down, making her meaning obvious. 'We're running late and need to get on. I'm sorry.'

She started to close the door, but I stuck my foot out.

'They have something of mine. It's a misunderstanding, they wouldn't have taken it if they knew. But I need it back.'

'Please will you remove your foot?'

'Just let me speak to them.'

The man said 'If you don't leave immediately we will be forced to call the police.'

I laughed. 'You won't be calling no police. Not when you've got that pair stashed inside.'

He pulled a phone out of his jacket pocket and held it poised like a weapon.

'Get away from our door now or I will call the police. What will it be?'

For the first time, I doubted. Maybe they had them hidden away somewhere else. I could be banged up for harassment or something, and there'd be no chance of getting the ring back.

'Ok,' I said. 'I'll go now, but I'll be back. Like I said, I just want my property back.'

I moved my foot and the woman slammed the door in my face.

I opened my eyes and saw flowers. Closed them again. I was in bed but I had all my clothes on and it was really warm. The sun was shining right on my head, I could feel it. I opened my eyes again. The flowers were on wallpaper. It came back to me. Sally's house, Old Barn. This was my new bedroom.

But when I went to sleep the sun wasn't shining through the window. I threw off the covers. The curtains were thin cotton and didn't fit the window very well, so the sun could get through them and round the edges too. I pulled them back and look out. It looked different. I couldn't quite work out what it was, but supposed it must be the sun making everything look fresher and brighter.

When I went downstairs I realised it was because it was morning. I went up for a nap yesterday after lunch and the sun was behind the house, casting shadows across the fields. I had slept right through, afternoon, evening, night and now it was the next day and the sun was shining from the other side of the valley.

'Good morning.' Sally was in the kitchen with her sleeves rolled up. Her arms were in a big bowl next to the sink.

'Sorry. I must have been beat.'

29

'You look refreshed. You have colour in your cheeks.'

I put my hands to my face, not sure what to say.

'Would you like some coffee and toast?'

I nodded.

The coffee was made from fresh beans that Sally had ground herself, and the toast was rye bread. I ate it with butter and ginger marmalade. I'd not eaten food like this since Gran died.

Sally went back to the bowl by the sink. I couldn't see over the rim, but it sounded like there was water in it. From the way her arms moved, squeezing and kneading, I thought she was washing something.

'Yesterday I wondered if you were running away from love,' she said after a minute.

'Maybe I am.'

'No. Whatever's the matter with you, food and sleep are working wonders. You look like a different person.'

I didn't know what she was on about, so I stuffed more toast and marmalade into my mouth and kept chewing.

'You're a very pretty girl. Lost love takes all your colour away, and no amount of sleep can bring it back.'

She was quite pale. I supposed someone must have dumped her and she hadn't got over it. Confused it with anaemia.

'What are you doing in that bowl?'

'It's time to feed the roses,' she said.

I went over and looked in the bowl and nearly spat my toast back out again.

They were in there, all those tampons from the upstairs bathroom, and she was squeezing them in the water, which was getting redder and redder.

I could smell it now as well.

'Love takes away all your colour, but I like to give some back to my roses. I don't want them to start fading like me.'

I watched fascinated as she took the tampons out of the water one at a time, squeezing them hard over the bowl before dropping them in the bin.

'Come and see,' she said when she'd finished.

I followed her out of the back door. The garden went back a long way, and I could see trellises and rows of vegetables further away from the house. But this bottom bit, the nearest bit, was a rose garden. There were beds around the edges, and a round one in the middle, all crammed with rose bushes. I don't know anything about that sort of thing, but they looked pretty well looked after, neat, bushy, healthy. They were all covered in red blooms – no other colours, just red. And the smell of the bloody water disappeared into the sweet smell of thousands of flowers in the sunshine.

Sally carefully poured the contents of the bowl into a watering can, then she started watering all the rose bushes with her menstrual blood.

'If you're going to stay for a bit, maybe you'd like to help with the garden,' she said.

And I thought, no bloody way am I helping with that.

4. Lauren

I was still thinking about Richard when I got home and found Peter and Suky in the kitchen. They had their backs to me and didn't notice me straight away. Peter had taken off his college clothes, and his hair was silver in the afternoon sunshine. I loved the silkiness of his summer coat nearly as much as the dark, thick underfur which came though in the winter months. He was wearing a white t-shirt and laughing with Suky. The sound made me think of high pastures and long evenings when the light dwindles, slowly painting everything with shadows, and of coming home with the warmth of the sun carried in your skin. Then I remembered Richard's heavy black coat and dark sunglasses, blocking out the light and creating a different kind of warmth. My home seemed suddenly less familiar.

Suky saw me first.

'Hi Lauren, just the person we need. Taste this and tell me if it needs more sugar.'

She held out a cup of purple liquid she'd taken from the pan on the stove. Bilberry cordial, steaming hot.

'Peter thinks it needs to be sweeter, but that's just his childish sweet tooth. Tell me it's fine.'

I took a sip. It was hot and sharp – almost enough to make you wince, but not quite.

'It's fine. No more sugar.'

'See,' she said to Peter, 'you have to grow up, you have childish tastes.'

Peter smiled too, but he wasn't looking at Suky, he was trying to catch my eye.

'Lauren, I'm really sorry about earlier. The experiment took longer than we thought. I caught the bus so I'd get here at the same time as you.'

'The school bus?'

He nodded and held my gaze.

The last time Peter caught the school bus was more than two years ago. I was with him. It's always crowded on that bus and everyone has to squash up together in the aisles.

Some kid next to us trod on his boot and said 'Sorry, did that hurt? – Oh no, of course, you haven't got any toes have you?', and the other kids around all started sniggering. Peter didn't say anything, but he hasn't caught the bus since.

I relented and smiled at him. 'Sorry, I walked over the tops, so you beat me to it.'

There were four glass bottles standing in a bowl of hot water in the sink. Suky started emptying them out and drying them.

'Why are you doing that here, Suky?' I said. 'Is it for us?'

'Yes. Mr Lion called and said he had a whole freezer load from earlier in the summer, and would I make it into cordial. I thought rather than lugging the berries across town, then the bottles back after, I may as well do it here. That way I get to use Mr Lion's fantastic pans as well.'

'Is he here?'

'He's out walking Beauty at the moment.'

I sat down at the table and took an apple from the fruit bowl. While I ate it, Peter helped Suky pour the hot cordial into the bottles. The sun fell across the room, cut into squares by the lines of the window frame. When I closed my eyes the inside of my lids were bright orange.

'I met that boy from Hough Dean on the way home.'

Peter and Suky both looked up at me.

'What's he like?' asked Peter

I shrugged. 'Ok, a bit moody maybe. He wears a big black coat and shades all the time, like he thinks he's really cool. Says it's an eye condition.'

'Have they moved in already?' asked Peter

'Dunno. I didn't ask him. He walked back that way though.'

'Jimmy's working up there at the moment,' said Suky. 'They're having a new bathroom and a new kitchen, and putting in an en suite. He's been there all week – probably next week too.'

'What's it like?' I asked, and Peter said 'What're they like?' at exactly the same time.

Suky laughed.

'God, you two! What're you like? I don't know, but I might go up there tomorrow evening to pick Jimmy up. You can come with me if you want.'

Jimmy is Suky's boyfriend and my oldest friend.

Back when I was a baby, when my mother left and me and Dad moved in with Mr Lion, Jimmy used to come round all the time. He was twelve years old then and he was learning fire-eating and he came round to practice. Not that Mr Lion knew anything much about fire-eating, but he'd hung around that sort of stuff a lot in the past, and it didn't make him nervous like it did Jimmy's mum. He used to let Jimmy practice in the back yard.

Mr Lion would make a batch of almond cookies. They were Jimmy's favourites. By the time the cookies were mixed, baked in the oven in two batches, then cooled for half an hour on a wire tray, Jimmy would find he'd done just about enough practice, and he'd come and sit with us in the kitchen and someone would brew a pot of tea.

The thing about Jimmy is that hot air passes through his mouth in both directions, and always has done. He practiced fire-eating every day until he became world class at it. I really mean world class: he spends half the year travelling all over Europe – sometimes further – with the top circus performers. His stage name is Pyrotastic. But the hot air, it's not a one way passage: it comes back out again. I never known anyone who talked as much as Jimmy.

He talked to Mr Lion and my dad of course, but sometimes they were busy doing stuff and Jimmy was left alone with me. So while I sat in my baby chair or crawled around on the floor with bricks and board books he talked to me and, because I couldn't say anything back and he thought I probably didn't understand, he'd tell me things he'd not tell anyone else. About the girls at school he fancied and the worry about his mum who he thought was dying. Back then, when I was crawling around on the carpet, it washed over me. But it became a habit for him, and as I grew older he kept on telling me his secrets, until I was six, eight, twelve, the sole recipient of the details of his love life, his mother's slow and lingering death, his self doubt, his triumphs. It became an essential part of life for both of us.

He met Suky when he went on a circus tour of Eastern Europe three years ago. She was part of the troupe as well, a trapeze artist from Kent. The night he first set eyes on her he texted me saying he'd met the love of his life. It was love at first sight for both of them. After the tour Suky moved up here with him straight away, and he's not looked at another woman since. Which is saying something for Jimmy, because before he met Suky he looked at lots of women and mostly didn't stick to looking if he could help it, and it got him into a fair bit of trouble.

Now he'd only go on tour if Suky was in the same troupe. When he wasn't away, he worked as a plumber for a local business, and that's what he was doing up at Hough Dean.

Later, when Peter had left and I wished he hadn't, when I was lying on my bed and my fingers could still feel the soft hair on his haunches and my lips still felt bruised from his kisses, I decided to phone Jimmy. It might have been different if I had a mother. When I'm down or confused I might talk to her. But then again, Peter's my boyfriend, and I'm sure there are things you don't talk to your mother about.

Jimmy was full of good common sense.

'Laurie love, you're only seventeen, you've got all the time in the world. He's a lovely lad, but you can see how it is for him. He wants to be sure that's what you want. He knows he's different.'

I groaned. 'God, we all know that. He won't let us forget it. How many times do I have to tell him it's him I want?'

'And in your house, under the same roof as your dad. That might make him feel a bit uncomfortable. Maybe if you were somewhere else, a bit more neutral.'

'What, like your place?'

'No. You're not using our flat as your shag pad. I'd never be able to look your dad in the eye again. Or Mr Lion. No, I meant somewhere else – his sort of place – out in the open.'

'Hmm, maybe. But it would have to be soon. Summer's nearly over.'

'Well, just stop waiting for him, Laurie. You'll have to make the first move.'

'Ok, Jimmy, I will. I promise.' I picked up a pencil and drew a circle on my knee. 'Suky was round today.'

'Was she?'

I wondered if I detected something odd in Jimmy's voice.

'She said you're working up at Hough Dean.'

'Oh, yeah, I am. Is that what she came round for?'

'No. She was making some cordial for Mr Lion.

'Oh.'

'So, what's it like?'

'The cordial?'

'No, idiot! Hough Dean. What's it like at Hough Dean?'

'Oh right! It's a bit of a mess at the moment. But it will be something special when it's finished.'

'What about the people – the owners?'

'Hardly see them. The woman comes and looks sometimes to see how it's going. She's a bit weird – never takes off her sunglasses. Nice bum though.'

'What about her son?'

'I've never seen him. He's either out or he's in his room. Not one for socialising.'

'I've met him.'

'You know him?'

I laughed. 'No. Not really. He seems interesting though.'

'Does he now? Should I warn Peter?'

'No, not like that. But I think he's travelled a lot. There's no one else around here like him.'

'I think I will warn Peter.'

'Watch it Jimmy, or I'll tell Suky you think his mum has a nice bum.'

The next day Peter went running after college with his dad, so just me and Suky went up to Hough Dean. I went round to their place after I'd dropped off my stuff at home.

Suky was still in the kitchen finishing off some jam. If you work half the year in the circus, you have to find something else to do the rest of the year. Suky had set up her own business making jam and cordials, the sort you find in little shops with fancy labels on. She was doing quite well. I helped her pour the jam into the waiting jars, then she covered them with muslin to keep off flies while they cooled down, and we got in her van and set off to Hough Dean.

Suky and Jimmy are quite alike. They both talk a lot. I sometimes wonder if either of them ever shuts up for long enough to listen to the other. They're always laughing and don't take anything in life that seriously, other than performance and each other. But as we drove through town Suky was silent, and on the lane up to the Craggs she still hadn't said anything.

'You ok, Suky?'

She let out a long juddering sigh, and I realised how tense her shoulders had been. Then she pulled over to the side of the road, stopped the van and put her face in her hands.

'Oh Lauren, I think Jimmy's seeing another woman.'

'Don't be silly.'

That slipped out of my mouth before I could stop myself. But it did seem ridiculous. I mean, before Jimmy met Suky, he was always looking for the right girl. Girls liked Jimmy. He was funny and good looking and the fire-eating gave him an edge of danger. Jimmy liked girls in the same way that a child likes sweets, they tasted good and made him feel happy. But I knew, because he told me, that every time, with every new girl, he hoped she would be The One. He wanted to fall in love and settle down. And when they turned out to be just a momentary pleasure followed by a sugar rush and the vague queasiness of over indulgence, he would vow to stop playing the field. He'd tell me that that was it, he was going to keep himself pure now, stop picking in the sweet shop and wait for the girl of his dreams to come along. He never doubted that she would.

So when he met Suky, and they loved each other, he wasn't surprised, but felt he'd reached a milestone. He grew up. His sweet shop days were behind him. I listened to him for hours on end telling me how perfect Suky was, how no other woman he'd ever met could match her, how happy she made him, how he would walk through fire as well as eat it for her. There was no way I believed he would jeopardise that.

I was about to say something of this to Suky when I remembered how Jimmy had been on the phone last night, and I said instead, 'Sorry. Why do you think so?'

And she told me how he had started coming back late sometimes when he'd been out for a drink with his friends. Not that often, maybe once or twice a month. Five or six times altogether. He'd creep back into the house long after the pubs were closed. She'd pretend to be asleep and he'd slip into bed beside her, and she thought she could smell something on him. Not as strong as perfume, but perhaps shampoo or body lotion. In the morning when she asked him, he'd lie about the time he'd got in – say he'd stayed for a last one after closing time. He'd be a bit cagey over breakfast, keen to get off to work. By the time he got home at the end of the day he was back to normal.

The first couple of times she'd relaxed, decided to believe him. Explain it away with a lock-in at the pub and air freshener in the pub toilets.

But it had happened again, the night before last, and she couldn't really believe that the White Horse had regular lock-ins midweek, and having sniffed it again, she was sure the smell wasn't air freshener. It had a hint of jasmine in it.

I said, 'Do you want me to talk to him?'

Suky sighed again, and her body was like a rag doll in the van's high driving seat.

'Would you mind? I'm not asking you to come telling tales or anything. I know he's your friend. But I just want to know if I should worry or not. We're so happy the rest of the time.'

After about half a mile, the woods came to an end and the track veered to the right, bounded by open grassland which rolled away for a distance before rising steeply. Hough Dean was in what I had learned at school was called a hanging valley, and the farm was nestled at the far end, with hills surrounding it on three sides.

When we arrived Jimmy and his workmates were out in the front yard stripped to the waist. They'd finished work for the day and were smoking cigarettes at the back of one of the vans. It was hot and their skin glistened with sweat.

'Hey, what a reception committee!' said Suky. 'Can I take a photograph?'

I laughed, and the men exaggerated their poses while she pretended to take their picture. The yard was a building site. Nails, wood shavings and random pieces of plastic littered the dusty ground. As well as the two vans there was the black Porsche I'd seen the other day.

Jimmy started telling Suky about an amusing accident that had happened earlier in the day. I thought about the window at the back of the house.

'Is it ok if I go and have a look round the back?'

Jimmy shrugged. 'I guess.'

I found it quickly enough. The elder tree next to the house was in full leaf. It had grown in the intervening years and cast a dense shade. Beyond it was the back garden, but this corner was secluded, dark and silent. The window was no longer a broken pane. The frame had been replaced with polished pine and fitted with double glazing and a lock. This hot afternoon it was slightly open, held on its catch, the bottom of the window just lower than my shoulder.

I peered in. It was dark compared to the daylight outside, and I couldn't see anything.

I don't know what compelled me. Maybe the previous failed attempt, and wanting to tell Peter. I undid the latch so the window swung fully open and hoiked myself up onto the ledge. The elder tree rustled its leaves, but I took no notice of it.

I wriggled forward, pushing at the wall with my toes for leverage. Gradually my upper body moved forward into the room.

I probably got just about as far in as I did the last time. But it wasn't the smell that stopped me – everything smelled new. I put my hands down on the work surface to stop myself falling forwards, the window catch pressing hard against my groin, and realised Richard was in the room.

He wasn't near the window, but in a dark corner where he blended into the shadows. In one hand he held a glass and in the other a pint of milk. He was standing by the fridge watching me, and he wasn't wearing his sunglasses.

I noticed three things simultaneously.

First that the milk was full cream. I didn't know anyone that used full cream milk and wondered, when I saw it in the shops, who bought it.

Secondly Richard was smiling. He was obviously amused at my clumsy and ridiculous attempt to break into his house.

But the things that struck me most, which distracted me even from the unbearable position I'd been caught in, were his eyes. I'd had my doubts about the supposed eye condition, thinking it was just part of some ridiculous pose. Now my doubts disappeared. The irises were blue, but not much darker than the milk in his glass. I'd never seen such pale eyes before. The whites were badly bloodshot, the lids heavy to the point of looking swollen, and fringed with lashes whose dark length looked indecent against the blue pallor.

'Hi Lauren,' he said. 'Would you like a glass of milk?'

I gasped and pushed myself quickly back out of the window. The catch caught the hem of my top and pulled it up as I slid, so I landed with my feet on the ground and my top round my ears, revealing my bra to anyone who cared to look.

I expected him to come to the window, but he didn't. The room inside reverted to darkness. I unhooked myself and scurried round the building back to the others.

5. Peter

Peter's physics teacher said he was gifted. Now he was in sixth form he sometimes had to talk her through his thought processes as she couldn't follow the leaps his mind made. He didn't go step by step, he just knew. This idea connected to that, this answer belonged to that question. The same way he knew that if he leapt from this rock his hooves would land neatly on that boulder. He could calculate the slippage, factor in ice or rainfall, in a fraction of a second. He never fell.

His dad had never taught him, not in words. As soon as Peter could run, they'd run together, and Peter had picked it up, whether by instinct or by following his dad's example he couldn't say. In the lab he'd moved beyond anything his teacher could tell him. She muttered about Cambridge University, scholarships, opportunities. He blanked her and focused on the work in hand.

Running with his dad was as easy as sleeping. His limbs relaxed, his haunches carried him effortlessly up steep wooded tracks, across open expanses of moorland, over peaks and down slopes that were almost vertical. Purple heather and bilberry brushed his thighs as he passed. He thought of Lauren in the kitchen, the sun lighting her pale hair with gold fire, as though she and it were made of the same substance. She was so fragile.

When he ran with Lauren he had to slow his pace to a trot, think about the path ahead, watch out for stones or hollows which might be stumbling blocks for her feet – so soft inside her boots – protected only by slippery rubber soles. She seemed almost translucent with the sun behind her. He sometimes thought she was a mirage, that one day he would reach for her and find she had gone.

But she was strong too. Strong like a sapling, like the new growth of spring forcing itself though the frozen ground. She could hold herself amongst the other kids, tell Joel Wetherby where to get off. Nobody at school ever picked on her. She was the golden girl, the one all the boys fancied, all the girls wanted to be, holding her head high, her healthy, blonde hair swinging between her shoulder blades.

When they were children he'd never questioned it. He'd accepted her friendship the same way as he took warmth from the sun, water from the mountain stream, love from his father. Now he knew it was a gift from the gods.

6. Ali

When I was eleven, our class went on a school trip to this big house with loads of land where they'd made stuff out of rope between the trees for us to climb on. The food was crap and the rooms were really cold with rickety bunk beds, and I had to share with the other girls, who had names like Jessica and Alice and talked about ponies and boys. A couple of them had mobile phones. But I could turn my back on them and go to sleep, and in the day, outside, it was all right. I found that I could climb higher than any of the others – even the boys – and I could get to a place up high where nothing really mattered. Best of all, it was time away from home.

It was only two nights. The second morning we had to pack all our gear and get back on the coach and go home. Some of the kids were crying because they'd missed their mums so much. They made me feel sick and I didn't look at them. I sat near the back of the coach on my own and looked out of the window. I thought about my gran. She hadn't done any cooking for a while. When I went round after school she still gave me stuff – biscuits and muffins and toast – but it was all out of packets. Mum said she was getting old and wouldn't last much longer – she probably just wanted her money. Maybe Gran was tired. I could ask her if she wanted me to do some cooking. She could teach me.

It was Saturday morning. When we got back to school, the buildings were empty and doors locked, but parents were meeting their kids in the bus layby. Mum was there with Emma. I was surprised: I thought they'd be out shopping and I would have to get the bus home. But here they were with big fake smiles, pretending to do the 'oh we've missed you so much, darling' act that all the other families were doing.

Emma's my sister. She's three years older than me and she's like a smaller version of my Mum. They both have blonde hair and small feet and they swap lip gloss and talk about celebrity makeovers and reality TV. She's just what my mum wanted in a daughter, so I don't know what possessed her to have another one.

'Alicia.' My mum said it 'Aleesha'. 'We've got such a surprise for you. Haven't we Emma?'

Emma gave me one of her supersweet smiles.

'Oh yeah! A real big surprise. Aleeesha.'

I felt myself going cold inside. She knew I hated being called anything except Ali, and that I hated it when she did fake American stuff. But that was just normal wind-up-your-sister type behaviour. That morning I could see there was something else. Underneath the saccharine there was something truly evil squirming with glee. I hoped that whatever it was had nothing to do with Gran.

I didn't say anything on the way home and they didn't ask me about the trip. Emma sat in the front with Mum and they talked about some telly programme they'd watched about house makeovers. That's what really grabs them, mum and Emma. Interior decoration. Cushions and rugs and curtains and all that stuff to do with fabrics and patterns. Mum even talks sometimes about setting up a business. They've changed the living room twice in the last three years, and last month they completely redid Emma's bedroom. They're addicted to it on the telly. Say they're 'shopping for ideas'. Every now and then, Emma threw me a glance over her shoulder, and her face would start to break into a smile and she'd turn away again.

We drove straight home, which was a relief. Probably not about Gran then – Gran never came to our house.

When we pulled up in the drive it was empty.

'Where's Dad?'

'Playing golf.'

Dad worked Monday to Friday, often ten hours a day. Came home, went out again to play squash or poker. At the weekends, golf, extra business meetings, car track days. He didn't know what went on in our house – thought that was my mum's domain. And that's the way she liked it.

'Put your bag down, Alicia,' Mum said in the kitchen.

'I'll take it up to my room.'

'No, just put it here for now. We've got something to show you.'

When we were small and Emma was excited about something she used to hop from one foot to the other like she needed a wee. She was finding it hard to keep from doing that now. She was sort of lurching from side to side.

'Come with us. Upstairs.'

They both went ahead of me and turned left on the landing. Towards my room. I reached the top step and Mum's hand was on my door handle.

'Close your eyes, Alicia.'

Emma was openly grinning now, right across her face like a split peach. I wanted to smack her hard with the back of my arm. I closed my eyes.

'Da da!' Mum sang.

She flung the door open and I could hear it crash back against the wall, which meant my giant teddy wasn't there where it should be. The giant teddy Dad gave me when I was three and he won it in a raffle at work.

'Open your eyes now, Alicia.'

I so did not want to look. I wanted to curl up and lie on the floor right there on the landing, with my lashes firmly glued to my cheeks in comforting blackness. I wanted to go to sleep and wake up to find this wasn't happening.

I opened my eyes.

My room was completely transformed.

All the furniture was new. There was a platform bed with a ladder up to it, covered in brand new bedding in purple and black. Underneath the bed was a squidgy sofa covered in black plastic and a long furry purple rug. There was a desk and a chair and a computer, and a set of drawers and cupboards in black with wiggly lines where there should have been straight ones. The walls had been painted a pale violet and the woodwork was silver. There was black carpet on the floor.

I stood and stared at it. Mum and Emma were both looking at me. Mum thought I'd be pleased; Emma knew exactly what I'd think. They were both waiting for me to say something.

'Where are my things?' I said eventually.

'We've got you new things,' Mum said. 'You're nearly a teenager now, and I realised that all your things were kids things. Toys and kiddie books and all your old school books from primary school. Emma's got rid of all her old stuff, and I realised that you needed new things now you're at a new school. Emma helped me. We got rid of all the old junk, and we've got you a computer – with loads of games on – and some books for teenagers and school stuff as well. We went to IKEA and chose all this especially for you. Emma thought you'd like it.'

'It's a bit emo,' Emma said, 'like you.'

I looked at her and I could see the lights dancing behind her eyes. This was her moment of triumph. She'd been waging a lets-wipe-Ali-off-the-face-of-the-planet campaign ever since I'd been rude enough to upset her equilibrium by being born, and now she'd finally won. This wasn't my room. This was the slightly troublesome – but hey, let's indulge her – younger sister's room. This was a room for a cliché, not a person.

I smiled at my mum.

'Thanks Mum,' I said.

I didn't go in. I walked back down the stairs and picked up my bag and went to Gran's house.

Gran couldn't do anything of course. She had no say in our house, and all my stuff had gone to the tip anyway. But she put her arm around me and let me cry, and understood when I told her how I always said goodnight to my giant teddy and I'd missed him while I was on the trip, and now he was gone and I didn't even get to say goodbye.

I didn't want to go home, ever. But Gran told me that I'd have to. That until I was sixteen Mum and Dad were my legal guardians and that was my home, and that even if they let her, she couldn't have me come and live with her, because she was finding things harder these days, and she wasn't up to taking care of another person as well as herself. I didn't want to hear any of this, especially the last part. Gran gave me a glass of milk and some chocolate cookies, and then she disappeared upstairs.

When she came back down she gave me the ring. It was her engagement ring and she hadn't been able to wear it for years because her knuckles had got too big. She said it was for me, something to keep as my very own. I didn't have to tell anyone about it and, although it wouldn't replace the giant teddy, she hoped it would help me feel better.

I held it in the palm of my hand and hugged her tight until she said I was hurting her and I had to let go.

I pulled the thong out from under my shirt and held the ring out to show Sally.

'It's lovely,' she said.

We were having a cup of tea in the kitchen before going back out to work in the garden. Sally had given me some jobs to do.

'I've got an engagement ring,' she said, 'but mine has rubies.'

I looked at her hands holding the mug of tea and saw she was wearing a wedding ring, though it looked like it was made of silver, not gold.

She saw where I was looking and stretched her hand out in front of her, spreading her fingers and moving the finger with the silver ring.

'Yes, I was married,' she said, although I hadn't asked her. 'My husband left me seventeen years ago. He went to live with my sister, Cassie.'

She said it matter of factly, like she was talking about the weather or something, but her hand was shaking a bit.

'Bitch from hell.' She said this so quietly that I wasn't even sure if I heard it right. I looked at her face and it was really still, her eyes focused on her held out hand.

Then she looked up and smiled, lifted her mug and swallowed the last of her tea.

'Shall we get back to work?' she said.

Sally had a patch planted with carrots and beetroot which were ready to dig up. She wanted me get them out then dig the ground over ready to sow a crop of winter lettuce as green manure.

I nearly asked her what the fuck she meant, but I didn't know if I could be bothered with the answer, so I just got the spade and started digging round the carrot plants.

She didn't show me how. She'd gone off to another part of the garden to do something else. I'd never done any gardening before. The first time I put the spade in too close and sliced straight through a carrot. Next one I dug a bit further away and a great clod of earth came up. I could see the carrots there in the soil, but they'd got dirt all around them. The orange finger shapes showing through the dirt made me feel a bit icky, so I dumped the whole clod on the side of the path and went to the next one.

Soon there was a heap of earth and the ground had loads of holes in it. I wasn't sure I was doing it right, but I carried on anyway. There were worms in the soil, and other creatures. Long black slidey things with millions of legs, fat white slugs, red ants, woodlice. I've never been scared of creepy crawlies – not like Emma, who would scream the house down if she ever saw a spider – but these weird things suddenly appearing in the soil made me feel strange. Like there was this whole world of life just there in the ground, right next to my feet, which I don't normally see. The digging was disturbing it, bringing it to the surface and I didn't like it very much.

When I got to the end of the row I leaned on the spade and looked up. The garden sloped up behind the house, and from here you could see over the roof and across the valley. On the other side there were woods about halfway up, then bare land. Not fields with cows or anything, but brown land with rocks here and there and nothing on it. I supposed it was the moors.

Along the side of the carrot patch there were apple trees. I looked at them to see if they were good for climbing. I've always loved climbing trees. They're great for hiding in. People never seem to look up so, even if the leaves don't completely hide you, they hardly ever notice you're there.

It was Emma's twelfth birthday and she'd had a party. She and most of the girls in her class had been bowling, then they'd come back to our house and hung around having milkshakes and cake and putting on make up. I'd been at Gran's earlier but she'd had to go out, and when I got back there were still some of them hanging around so I went out to the garden with a book and climbed my favourite pear tree.

I was nearly at the end of the book when I heard Mum and Emma.

'Have they all gone now, love?'

'Yeah. Sophie's dad just came for her.'

I looked down through the branches. Mum was collecting up things that had been left in the garden – empty ice-cream bowls and glasses, sweet wrappers. I'm sure if I'd left stuff like that in the garden I'd have been in trouble. Emma was bending over backwards, her blonde hair hanging down to the ground, her hands holding the back of her calves. She was good at gymnastics.

'Mum.' She walked her hands up her legs and back to standing.

'Yes love?'

'Did you see what Gran gave me for my birthday?'

I'd been there when she opened it at breakfast time. It was a book of traditional Yorkshire recipes. Gran had written inside it that she hoped Emma would enjoy making some of the things she used to eat as a girl, and how it was good to keep the old traditions alive. Emma was not impressed. She'd flung it aside and grabbed the next present on the pile.

My mum sighed and put the things she was carrying on the garden table.

'Your gran's lonely here, love. She misses her friends and she misses Yorkshire. She lived there all her life until she moved here, you know.'

'Why did she move here then?'

'To be near us. We're her family. I sometimes wish she hadn't. It was easier when she was further away: we could visit her on our own terms then, rather than feeling we have to include her all the time.'

'Do you miss Yorkshire?'

'God no! I never felt at home there. This is my place. Yorkshire's your gran's and maybe she should have stayed, but seeing as she's here we have to make the best of it. Perhaps you could make something from that book for her one day.'

Emma snorted and threw herself forward into a handstand, walked a few steps, then flipped gracefully over into a crab.

'Do you think Ali would like Yorkshire?'

My mum considered this for a moment.

'Probably. She's a lot like your gran. Strange, really. I can't see any of me or your dad in her.'

They went in after that but I stayed in the tree, thinking. I wished I could make something for Gran from the book, but it was Emma's book so I'd never even be allowed to look at it. I knew what Mum meant about not belonging, but I'd just thought that was life. It hadn't occurred to me that there might be somewhere I did fit in. I wondered if I could get Gran to take me to Yorkshire.

A tree seemed like the natural place for a hideout. After they'd shut the door in my face I scanned the road, walked up and down for a bit. There were trees planted all along the pavement. The colours were thinking about turning, but they hadn't started properly yet and the trees still had loads of leaves. The problem was, they had been pruned so the branches didn't start until quite high up the trunk, and there was no way I could shin up without someone noticing me.

Opposite there was a place set back from the road – a square building like a low block of flats. There was a car park at the front, and a wall around it with iron gates. The sign on the gates said Restview Residential. I did a bit of a recce. There was no one about. The wall was about four feet high, and a couple of the trees from the street had branches that reached right over. It seemed like the best bet.

I pushed one of the gates and it swung open. I closed it quietly behind me and made my way along the edge of the wall to the furthest tree. The trickiest bit was getting onto the wall. Four feet doesn't sound that high, but there wasn't much of a toehold between the bricks. It was a case of pulling myself up with my hands and making sure the momentum didn't send me hurtling over the other side. Effort versus balance. But I was soon up, and I used the branches of the tree to steady myself as I got up on my feet. I looked back at Restview Residential. There was an old guy standing in one of the windows watching me. He didn't look too bothered. I smiled and waved at him and he waved back.

After that it was easy. Me and trees, we're old friends. Through the branches on the other side I had a great view of the front of the house. And surrounded by leaves, eight foot up in the air, there's no way anyone was going to spot me.

I didn't have to wait long, either. It was only about half an hour before the woman came out, still wearing the grey trousers and navy jumper, now with a matching grey jacket. She clicked the car remote and a black Mini on the kerb flashed into life. Before she got into it the man rushed out of the flat after her. I couldn't make out what they were saying, but I could tell that they weren't in agreement.

It seemed like he was pleading, or coaxing, or at least asking for something. She turned and snapped at him angrily, then he became angry too. Because they were out in the street they were trying to keep their voices down, but their body language told me all I needed to know.

She got into her car and drove away and he went back inside. As he walked through the door he lifted his hands to his head as though he was pulling at his hair and I nearly laughed. Five minutes later he came out with a jacket on and carrying a briefcase. He paused for a moment in the open doorway and looked back. Then he slammed the door, got into a red Nissan and drove off.

I waited ten minutes, then jumped down from the tree and headed back into town.

7. Lauren

The day had been humid and at about four o'clock there was a fully fledged downpour, the sort that makes you want to dance in the grass and soaks you to the skin in seconds. It rained like that for about an hour and then it stopped, and I asked if I could go and play with Peter. Dad was upstairs marking and Mr Lion said yes, so I went into the woods and all the plants were singing together, like a choir, but they were so excited that some of them kept going off on their own melodies, screeching with exuberance. I sat on the stone waiting for Peter, and by the time he arrived I was crying with laughter.

He said, 'What's funny?'

'Listen,' I said, 'The Himalayan balsam's completely out of tune.'

He looked strangely at me.

'Can't you hear it?' I asked.

'No.'

'They're so funny,' I said, 'and so loud. You must be able to.'

'Lauren, plants don't make a noise, no one can hear them.'

'But they do, they're always telling me things.'

I looked at his face then and knew he was telling the truth. We both looked at his goat legs and we held hands. I think we must have been about seven.

I opened my eyes and closed them again. It wasn't light, not properly. Why was I even awake? My alarm wasn't set to go off for ages and I never wake up before the alarm. I turned over and curled around my pillow, pulled the covers up over my ears.

Then I opened my eyes again and sat up. There was a noise. I sat still and listened. The house was silent now. Maybe Beauty was moving around downstairs – but that didn't usually wake me.

It came again, and now that I was awake and paying attention I could tell what it was. Someone was throwing gravel at my window. I pulled back the curtains and looked out. It was grey and misty and the sun wasn't up yet.

I opened the window and leaned out.

'Peter?'

His face was turned towards me and I could just make out that he was smiling.

'Get dressed and come down,' he called in a loud whisper. 'We're going for a walk.'

The dawn air coming through the window was freezing against my bed-warm skin and I could feel the seductive draw of the duvet.

'I'll wait at the front,' Peter called, and then he disappeared. I took a deep breath and the air that came into my lungs was damp with mist. The plants sighed and settled. I wondered how long he'd wait if I didn't appear, whether he'd come back and throw more gravel.

Five minutes later I was shivering at the front of our house in jeans and anorak. Peter threw his arm around my shoulders and kissed me. He wasn't wearing anything.

'Aren't you cold?' I shrugged up against him. He didn't feel cold. His skin was warm and damp with sweat.

He took my hand and set off along the street pulling me after him.

'Me and Dad have been up all night,' he said. 'He's off to Greece later today to stay with Mum. We ran up to the Dales and only just got back.'

They do that sometimes, go night-running. They can run for miles with their strong hind legs, and they cover ridiculous distances. I've asked once or twice if I can go with them but, although they smile and say maybe, I know I can't. Not the way they do it. There's no way I'd be able to keep up.

'Where are we going?'

'Just to the woods.'

We went in through the bottom path and the mist was even thicker. I could see Peter next to me, but beyond him the trees were dark shapes looming and fading. They were silent.

'There's something I wanted to show you,' Peter said.

The footpath showed itself for a foot or two in front, closed again behind us. I grabbed hold of Peter's arm. The world was asleep and there were just the two of us in this small patch of world rubbed clear of grey. We were nearly at the pond.

'Listen,' Peter whispered.

I stood still and realised my coat had been rustling. Now that it stopped, the stillness of the wood expanded. I could hear other noises. Small scurryings in the undergrowth. Leaves turning in their sleep. Ducks by the pond murmuring to each other, and a rush of water as one of them made a dash at another.

Peter tugged my hand and we walked on, slowly now, each foot placed carefully down so as not to make a noise. I could see the gleam of the water beside the path before the mist swallowed it.

'There.' Peter stopped suddenly and his voice was barely audible.

I followed his gaze. The brown mud of the path, the silver glint of water, the mist.

Then there was a movement and I saw the heron. Almost invisible, it stood upright, head raised, looking across the water. It was nearly as tall as our shoulders, and only five feet away. I leaned closer to Peter and watched the bird. We were barely breathing. Its eyes were orange and its beak sharp.

It didn't seem to notice us, but suddenly it bunched its feathers, gathered its wings, lifted up out of the water with a couple of large flaps and disappeared back into the mist. I could see its legs dangling in the air for a second, black lines against the grey, then it was gone and the woods were silent. Peter hugged me and I turned to kiss him, wound my arms round his neck and pressed my body against his. His fur was damp, but his skin was shiny with moisture, slippery beneath my fingers.

'I know a place we can go,' he whispered into my ear, 'if you want.'

I laughed and hugged him tighter, kissed his mouth, his neck, his ears.

'Yes, I want.'

In the woods there are two trees, a hawthorn and a young oak, which have grown together, their trunks entwined. They're not the same tree, but if you were to cut one away, the other would still coil around the empty space. In time it might fill out, gain its own strength, but it would always have that twist, that memory held in the turn of its trunk, that whisper in its leaves that once there used to be something else. It might happen that the two trees, growing close like that, would crowd each other out – one would take the other's space, steal its nutrients, choke it to death. Or they may grow to accommodate each other, bending and twisting more as the years go by, until it's only by the difference in leaf and bark that it's possible to show which limb belongs to which tree.

By nine o'clock the sun had risen and burned off the mist. The sky was blue and clear. A fresh new day. I'd left Peter sleeping in the woods. After he and his Dad have been night running he sleeps for hours – sometimes right through. He might miss a day at college but he catches up quickly enough.

I had history that morning, and we were working in the library on our projects. We had to decide what topic we were going to do, and Miss wanted us to work in pairs, looking for ideas. The college library held the local archives and there was often someone from the local history society on hand. I arrived a few minutes late and everyone had already paired up, so I headed into the aisles on my own and found Richard looking through a box of old newspapers.

I hadn't seen him since the day I'd tried to climb in through his kitchen window.

'Hiya Lauren,' he said.

I looked at him, trying to work out if he was laughing at me, but with those shades on I couldn't tell. I decided not to worry about it. It was only half past nine, but I'd been up for four hours and already it was the best day of my life.

'Hiya Richard. What you doing here?'

'Just a bit of research,' he waved the paper in his hand.

'Are you a student here?'

'No, just using the archives.'

'Oh.' I nodded and started to look along the shelves at the box files and heavy bound books. He read his newspaper. I couldn't see the date, but it was pretty old – columns of tiny print and no photos. He looked up and smiled at me.

'Have the builders gone yet?' I said.

'Most of them. There's just the plumber.'

'Jimmy?'

'Yeah. Mum decided she wanted to change the taps and god knows what. I think she just wants to have people about the place so she dreams up stuff for them to do.'

'Jimmy'll do a good job.'

'He should be careful. If Mum takes a liking to him, she'll be calling him out all the time.'

'He can look after himself.'

I delved into my bag and got a pen and notebook.

'I've got to choose a project,' I said.

'Any ideas?'

'I was thinking of doing Unitarianism in the nineteenth century.' I'd told a couple of my friends who'd looked at me blankly and I'd had to explain.

Richard nodded. 'Yeah, that will be interesting. Try looking at the links with freemasons too.'

'Thanks. I will do.'

I took down a bound copy of the proceedings of the town council from 1850 and looked through the index.

'There's a party tonight, down at Canal Bank,' I told Richard.

'Whose party?'

'Oh, anyone's, everyone's. It's where the houseboats are moored, in the communal space – everyone mucks in, brings stuff, you know. Half the town will probably be there.'

'Are you inviting me?'

I turned and looked at him, and encountered my reflected self in his sunglasses. His mouth was twisted into what I suppose was a smile.

'I guess so. But it's like I said: everyone can come. I'll be there with Peter.'

'Ah, Peter the Invisible Boyfriend.'

Now he was definitely smiling. I looked away, annoyed despite my resolution not to let him get to me.

'Look, I was just telling you about it in case you'd like to come. You being new round here, I thought it would be a chance to get to know people. It's up to you if you come or not.'

'Thank you Lauren,' he said, and now he sounded sincere, 'I'd love to.'

The thing about having world class circus performers living in your town and, even better, as your friends, is that they need an audience to try out their acts on. Since Suky and Jimmy have been a couple they've been working on a performance to do together. So far they haven't done it in the wider world – they are still known as Spangled Suky the High Wire Supreme, and Pyrotastic – and as far as the audiences of Europe are concerned they are two entirely separate acts. Here in Hawden though, we've seen their double act grow and develop.

It started with them performing side by side – her spinning cartwheels along a wire while he paced around below breathing fire like a restless dragon. That was cool. But every time there's a communal event or a party, they perform for us again and each time it's changed, become more integrated. Their performances aren't side by side any more, but intertwined, dependent on one another.

It was twilight down by the canal and there was a big pot of chilli which everyone dipped into, and someone produced jugs of sangria. There was music on and Mr Lion was sitting at the base of a tree rolling a spliff with Beauty on his feet. I leaned against Peter and we watched Jimmy making the final preparations for the performance.

The two bridges weren't far apart – maybe 300 feet – and they'd strung a wire up from one to the other in a line down the middle of the canal. Before they put it up they'd dragged it though a bowl of liquid, which I wasn't near enough to see or smell properly, but I guessed it was petrol or something equally flammable.

Suky was wearing an orange leotard sewn all over with sequins so she shimmered. She had sequins on her legs and arms too: orange, red, gold and silver, stuck to her skin in swirling patterns that rose and twisted from her ankles and wrists, so that as she walked she looked as though darts of fire were flickering across her limbs. She had her hair up and her face was heavily made up in the same shades of red, orange and silver.

Jimmy was wearing what he always wears for fire-eating: not very much. Just a pair of tatty old khaki shorts which come down to his knees. But he looked nearly as decorative as Suky, because his torso, upper arms, back and legs are covered in tattoos. Dragons, Celtic patterns, Chinese calligraphy, mermaids and loads more, all in green and black, no other colours.

The wire was pulled taut. Suky climbed on to the wall of the bridge and stood legs slightly apart, hands on her hips. Someone turned the music down and suddenly all eyes were on her. There was the hush of everyone collectively holding their breath.

Jimmy stood behind her on the bridge and handed her a flaming torch. She bent at the waist and held the torch out at arms length so that it touched and lit another torch which was attached to the bridge. She pirouetted and repeated the movement to light a third torch. She turned and beckoned to Jimmy who climbed up next to her. He stood in the centre, smiled at Suky, then stepped out onto the wire.

Everyone gasped. None of us had seen Jimmy walk the wire before.

He took a step, then another, his arms held out for balance. Then he turned and bent at the waist in the same way that Suky had. She held out the flaming torch to Jimmy. He took it in his mouth.

He straightened up and turned towards us, took two more torches out of the waistband of his shorts and lit them from the one in his mouth. Then, with a flaming torch in each hand and one in his teeth, his head bent backwards so that the torch stayed upright, he started to edge his way slowly along the wire.

At first we were quiet, but then someone started to clap, and gradually everyone joined in, clapping the rhythm of Jimmy's feet as they moved along the wire. The audience was nearer the second bridge and when Jimmy was about level with us he stopped and turned so he faced Suky who was still standing on the bridge at the other end. He began to juggle the three torches as Suky stepped out onto the wire.

She made his tentative steps seem like those of a lumbering elephant. She skipped out, stopping, bending, her hand movements reminiscent of Indian dancers'. She did a cartwheel, she leapt and danced. Jimmy was a study in concentration, keeping the torches in the air, keeping his balance on the wire which shook as Suky moved. The flames reflected in the dark water beneath.

Suky approached Jimmy. She darted at him with mischievous movements. He ignored her. She grabbed out and tried to steal one of his torches and he growled at her in mock anger. She tried again and succeeded. He was juggling with two torches, and she waved the third in the air. The audience was cheering her on. Encouraged, she tried again, and grabbed hold of a second torch.

The audience cheered and shouted for Suky. Jimmy, left with one torch only, opened his mouth and closed his lips around the flames. When he removed it the torch was extinguished.

Suky stood in front of him waving a lit torch in each hand. She bent and inserted the ends of them between her toes, danced a teasing little dance with flames at her feet.

He stared at her for a moment, his face lit with the orange glow of the torches, then he opened his mouth and breathed out a jet of fire. It hit the wire between him and Suky and set it alight.

Suky, with a lit torch still held between the first and second toes of each foot, cartwheeled the length of the wire back to the bridge, pursued by the line of fire. The spectacle was amazing. Darkness had fallen and the flames formed a circle around her, the sequins on her clothes catching the light and shattering it into a thousand drops of fire. Beneath, the canal was filled with dancing lights, and the flaming line of the wire chased after her.

She reached the bridge, did a back flip and landed with her feet on the bridge, facing Jimmy. The wire stopped burning, but she still held the flares in her toes. She removed them one at a time and threw them to Jimmy. He caught them, relit the third flare, then, juggling again, walked back along the wire to Suky. She held her hand out to him. He stepped on to the bridge, turned, and hand in hand and torch in hand, they bowed.

We cheered and shouted and whistled.

'That was amazing.'

Richard was standing next to me.

'They always are.'

He wasn't wearing his sunglasses and his eyes looked almost normal. He was watching Jimmy and Suky as they bowed on the bridge, and their flames were reflected in miniature in his irises.

'I saw Jimmy once before,' he said, 'in Istanbul, when he was performing with the Moscow State Circus.'

'Wow. That must have been amazing.'

'It was. But if he did that stuff with Suky, people would go crazy for it.'

'They're pretty cool together. What were you doing in Istanbul?

'Oh, I stayed there for a while with Mum. It's an amazing city. Have you been?'

I shook my head.

Jimmy and Suky jumped down off the wall and put the torches out. It had got dark during the performance and someone switched on the fairy lights that were strung through the trees. I looked for Peter so I could introduce him to Richard, but he had disappeared.

'Do you like the circus then?' I asked.

'I love it!' He was holding his coat over his shoulder, his finger through the loop, and he was wearing jeans and a t-shirt. His hair was pushed back from his face and he looked younger than when I'd seen him before. 'I go to the circus wherever I can. We've travelled quite a bit, and it's always one of the first things I look for when we arrive anywhere.'

'What's your favourite act?'

'Clowns. I love all of it, the ringmaster and the trapeze girls and the lion tamers, the spangles and the spectacle. But the clowns are my favourite. There have been some wonderful clowns. Have you heard of the Great Bartolomeo?'

'Someone who knows his circus history I see,' said a voice behind me.

It was Jimmy, sooty and streaked with sweat, in his khaki shorts and a clean red t shirt.

'I know some. Bartolomeo was fabulous, but underneath the paint he was very sad. His wife and children were put into a concentration camp during the war. He was on tour and never saw them again.'

Jimmy looked surprised. 'I didn't know that. I thought I knew all there was to know about famous circus performers. I can see I'll have to pick your brains. I'm Jimmy by the way.'

He held out his hand and Richard took it.

'Richard. You've been working up at our house haven't you?'

Jimmy peered at him in the half light. 'Oh it's you. I've only seen you from a distance before.'

'I guess you must be about finished up there by now,' I said.

'No. That is, we've finished what we were doing, but Meg has asked me to do some work in the attic. She wants to turn it into some sort of flat or den with its own bathroom, and she's asked me to stay on to do the work.'

'Is that for you?' I ask Richard.

'I don't know what it's for. Just another of Mum's projects. Probably just an excuse to keep Jimmy about the place. I told you she'd taken a shine to him.'

'Who's taken a shine to him?'

Suky squeezed herself in between Jimmy and Richard, still in her shining leotard. Jimmy put his arm round her.

'This is Richard, the lad from up at Hough Dean I told you about.'

'Hiya.' Suky turned to me. 'I thought I saw Peter. Has he gone?'

I looked around at the groups of people chatting in huddles, those milling around over by the food tent. I couldn't see Peter anywhere.

'He was here. He must be around somewhere.'

'Maybe he's avoiding me,' said Richard with a grin.

8. Peter

Off the peg clothes never really worked for Mr Lion. He had his clothes made by a tailor, and he made an appointment with him for Peter. When Peter told his dad, he said they could charge it to his account. Lauren said she'd never seen his dad in clothes, was surprised he had an account at a bespoke tailor. But Peter had seen him at airports, and sometimes dressed up to go out on the town with his mum when they were in Greece. His dad had seen all of fashion's twists and turns, and when he decided to wear clothes he did it well.

The tailor looked Peter up and down and said, 'Wonderful! Wonderful!' He walked around him in a circle, pinched him at the waist, patted his shoulders. 'Italian cut, that's what you need: high waist, tailored around the hip, tapering down the legs. I recommend polish for the hooves.'

Peter frowned and looked down at his feet. He didn't want to be there. He didn't want any of this. When Lauren said 'What are you wearing for the prom, Peter?' he'd said, 'Do we have to go?' and she'd pulled a face at him, one that told him she was going whether he was or not. He basically had the choice of going with her or spending the evening thinking about her there without him.

'Wouldn't it be better to wear shoes?' he said to the tailor.

'Goodness me no! You have such an advantage. It's such a shame, such a waste of perfect tailoring to stick a great pair of feet at the end of a nicely tapered trouser leg. But with you, we can narrow it down to the hoof at the bottom and the line will be perfect, perfect. Such a pleasure to work with such a fine young gentleman. Wonderful.'

He whipped about Peter with his tape measure, making notes and breathing with a whistle in his breath, and soon he was done. He said to come back in one week for a fitting.

Peter went alone for the fitting – Lauren was playing hockey that evening – so she didn't see the suit until the night before the prom when he picked it up and went round to her house.

'Let's see it on,' she said.

'You too,' said Peter.

They went into separate rooms to change. Peter was ready first and he went to the bottom of the stairs to wait for her. When she appeared he stopped breathing. Her dress was red velvet. It clung and pushed her breasts together. Her curves were convex and concave. He gulped in air.

'You're beautiful,' he said.

'Tomorrow I'll have my hair and face done.'

But this was how he'd remember her, her face pale, her fair hair tumbling about her shoulders as she descended the stairs. He held out his hand and she took it as she reached him, let him pull her to him and kiss her.

The tailor was right. The suit fitted him perfectly and shoes would have ruined it. Nobody laughed at him at the prom – he even caught some admiring glances thrown his way. When Joel Wetherby walked by Peter put his arm around Lauren, and although Joel looked at Peter's feet he didn't say anything about them. He looked at Peter's fingers resting on Lauren's waist and said, 'Nice suit.'

And although Lauren couldn't persuade Peter to dance, he was pleased that he had gone.

That was over a year ago. Lauren was at another party now. Peter sat in the darkness at the top of the hill. The moonless night spread thick and black in every direction; even the stars were hidden behind a layer of high cloud. Peter crouched on his haunches, pushed his fingers into his hair and probed at his skull with his fingertips.

9. Ali

After a while Sally came over and looked at my cloddy lumps and laughed. She showed me how to shake off the dirt and we collected all the carrots in a big wicker basket. Then we raked and levelled the soil. She didn't say much and I liked it that way.

She'd made stew earlier and at around six we went in and ate it with some bread, but we were soon out again, in the evening air, clipping and cutting and collecting berries from the brambles at the end of the garden. I was covered in scratches and my hands were dry and stained from the sap and dirt. I can't say I really took to gardening.

As the sun reached the hills behind, making our shadows long and skinny across the grass, I stopped and listened. There was music somewhere down below. Sally noticed me.

'Sound travels up the valley. Someone's having a party, but it's a long way off.'

I shrugged, and stretched out for some glistening blackberries just beyond my reach. I squished one, then I pricked my finger on the bramble and swore beneath my breath as a bead of blood formed. I put my finger in my mouth and listened again. There was a good bass sound, but it was too distant to be able to tell what they were playing.

Sally watched me.

'They often have parties down by the canal, not far from the turn off. It's about a mile away.'

'It must be pretty loud if you can hear it right up here.'

'I suppose so. I never go down.'

I looked at my finger and the blood had stopped coming. I'd had enough of the garden. I'd collected half an ice cream tub full of berries. Sally had picked loads more.

'Why don't you go?'

I could hear the far off beat pulsing with my blood.

'Would it be ok?'

'As long as you don't bring anyone back here with you.'

I didn't help take the berries in or tidy up. I kissed her on the cheek and headed off down the hill, not wanting to miss anything.

I could just about make out which way the track went in the failing light, and the music kept me moving in the right direction. When I reached the edge of the town, the noise got much louder. I could make out a song and beneath it, the chatter of voices.

I was nervous. I'd been out a lot in the years since I left home – clubs, warehouse parties, house parties. But they were all in the city. Mostly I knew someone there, and even if I didn't, I knew the type of people, I understood the vibe. Here I didn't know what to expect.

The road ahead of me had no street lamps. It led down to the canal and I walked slowly, listening. There were shouts of laughter and the beat was continuous. But I could feel silence filling the woods behind me. I was between the two and for the moment it seemed like a safe place to be.

The road wound down the hill and crossed the canal at a bridge. As I rounded a bend I could see people on the canal bank, a marquee and another tent, and the smell of food wafted along the water. There were fairy lights strung up, and the next bridge was lit with flaming torches.

This one was in darkness, and on the other side of the canal was a wooded slope. I decided that, for the time being, I could watch from there.

I crossed the bridge in the shadows. On the other side I left the road and made my way between the trees. There was a strange smell, like mushrooms, and twigs brushed against my face. I didn't like it much, but I could see the dark shine of the water on my left, reflecting the lights from the party, and it was ok knowing there were people on the other side.

There was a big tree near the bank and its trunk split a couple of feet from the ground, so I hoisted myself up into the ready made seat.

Nothing much was happening. People stood in groups chatting, drinking and smoking. A lot of them wore woolly jumpers and cardigans in bright colours, and occasionally someone would dance a few steps to the music – but it was early yet. There was a food tent with enormous saucepans on gas burners, and that was where the most people were gathered. I wasn't hungry after eating Sally's stew, but the smells coming across the canal were amazing.

After about twenty minutes I thought I'd go over. I could probably get by without attracting too much attention, get a plate of food and sit somewhere inconspicuous, wait for someone to offer me a spliff. It was getting cold sitting still in the tree and my back was aching,

I shifted my weight and glanced behind me, and that was when I realised I wasn't alone. There was someone standing three or four meters away from me, just inside the trees. I was pretty sure it was a man. He was facing away from the water looking towards the trees and standing incredibly still. I realised two things – one, he didn't know I was there, and two, he was watching something intently.

Slowly as I could I turned my body round in the tree. The lights from the party didn't reach this far and I was in darkness. As long as I didn't make any sound I should be able to move without attracting his attention. I could hear the blood pounding in my ears and the music suddenly seemed less important, further away, the canal a watery divide between the twinkling lights and this earthy blackness. Now that I had my back to the party, the life of the woodland around me seemed strange and invisible, bold and strong in the dark. The man hadn't moved. I looked beyond him.

There was an area less dense than the rest. As I watched, my eyes adjusted and I could pick out the individual tree trunks, the dark spaces which separated them. I moved my eyes from one to the next, looking hard at the darkest parts. There was nothing.

I glanced back at the man. He must have moved, because the light from the canal no longer picked him out. He was in deep shadow, and standing so still I would never have noticed him if I hadn't known he was there. I couldn't get to the bridge without passing him, and couldn't get out of the tree without making a noise.

Then the stillness was torn apart with the sound of something racing through the undergrowth. It ran full pelt out of the trees and across the clearing, its feet pounding, crashed straight into a tree trunk and fell in a heap on the ground. There was the noise of someone crying quite noisily with harsh ragged breaths that went on for a few minutes. The man in the trees didn't move.

I peered into the darkness. Neither the man nor the other creature seemed to know that I was there, and I thought it was probably better if it stayed that way. I pushed my body against the sinews of the tree.

The creature was back on its feet and running again, straight across the clearing into another tree. This time I could see more clearly. It was a boy or a young man, naked on the top half of his body and he was ramming the top of his head against the trunk of the tree. He butted it three or four times, turned and ran full pelt again at another tree and did the same. A frenzy had taken hold of him. He ran from tree to tree driving his head against the bark. Caught momentarily in the light from across the river I could see his face was streaming with blood that ran down his shoulders and onto his chest. His hair was matted and shining. He was making a noise that sounded like a cross between a sob and the bark of a dog, and his breath was ragged in his chest.

Then he was running straight towards the tree where I was sitting. I hugged my body and waited for the impact. It never came. He ran straight past me, out of the clearing and into the darkness of the woods further up the hill. The sound of his crashing feet continued for what seemed like an age before it faded away and silence returned to the clearing.

I became aware of the music still carrying across the water. No one at the party had heard a thing.

'What the hell was that about?'

My heart started pounding again and I looked to my right. The figure in the trees had come closer to me and now I could see that it was someone of about my age and he was talking to me as though he'd known I was there all the time.

I tried to speak, but my voice didn't come out. I cleared my throat and tried again.

'Did you know him?'

He shook his head and held out his hand.

'No, I don't know who he was, but he was pretty freaked. I'm Richard by the way.'

I put my arm forward, thinking he wanted to shake hands, but as soon as my hand was in his he pulled so I was off balance and had no choice but to jump out of the tree, and then I was standing right next to him and I could feel the rough weave of his coat against the skin of my arms. I took a step back and was pinned against the tree.

'Ali,' I said, shaking his hand, then trying to extricate my fingers. 'I was trying to decide whether or not to go to the party.'

He smiled then and stood back so there was a more comfortable space between us.

'Why don't we go together?' he said.

I couldn't see a good reason to refuse, so I followed him back through the trees to the road. He walked faster than I would have done on my own.

On the bridge he took my arm, and suddenly it felt all right. I did know someone at the party after all. We walked together to the marquee and nobody turned to look at us.

'I'll get you a beer,' Richard said, and went over to the table where they were doling out drinks. I turned to look about me, happy now, a part of it.

That was when I saw them. Smith and Jeannie. They were standing by the torchlit bridge, smoking and looking around. They looked ill at ease, scanning the crowd, watchful and restless where everyone else was laid back and chilled. They were trying to blend in and failing miserably as they looked right and left with darting eyes, dragging on their fags.

They hadn't seen me. They wouldn't still be standing there if they had. There was a way I could slip out, behind the food tent and back up to the road. Richard was still inside the marquee getting my beer, but there was no way I was sticking around. He'd have to give it to someone else.

10. Ali

When I got to the road I ran. The road wasn't lit but there was just about enough light and I ran as fast as I could. Which wasn't very fast or for very long because I've never been a runner. I can walk forever through the city and not get tired. But that's mostly flat, and this road wound itself up the hillside pretty steeply. I'd probably only run a few hundred yards when I had to stop and put my hands on my knees and the breath in my lungs was like a rush of gravel. I was just by the turn up to Sally's. I looked behind me and there didn't seem to be anyone there, so once I'd got my breath back I headed into the dark.

My eyes had kind of accustomed themselves to seeing by the light of the stars, but the darkness here pooled beneath the trees on both sides. I followed the track, looking straight ahead, until the branches crowded in and cast their darkness over the road so thickly I couldn't see anything. I tried to keep breathing. My steps got slower and slower.

I walked into something hard.

I put my hands out. It was rough and cold on the sides and soft and wet on the top. It stretched out at waist height in both directions barring my way. It was the stone wall that ran along the side of the road, and the wet stuff was moss. I'd walked right into it. I stood still and thought about the other side of the track and what would have happened if I'd accidentally veered off that way and how many hundreds of feet the drop was.

I turned, keeping my back against the wall, slowly bent my knees and dropped into a crouching position.

It was completely black in both directions, and even if I felt safe enough to retrace my steps back to where it was lighter,

Smith and Jeannie were waiting down there and that would be just as bad as stepping into the void.

I could feel wet moss at the back of my neck, and I heard a scream which might have been an owl. The sweat I'd worked up from running was turning icy cold across the top of my back and between my breasts. I hugged myself and rubbed up and down my arms with my hands.

I could still hear the music from the party, but I was listening to other sounds. The rush of the stream at the bottom of the ravine, the trees creaking their branches, rustles and squawks that startled and alarmed me. I told myself it was just small animals and birds, nothing to worry about, but I jumped every time.

I wondered if it was possible to sleep here like this, cold and scared, and then I wondered where Smith and Jeannie would spend the night, and how they'd managed to track me here so quickly. It was only the day before yesterday I'd left Leeds.

When I got back to the city centre, the first place I went was the indoor market. It's a grotty place with lots of empty shops and junkie kids hanging around in doorways, and I wouldn't go there except for this one shop. It sold wool and ribbons and thread, thimbles, zips and buttons, and it said 'Haberdashers' on the window in white fancy letters. It had wooden floors and a wooden counter and looked like it had been there for ever. So did the woman who worked there, who must have been well past retiring age and had a face like a walnut.

The first time I went in just to look around and the woman smiled at me. I'd looked at the threads arranged in colour order and the shapes of the buttons, and wanted to cry. The woman watched me.

'Are you ok, love?' she asked.

I nodded, and then I left because I didn't want to cry in front of her. But I went back every now and then and she was always kind to me, and once she offered to teach me to sew but I refused. One time I noticed she had a couple of tubs of scarves, the sort that old ladies tie round their heads, and one of the designs was of horses galloping across a field, and I knew that Jeannie had been there because she had a scarf just the same which she always tied her hair up with. I couldn't imagine Jeannie in that shop and hoped she'd paid for the scarf and not just nicked it. I knew that once the lady was too old to run the shop it would close, and there would be nowhere like it in the city.

She didn't open every day, but luckily it was one of her open days. I pushed the door open and the little bell above it rang like it always does. The lady looked up and saw it was me and smiled.

'Hello love,' she said.

I mumbled hello back and grinned at her, but I couldn't think of anything else to say, so I started looking around the shop. I had a tenner in my pocket. It was all I had between me and starvation for the next few days, but I wasn't going to spend it on food. I glanced at the baskets with the scarves and saw that they were still mostly full and, better, there were still some with the horse design on. I'd never looked at the price before and I hoped I'd have enough. There was a piece of card attached to the side and it said £3.50. I thought that was pretty cheap and that the lady might do better with her shop if she charged a bit more. But it was good for me.

The threads and the needles and embroidery silks were beautiful, but also bewildering. I wouldn't have a bloody clue where to start. It would be easy to nick them, and one of those instruction books from the shelf below. But I didn't want to steal in this shop.

Then something caught my eye. In between the threads and the wool there was a rack of knitting needles, and on the bottom row were some crochet hooks. And I was back at my Gran's house, and it was a wet afternoon in autumn before she started to get ill and slow.

Gran was sitting by her window knitting. She was always knitting. It was like a part of her, the ball of wool in her lap, the needles clacking and the woollen thing growing from them with its miraculous pattern of cables and small neat stitches. That afternoon I was bored and kicking my heels, wishing I could go outside. Gran suggested that I read my book but I didn't want to, and I was pacing the room, picking things up and putting them down and sighing loudly. For a while Gran ignored me, then after a while she put her knitting aside and said,

'Ok Ali, why don't we do something together? Why don't I teach you to crochet?'

And that's what she did. She found two crochet hooks from the depths of her knitting bag, one for me and one for her. I looked at the strangely short and deformed single needle, and wondered how on earth I was supposed to make anything with it. But Gran gave me a ball of green wool and showed me what to do and by the end of the afternoon I'd made a small round doily thing. Gran said you could use it to stand a teapot on, so I gave it to her, and she had it in her kitchen right up to when she died.

And for the rest of that winter I crocheted. I made a hat and a cushion cover and even a poncho which I gave to Emma for Christmas. She put it away in her wardrobe and it was never seen again. It was my craze for the whole winter. I went round to Gran's and we sat by her fire and she knitted and I crocheted. Somehow, when the spring came my enthusiasm waned and I never took it up again.

I picked up a crochet hook and looked at it. I wondered if I could still remember how to do it. It was probably one of those things like bike riding that you never forgot. I chose a ball of rust orange wool and took it with the crochet hook to the counter.

'I'll take these,' I said to the lady, a bit too loudly.

She picked up the hook and the wool and looked at them.

'This is quite a chunky yarn,' she said to me, 'You might want to get a larger hook.'

I hadn't realised they came in sizes. She came over with me and looked at the different hooks, and held out a piece of the wool and helped me to choose the right size. The wool and the crochet hook together came to £5.15.

Just as I was about to pay, I picked up one of the horse scarves and said, 'Oh, I'll have this as well.'

She folded it and put it in a brown paper bag with the wool and the crochet hook, and I paid her most of the money I had in the world. There was enough left over for a bag of chips. I didn't want to leave.

She said, 'Good luck dearie. Do you know how to crochet?'

And I said 'Yes, my Gran taught me.'

She smiled at that, and I found myself saying, 'But she's dead now.'

'That's a shame, love,' she said. 'But do come and show me what you make won't you.'

I said I would and felt awful for lying.

The wool and the crochet hook were still in my backpack which was now sitting in my bedroom at Sally's house on the other side of these woods. There was a breeze getting up, blowing gusts through the trees, making everything shake. Then I heard a crunching noise that might have been a footstep on gravel and every part of me went still. I didn't even breathe as I listened. If I didn't move, would they walk past without noticing me? Did I want them to?

After a couple of minutes I relaxed. There were no more footsteps. Maybe it had been a tree knocking its branches or something falling over.

I thought about crocheting. I imagined the hook in my right hand and the yarn in my left and the warm feel of the ball of wool sitting in my lap, turning and twisting as I worked. I imagined my hands making the movements, the hook grasping the stitches it wanted, letting the others slide over its round end, creating a pattern of rosettes and holes. I watched it grow.

After the Haberdashers I went straight to the police station. On the way I removed the horse scarf from the paper bag and dropped it in a puddle. I picked it up, wrung it out and screwed it up tight into a ball in my fist, then shook it open. It was now creased, dirty and damp, which was just what I wanted.

At the police station I told them I knew they were looking for Smith and Jeannie and that I knew where they were. They looked at me suspiciously, wondering why I'd tell them, what was in it for me.

'They've stolen something of mine,' I said, 'and I want to get it back.'

The desk officer made a phone call and some other policemen took me to an office where they asked me questions. I showed them the horse scarf and said it was Jeannie's and that I'd found it in the garden of the house where they were hiding, that it must have fallen out of her hair.

'She always wears it. I expect she'd not tied it very tightly because she had to get out quick in the raid.'

One of the policemen took the scarf out of the office and a few minutes later he came back. He and the other man exchanged glances and the one who'd been out gave a tight little nod. After that it wasn't long before I was being put in a police car and we were driving across the city with a police van following behind.

The house looked just the same as when I'd left it earlier. The blinds were all down and both the cars were still missing. The policemen looked at me.

'You're sure this is the house?'

I nodded

They told me to stay in the car. There were seven of them, all dressed in black police uniforms with truncheons in their belts. A couple of them had their hands on their truncheons, ready, and I felt a bit sorry for Smith and Jeannie, who'd always been kind to me. But then I remembered Gran's ring and my thoughts went hard again.

First the police knocked on the door really loud and shouted, 'This is the Police, open up.' Curtains twitched in other houses, but this one stayed silent and still. After a couple of minutes they kicked the door in. Just like that.

Thirty seconds later Smith and Jeannie jumped out of a window. They'd obviously been in bed. He was only wearing a pair of jeans, and she was wearing a green vest top and black leggings, Gran's ring on its thong around her neck, Smith's shoes in her hand. I was out of the car before I could think. I dived on her and we both fell to the ground.

All I was bothered about was the ring. I grabbed at the thong. She was underneath me and she was twisting and turning like an animal, scratching and biting at me. I tried to avoid her teeth, but the main thing was the ring, and as soon as I had a good purchase I gave a yank and the thong snapped. She yelled because it dug into her neck and hurt her. Then someone was lifting me from behind, and a police officer took hold of Jeannie and snapped some handcuffs on her. I didn't know what would happen next, but I didn't really care because I had Gran's ring held tightly in my fist.

There it was again, slower this time, like someone putting their foot down very slowly, heel first. I held my breath, and there was the other foot. It was definitely a person. Then the attempt at silence was abandoned and they were walking quickly along the track towards me.

I squeezed myself back against the wall, closed my eyes and waited.

The footsteps drew level with me, went past, and stopped. Silence again. Except this time I knew there was someone there just a few feet away standing still and waiting like me. I could hear the music from the party down in the valley and I almost wished I was there where the danger was known and understood. An animal scuttled further up the slope and knocked a stone that came bouncing down the hill and onto the track, landing somewhere between us.

There was the sound of shuffling feet, movement.

'Hello?'

They might be as scared as me. But the voice didn't sound scared. I tried to breathe as quietly as I could. Water from the moss on the wall was trickling down my back, but I didn't move.

'It's me, Richard. Is that you?'

And suddenly I was laughing and I was on my feet and I couldn't stop talking.

'Oh god, I'm so glad it's you. I was terrified. I didn't know who you were but I couldn't see a thing and I walked into the wall at the side of the path because I couldn't see which way the path went and then I thought what if I'd done that on the other side and fallen down the cliff so I couldn't move and I didn't know what to do and I was so scared.'

I started crying and Richard put his arms and his coat around me and he was stroking my hair and it felt really comforting.

'It's ok,' he said.

I cried a bit more and realised that his shirt was getting wet, so I straightened myself up and he dropped his arms so that we were standing close but not touching any more.

'I've brought you that beer,' he said. He took a can out of the pocket of his coat and handed it to me.

I took it and laughed again.

'Thank you,' I snapped the can open and took a swig. 'Sorry I disappeared. I didn't know anyone there and I felt a bit uncomfortable.'

'Nothing to do with those two standing over by the bridge then, watching everyone like hawks?'

'Oh. Did you see them?'

'Yes. But they didn't see you, so don't worry.'

'Well, we have some history.'

'They don't look like the sort of people you want coming after you.'

'No. That's why I left. But then I got a bit... well, stuck.'

'Shall I walk you home?'

I looked up at where his face might be. 'Would you mind? I mean, won't you miss the party?'

'The party will keep going for hours. I can go back. Where are you staying?'

'Up the valley, at Old Barn.'

He took my arm and started walking up the hill, and I found that walking up the track in the dark was really fun. I had the beer in my right hand and Richard on the left, and he seemed to know exactly where he was going and didn't falter at all, and when I stumbled over a boulder in the path it was funny, not scary. He told me about the circus act that they'd had earlier at the party and what fantastic performers they were.

'Jimmy, the fire eater Pyrotastic, he's working for my mum doing some work in our house. It's amazing that someone who can do that sort of thing has to have an ordinary job as well. He should be on the telly. He should be world famous.'

'I suppose there's not that much demand for fire eaters. Not like every night.'

'I'd watch him every night.'

He started telling me about different circus acts he'd seen and which were his favourites, and suddenly we were out above the trees and I could see the stars and I could see Richard walking along beside me and the track winding up through the fields.

'I'll be ok from here,' I said.

'Are you sure?'

I nodded and he smiled at me and fished another beer out of his enormous coat pocket.

'Here you can have mine too.'

He kissed me on the cheek, turned and vanished back into the trees leaving me with a can of beer in each hand. One was warmed by my body heat, but the other was as cold as the earth.

11. Lauren

Around midnight I realised Peter wasn't coming back to the party and I decided to go and look for him. People were starting to dance and others settled in groups, chatting and smoking. Richard was down by the bridge talking to a couple I didn't know. I didn't think anyone would miss me.

I thought I'd head up to the woods where we'd seen the heron. That was only this morning, but it seemed like a lifetime ago. The woods were on the other side of town from the canal, and I was walking quite quickly past the end of our street, when I thought I heard someone say my name. I looked round but there was no one about, and the trees were silent. I decided to pop home first.

The garden was quiet. Most of the flowers were over, now that summer was gone. The Japanese anemones were bobbing their sleepy heads, and in the herb garden purple Echinacea preened itself in the starlight. I touched its petals, rubbed wormwood leaves between my fingers and smelled the sharp sap on my skin. Before long most of these plants would have died back, leaving only their roots, some seeds and bare twigs scattered through the soil to await the spring. The lemon verbena brushed against my legs, marking me with its scent, telling me someone had passed by.

Mr Lion keeps a spare key under a stone in the rockery. It wasn't there and the back door was open.

I didn't turn on any lights. I tiptoed up the stairs and into my room.

Peter was sitting on the floor next to my bed. I could just make out his silhouette, chin on his knees, hands on his head.

He was silent, but I could tell he was breathing deeply from the way his shoulders were moving.

I sat down next to him.

'Peter?'

He didn't move, so I put my arms across his shoulders. He wasn't wearing anything and his skin was damp and sticky. I cupped the point of his shoulder in my palm and pulled him towards me.

'Are you ok?'

He lifted his head and looked at me and the light from the window shone on his face. He was streaked with dirt and something else. I touched his cheeks. They were wet and warm. I put my finger in my mouth and tasted blood.

Everything in the room was very still. I could barely hear us breathing.

Peter took hold of my wrist, lifted it and placed my hand on the top of his head. At first I was only aware of the blood, thickly matted in his hair and oozing between my fingers. It was cold and slimy and I wanted to pull my hand away. But as I moved my fingers I felt something else. The warm hardness of bone, a round base attached to his skull narrowing to a sharp point a quarter of an inch higher. I lifted my other hand and felt both sides of his head, rolling my fingertips across the points of the newly emerged horns.

'Peter!' I whispered.

He pulled me hard against him and I could taste the salt of sweat and blood in his kiss.

It was different this time. This morning we had talked to each other about what we were doing and laughed in the mist. This time was wordless, fierce and completely thrilling. My fingers grasped at the hair on his thighs and I tasted blood when he kissed me, felt the hard knock of his horns against my neck when he lowered his head. I arched my body against him and shouted out and it was a good thing that everyone else was down at the canal bank and we were alone.

Afterwards he fell limp on top of me and after a few minutes he rolled to one side. One of his hands lay on my right breast.

'I'm sorry,' he said, his voice muffled by my hair.

I kissed him on the lips.

'I'm not sorry,' I said.

We lay like that for a long time with the light from outside making shadows on our skin. There was no sound except for the intermittent cry of an owl. I don't think either of us slept, but we lay still and didn't move, and I could feel the sweat and blood drying on my skin, the wetness between my legs.

I got cold. I sat up and put my hand on his hindquarters where the hair was damp and gritty.

'Let's have a bath,' I said.

He didn't move while I ran the hot water and dripped in oil of vetiver and rosemary. But when the bath was good and deep, I took his hands and he let me pull him up and lead him to the bathroom. He stepped into the hot water and his hooves slipped on the enamel. I grabbed hold of him to steady him and we both laughed.

The water was soon deep red with his blood. I rubbed shampoo into his hair and it covered my hands in red foam. I took the plug out, pulled the shower curtain around the bath and turned the hot jet of clean water onto him. Soon his hair was free of blood, and I could rub at the dried crusts that had formed around his ears and forehead and at the base of his horns. When the water was running clear again, we refilled the bath and lay back in the hot water, his legs either side of me, my toes in his fur. We looked into each other's eyes and my toes moved up his thighs. Before long he came up to my end of the bath and we did it again, slowly this time, trying not to make the water slosh over the side of the bath.

Then we washed and dried ourselves and wrapped ourselves up in a couple of Mr Lion's enormous white towels and went downstairs.

Peter built a fire in the grate and I went to the kitchen and found half a bottle of wine and a couple of glasses.

An hour or so later Mr Lion came home and found us curled up under a blanket in front of the fire, watching patterns of light dance across the room and get lost in the shadows. He fetched some brandy and sat down in his armchair to roll another spliff. He said he'd left when the party was in full flow.

The three of us sat in silence and Mr Lion's smoke curled into the room, its smell mingling with the apple smoke from the fire. My limbs felt heavy and warm and I sank against Peter who had his arm around my shoulders.

'Is Dad still at the party?'

Mr Lion nodded. 'He was talking to Jimmy when I left.' He took another drag and slowly exhaled. 'I don't suppose he'll be long, though.'

He was staring at the photo of my mother on the mantelpiece.

The first time I remember asking about her I must have been four years old. I'd fallen over at nursery school and grazed my knee. I'd fallen so many times before, in the woods, in the back garden, in the street, but this was different. My dad wasn't there. He'd left me in this place with strangers. The other children had snotty noses and mothers who tucked their hair behind their ears. It seemed like a personal affront.

When Dad came to pick me up at lunchtime I was angry and red-faced, but he wasn't as guilt-stricken as I'd expected. He didn't promise to never leave me there again. He laughed and said, 'Been in the wars, Lauren?'

So when we got home I said it, the thing nobody ever said. He sat me on a tall chair while he dabbed at the wound with damp cotton wool, and I said, 'Why haven't I got a mummy?'

He carried on wiping my knee, threw the cotton wool in the bin and said, 'You do have a mummy, Lauren.'

'Well, where is she then?'

'She had to go.'

'Did she love me like the other mummies? Did she buy me a pink lunchbox?'

'Yes, she loved you.'

'Well why did she have to go? I think she'd still be here if she loved me. I think she must hate us.'

'Do you want a pink lunchbox? We could go to town on Saturday and look.'

'Is she dead?'

'No, she's not dead.'

'What does she look like?'

So he showed me the photograph of Cassie, my mother. It was always there, on the mantelpiece, and I must have seen it a thousand times, but never realised it was any more important than the poster of James Brown on the kitchen wall or the painting of a naked woman crouching at the bottom of the stairs, or the photos of African children in the bathroom.

I looked at it now like I had that day.

She was smiling. No, laughing. She was outside, wearing a raincoat, looking at the camera, and her hair had blown into her face. Her eyes were the same colour blue as mine and she looked happy.

'Peter wants me to go to Greece with him in the summer,' I told Mr Lion, 'to meet his mum.'

Mr Lion nodded his head and the light from the fire glinted on his mane. He offered me the spliff and I took it. I don't often, because I hate the taste of the tobacco, but it seemed like a good moment, with the soft heat of Peter's legs against mine beneath the blanket. The only light came from the fire. I breathed and felt my muscles relaxing. I felt like warm wax. I passed the spliff on to Peter.

Mr Lion looked at the photo again. 'They said she had postnatal depression.'

Nobody ever speaks about my mother in this house. Dad didn't tell me anything else, just that she'd been ill, and to remember that she loved me.

I remembered it, but I didn't feel it. I looked for it in her face, gazing into her eyes for some sort of recognition, something she had to give me. The curl of her hair or the curve of her nose or the whorls of her left ear, side on to the camera. All I could see was that she loved my Dad who took the picture, and I wondered how she could have left him after she'd smiled at him in that way. When she left the only thing that had changed was me. I was there. A three-month-old baby and she just packed her bags and left.

Mr Lion looked at me. 'She carried you about in a sling and wouldn't let you go. Even your dad had a hard time prising you off her.'

I pressed against Peter and he tightened his arm around me. I tried to say something, but no sound came out.

Peter said 'What happened?'

Mr Lion shrugged. 'She started crying a lot. She said she wanted you to sleep in a different room, and she stopped feeding you, so you had to have a bottle. They didn't live with me then, so I only saw her sometimes, but she would look at you and Andy as though her heart was breaking. Then she was gone. Andy moved in here with me because he couldn't bear to be in the house without her.'

The back door opened and someone turned on the kitchen light, sending a flood of yellow through the open doorway. There was laughter and the clink of bottles. A draught of cold air made the flames dance wildly.

I looked at Peter.

'We better go and get some clothes on.'

Wrapped in blankets we shuffled across the room. We couldn't move our legs high enough to climb the stairs so we had to lift our skirts and we started giggling.

We were halfway up the stairs when Mr Lion spoke to us again. The people in the kitchen were getting louder so I only just caught it.

He said, 'I saw her today. She's back in the old house.'

Then someone switched the light on and the shadows vanished. We dashed upstairs before anyone saw us.

Peter didn't want to come back down again. He was knackered and the spliff had finished him off. I don't think he'd heard what Mr Lion said. He wanted me to curl up with him in bed, but my mind was buzzing and I knew I would lie there with questions flying round my head. So I pulled on my jeans and a jumper and went back downstairs.

They were all in the living room. Mr Lion was still in his chair gazing into the fire and didn't look as though he'd moved. Nobody was talking. Jimmy and Suky were on the sofa and Dad was in his chair looking at his hands.

Richard was sitting on the floor, and so were the couple from the party. They sat close together, watching everyone. He had short brown hair and two nose rings. She had bleached dreads tied back with a scarf, thick black make up and a piercing between her nose and the left corner of her mouth. She was really beautiful.

The other person there was Steph who works in the post office. She's seven years older than me and she used to babysit for me sometimes when I was a kid. She's really nice, but she's quiet and not much of a party-girl so I was surprised to see her.

Still nobody spoke. I looked at Mr Lion and he raised his eyebrows.

The girl on the floor said, 'Anyone want some MD?'

Dad stood up. 'I'm going to bed,' he said.

Jimmy looked round the room and caught my eye. 'We could go to ours,' he said, 'so we don't keep you awake, Andy.'

Dad shrugged. 'Whatever.'

'I'll get my coat,' I said.

'Are you going?'

'Yeah, I think I will.'

'Well, be careful,' he said. He looked at the three sitting on the floor. He obviously didn't like the look of them.

'Ok, Dad.'

Peter was fast asleep under my duvet, his lashes soft on his cheeks. I leaned over to kiss him and noticed a couple of beads of fresh blood at the base of one of his horns. I flicked my tongue and licked them off. I kissed first one closed eye and then the other. Peter murmured in his sleep but didn't move.

Downstairs the others were waiting for me. Steph said she thought she'd better go home, though she lingered a bit as though she wanted to us to persuade her otherwise. When we reached the end of our street she went on her way looking a bit forlorn.

Jimmy was walking ahead with Suky, and the couple, who were called Smith and Jeannie, had their arms around each other, so when Richard offered me his arm I said, 'Why, thank you kind sir,' and we walked through the night quiet streets like a Victorian gallant and his lady.

I remember a woman once came to the door asking for my dad, who wasn't in. Mr Lion told her to come another time, but she was really persistent and kept asking questions and I could hear Mr Lion getting more and more annoyed.

She said something which sounded like 'Are you sure she's still alive?'

I came into the hallway and peeped round the door and she spotted me.

'Is that her daughter?' she said, and Mr Lion roared. His mouth opened and his teeth were huge, his tongue was bright red and his lips were black. His claws extended and the woman on the doorstep stepped back very quickly.

'Are you the only one here with that little girl?' she said.

Mr Lion took a step forward and roared again. The noise made my hair prick against my head and I felt alive and excited. The woman walked quickly away down the path, turning at the road to look back. I'd gone up to the doorway and was holding on to Mr Lion's leg and I could see his claws were still out, although they were gradually retracting.

The woman fumbled in her bag and pulled out a camera and Mr Lion growled again. Not loud, but loud enough for her to hear and she leapt into her car and drove away.

I said, 'I didn't know you could do that Mr Lion. Will you do it again?'

But he wouldn't. We went back into the house and he put Ray Gant's *Don't You Leave Me Baby* on the record player, and we pretended to sing along and laughed and laughed.

12. Ali

When Smith jumped out of the window the police came out of the house like greyhounds from a cage. But the rabbit was faster and had a good start and he knew the twists and turns and back alleys better than them. The officers who had stayed behind to separate me and Jeannie took her down to the police cars. She was kicking and fighting and it took both of them to hold her. I was alone in the garden, Gran's ring still clutched in my hand.

I could feel my heart beating.

I saw Smith's trainers in the grass where Jeannie had dropped them.

Smith wears thick soles – ridiculously thick, as though he had some sort of height complex and wanted to make himself taller. Or it could have been a fashion thing. But it didn't quite go with the rest of what he wore – skinny jeans and jumpers with holes, leather jacket. These shiny black trainers with their orange flashes and soles like bicycle tyres didn't seem like him.

I knew why. I'd seen him once, when he thought I was asleep, taking out the inner soles to uncover the compartment below. The place where he hid his stash, his money, his knife. Whatever.

They were two feet away from me.

I looked towards the street. I could hear Jeannie shouting and the two police officers talking to her. The others were all off chasing the rabbit.

I grabbed the shoes. The left innersole was stuck tight, so I tried the right and it came away easily in my hand. Underneath, fitted neatly between the ridges of the shoe, were two items: a plastic bag of pills and a fat roll of twenty pound notes. I thought for a second, then I took the notes and stuffed them in my pocket, fitted the insole quickly back into the shoe.

I threw them into the bushes, turned around and there was one of the policemen standing inside the garden looking at me.

He said 'We're going back to the station now. I think you'd better come with us.' He didn't look unfriendly, though, and he didn't even look to where I'd thrown the shoes.

At the police station they asked me some more questions and I told them that Jeannie had taken my Gran's ring and I showed it to them, still clasped in my hand. They asked me about the squat and stuff that Smith gets up to and what acquaintances he might have. But I didn't tell them anything, because that had nothing to do with Gran's ring and I wasn't going to tell them things they didn't need to know.

Then they let me go. I was surprised. I thought they'd search me and find the money or even take Gran's ring away again. But they said thank you for your cooperation, and let me go just like that.

When I was walking down the steps someone called my name. I turned around and it was the same policeman who'd appeared in the garden when I'd just taken the money out of Smith's shoe. He was quite young, and if he hadn't been stuffed into that uniform he might have been fit. I waited and he caught up with me.

He said 'We're not going to be able to hold her, you know.'

I looked at him. 'Jeannie?'

'We've got nothing on her. Only her boyfriend, and he got away.'

'So you're letting her go?'

'We'll have to. We can only hold her for a few hours. Then she'll be out.'

'Ok.'

'Leeds isn't that big a place really, when someone is looking for you.'

'No.' He had really nice eyes, brown and deep, and I almost wished he was my type. 'Thanks for telling me,' I said. 'Bye.'

I walked off, leaving him on the steps looking after me.

In the train station I locked myself in the bogs so I could count the money. There were ninety-seven crisp new twenties. One thousand, nine hundred and forty pounds. I'd never seen that much money, let alone held it in my hand. I peeled off five of them and put them in my jeans, then stuffed the rest right down at the bottom of my rucksack underneath my copy of *Nicholas Nickleby* that I was half way through reading.

I caught a train to Wakefield, then Huddersfield, then Manchester, then Skipton and so on, circling around, moving about, trying my best not to leave a trail. Until eventually I ended up in Hawden, the town my Gran came from. Well, almost. She lived in the village up the hill, Hawtenstall, over the ridge from Old Barn where I was now living with Sally.

The morning after the party I came downstairs and Sally was at the kitchen table slapping a piece of dough about in some flour. She was thumping and whacking it like she was really pissed off.

I noticed my book was on the table, just out of the circle of flour, but I didn't think I'd left it there. I might have left it on the end of the sofa in the living room. Was she angry because I'd left my stuff lying about?

'Good morning,' I said.

She spun round. Her hair was down, and its kinks and curls stood out at all angles from her head. She had streaks of flour in her hair and on her face. Her eyes were shining and wild. It was pretty early when I got back from the party. I tiptoed in and didn't disturb her. I didn't bring anyone back. I hadn't done anything to annoy her.

'Ali.' It came out like a hiss.

'Hi Sally, are you making bread?'

She looked at her flour covered hands for a moment, but didn't answer my question. She stared hard at my face.

'Who are you?' she said.

'Who am I?' Maybe she really was mad. 'I'm Ali. You know, I was helping you with the garden yesterday. You said I could stay...'

'*She* sent you didn't she.' Her voice was harsh and loud.

'Er... She? Who do you mean? No one sent me.'

'She!' Sally snatched my book off the table and brandished it at me. 'She sent you!'

It was a tatty old black classic I'd picked up in a charity shop. Paid for actually. I hadn't read that much – only about seventy pages – but there was nothing in it so far that could explain this kind of outburst. I shrugged and shook my head.

'Sally, I don't know what you're talking about.'

She opened the book and thrust it at me. On the flyleaf I had written my name – Ali Greenwood. Officially I have my dad's name, which is Parker, but I quite often use mum's because I like it better.

'I've been nursing a viper in my bosom,' Sally said.

I took the book out of her hand, stepped round her and walked across the room. I sat down at the other side of the table. She followed me with her eyes. She was shining, almost vibrating, sparks coming off her.

'Ali Greenwood – that's me. I was hiding and you let me stay here. That's all.'

Her mouth was twitching and for a moment I thought she was going to laugh.

'Frances,' she spat out. 'Frances Greenwood sent you.'

'Frances Greenwood?'

'What does she want?'

'Frances Greenwood was my Gran.'

'I knew it!' She slapped her right thigh with her floury hands leaving streaks on her jeans. 'A viper! Born of a viper's blood. Where is she? Has she come back?'

I'd kind of hoped that while I was here I might meet some people who'd known my gran, who could talk to me about her, tell me stuff about her and her past. This wasn't really what I'd expected.

'Gran is dead,' I said, and I was annoyed to feel tears welling up in my eyes. 'She's been dead for six years. This is her ring.'

I pulled the string on my neck and held it out. Sally looked at it warily, as though it might leap out and bite her. She didn't take her eyes off it when she spoke.

'You are her successor. You've come back to carry on her work.'

'No!' I jumped on to my feet and shouted. 'She didn't have any work. She was a lovely old lady and I miss her. Shut up, shut up!'

I ran out of the room and up the stairs and threw myself on the bed. I found myself crying in a way I never had when Gran died. My whole body bent in two and hoarse sobs hurt my throat. A detached part of myself watched with horror. I told myself, pull yourself together girl, don't let her see she's got to you, and after a while I quietened down. I lay still on the bed, my face pressed against the wet pillow.

When I walked back into the kitchen with my bag there was a man sitting at the table eating a plate of bacon and eggs. There was no sign of the dough or the flour, only a warm yeasty smell underneath the sharp tang of bacon.

'Morning,' he said to me, and shoved a forkful of food into his mouth.

Sally walked through the back door and as she walked past the man squeezed her bum. She grinned and I could see that she was still shining, though the anger had gone. She smiled at me and I wondered if I'd imagined the whole conversation.

'Ali, would you like some coffee?'

I shook my head and turned to leave.

'Sit down girl and have some breakfast.'

It was the man who spoke. He was a fat man with a bald head and the features of his face all seemed too big: fleshy lips, a wide thick nose and big eyes that were green, fringed and beautiful like a girl's. He should have been repulsive, but his good humour brought everything together as part of a really pleasant whole. It was impossible to resist him.

'Sally has got some toast on, haven't you love?' He smiled at her and she squirmed like a cat. 'Get some food inside you and everything will feel better.'

Sally poured coffee into a mug and handed it to me.

She said 'Sorry Ali, I was a bit out of order.'

I didn't really have a choice. I took the coffee from her, slid my bag off my shoulder and sat on a chair. I was curious too. I wanted to know who this bloke was and what he was doing here.

He shovelled the rest of his eggs and bacon into his mouth. It smelled good. Sally put a rack of toast between us and butter and marmalade, then she gave us both a plate and a knife and sat down opposite the man. She gazed at him. Her eyes had gone soft and violet coloured. I guessed I'd missed the main course.

I spread a piece of toast with butter.

'I should introduce you.' Sally was talking to me but she couldn't take her eyes off the man. 'This is Terry, my husband.'

They were focused totally on each other. She had her chin resting in her cupped hands, and he was managing to get the last of the bacon and eggs into his mouth whilst looking only at her.

'But I thought you said...'

'That he'd left me. He did. He left me seventeen years ago.'

'Seventeen years, eight months and fourteen days,' he said. 'But now I'm back.'

'I've missed you every day.'

His plate was empty. He put down the knife and fork and pushed it away from him. With his other hand he took a piece of toast. He did all of this without taking his gaze away from Sally. She refilled his coffee mug and passed it to him. He trapped her hand in his.

'He came back last night,' Sally said. 'I'd been waiting for him all these years.'

She turned and looked at me.

'I thought it was because of you. You turning up, and then Terry. It's too much of a coincidence. You being her granddaughter. I was scared I was going to lose him again.'

I didn't say anything. I wanted to know what Sally knew about Gran, why she hated her so much, but I didn't want to start crying again.

Sally was looking at her husband, who was eating marmalade and toast.

He said 'I'm back to stay, Sally. You've got me for good now.'

'Unless anyone sends you away again.'

He munched his toast.

I thought about what it would be like now he was here, the two of them. And I wondered if Sally would go off on one about my gran again.

'I'm just going to take my bag upstairs,' I said. They didn't turn as I left the room.

I didn't go upstairs, though. I slipped quietly out of the front door and closed it behind me. It was time to go and find answers somewhere else.

Part Two

BEGINNINGS

13. Richard, 1889

I kept my eyes closed as I climbed. If I opened them there would be no difference. The blackness in the stairwell was as complete as that behind my eyes, and I didn't want to see it. The last time had been terrifying, and I thought that if the darkness was of my own making it would be more bearable. I kept my hand on the wall to my right, feeling the curve in the cold stone as it spiralled upwards. I went slowly, feeling with my foot for each step.

I knew the climb took only a couple of minutes, but it seemed longer before I felt the wind lift my hair and I emerged at the top. It was a fine day and the sun was hot on the heather, but even so there was wind up here. The last time I'd felt as though the gale would gather me up and blow me like a sparrow across hills and valleys right into Lancashire. That time I clung to the balustrade, torn between fear of the wind and fear of the darkness awaiting me on the climb back down. Today the wind was of a different nature, a breeze carrying the warmth of hot grasses and dry stream beds, the smell of warmed heather and the sound of bees. I walked around the four sides of the balcony, able this time to do what I was supposed to the last: survey the grandeur and the vastness of the landscape from this high vantage point. In each direction, to all four compass points, the land rolled away to unimaginable distance, myself at the centre, the world at my feet. That was what they had wanted me to experience. In actuality I had pressed against the stone, crept around barely looking, filled with awe for the ferocity of the elements, but feeling no power within myself. It was only now, on this hot summer's day, that I got an inkling. Awe with no fear. I was meant to be a part of this greatness, not subject to it. I should stand tall and let the wind fill my clothes, lift my hair by the roots, feel I had dominion over this land, rather than grovel and cling to the walls. It was easier in the sunshine.

Over the next few weeks this monument was to become my place of work and I would become familiar with it in all of its moods. The renovations shouldn't take us beyond the summer months, but I couldn't hope that this fine spell would last. July is oft beset with storms and winds and I knew that Mr S would expect me to work whatever the weather.

Having circled the monument and come back to the top of the stairs, I was reluctant to return to the darkness. I leaned my back against the stone and let my legs fold beneath me, sliding down until my buttocks reached the stone floor. Through the balustrades I could see stripes of land and sky, blue at the top, green below, framed by grey stone. I ran my fingers across the floor and my limbs had lines of light and shade. The stone had not absorbed the sun's warmth, was cold and impermeable, letting through neither heat nor light. It occurred to me that if the square upon which I sat were removed, the stairwell would be illuminated.

I sat for a long time, perhaps an hour, listening to the sounds of the moorland before I heard voices from further down the hill. I stood and looked, and three boys were running, shouting, chasing each other with laughter. One of them was carrying a bucket. They ran right up to the monument, and then in circles around it, but they didn't step into the dark and climb the stairs, and they didn't notice me watching them. They were ten or eleven years old, out on the moors and free.

Before they ran off I heard one of them say 'I dares ya,' but they all laughed and they weren't serious. I saw their bare legs flying down the path, their boots a jumble of scuffed black and brown leather flashing against the dry ground. It wasn't long since I was their age, and suddenly I wanted to follow them, be a part of their rough and tumble even if only from a distance.

I ran down the stairs, trailing my hand on the wall behind me, keeping to the wide side of the steps, too fast to let the dark enter my consciousness, blinded anyhow by the sudden change from sunlight to dark. My eyes hadn't had time to adjust before I was out again, my feet on solid ground, my legs running like the boys' across the hilltop. They were out of sight, but they'd gone in the direction of the reservoir and I went that way too.

The path lies across the wide sweep of hillside like a piece of dropped thread on the heather. I could see the three of them still running while my breath was ragged in my chest. Knowing what I do now about the dangers of the smoke that billowed from the chimneys across the valley day in day out, I'm surprised that the boys could run. But their youth stood them in good stead and the gap between us widened as they got nearer to the reservoir. By the time I reached the lip of hill the boys were on the other side, already embroiled in their next adventure.

Two of them had stripped down to their undergarments and were talking excitedly to the third, waving their hands about and gesturing towards the water with their heads. The third and smallest boy was obviously reluctant, but after a few minutes he sat down on the ground and began to unlace his boots.

I smiled and sat down on a rock. The surface of the reservoir was smooth and reflected the sky perfectly, the few white drifting clouds as clear and soft in the water as they were in the sky. I could feel the sun warm on my back. I had nothing else I had to be doing that day – the only day where I could please myself for some time to come.

The two boys were knee deep in the water by the time the youngest had folded his clothes into a neat pile next to his bucket. They held out their hands to him and he tiptoed in. I remembered rare excursions with my sisters. The cold bite of the water when I dipped my toe, then the cool smoothness as it swallowed my whole foot, the circles of water lapping higher and higher up my legs as I ventured out.

The boys were going further than I had ever dared. The older two were holding the smaller one by the hands and pulling him, and I could hear their shrieks of laughter rolling across the water, his voice lower, murmuring dissent beneath their high spirits. I wondered if they could swim. Not many people could in the whole valley. I had learned when I worked up at Gibson's for a short time after my dad died and Mr Gibson put me in charge of cleaning the millpond. He had made me stay on late every night for a week, splashing about at the end of a rope until I had learned not to drown.

One of the boys seemed to trip or slip on something. He shouted and disappeared under the water. Before I grasped what was happening the other two were in trouble as well, the second of the bigger boys sinking suddenly so that only the top of his head was showing, and the smaller one splashing wildly, flailing his arms in an attempt to tread water. I knelt, unlaced my boots and threw off my jacket. By the time I stood up the surface of the water was smooth and there was no sign that there had ever been any boys at all. Except of course the three piles of clothes, two higgledy-piggledy and one neat, on the rocky beach.

I ran to the wall edge where the water was the deepest. As I dived I realised I wasn't alone. Another young man had stripped off his jacket and trousers and was diving in on the other side of the reservoir.

It was shockingly cold and I couldn't hold my breath for long underwater. I surfaced and swam towards the point where I'd seen the boys disappear. The other man was doing the same. When we reached the place we nodded at each other and then dived under. The water was clouded with mud as though there had been a disturbance or a struggle. It was impossible to see anything and the particles got into my eyes and nose. I tried flailing my arms about to see if I could find anything by touch, but the air was bursting in my chest. I had to shoot to the surface again and let it out in great gasps.

The other young man surfaced a few seconds after me. We both trod water, unable to speak for the rush of breath in our lungs. Then one of my feet hit something hard and I explored it with my toes. There was a ridge under the water. I put both my feet on it and pushed against it and I rose up into a standing position, my feet on solid ground, the water only reaching to my waist.

'It falls away,' I said.

The other man nodded. 'It gets deep here suddenly. They were out of their depth.'

'They couldn't swim.'

It had been a few minutes now since the boys had disappeared and the only disturbance to the water was made by the two of us. We both knew the worst had happened. This time I filled my lungs full of air before I dived and kept my eyes half closed against the motes in the water. I was under for longer than I'd ever been before, feeling with my arms and my legs for any sign of the three young boys, but I found nothing. The murk was such that even if I had been only a foot or two away I could have missed them.

I burst to the surface and the other man was just behind me.

'It's hopeless,' he said. His voice was soft and low.

'We should raise the alarm.'

'It's too late to save them.'

We swam back to the opposite sides of the reservoir where we had each left our clothes. I thought I would let the sun dry my underclothes a little before I dressed. As I turned, I noticed a third man descending on the far side from the path to the Basin Stone. He was walking quite fast. He reached the beach and stopped short as he noticed the piles of clothes left by the boys. He crouched and looked at them, reached out his hand and turned them over. He looked out across the water which was lying still and innocent as a sleeping cat in the warmth of the sun, reflecting the blue of the skies. For a few moments he knelt there as though contemplating the meaning of what he had discovered, then he was on his feet and running, back in the direction he had come. He hadn't noticed either me or my companion on the other side.

We met on the beach. I was carrying my clothes but he had put his shirt and trousers back on top of his wet underclothes. It must have been very uncomfortable. We sat next to each other on a large rock and looked at the reservoir. I noticed there was water running down his cheeks. It might have come from his wet hair, but I thought not.

'What a waste of life,' he said, and again I was struck by the softness of his voice.

I looked at him more closely, and drew in my breath.

'Good grief, you're a woman!'

She smiled at me through her tears. I would never have mistaken her for a man if I had met her under different circumstances. Her clothes were a man's and her hair was cropped short like a man's, but her cheeks were smooth and hairless, and I have never met a man as pretty as she was. Her smile creased her skin into tiny lines around her eyes and mouth and I saw she was past the first flush of youth, and quite possibly the second too, though she was strong and vigorous.

'I thought you would have noticed, having seen me undressed.'

I flushed and felt the heat in my face. 'I was thinking only of the boys.'

Her smile faded.

'The gentleman who was here,' she gestured with her arms, 'he will be raising the alarm now.'

'Yes. He will bring help. Boats and poles. They will find the bodies.'

She looked thoughtful.

'I might not stay.' She looked at me almost defiantly, as though I might contradict her. 'There's nothing we can do now. And if many people come they will see me...' She looked down at her male garments and I understood. Her disguise was only effective from a distance. Once you looked closely her gender was clear and, even with the tragedy at hand to fill people's minds, questions would be asked.

I nodded. 'I will stay. I might be of some help if they need someone who can swim.'

It would take at least an hour for help to arrive and we sat for a while letting the sun and breeze dry our clothes. I wondered if I ought to put my trousers and shirt back on now that I knew she was a woman, but somehow the normal social niceties didn't seem relevant. The shock of the boys' drowning threw a cast over the day which would have made embarrassment seem frivolous. If she had been a young woman I might have felt differently, but she was probably around the same age as Mr S, or as my own parents would be if they were still alive.

When the sun had passed the highest point in the sky and our clothes had dried enough that they didn't stick to the skin, she left. I watched her disappear along the path I'd walked earlier. Then, I had felt carefree, enjoying a day to myself before the work of the coming weeks. She walked lightly, but the tears were still running down her cheeks.

I put my clothes back on. It wouldn't do for the search party to find me sitting here in my underclothes.

As I waited, I wondered if these three boys had families, mothers and fathers and siblings who would grieve for them, or if they were orphans like myself. And I wondered if I would meet the woman again. I hoped I would.

14. Lauren

I was eleven or twelve. Mr Lion was having one of those afternoons when he played records in the back room with the doors open onto the back garden and a spliff constantly on the go. He didn't talk or involve me. I lay on the carpet near where the curtains touched the floor and kicked my legs behind me. Sometimes he put on one of my favourites. Dad came in to smoke with him. They drank beer and made comments about the musicians and the record companies. I didn't listen to them, only to the music.

This particular afternoon he put on a new record. Mr Lion haunted charity shops, markets and jumble sales, looking for new stuff, so there were often songs I hadn't heard before. This was something else, though. The moment the needle touched the vinyl I could feel the difference in the garden. The plants were paying attention. It was music I'd heard outside that no one else seemed to notice. It was the sound of a hot day after weeks of hot days, of dried earth and empty stream beds, of dried grass and plants desperate for water. The singer had a longing for rain and sang in the voice of the grass.

'Who's this?' I asked.

'It's Tallara Graham,' said Mr Lion.

'Do you like it?' Dad asked, sounding surprised.

'I love it.'

Mr Lion told me she was from Australia, an orphaned aboriginal girl who was brought up by white farmers. A three-year drought meant they nearly had to sell up, but then she began to sing and things turned around for them. The rain came and the cattle began to thrive. The crops grew and grew.

People wanted to buy her music and the family became the most successful farmers in the area. She was wooed by record companies and taken to New York, where she was murdered in an alleyway by a thief with a knife. The white family grieved, but they played her music and the farm continued to thrive.

I listened to the story and something settled in me. I may not have a mother, but here was an aboriginal girl who sang the song of parched grass from across the world, across the span of years, across death itself. I was not the only one who could hear.

Later I crept off to the woods and called for Peter, and when he came I sang him the song of the aboriginal girl.

He said 'That's your song. You sing like that all the time.'

I smiled. 'Let's go and build a dam in the woods.'

So we did and Peter caught a fish. We built a fire, and cooked the fish on hot slabs and ate it with our fingers, wrapped in ramsons. I took some roots home to plant beneath the hawthorn in my herb garden.

A vase of flowers had appeared on the front windowsill of our old house. In the evening the curtains were closed and the lights on. There was a bag of rubbish at the end of the path on bin day. She wasn't trying to hide.

I watched Dad. He must have known, there's no way he couldn't have, but he didn't say anything. There might have been a slight edge to him, a brittleness in his voice, a hint of awkwardness in his movements, but it might just have been that I was looking for it.

I had to walk past the house on the way to the bus stop or into town. Some days I took a detour and tried to forget she was there. Other days I went past slowly, looking out for new signs of her presence. Once I saw a figure moving across one of the upstairs rooms and I ran.

She left when I was a small baby and she wasn't part of my world. I didn't think I had any feelings for her at all. The force of my anger took me by surprise.

How dare she leave this great empty space in our lives, this empty house full of memories and the hopes of a young family? All these years. Then just come back and take up residence as though nothing had happened, as though it was her right. I knew this was just the beginning. Now she was living in the house, in the town, our lives would never be the same.

Two days later I got home from college and Dad was in the kitchen singing. He was washing up, his arms in the suds, singing some old song along with the radio. There was a pink rose on the table in a glass of water. My dad never sings. I put my bag down on the chair and backed out of the kitchen. He turned just as I closed the door quietly behind me.

'Lauren?'

But I was running down the road and through the town. I had to find Peter. I could talk to Peter.

He'd been at college that day and I didn't know if he'd be back yet: he often stayed to do extra work, finish off things they'd not completed in the lesson. I'd go to the woods, to our stone, and wait for him. He'd turn up sooner or later.

Peter's mum lives in Greece. When Peter was born she married his dad and came to live with them here in Hawden, but she couldn't cope with the cold. She was like a hothouse flower put out in the winter's frost. She wilted and blackened at the edges. She was ill all the time and refused point blank to leave the house while the hours of daylight were fewer than ten. She stayed inside with the heating on full blast, her baby sweating in layer upon layer of blankets.

His dad had never lived in a house before. He bought it for her as a wedding present, and now he struggled to stay inside its four walls. He would go out late at night when the dry heat felt like it was slowly cooking his muscles into meat and he couldn't stand it any longer. In his hideout in the hills, the cold air in his nostrils and the warmth of animal skin to protect against its bite, he would lie down and sleep, only to awaken in the morning to loneliness.

It went on for about a year I think. It was then that it became obvious which of his parents Peter took after. The soft down on his baby legs grew thicker and he kicked hard at his blankets, crawled towards any door that opened to the outside air. Everyone knew it couldn't go on.

One day she packed her bags and left. Peter and his dad went with her to the airport and they hugged and kissed and promised undying love. She went back to her homeland where she lives in a white house with the doors and windows open and sweet warm air wafting down from the mountains. He sold the house in town and moved back into the hills with baby Peter. But they visit Greece all the time, his dad even more than Peter. His parents are still in love.

I thought about my dad singing at the sink and wondered what it was like to have two parents who both loved you, even if they had to live in different worlds.

I hoped Peter would come soon. I wanted to ask him how you spoke to a mother who wasn't there for you, who never tied your shoelaces or kissed the top of your head in the school playground or made you cheese on toast after school. How did Peter deal with resentment? Did he even have any? He never spoke about his mother with anything but affection.

The day after the party by the canal I'd been for a walk with Richard. We were looking for a girl he'd met because we'd learned some information she might like to know.

At Jimmy and Suky's that night, Smith and Jeannie had got quite talkative. They were looking for this girl called Ali. I hadn't seen her, nor had Jimmy and Suky, and Richard said he hadn't either. She'd stolen some money from them.

'It was Jeannie's fault,' Smith said. 'If she hadn't taken Ali's ring we wouldn't be in this mess.'

Jeannie grinned. 'It was an impulse.'

'Yeah, and your impulse got us into this situation.' He turned back to us. 'The police raided our place, but Ali was nothing to do with that. She just crashed there, and she ran when we all did. That would have been it if madam here hadn't taken fancy to something shiny as she ran past.'

'Silly bitch shouldn't a left it there. I dint take it on purpose. I didn't think.'

'That's your problem, you never think.'

I looked up to catch Jimmy's eye. I knew he'd be loving this story. But he had his arms around Suky and wasn't looking my way. It was Richard that grinned at me.

'So what happened?' he asked.

Smith continued. 'It turned out that Ali was very attached to this ring, and she got the police onto us. I don't blame her. She's got no reason to be loyal, and she wanted her property back. She put up a proper fight, didn't she Jeannie?'

Jeannie pulled the neck of her top aside and there were some ugly red marks, like burns.

'Almost garotted me in the process, the cow. It hurt like hell.'

'It's your own fault,' Smith said, but he put out his hand and touched her lightly on the back of her neck and she smiled at him as though he'd given her a compliment.

'Anyhow, I legged it out the window in just me kecks and the police were all after me, except the ones that stayed to arrest Jeannie. Ali decided to go through me stuff. I'd have done the same. She was mad at us and she didn't take everything she found either. Just some money.'

'Is that why you're after her, to get the money back?' I asked. 'Was it a lot?'

Smith shrugged. 'No, not that much. About two grand.'

I opened my eyes a bit wider. It seemed a lot to me.

'It's not the cash. It's a pisser to lose it, but not the end of the world. It's just that there's something written on one of the notes.'

'What sort of thing?' Richard asked. We were all sitting forward, listening. 'A message?'

'No, a code. It's a deal I was doing – that's why the police were after me in the first place. They think I've hidden the stuff, but actually I haven't picked it up yet. I need this code and it's written on one of those notes. That's why I need to find her, the stuff's worth a hell of a lot more than two grand.'

'So if you got the code, you'd let her keep the money?' Richard asked.

'Why, d'ya know where she is?' Jeannie asked staring at him.

He shook his head. 'I just wondered.'

'I want the code,' Smith said.

'I want to slap her fucking face,' said Jeannie.

They told us they'd followed her this far, but lost her when they got to Hawden.

'She left a trail as wide as an aeroplane. But she's gone to ground here.'

We asked them lots of questions, and they told us what they knew about Ali, which was not much really, except that she was 'a nice kid'. They wouldn't tell us what it was they needed the code for, but I supposed it was drugs. Eventually we exhausted the subject, and by then the MDMA had kicked in and we lost interest in talking quite so much.

It was getting light when I went home. Richard walked with me.

'I know where Ali is,' he said

'Who?'

'The girl those two were talking about. She was at the party last night, but she saw them and ran away. I talked to her. I know where she's staying.'

'You're joking!'

'No. It's true. I'll walk up tomorrow and tell her about the code. Do you want to come?'

So the next day I met Richard in the square and we walked along the canal, then headed up through the valley.

'There's a house up here called Old Barn,' I said to Richard. 'It's where my mum grew up.'

'That's where we're going,' said Richard.

He walked on a few steps before he realised I'd stopped.

'What's the matter?'

'I can't go to Old Barn. My aunt lives there and she hates me.'

'Why?'

'I don't know. She's never met me really. She hates my dad too, and my mum. Most likely Mr Lion as well. I think she hates most people, but especially us.'

'Maybe it's time to make up.'

'I don't think so. She's crazy.'

But he took my arm and tugged gently, and grudgingly my feet shuffled along the loose stones on the path.

'She might not even be there.' I didn't know if he meant the girl or my aunt.

We didn't see either of them. We knocked on the front door at Old Barn and waited. I was about to suggest we went round the back as nobody uses their front doors round here, when it was opened by a man. He was a big man, fat and tall, but he stood right back in the gloom of the hall holding on to the door. We had to peer to see him.

'What do you want?' he said, and his voice was deep but thin.

Richard took a step forward and the man backed further away.

'We're looking for Ali, is she here?'

'She's gone.'

'Do you know when she'll be back?'

'She's taken her things and gone. You won't find her here.'

He started to close the door, but Richard leaned forward into the gloom.

'Where has she gone?'

'I've no idea.' This time he succeeded in closing the door in our faces.

'Who was that?' asked Richard. I could see myself reflected in his sunglasses.

'I haven't got a fucking clue.'

At school, in history, we learned about white witches who knew the lore of plants and the doctrine of signatures. I thought about the witches as children playing in the woods. How when they hurt themselves they heard the wild comfrey offering its leaves as a bandage. How they knew which berries were safe to eat and which herbs would kill a cat. Which was the poisonous part of a yew tree and how much you needed to make the teacher sick.

I knew that marigolds and nasturtiums didn't really get on, and delphiniums found lupins irritating. I liked to listen to the plants in my garden. The roses whispered, wishing the others would all be quiet. The vegetables sang songs of soup and frittatas. The onions told dirty jokes which made the cauliflowers laugh. The roses blushed and the runner beans tutted and turned away. But my favourite was the herb garden with its secrets of light and dark.

I grew plants for the pot and plants for healing. Most of them could be dangerous in the wrong amounts. Some would give you the runs, a rash, or hallucinations. Some could kill a person. I knew them all, they talked to me. They told me their powers.

Someone was coming up the path, but it wasn't Peter. As he came nearer I recognised the footfall and the soft sound of Richard's boots on the hard ground. I shrank back behind the stone so I was hidden from sight. The brambles hissed in my ears. I didn't want to give away this place, didn't want to share it with anyone except Peter.

I thought about Richard's mother, Meg, with her Porsche. She wasn't a run-of-the-mill school playground sort of mum. I bet she never took him to a toddler group. And where was his father? His home life wasn't very ordinary either.

I waited until he was almost out of sight, then I slipped out onto the path and ran after him.

He heard me as I approached and stood back to let me pass, leaning into a rowan tree which shivered its branches.

'I was running to catch you up,' I said, ignoring the rowan.

'I was taking the short cut up to Heath.'

'Do you mind if I walk with you?'

'I would be delighted.'

I looked at him, but I didn't think he was taking the piss. It was hard to tell when you couldn't see his eyes. Sometimes his language was just a bit odd, a bit old for him. I supposed it was because he'd lived in different places.

15. Peter

Peter was in the lab when he heard her whistle. Even though it was two miles away and there was a massive hill in the way, his ears picked up the sound. He turned off the light generator and laid a mirrored sheet flat on the desk.

'I have to go,' he said to his teacher.

She looked up from her marking. His equipment was spread out across the workbench where Year Twelve students would need to sit in the morning.

'I'll come in early and tidy up,' he said. 'Sorry, it's urgent.'

She didn't mention that fact that his phone hadn't rung, that he hadn't even looked at it, that no one had come with a message. Nothing had happened to disturb the still afternoon air of the laboratory. She just smiled.

He went straight across country, skidding down steep slopes between birch trees, leaping streams, bounding through heather and bog on the tops. The black mud spattered his haunches. He didn't always answer her whistle. If he was very far away, or in the middle of something, he'd text, catch up with her as soon as he could. But Cassie was back in town, living in the house where Lauren had spent her first few months of life. The mother she hadn't seen since she was a tiny baby. He knew Lauren was upset.

It couldn't have been more than twenty minutes since the whistle when he got there. The stone was empty, though still warm in the middle where she'd sat. He heard voices and looked down towards the main path. The leaves of the wych elms were quivering, and he wondered what they were saying. Lauren wasn't listening to them. She was walking away and Richard

117

was walking at her side, wearing his long black coat, his shiny hair the blue-black normally only found on crows and goths.

He heard her laughter dancing across the surface of the pond. The ducks swam through it, ruffling their feathers in the sunshine.

16. Lauren

I lifted the knocker and then let it quietly down again. She probably hadn't seen me yet. I could just walk away and forget about it. I didn't have to do it. Winter jasmine was growing in the front garden but it was quiet. I closed my eyes and took a deep breath, then knocked on the door.

The sound was thin and I wondered if it would carry through the house, if she would hear it. She might not open the door to just anyone, she might check who it was first from behind the curtain at the upstairs window. It was possible she was up there looking at me now wondering who I was. I was a baby last time she saw me.

The door opened.

She was older but she was still the woman from the photo. Her hair was tied back in a pony tail and she wore jeans with a dark blue jumper. Our eyes met and I knew that she hadn't been looking out of the window and that seeing me standing there was a real shock to her. Neither of us said anything. After a moment she stood back and opened the door wider as an invitation for me to come into the hall.

I stepped in to what was once my family home. I hadn't been inside since I was a baby. She closed the door behind me and leaned against it for moment as though she needed support. Then she straightened up. 'Come on through,' she said.

I didn't recognise her voice. I followed her into the room.

She was very tense. She stood near the window and I looked at the room. On one side was a bookcase which stretched half the length of the wall and reached up to about waist height.

The top of it was covered in framed photographs and they were all of me.

They weren't arranged in chronological order, but they covered practically the whole of my life. All of my school photos and others too, familiar photos from holidays with Dad and Mr Lion, me holding an ice-cream on the beach at Whitby, me spinning a hoop round my waist in the garden, me wearing a cycle helmet and grinning from ear to ear next to my bike that I'd just learned to ride. Even one of me waving a piece of paper in the air which had my GCSE results. That one was taken last year.

I looked at her.

'Your dad sent me the pictures. I'd asked him to.'

'He knew where you were?'

'He sent them to a post office box. He knew the town, that was all.'

I thought about that. He could have gone there and looked for her. It might have been like looking for a needle in a haystack, especially if it was a big town. I suppose it would have been a bit stalker-ish as well, and if she didn't want him then his pride would have stopped him. But he might have done it for me. She was obviously interested in her daughter, which was a whole lot more than I'd expected. It was a bit freaky to think this woman had been watching me all these years from afar, watching me grow up in still pictures. That she was so familiar with my face, when I knew her from just one photo.

I went over to the bookcase and picked up the picture that was in the middle, sort of like a centrepiece. It was of my mum and my dad and me. I was a baby and I had a grimace on my face. My mum was holding me on her lap and Dad was sitting with his arm round her. She was looking at me and he was looking at her and their eyes were shining. They were the perfect family.

I couldn't say anything but I had loads of questions buzzing through my brain. How could you have this and throw it away?

I wanted to shout it. Why did you have to hurt Dad so much? How is it I'm nearly eighteen years old and I don't even know you?

She stood next to me and looked at the photo.

'We were very happy,' she said.

I swallowed. I didn't want my voice to break when it came out. I wanted it to be strong and steady and I had to wait a moment before I was ready.

'We're happy now. Dad and Mr Lion and me. We're a good family.'

She looked me in the face, her eyes intent, watching me.

'Andy is a good man,' she said. 'A lovely man.'

I thought she was going to say more but her voice was unsteady too.

I noticed the way her face moved as she breathed and swallowed, how when she blinked little lines appeared for a second around her eyes. How the emotion she was feeling had made her flushed and she gave off a faint pleasant smell of sweat mingled with perfume. The picture of her above our fireplace did none of these things.

'I have to go,' I said.

She didn't try to stop me. I slammed the front door behind me, and then I ran, right across town to the park where I found a bench in the rose garden and sat on it with my head in my hands and my heart racing.

If anyone asked me, I'd have said that I wanted to get to know her and talk to her. But really I wanted to be angry with her. I'd gone there with confrontation at the back of my mind and hoped that I'd find evidence of her badness. I was so angry already, I wanted something to bolster that, to justify and feed my anger. But she'd just seemed scared. Scared of what I might say and more than that, that I wouldn't like her. She wanted me to like her. I didn't know if I could cope with the evil queen suddenly turning out to be an ordinary woman after all.

There were a few straggly late blossoms in the rose garden and the warm autumn sunshine released their perfume into the air. I listened to their murmurings, pressed my fingers against my eyelids and breathed in.

'What's up chick?' Jimmy sat down on the bench next to me. He put his hand over mine and squeezed it. 'You ok?'

I shrugged.

He smiled at me and I looked at his face. It was familiar in the way that my mother's wasn't. I knew what every movement of his eyes or mouth would do to the muscles in his cheeks and jaw. I could tell if he was happy or sad from tiny movements at the edge of his mouth and the light at the back of his eyes. I snuggled up against him and he put his arm around me.

'Do you miss your mother?' I asked him.

'Mum? Oh I don't know,' he said. 'It's years now since she passed on. I used to miss her a lot, but it's kind of become normal now, her not being around. I don't think about her that often.'

'But you've got good memories of her.'

'Good and bad. She was ill for years and she was a whingey old bag a lot of the time. But she was a sweetie too.'

A woman came into the garden with a pushchair. She'd just come out of the post office which was right next to the entrance to the rose garden, and she was carrying a large brown paper parcel. She was struggling. She carried it under one arm and was pushing with the other arm, but the pushchair wasn't going in a straight line. She crouched down and looked in the tray beneath the child's seat, but it was already full. She tried moving the stuff about, but it was a waste of time because the parcel was too big to fit there even if it was empty. She walked round to the front of the pushchair and spoke to the child.

'I don't have any memories of my mum at all.'

Jimmy knew my face as well I knew his; there was no use pretending anything with him.

'Have you seen her?'

I nodded. The woman put the parcel on the ground, took the child out of the pushchair, strapped the parcel into the seat and lifted the child onto her hip.

'I went round to the house. You know she's living there now?'

'Yes.' The arrangement worked. She still only had one hand for the pushchair, but it was lighter now, and the child fitted snugly against her. The woman disappeared into the park. 'I saw her in the market the other day.'

'Oh Jimmy!'

I laid my head on his shoulder. An old man pottered by with his dog. The dog had silver hair around its chops and waddled slowly behind its owner.

'I don't know what to think or what I should be feeling. I was angry, but when I met her that just vanished and I couldn't be angry with her.'

'Just let it happen,' Jimmy said.

'But why is she here? Why has she come back now?'

'You'll find out in good time.'

He was right. I should stop worrying and let the situation unfold itself. I leaned against him and breathed in the rose scent. A postman came dashing into the garden with his fluorescent bag slung over his back. Half way across he broke into a run. I remembered the conversation I'd had with Suky that day on the way up to Hough Dean.

'How about you anyway?' I asked Jimmy. 'What you up to?'

'I'm still working for Meg Crossley. There's a lot of work. It's been standing empty for way too long.'

'She likes you.'

'I don't think I irritate her as much as some. She doesn't suffer fools. If she minded me being around, she wouldn't have the work done. She'd rather have the mess.'

'What does Suky think?'

He turned on the seat so I had to lift my head off his shoulder and he looked at my face.

'Suky? Suky thinks it's great that I've got some work. She's pleased. Why?'

I shrugged. 'I just wondered.' He was still looking at me and I knew I'd puzzled him. 'So everything is fine with you and Suky then?'

'Of course it is.'

The trouble with knowing someone that well is that you can't lie to them. His eyes met mine but held something back. His voice didn't ring clear.

'What is it Jimmy?'

He slumped back against the wooden bench. 'She thinks I'm up to something. Something extra curricular.'

'And?'

'She hasn't said anything to me. It's just kind of there at the moment. Unspoken between us.'

'Why does she think it?'

He looked down at his hands in his lap, then up again across the garden.

'I've been home late a few times. I guess she's putting two and two together.'

'Is four the right answer?'

Jimmy didn't say anything, which is quite unusual for him. I was surprised. I'd been sure Suky's suspicions would turn out to be groundless, that there would be some other explanation. She was so precious to him I couldn't believe he'd endanger what he had with her.

'Is it Meg Crossley?' I asked.

'God no!' He looked aghast. 'She's good for her age, but… no, how could you think that? I don't even like her.'

'Well who is it then?'

Again the uncomfortable silence. I noticed him looking towards the entrance. A man was just walking through in the direction of the post office. Jimmy was trying to keep his face still so it didn't give anything away, but it wasn't working. His eye flickered and he swallowed so his cheeks sucked in a little. He'd come from that direction himself.

'Steph?'

He looked quickly at me then away again and still said nothing. Steph had dark blonde hair which she mostly wore scraped back into a ponytail, and she wore grey jersey skirts, soft blouses and cardigans. At least she did for working at the post office. I remembered her coming back to ours that night of the party. I'd never have thought of her and Jimmy in a million years.

'It's not what you think,' Jimmy said.

'What is it then?'

He shook his head and opened his hands.

'I can't tell you about it here.'

I stood up. 'Come round to our house and have some tea.'

'Ok. You can tell me all about you and Peter, too. Something's changed with you two as well. Something good, I think.'

He gave me a knowing look and I grinned.

Nobody was in and the house was empty. I made a pot of tea and we sat at the kitchen table with mugs full and steaming.

'It started a few months back,' Jimmy said. He looked more comfortable now. The admission was made and he had a story to tell me. 'I was in the White Horse chatting to folk, like you do. Steph was there with a couple of friends. One of them had a birthday and they'd all drunk quite a bit and the conversation got round to sex. There was quite a group of us sitting around the corner near the fire, Steph and her friends and me and five or six other people. Her friends were really loud and started talking about orgasms. It all got a bit silly and out of hand and one of them started making a load of noise and the barman was giving us looks. Steph didn't say anything, though she laughed a lot and she was a bit flushed from drinking.

'In the end one of her friends had too much and was ill, so the other one took her home, but Steph stayed. It was getting

125

on and gradually people peeled off and went home, until it was just me and her. I was doing my normal thing, talking. I think I was telling her about the circus. And she was listening with these big eyes like it was the best story she'd ever heard.'

'Like Desdemona.'

'What?'

'That's why Desdemona fell in love with Othello: because of the stories he told.'

He took a gulp of his tea.

'Well I don't know about love.'

'Go on then, what happened next? As if I can't guess.'

'I doubt you can.'

I raised my eyebrows.

'We got more drinks in and Steph moved a bit closer to me on the seat, and I thought the same as you're thinking and decided I'd better make a quick exit. But she didn't make any moves or anything. She said, please keep talking Jimmy, so I did. I mean, I'd had a few and usually people are telling me to shut up by that time of night. I don't even remember now what I was saying, I was just blithering on about various people I've known and places I've been.'

'And she was lapping it up.'

'Anyway, by the time we'd finished our drinks they were kicking people out and Steph asked if I'd come round to hers for a nightcap. It seemed like a good idea. I was on a roll and another drink seemed like a plan. I told myself I didn't have to do anything else.'

'Hmmm.'

'At her place she only had white wine so she poured a couple of glasses. Then she told me what she wanted.'

He stopped and drank his tea.

'Go on then, what did she want?'

'She told me... Laurie, you've got to promise that you won't tell this to anyone else. I shouldn't be telling you.'

'Ok, I promise.' I wondered if I ought to cross my fingers, thinking of Suky, but my hands were wrapped around my mug and I couldn't.

'She told me she'd never had an orgasm.'

'What, never?'

'Never, not with anyone, not even by herself.'

'But she's like, how old?'

'She's twenty-four. She'd never had one and it really bothered her.'

'And she thought you...' That was some line.

'She said she'd been getting really turned on by me talking and she thought if I carried on...'

'While...?'

'No, she didn't want me to do anything else. I put my arm around her and put my mouth close to her ear, but that was it.'

'And? Did she?'

'It was amazing. I just kept talking in her ear and she went very still for a while, and then she started moving her hips and moaning. Well, you know. Her head moved a bit, so I put a hand on her shoulder to keep her still and carried on talking into her ear, until she stopped. She was really sweaty.'

'Then what happened?'

'Nothing. I mean, she was really emotional and cried a bit and kept saying thank you. But we didn't do anything else. We finished the wine and I went home.'

'And you've been seeing her since?'

'Not much. A few times when we've both been out and bumped into each other. We haven't planned to meet.'

'And you always just... talk?'

'Yup, just talk.'

He was probably telling the truth. I mean, if I was to break my promise and tell Suky, I don't think she'd be too impressed. He was seeing another woman for sexual purposes, even if they never actually had sex. Or took their clothes off.

'Hasn't she been tempted to try anything else? I mean, since...'

'Normal sex doesn't really appeal to her.'

'That's bloody weird, Jimmy.'

I poured some more tea from the pot. Then I thought of something.

'Hadn't you just come from the post office when I met you earlier?'

He nodded and looked a bit shamefaced. 'I pop in sometimes, if I'm passing, and tease her a bit. If it's not busy and there's no queue. I go in and buy a stamp and I tell her stuff – anecdotes or whatever. The other staff think I'm just being chatty, and she gives me these evil glares. She likes it though.'

'Jimmy, I just don't believe you sometimes.'

He looked at me anxiously and I grinned. What else could I do?

Then the door opened and Dad came in. He was whistling, and the smile vanished from my face.

17. Meg, 1889

Seeing those boys drown at Gaddings Dam was one of the worst days. It was only nine weeks since Charles had died, and I was flooded with memories of him as a boy of that age. I missed my child, with his huge and unrestrained appetite for living and learning, and I missed the man, strong and determined, devout in his belief in science, which he claimed would be the new religion. When he was older, we had long night-time talks about the theories of Mr Darwin, chess games that lasted for days on end and rambles across the moors looking for plants, fungi, liverworts, whatever it was that obsessed him at the time.

The day of the drowning I'd been hoping that a stride on the moors in the fresh air would bring colour to my cheeks and make me forget, if only for a short time. I walked for miles, over to Blackstone Edge and back up to Broadhead Clough before heading back to Langfield Moor. I felt energised, but it was an effort to keep the thoughts at bay. When memories threatened to crowd in I increased my pace and concentrated on the path beneath my feet. Eventually I was tired and sat down to rest.

I was wearing some of Charles' clothes. It can make things simpler, as long as you don't get too close to people. No one feels the need to protect and accompany you the way they do if they see a woman alone on the moors. Also, I feel more comfortable wearing the spectacles with men's clothes when I'm in public, and it was too bright a day to be abroad without them.

I saw the three boys come scampering along the path, and to my shame I thought about how young and vigorous they were and how the blood ran strongly in their veins. They went into the water and I smiled at their antics.

Soon afterwards I saw the young man arrive and settle on the other side of the water, and was glad that he hadn't noticed me.

The drowning happened so fast. Despite my baser instincts, I wanted to find those boys alive, to pull their little limp bodies from the reservoir and pump the water out of them, fill them with life-giving air. But we couldn't find them, and after a while there was no point in searching any more because the chance of life had gone.

That's when the tears started. I hadn't cried when Charles died, or in the intervening weeks. There had been a numbness as though my heart were encased in rock. Now, with the mad chase into the water, the frantic diving and the hopeless realisation, the rock had crumbled away.

The three dead boys would have mothers who would soon be grieving and keening, and they would never have the pleasure of seeing their boys grow into strong young men, of watching them make their way in the world. I had that with Charles. I grew to know Charles as a friend, one of the best friends I've ever had. The tears rolled down my face unchecked.

The young man looked at me curiously. He had only just realised my gender, but his face didn't hold criticism, only interest and some sympathy. He was young, not many years older than the drowned boys. He was dripping wet in his underwear, but he didn't rush to put his clothes on as I think most men would have done, and I liked that about him. But I couldn't stay, and the tears weren't stopping.

They didn't stop that day or even that week. I kept to the house during daylight as the salt irritated my eyes and made them red and raw, and sunlight was painful even with the glasses. I kept the curtains drawn and occasionally ventured out after dark when hunger got the better of me. Charles had gone and there was no one else I could talk to. My bodice became salt streaked, my cheeks lined with white.

One day I woke up and my pillow was dry. I put my fingers to my face and found the rims of my eyes were crusted, swollen and sore, but there were no more tears. It was mid afternoon. The sun would be high in the summer sky, but I had an urge to go outside.

I bathed my face in tepid water until the sores softened and my skin regained enough flexibility to grimace at myself in the glass. I dressed in Charles' clothes, placed the tinted spectacles on my face, and ventured out.

For ten days I had been living in dim light behind drawn curtains and the soft dark of night. The harsh brightness brought bile to my throat. I stood on the step, tempted to scuttle back inside and wait until nightfall. But I remembered Charles's rejection of my way of life. He didn't want to live hiding in shadows, never able to bare his face to the honest light of the sun. I took a deep breath and stepped out.

My feet took me in the direction of the monument and the reservoir. I wanted news of the drowned boys and, although it was unlikely anyone would be about on a working day, I could think of nowhere else to go. I couldn't walk into town and buy a newspaper. Not enough time had passed for memories there to fade.

As I approached the monument I became aware of a noise: tapping and scraping. It was coming from the edifice itself. I looked up, my hand shielding my eyes from the worst of the sun's glare, and saw a man suspended on a rope right up at the top. I couldn't see exactly what he was doing, but his movements didn't seem to fit with the sounds I could hear. I walked around the base, but couldn't see anyone else.

I had been inside the monument a few times, when my new life was raw upon me and I had a need for the cover of darkness. By taking away one of the senses my actions seemed to take place in fewer dimensions and have less reality. If I couldn't actually see what I did I could pretend I hadn't done it.

When I became accustomed to that life, however, I no longer had need of pretence.

I entered the stairwell and walked up the stairs. Halfway up, I was plunged into blackness, but after a few steps a shaft of light pierced the gloom. I climbed to the balcony and found the source of the tapping noise.

A young man in workman's clothing was making a hole in the floor, using a chisel and hammer to chip and scrape at the hard stone.

'That looks like a thankless task,' I said.

He looked up, dust from the stone flying up around him in a cloud, and I recognised the young man from the reservoir. Like mine, his eyes were bloodshot, the rims swollen and raw.

Charles was fretful that night. When I tried to hand him to the nurse he clung to my dress with tiny fingers and said 'I want mummy.'

The nurse tried to be strict with him. 'Now don't be a silly boy, you know your mother has to go out and you will see her in the morning.'

He buried his face into my neck and nuzzled there, his breath hot on my neck, and I knew I couldn't give him up.

'I'll take him with me,' I said, and the nurse's face tightened.

'Mistress, it will be too cold up there for a little boy.'

I knew she thought I was wrong to attend the ceremony myself, that I should leave such things to the menfolk. But I had no menfolk, only Charles. I asked the nurse to fetch his coat and she went off with a face like a sour plum. I wondered if I should let her go. There was nothing she did that I couldn't do myself. It was only propriety which dictated I should not demean myself with certain tasks. But propriety interested me less and less these days, and up here on the moor there were no neighbours to watch and comment.

Charles never liked me to leave him with the nurse and was always calmer when I held him myself. I found great comfort in this.

His father, my husband Daniel Crossley, was killed at war when Charles was but four months in my belly. Ours had been a great love match. Although not wholly disapproved by our families, neither of us were first choice for our in-laws, but nothing could have dissuaded us. We were so hungry for each other we would have married even if it had landed us in poverty and disgrace. Our families gave permission and we moved to this house high on the moor, far from everyone. We had only two servants: a maid, and a boy who worked in the kitchen and stable. We paid little attention to them, only to each other. It was the most perfect time. The two of us lived in a bubble of happiness so intense that sometimes I would break down and cry in great gulping sobs, and Daniel would stroke my hair and feed me squares of sweet chocolate.

It lasted less than a year. A tiny portion of the life I have lived. Yet I would happily give up everything, past and future, to live that time again. Even Charles. Even Richard. No one came near him in my affections until I met Andy.

He was called to war and he left for France and I never saw him again. My Daniel. He never even knew that I was carrying our child.

When the Quakers came knocking on my door after the war was over, asking for contributions to a monument, I was happy to help. Its purpose was to celebrate peace rather than war. I had nothing else I wanted to spend my money on. I hated the war that had taken Daniel from me and I hated the country that needed him. The Quakers were surprised at my generosity.

It wasn't only the Quakers involved, of course, as I realised when the planning got under way.

I found I wanted to offer more than money. My grief over Daniel's loss had been so devastating that I had sunk into apathy. If it hadn't been for the child I was carrying, I might have been tempted to take my life in the hopes of finding Daniel in the next world, or at least sinking into pain-free oblivion. Even after

Charles was born, the world continued grey and empty. As soon as I handed the child to the nurse I sank back into listlessness.

This project brought me back to life. It gave me something to focus on and something to do. I wanted to be actively involved. There were difficulties of course, because of my gender, but I threatened to withdraw my funding if they didn't include me. That would have delayed the project significantly so they gave in. On my behalf, meetings had to be moved from the Masonic Lodge to the Town Hall, and some of the other committee members cast me resentful glances.

The opening ceremony had to be changed to accommodate my presence as well. I wouldn't back down. We marched up the hill to the monument together. Some of them wore their regalia and carried swords, and I carried Charles on my hip. The Master of Ceremonies looked aghast when I arrived with the boy in my arms, but there was nothing he could do.

They hoped I would stand back, let them hold ceremony whilst I kept my distance, but that was not my plan and I thrust myself into the thick of it, which was how the accident happened.

The Master of Ceremonies lifted his sword high into the air and the weight of it made him lose his footing slightly. He shifted his arms in an attempt to regain his balance, and the blade came slicing through the air into poor Charles's head.

There was a dreadful silence which seemed to go on forever before the child's wailing filled the air. Blood was gushing from the wound, dripping onto his shirt and collar and onto my dress. I gasped, then lifted my skirts and ran.

The nurse was shocked when we arrived home covered in gore and together we examined the wound. It wasn't deep, but the boy had lost a lot of blood from his small body and he was weak and pale. He was not unconscious, but his crying had stopped and he was listless, letting us move him as we wished. His eyes were dull and he didn't speak. I could see the nurse was worried.

That night we took it in turns to sit with him. I put him to bed in my own room that I had shared with Daniel. The bleeding had stopped and we had bandaged his head. He slept, unmoving, his body so small in the vast bed. I was scared that Death was going to take another from me. I paced the room and gazed out across the moors to the starry sky. It was a moonlit night and the new monument showed up as a dark pointed silhouette.

It was during my second watch, in the small hours of the morning, that Death came. I heard him first, a soft swishing sound at the window. When I looked I saw a dark shape moving like a wraith. He had come for Charles and my heart filled with anger. I rushed to the bed and threw my body across my child's. His skin was cold, but when I placed my ear against his chest I could hear his heart still beating faintly. I held him against me, hoping to give him some of my own warmth.

The window opened with a loud crash as the frame was thrust back against the wall, and cold air rushed into the room. The dark shape circled the bed and Charles' heartbeat was getting weaker and weaker. The end had come for him.

I was desperate. Death had taken Daniel from me, and was now going to take Charles, his child. I screamed aloud.

'Don't take him. Please don't take him.'

The shape still circled. Charles was cold, his heartbeat barely a murmur.

Then I heard the voice.

'He has been marked. I come to collect my own.'

I screamed again.

'No, please. He is but a child. Take me instead.'

A stillness fell over the room. Nothing moved in the darkness. I held Charles' body to my chest and looked about the room wildly.

'Are you still there? Do you hear me? Take me instead.'

Death loomed up before me and spoke in his soft voice.

'If you give yourself to me voluntarily, I can do with you what I want.'

'I don't care. Spare my boy.'

'I may make you one like myself, or one of the other countless beings of this world who neither live nor receive the comfort of death.'

'Please, he is nearly gone. Give him back his life and take mine.'

Death thrust his face in mine and I saw into the depths of his eyes. In them I could see the years stretching ahead of me and I knew that I would never see Daniel again in this life or any other, and that my life would go on and on and on. But I would not have him steal my son as well as my husband, and I stared back unblinking.

Death's lips brushed against mine. 'So be it, my angel,' he said.

And I sank back into blackness.

The young man blinked at me as the dust cloud dispersed.

'You!' he said. 'I'd almost convinced myself you were a dream.'

'Well you must be dreaming again, for here I am. What are you doing?'

'Making a skylight for the stairwell. We're doing some repairs.'

'So no more plunging into the dark.'

He frowned. 'That was a stupid idea anyway.'

'You've decided to be the bringer of light?'

He grinned. 'Mr S is making me do this in my lunch breaks, as it's not actually a repair, and it was my idea.'

I looked up to where the older man was suspended from a rope.

'He's fixing on a lightning conductor.'

'He won't mind you talking to me?'

'It's my lunch break.'

I looked about, but there didn't seem to be signs of any food. He was thin. I wondered who looked after him.

'What happened with those boys?' I asked.

He looked at me with surprise. It had probably been the talk of the town, filling the newspapers. He would have expected me to know all the details.

'They got them out, eventually. A policeman dived in, and some others and I went back in too. It was the next morning when they found them. They were all dead.'

I turned away. 'Their poor mothers.'

'We did what we could, you and I,' the young man said. 'We couldn't have saved them.'

His words were a question. It must have been preying on his mind.

'It was too late even before we hit the water,' I said.

'I saw them up here,' he said. 'They were running and laughing.'

He rubbed at his sore eyes with the back of his wrist.

'You should have some protection for your eyes. All that stone dust might damage your sight.'

'I do have some.' He indicated a pair of goggles on the top of his work bag a few yards away. I picked them up and held them out to him, but he didn't take them.

'It seems that pain is my lot in life so I may as well embrace it.'

I laughed. 'That sounds very bitter for one so young.'

He shrugged. 'I'm alone.'

'I am alone too. Is your solitary situation new to you?'

'I was to be married but my betrothed has forsaken me for another. My family are all dead. I lodge with Mr S at the stonemason's yard. That's my life now.'

He was young and life would change for him.

But an idea had entered my head.

Charles had been my friend and companion throughout his life until his death of old age. I no longer had a son and I missed him sorely.

I sat down on the stone floor next to the hole the young man was making.

'What's your name?' I asked him.

'Richard.'

'Richard, tell me about yourself. What are your dreams?'

18. Richard

The first bite is just a beginning and usually also the end. The first bite binds the victim to you only lightly. Until the wound has healed they will dwell on you in their thoughts. They may seek out your company and they will feel a physical bond as their blood feeds your body. By the time the skin has closed over, their blood will have nourished you and you will have no further need of each other. If you are a stranger to them and never return, you will remain only as a memory or a fragment of a dream.

The second bite has a bond of iron and can only occur when the first wound is completely healed. This is the bite that makes the victim want you. They will turn to you with their body and their soul and they will seek you out, desperate if they can't find you. They will follow you across desert or mountain or snowy wastes. They will offer themselves to you, prostrate themselves before you. While their blood is in your body they will desire you like a powerful drug. They will hunger for your teeth. But if you bite them a third time before the second wound has healed they will die. The second bite is not to be undertaken lightly, best done only as part of a turning. After the wound heals, the victim's desperate hunger will fade, but will never completely leave them. They may live a normal life, but they will carry with them a yearning for something else, which they will never quite understand.

In a turning, the second bite must completely heal before the third can be attempted. The third bite will complete the process.

I've had a hundred and twenty years of first bites. I've never turned anyone. I take what I need for food then leave, and I rarely see the victim again. It's mostly girls and they're usually drunk. That way they don't remember clearly, they think the wound must have occurred during some drunken accident. I live as a scrap of memory in the minds of thousands who have nourished me.

My constant companion has been my 'mother' Meg, and we have travelled the world together. We have lived in cities and deserts, forests and ghettos. We have travelled in the Americas, crossed the African plains, followed the circus through China and Russia and gone walkabout in Australia. We have wandered the battlefields of two world wars, feeding on the dying. Sometimes we have joined with others of our kind in ones or twos or even small communities hidden in the depths of the largest cities. Twice Meg has turned a man who she thought to make a third in our small family, but neither of them stayed. They went their own way when it became clear how much Meg demanded from them in intensity and devotion. They could not satisfy her, could not be the lover she desired. So they left us and we were once again mother and son.

Life had been full of interest and I'd seen and done many things, but recently I had become restless. Meg sometimes went off on her own and then I was lonely. I began to hate my victims, young girls and boys who were happy to throw their arms around me and receive my kiss on their neck in return for a couple of vodkas. Who would wake the next day rubbing the soreness of their skin with the vague memory of a tall dark stranger. And even that memory would fade over a week or two. I wanted someone who wanted me.

It wasn't a new feeling to me, of course. I had been desperate for love before Meg found me. My fiancée, Laura, had left me for another, a lad whose father had a lathe and who had good prospects and strong thighs. I was devastated, but it would have passed. If Meg hadn't turned up when she did, I would have found another girl, because life ran strongly in my veins. I think I missed the romps with Laura behind the hawthorn hedge at sunset more than anything else about her. When I tried to remember her I could summon up a length of inner thigh, milk white and covered with the finest hairs that glinted in the evening sunlight; a fall of blonde hair across my belly; the crease and roll of flesh where her breasts rose beneath her arms. I could remember her laugh and her intake of breath. But I couldn't see her face or remember anything we had talked about.

We were in Paris living in a small commune near the Père Lachaise cemetery. I had been out the night before at a club and I was satiated. I slept deeply into the day and woke before nightfall. I had dreamed and the sensations from my dream filled my waking mind. I was walking through woodland and I knew the path well. There were bluebells and there was a girl beside me holding my hand. I couldn't turn to look at her, but I could feel the warmth of her palm against mine, the grasp of her finger tips on the back of my hand. I tried to see more of her, but my head would not move. In my peripheral vision I thought I could see blonde hair swaying as she walked, but she was half a step behind me and I wasn't sure. When I woke I put my hands together. My right palm was warm and tingled from the girl's touch.

The feeling stayed with me all through that night in the centre of Paris. I stretched my fingers and felt human warmth in my palms. When I lay down to rest in the early hours of the morning I hoped to dream the dream again, but didn't. I woke with longing in my palms and an empty hunger in my chest.

I went in search of Meg and told her that I wanted to go home.

19. Lauren

At breakfast Dad said he thought we needed to talk and my heart sank. It was bound to be about my mum. I gave him a quick smile and said I wasn't sure what I was doing later.

So when Richard texted to ask if I wanted to walk up to the monument after college, I jumped at it.

'I've been reading about stonemasons,' he told me when we met in town.

'Not freemasons?'

'Hmmm, sometimes the same thing,' he said. 'The monument could come into your project too. It was built by Unitarians.'

I looked at him in surprise. 'Yes, I just found that out.'

I had a couple of frees on Wednesday afternoon so there was plenty of time before it got dark, and the sun was shining. A stroll on the moors sounded like a fine idea.

We set off through the Field Estate which covers the lower sweep of the hill. Although Richard remembered some things about the place pretty well, other things confused him. As we walked along the track at the back of the houses he said 'Are you sure this is the way?' and I laughed. I'd come this way more times than I could remember. When the path rose up higher than the houses he seemed to get his bearings.

I was surprised at his speed again. I asked him to slow down at one point when the path veered up steeply. He laughed and held out his hand.

'Come on, I'll pull you up.'

I hesitated. Going for a walk with him was one thing, going for a walk holding hands was another.

'Just up the hill.'

'Ok.'

I put my hand in his and his fingers closed around mine. We were still in the woods and the beech trees were whispering into the spaces beneath them. I didn't want to listen. Richard's hands were large and cool and, although he didn't seemed to be pulling me very hard, the hill did seem a lot easier, almost effortless.

'I walk a lot,' he said. 'I have strong legs.'

After the beech woods, the path rises steeply past an old stone farmhouse and then turns to the right and levels out. It continues at this height for a mile or so before rising again up to Langfield Moor. When it levelled I tugged at my hand and he let it go. He rubbed his palms together.

'You have warm hands,' he said.

I liked it better when he was being sarcastic. I knew how to answer him then.

'I'll race you to that stile,' I said, and ran.

At first I thought he wasn't going to race. I ran and he stayed behind. At least I could stop and wait for him at the stile, get my breath back. But then when I was nearly there he sped past me. He wasn't wearing his black coat today. He was wearing a leather jacket which zipped up at the front, and jeans, and as he ran I noticed how long his legs were, how powerful he looked when he moved. He reminded me of a deer running in the forest, or maybe a big cat. I thought about Peter. He's really fast, but I thought Richard would give him a run for his money. It would probably depend on the terrain. Peter is nimble and his hooves mean that he can leap and race across country and on stony ground. On the flat Richard might be able to beat him.

He was waiting for me at the stile.

'You're fast.'

'I can't resist a challenge,' he said.

We walked at a pace after that, side by side but no more hand holding, even when the path got steep again. He was different today. I kept my gaze on the path in front of me. He still wore his sunglasses so his eyes were covered, but I felt that if I looked at him I might say something with my own.

It was cold on the moor even though the sun was shining, and the heather was wailing in the wind. We walked around the base of the monument and leaned into the gusts. Sometimes up there you think you'll blow right away, and when you can't bear it any more it's time to go inside. The stone staircase spirals up the centre, plunges you into darkness, then thrusts you out again into a higher level.

Richard said he wanted to go up first. He asked me to wait at the bottom and watch for him to appear before I started coming up.

'Why?' I asked.

'Just humour me,' he said.

I hugged my coat around me. It was freezing, but Richard didn't seem to be bothered by the cold. I hopped from foot to foot and kept looking up but the sky made my eyes water. I wouldn't hear him if he shouted. The wind would carry his voice off as soon as it left his lips.

It seemed ages but eventually he was there, waving at me over the stone balustrade. I raced around to the other side and into the stairwell. The wind stopped instantly. I could hear it, but it was on the other side of thick stone walls and I was enclosed in stillness. I was warmer already.

I always loved doing this. There's the point, half way up, where everything closes down and it's pitch black. I've been here with friends and torches, once even with a candle that flickered and made shapes on the black walls, but it's best without. The darkness is utter and complete but momentary. Two steps, or three and then there's a glimmer of light from above.

Today the glimmer didn't come. I took another step and it was still dark. I stopped and felt the stone wall on my right. I slid my foot to the left and felt the narrowing of the step towards the centre of the spiral. I closed my eyes, swallowed and opened them. It was utterly dark. I leaned my shoulder against the wall and felt for the next step with my foot, then the next. Three steps and still no light. What had he done? I could feel something growing in my chest and I was scared to move in case it got too big. But I couldn't stay here in the dark. I breathed in and felt again with my foot, moved up another step. At least I think I did, though it was hard to tell what my movements were in the blackness. I was disorientated.

I have no idea how long it took me to walk up the stairs. I lost track of time as well as anything else. It can't have been long. It only takes a minute or so normally, and even going that slowly it can't have been more than two or three. But I can't believe it was only three minutes of my life. By the time the light appeared I'd stopped hoping for it. It crept around the central column towards me as I neared the top of the steps. Then there were a few steps growing brighter each time before rounding into full sunshine and Richard was standing there with a grin on his face.

His smile faded when he looked at me, and I fell against him shaking. He held me.

He said, 'I'm sorry.'

I could feel that I was crying and my wet face slid against the leather of his jacket.

'I'm really sorry.'

He showed me what he'd done. There's a square hole cut into the stone floor of the balcony, covered with an open grid, its purpose to act as a skylight for the stairwell. He'd covered it up with a slab of stone.

'Why did you do that?' I asked him.

'It's how it used to be, when they first built the monument. It was symbolic, the dark climb, then the amazing view. Like blindfolding. Masonic.'

'How do you know?'

'I've been reading about it. This hole was cut much later, when they were doing repairs.'

'You should have told me.'

'Yes. I'm sorry. I didn't think you'd be scared.'

He moved the stone and leaned it against the central column.

'Did you carry that up?' I asked him.

He shrugged.

'I found it,' he said. 'Let's go back down.'

He held out his hand and I took it. The light shone through the grid. We followed the curve of stairs and the light dimmed. A few steps more and it went completely. I breathed in. My hand was inside Richard's and he was in front of me, my body slightly twisted as I followed him along the widest edge. When I took another step he hadn't moved forward. We were both on the same step and he had turned round so our faces collided. In the pitch black he kissed me. I could feel his teeth on my gums, his warm tongue. He kissed my face, my ears, my neck. His skin was smooth against mine and I pushed him away.

'No. No, this isn't right.'

He held me against his body, his face buried in my hair. My fear of the dark had evaporated.

'Richard, we should go.'

I pushed his chest with my hands and he stepped back. Another step and the light was coming up from below.

Back outside we laughed and ran, down the hill away from the wind's ferocity. The heather screamed after us and I ran faster. By the time we reached the track the day had shifted back into place. I looked at Richard as we walked, fast along the path now so we could get back down before nightfall. He was very good looking, but I couldn't imagine him kissing me.

When we reached the town it was nearly dark. Richard took off his sunglasses and put them in his pocket. His eyes were blue and clear. He caught me looking.

'I'd better go home,' I said.

'Ok.'

We were standing near the entrance to the park on Market Street and neither of us moved.

'Thanks...'

'Thanks to you too. Sorry I scared you.' He reached out and touched me lightly on the neck.

'No, I was silly. It was only dark.' Then I remembered Dad waiting at home to talk to me and I had an idea. 'Richard, do you want to come for dinner?'

He smiled. 'Sorry Lauren, I can't. Another time.'

He leaned in, kissed me on the cheek and left.

I watched him walk away and put my fingers on my neck where he'd touched me.

Everything's starting to die back in the garden. The ramsons have disappeared and are now just roots and bulbs beneath the soil waiting for next year. The wormwood has grown leggy and the foxgloves and poppies have mulched into the ground. I collected their seeds by hand when they were at their summer ripest. The vervain will soon be bare stalks and the monkshood leaves have turned black, their roots dormant now for winter.

Mr Lion was pan-frying salmon steaks and the smell filled the kitchen. Dad was laying the table. They both looked up when I walked in.

'Hi Lauren,' said Mr Lion.

I threw my coat over the back of a chair.

'Hang it on the peg, love,' said Dad. 'We're going to eat in a minute.'

'Hiya,' I said.

I hung the coat up and sat down on the chair.

'Do you think you could get some plates out?' Dad said, and his lips went into a straight line. Sometimes that meant he was angry, but right now he looked nervous. Mr Lion was busy at the cooker and had his back to us. There was clearly no escaping The Conversation.

I got three plates out and Mr Lion served up salmon steaks with red peppercorns, gratin dauphinoise and broccoli with garlic. I sat at the table and looked at my plate. Mr Lion poured us all a glass of wine. If he was trying to soften me up with food and drink he was going about it the right way.

I took a sip of wine then a mouthful of salmon. It melted into oily softness in my mouth. A peppercorn burst its flavour between my teeth and my tongue tingled. I kept my eyes on my plate.

'Lauren.'

'Mmm.' I ate a forkful of potatoes.

'Lauren, look at me when I'm talking to you.'

I raised my eyes. Dad hadn't started his food.

'You should try this,' I said. 'It's fantastic, Mr Lion.'

Mr Lion was eating and watching. He smiled at me. Dad picked up his fork and looked at the food on his plate, then back at me.

'Lauren, your mother...'

I put a broccoli tree in my mouth. It was too big and I should have cut it in half. I chewed with my mouth closed and my cheek bulging.

'I know you've been to see your mother. She told me. You see, I've been seeing her.'

I swallowed the broccoli a bit too soon and it hurt my throat as it went down.

'Seeing her?'

'Well, no.' My dad was going red. 'We've met a couple of times and we've talked. About the past mostly.'

I rested my wrists on the table and waited. He swallowed.

'Things aren't always what they seem,' he said.

I pushed some salmon onto my fork and put it in my mouth without looking at it.

I shrugged.

'I want to invite her round. For a meal.'

'I'll make myself scarce.'

'No. I want you to be there. All of us. Mr Lion too, and Peter.'

'Peter?'

'He called round earlier,' said Mr Lion, 'looking for you.'

I suddenly wanted more than anything in the world to be with Peter.

'Did he say where he was going?' I asked.

Mr Lion shook his head.

'Well?' Dad still hadn't started eating. 'Will you be here?'

'Did he say he'd call back?'

Mr Lion cleared his throat. 'I got the impression he was off for a run.'

I slumped in my seat. He'd be miles away by now. If I hadn't gone with Richard I'd have been in when Peter called. I might have persuaded him to stay. I wanted to snuggle up next to him and feel his warm animal hair, rub my face against the stubble on his cheeks.

'Lauren, can I count on you?'

I sighed. 'Yes Dad, I'll be there. I'll ask Peter.'

'It's a week on Saturday, the third.'

'What do you want me to cook?' asked Mr Lion.

Dad sat up a bit straighter in his seat and pushed his shoulders back.

'Actually, I think *I* will cook,' he said.

20. Meg

It was his move. I watched him as he contemplated the board, completely absorbed, unaware. His hand was in his hair, teasing it into blond tufts. When he sweats his hair is darker. His eyes turn a darker shade of blue when he's in the throes of passion. So I imagined. I imagined the push and snap of incision. Would his blood gush forth or just leak a drop or two on the tongue before his skin closed over again, resealing him? I put out my hand and stroked the skin of his arm, brushed his cells with my fingerprints, our bodies already mingling. He looked up and there was excitement in his eyes. I scraped the back of his hand with my fingernail and he looked at it, looked back at my face, my lips. We were only a few inches away from each other. I could feel his breath on my face and I smiled.

He frowned and moved his arm away from me, leaned back. Then he took my bishop.

I thought, if he won't let me inside his skin, I might just help myself.

21. Ali

Hawtenstall is the village my gran came from, and that's where I was living. If you could call it living. That's where I was staying, hiding, only going out at night.

I'd found an old abandoned cottage. Part of it had collapsed, the roof had fallen in and a tree had grown up and was bursting through the roof. I found that a bit freaky actually. I never went into that part of the house and I didn't like looking at it. But the other half – I think there had only ever been two rooms – was a bit better. The roof was on, although there were a couple of holes where the slates had come off. The floor was littered with bits of rubble and animal droppings. Once there had been red tiles, but these had been taken up and there were just a few fragments here and there. There were holes in the floor. No one came this way much, and even if they did there was no way they'd come poking their nose in this old dump. There was a bit of wall sticking out where the fireplace used to be, and I could hide behind that if I needed to.

It was cold though, even in the daytime, which was now my night. I'd become nocturnal, sleeping all day and going out at night to forage. It wasn't easy. I'd found the place behind the supermarket down in Hawden where they threw out the out-of-date stuff at the end of the day, and that was the best place to go for food. I could live off it if I could get there often enough. But I had to get down to the town without being seen, and early enough that no one had got there before me and scoffed the lot. Weekends were a non-starter as there were people hanging around the town all night. I tried to get as much as I could on Wednesday and Thursday to last. It made for a strange diet. Last week I ate loads of blueberry chocolate muffin pie. Like loads, a whole pie every day. The first bit was fantastic, but by the fourth day I hated the sight of it. This week it's mini pork pies and coleslaw.

The third main problem, after staying hidden and finding food, was boredom. I'd finished *Nicholas Nickleby* and I needed another book to read. People don't tend to leave them outside. I checked the charity shops when I could and looked through the bags people leave on the doorstep. I'd found some useful things like jumpers and trousers, a blanket and even a pair of wellies. But no books so far. So I was delighted one morning, coming back up from the town in the early hours with my haul, to see that it was recycling day and everyone had put out their green bags full of paper. It wasn't even raining. I might find a newspaper or two that wasn't soggy.

I stashed the food at the cottage on a ledge by the bricked up window, out of the reach of foxes, then I went on a search for printed matter. It was really dark. I couldn't see what was in the bags and I didn't want to make a load of noise rustling through. They were mostly stuffed with packaging and junk mail, but there were a few newspapers here and there and I grabbed what I could. A carrier bag of what turned out to be dieting magazines made me laugh. I could give them a few tips.

After the houses I had to climb over a wall and cross two empty fields. The first was pockmarked with hoof prints and you had to step from hummock to hummock, trying not to twist your ankle. I was beginning to know my way in the dark, but with my arms full I walked around the edge. Behind my cottage was an enormous tree that showed up against the sky even on the darkest nights, and I used that as a marker.

When I got back it was too dark to read anything, so I ate some mini pork pies and then lay down and went to sleep. I'd never slept so much before, or had such an uncomfortable place to do it. I'd made a bed of sorts in the corner of the room by chipping away the sharp bits of tile and making a smooth hollow. I wore all of my clothes for warmth and the blanket from the charity shop. I'd got used to the hard floor; it was the cold that woke me up.

It was getting late in the year and the days were getting shorter all the time. When I woke it was grey outside and raining. I sat up in my bed and gathered my recycling treasure around me. As well as the bag of magazines I had fifteen newspapers, including four Sundays with all the sections, two of which were identical. There were three Guardians and two copies of the Sun, and the other six were all back issues of the local weekly paper, Hawden Times.

I ate a couple of pies and some coleslaw for breakfast. I would read for as long as I could see.

It never got really light that day. The rain was persistent and steady, and the world outside my open doorway was grey and damp. It was damp inside too and I wished I had some chocolate to eat. I read sports pages and financial pages and recipes and TV guides, and scrabbled in the bottom of my rucksack for a pencil so I could do a crossword. I saved the travel pages and book reviews for another day. Something to look forward to. By the time the light failed I'd still not got through all the Sundays.

It took me most of a week to read them all, even without the diet magazines. I knew I had to do something else and couldn't just hide out reading yesterday's news forever. I wanted to find out something about my gran for a start. But it felt kind of safe here, and I was reluctant to change anything. I could hide here on my own, grab more papers each recycling day, and become a current affairs expert in my lonely den, cut off from twenty-first century life.

It was an article in the Hawden Times that kicked me out of my lethargy. The paper was a few weeks old, and full of stories about talented children, proposed changes to the town and outraged locals. I was flicking through, unable to summon up much interest, when I saw picture of an elderly woman and a headline: Hawtenstall Mourns Library Hannah. The picture took up half a page. The woman had short cropped hair and was sitting next to a pile of books, smiling at the camera. I read on.

The Hawden Times is sad to report the passing of Hannah Chandler, librarian at Hawtenstall Library for nineteen years until she retired in 1991. During retirement she was an active member of the community. Hannah, a widow, died at home last Wednesday. She leaves one daughter, Amanda.

I used to go to the library at home. Mum never bought me books as she didn't read and so she didn't think of them. Gran sometimes did, but mostly I got my books from the library. Our librarian was quite scary. She wore a tweed skirt, and once she peered over her glasses and said, 'Are you sure you want to read this book? Don't you think it's a bit old for you?'

The book was Wuthering Heights. I ran to my gran's house with it under my arm and she told me about her friend, Hannah, who worked in a library, and how she would have loved it that I wanted to challenge myself, would have made suggestions of other books for me to read. I said I wished Hannah worked in our library.

This had to be the same woman. I stared at the picture and tried to imagine her and my gran being friends. Sharing a cup of tea or laughing at a joke. She looked like she might have been fun – there was a spark of mischief about her. I checked the date of the paper. It was over a month since she'd died.

I went on another newspaper raid the next night and set myself up with a new pile of papers to read. I found they had a dual function in that they also made good insulation. With them layered under and over my bed at night, I slept more cosily, and after I'd read each one I added it to my den. But as I read about atrocities and injustice at home and abroad, my mind kept coming back to Hannah. I wished she could have lived just a bit longer so I could have met her and talked to her about Gran. They had been friends. She wouldn't have hissed at me and ordered me out of the house like Sally. Would she?

On the way back from a night time food raid in the town I suddenly thought of the daughter, Amanda. She would have known Gran too. But how could I find her? I dug out the article and looked at it again, but there was no more information. I had no access to the internet. I couldn't go to the library. I didn't even know if Amanda had the same surname as Hannah. She might not live locally. The paper didn't say.

Then I remembered I'd found a phone directory amongst the pile of diet magazines. It was a slim chance: not many people were listed in the phone book these days. When I was a child they were big books an inch thick, and Gran said that they used to be even thicker in the past, that everyone used to be in the phone book. This one was about as thick as a short novel, though taller.

I looked up Chandler, A, and there was nothing. In fact there were only three Chandlers in the book at all and two of them were in Halifax. But there was an R. Chandler listed at 3, Church Cottages, Hawtenstall. I didn't know who R might be, but it was worth checking out at the very least.

The next trick was to find Church Cottages, and I thought the clue was probably in the name. I walked along the main street to where a cobbled lane led off to the old church. On one side were gravestones and the ruin of the church tower. On the other was a row of old terraced cottages. The sign on the end told me I was in the right place.

Number three looked empty. There were no curtains and, even though it was the middle of the night, the black windows gave it an abandoned look. I peered in the front and could see shapes in the dark. I walked to the end and round to the back of the terrace, where a path led between the cottages and the tiny back yards. I counted along until I was outside number three. A light from the churchyard was shining through from the front and I could see that the furniture had been piled at the side of the room. Someone was clearing out by the looks of things. Amanda? The house didn't look lived in and I doubted she was here. I tried the back door handle on the off chance, but it was locked.

I could break in. But I didn't know how to pick a lock and I didn't want to smash anything and wake the neighbours. I decided to go back to my cottage and eat and think about what to do next.

I was about to walk away when I noticed the back yard on the other side of the path. It was a tiny space – enough room for a wheelie bin and a few feet of washing line, nothing more. But next to the bin were two green bags stuffed with paper and two extra supermarket carrier bags, all put out for the recyclers later in the week.

It took two trips to carry it all across the fields, and when I finished I was knackered. I ate three Gruyère and leek tartlets and snuggled down in my newspaper bed.

The next day I looked through what I'd found. The green bags were full of old correspondence – some of it addressed to R Chandler and some of it to H. It looked like I'd hit the jackpot. Whoever R was, they didn't seem to want their stuff any more. Most of it was quite boring. Junk mail, bank statements, bills and offers from gas companies. My mum always used to say you couldn't recycle that sort of thing because your personal details were on them. I knew Hannah was dead, and maybe R was too, but I thought maybe Amanda could have used a shredder. It seemed a bit weird going through their private papers.

One of the carrier bags was stuffed with newspapers from earlier in the year. I added them to my stack.

The other was full of exercise books in different colours. I took one out and looked at it. It had Hannah's name written on the front in biro. Inside was page after page of small neat handwriting. There were dates every now and then and I realised that what I had was her diary. I wondered what sort of person Amanda was, and why she didn't want to keep her mother's diaries. Had she read them first? I rummaged through the bag.

There were about thirty books. I suddenly had loads of reading matter and a new person to get to know, even if she was dead.

Hannah Chandler moved to Hawtenstall from Halifax when she got married to Ray in 1965. She'd worked in a textile mill on the machines before that. The diaries didn't go back that far, but she mentioned the hard work and long hours, the camaraderie and the nights on the town with the girls. Married life in the village was very different. Ray worked in the mill as well, but Hannah gave up her job when they got married. In the notebook she vented her boredom and frustration. I don't suppose she ever told anyone else about these feelings. She probably appeared cheerful and content. She probably never told Ray what a boring lover he was, and I bet he didn't know that he wasn't her first. She must have kept her diaries hidden.

After two years they had Amanda. She gave Hannah something to do other than housework, but she didn't really take to motherhood. They didn't have any more children. Ray didn't seem to enjoy the sexual side of marriage and after Amanda was born he lost interest all together. Hannah didn't miss sleeping with Ray, but she remembered the fleeting excitement of her previous encounter. When she met Don in the park one day and he asked her out for a coffee, she went to the doctor and asked to go on the pill.

Life split into two parts for Hannah. She was a mother and wife. When Amanda started school she got a job in the local library and Amanda would read in the children's corner until it was time to close. Hannah became well known and respected in the village. Neither Amanda nor Ray grew any more interesting, but Hannah enjoyed life, chatting to customers who came into the library for piles of romances and adventures to take them away from the dull grey of long Yorkshire winters. And secretly there was another Hannah, known only to her lover. The diaries told me everything about Don, far more than I wanted to know.

I think the people of Hawtenstall would have been quite shocked to know what went on in her head and in her notebooks.

I read until it got too dark to see. Hannah had an easy way of writing, as though she were chatting to herself. I liked her and thought she would have been a nice friend to have at the library.

I put the notebooks back in their carrier bag to keep them dry and stood in the doorway looking out across the valley. I loved the view. Mostly I stayed back in the cottage, away from the door, so I didn't often see it in daylight. It wasn't daylight now, nor fully dark. You could still make out the folds and creases of the hills and valleys. The land was so different from where I'd grown up in Suffolk. There it was smooth, as though the earth had been layered over with a palette knife, covering a shape which was mostly flat with the occasional bump or slope. If you got up high you could see for miles

Gran said they call Yorkshire 'God's Own Country', but I'm not sure that he liked this bit of it. It was like he'd grabbed it, scrunched it up and thrown it away. The hills and valleys were crazy, one on top of the other and all of them really steep. The valley bottoms were mostly covered in woodland; above, the tops stuck out stark and proud. It made it an easy place to hide in, but you couldn't see people coming.

A few hundred yards down the hill from me the woods began, and that day there was a group of shapes just this side of the tree-line. I peered through the dusk and realised that they were deer, grazing. They hadn't noticed me and I stood very still in the doorway watching them. I'd seen deer in Suffolk, dead on the road or running across the path of a car in a mad dash for the other side, but I'd not watched them like this, just doing what deer do when they don't know anyone is watching them.

A star appeared in the sky above the woods. I felt very still. I looked at the deer, heads down, eating, occasionally moving a few steps and eating some more. The woods had become black behind them, but they were nothing to do with me. I didn't have to go there. The star was twinkling. I almost laughed. I hadn't realised stars really did that.

A dog came racing down the hill barking, and the deer turned tail and fled. I saw their white tails bobbing as they disappeared into the woods. The dog ran after them, but lost interest when they vanished. Someone behind the cottage called its name. I tried to keep the stillness in my limbs as I slunk back from the doorway, but it was no good. The dog spotted me and ran towards me, wagging its tail.

I crouched backwards into the far corner of the room. It was pretty dark now, and in here you couldn't see anything. Of course, dogs aren't bothered by that: they go by smell. It came running straight over to me and started butting at my knees with its nose. It was small and white, and its shape showed up faintly. It found my hand and tried to nuzzle into it.

Footsteps passed the cottage. The person was at the front now. He called the dog's name again, loud into the valley. The dog tried to prise my arm away from my knees with its head and made a low whimpering sound.

'Be quiet, Beauty,' I mouthed.

Someone was standing in the doorway; someone very tall with a mane of hair. He was silhouetted black against the lighter blackness of the outside sky.

'Beauty?'

The dog whimpered again and gave one last shove at my knees.

'Come on Beauty, are you there?'

His voice was higher now, and softer, appealing to the dog. It worked. Beauty gave up on me and scampered to the man in the doorway. He leaned down and fixed her lead to her collar, then he stood and stared for a few more seconds into the darkness of the cottage. I stopped breathing. I was still and silent and I was hidden in the darkness.

He shook his shoulders.

'Ok Beauty, lets get home now.'

I could hear them as they walked across the field, the man's feet swishing against the grass, and his voice as he talked to the dog in low tones. They went towards the woods. I started breathing again but I didn't move, not until they had had time to get all the way back down the valley into Hawden.

22. Lauren

In May there were foxgloves at the back of my herb garden. They are one of my favourite flowers. They stand so tall, so proud; unafraid of who they are. Their purple bells are rows of open mouths, spattered on the inside with black dots that look like seeds on the tongue. Their poison can be a powerful medicine if used carefully. At this time of the year they were just a mulch of dead leaves sinking back into the soil. I'd gathered their seeds earlier in the year.

I was lying on the floor in Jimmy and Suky's living room. Peter sat cross legged on the floor by my head, playing with my hair. He was spreading it at its full length all around my head like an enormous halo, like those you get in some old paintings that look like a gold plate stuck to the back of the person's head, but made of hair.

Jimmy and Suky were both on the sofa with cups of tea. He had his arm around her and she was curled against him with her feet tucked up. When we arrived Jimmy had let us in. He had bare feet, and his jeans and t-shirt were all skewwhiff as though he'd just thrown them on. Suky was upstairs and didn't come down for a few minutes. We hadn't disturbed them in the act but they were definitely basking in a glow. I wondered if he'd seen Steph recently.

'So, tell us all about it then,' Jimmy said.

Peter picked up one of the mugs of tea on the floor near us and drank some. I felt pinned down by the arrangement of my hair and didn't move.

'It was ok. Nobody cried or swore or threw their dinner at the wall.'

'What did you eat?'

I lifted my head and looked at Suky and my hair fell back into place on my neck.

'Aw, I spent ages doing that,' Peter complained.

'I can't lie on the floor all night. I'm not your doll.'

'Aren't you?' he asked in mock disappointment. I kissed him on the mouth.

'Hey, enough of that,' said Jimmy, and I grinned even more.

Peter's lips were warm. I suddenly thought of that day inside the monument and I remembered that Richard's lips were cold. I touched my neck.

'What did your dad cook?' Suky prompted.

'He only has five dinners he can cook, and tonight he cooked his special occasion meal. Chicken and Tarragon Risotto with Spinach and Potato Bake.'

'Oooh, rice *and* potatoes, carb overload.' She shook her head.

'Mmm. I wondered if she'd eaten it before, because he's been cooking it like forever. She made this sort of funny smile when he brought it out.'

'What's she like?' Suky asked.

'She's lovely.' Peter said, and pushed a strand of hair behind my ear.

I picked up my tea.

No, it was Richard's hands, not his lips, that were cold. Chilled by the wind up there probably.

'She talked to Peter about physics. She used to be a science teacher.'

'Is that how...'

'... she met my dad? Yes, they taught at the same school. A staffroom romance.'

'How sweet,' said Suky.

'Sickly.'

Jimmy was trailing his fingers up and down Suky's thigh and she snuggled against him.

Peter jabbed me in the ribs. 'Come on Lauren, she's making an effort.'

'Well, we all buggered off after we'd finished eating. Mr Lion had a gig in Brighouse and we came here. So the two of them are there all on their own now finishing off the wine.' I drank the rest of my tea with one gulp. 'I might stay somewhere else tonight.'

I looked at Peter. We'd not spent a whole night together before.

'I think you should go back and talk to her,' he said.

Half an hour later we were walking back again. Jimmy and Suky were obviously too loved up for us to stay there.

'I used to think I hated my mum,' Peter said. 'I was furious with her for leaving me and Dad. But in the end I realised it was ok. Dad didn't hate her. That's just who she is, she's not a motherly person. We get on really well now, like friends.'

'But she's meant to be your mother, not your friend.'

'She wasn't any good at it. Some people aren't.'

'Well my mother was, apparently, for five minutes before she did her vanishing act.'

I opened the kitchen door. Dad and my mum were sitting together at the table. They moved apart a bit when we came in. For a moment I was tempted to run straight up to my room and stay there. But they were all trying to make me confront her, so I thought what the hell.

Peter was putting the kettle on. I sat down at the table.

'So, you two are making up again, are you?'

Dad frowned and she looked puzzled.

'We've been talking through some things,' she said. 'Clearing up some misunderstandings.'

'What, like the misunderstanding that you were meant to be someone's wife and someone's mother?'

She flinched as though I'd hit her.

'Lauren, that's not fair.'

I turned to Dad. 'Why is it not fair? She comes swanning in here expecting us to forgive her, as though she'd just been out a bit longer at the shops or something. But it's my whole life longer. She's a stranger to me, why should I be nice to her?'

'You could do it for me.' His voice was quiet, and it had that note in it that I knew – the one that meant *I am your father and you will do as I say young lady*. But his face was sad, and that was what did it for me. He'd had enough sadness in his life. I didn't want to add to it.

I sat back in my chair.

'Is there any more wine?'

Dad relaxed his shoulders a bit.

Peter said 'You're not having tea then?'

'No, I'll have wine and be sociable.'

Peter fetched two glasses from the dishwasher and a bottle of wine from the shelf. He sat next to me.

'Have you come back to stay in Hawden?' he asked my mother.

She glanced sideways at Dad.

'I'd like to, but it's early days. We'll have to see how it goes.'

'We? You mean you and Dad?'

She looked at him again and he sat forward and put his hand on top of hers.

'Yes Lauren, me and Cass are going to see how it goes. There's a lot you don't understand. I barely understand it either. But I'm willing to try.'

She flashed him a smile. It was there and then it was gone, but we all saw it, and I realised she loved him. I thought she must have stopped loving Dad and that's why she'd gone away.

If it wasn't that, what made her leave?

I closed my eyes. Everything seemed wrong. Behind my eyelids there were sheets of colour flashing first one way and then the other, making me nauseous. I opened my eyes again and the room looked different. Everything in the same place, but as though someone had changed the lighting; swapped the bulb for a slightly brighter one, tinged with blue. I stared at my mother. I knew her features so well from the photograph. Now they moved and changed and it was as though a character had stepped out of a fairytale and become real. I could feel a falling sensation within my body and put my hands on the table for steadiness. No one noticed. The moment seemed to stretch on and on, but was only a second or two.

I could feel the touch of cold lips on mine. I grabbed Peter's hand and held it tight. The plants in my garden were dying back for the winter. Roots and twigs and seeds – that's all they had to offer me at this time of year.

'Is there a lot of work to be done in the house?' I heard Peter asking. 'It's been empty for a long time.'

'It's not too bad. A lot of dust. But Andy and Mr Lion have been keeping an eye on it.' She had a really nice voice, soft and quite deep. I wanted to hear her sing, or for her to go on talking while I curled up and went to sleep. 'I might do some redecorating, but not yet. I'm just taking it day by day for the moment.'

No point in decorating if it all goes wrong and you need to run away again.

'I'd really like it if you – both of you – would feel free to pop in. I'd like to get to know you.'

You would know me if you hadn't gone away, you silly bitch. I pressed my palm against Peter's and we both squeezed, our nails digging into the backs of each other's hands.

'Well, if you need any help with anything,' Peter was speaking for both of us and I was glad. I didn't trust myself to say anything nice. She and Dad seemed so far away, sitting at the other side of the table, as if I was looking at them down a tunnel.

Dad leaned forward. 'Lauren, thank you for being here this evening.'

I smiled at him but I couldn't speak.

'I know everything is strange at the moment. It's hard for you.'

I parted my lips. 'I'm tired now. Do you mind if I go to bed?'

Dad looked at my wine, which I hadn't touched, then he shrugged. 'Ok, school day tomorrow.'

I stood up and tugged at Peter's hand. 'Come with me?'

He stood up and said goodnight to both of my parents. I kissed my Dad on the forehead, something I did every night. He ruffled my hair and said 'night, sweetie,' and I noticed my mum looking at us.

'Goodnight,' I said to her.

She nodded but she couldn't say anything because she was crying.

Upstairs Peter undressed me and kissed me at the base of my throat and his breath was warm. His hands ran down the sides of my body, leaving a trail of heat, and he pressed the length of his body against mine. His haunches were soft against the skin of my legs. I held on to him, my arms wrapped round his back and my face pushed into his shoulder.

'Lauren, it's ok.'

He stroked my hair and ran his fingertips down my spine.

We stood like that for ages. He was so warm and so perfect I wanted to stay there forever. Outside of this moment everything was uncertain. Peter put his hands on either side of my head and lifted it so he could look at me. He licked the tears off my face and kissed my wet eyelids.

'I love you, Peter.'

I wanted to say it.

He kissed my lips then, and one of his arms slid down my back. He pulled me hard against him and his excitement passed into me as we opened our mouths to each other. He nudged me backwards towards the bed and we tumbled on to it, laughing for a second before grasping again for each other's bodies. We made love and I forgot everything that had happened and everything

I knew. Afterwards, I held on to Peter with my legs wrapped around him, ankles crossed behind his thighs, unwilling to let him go. His face was above mine and it looked naked. I was so happy that he let me see him like that.

'I love you too, Lauren,' he said.

I let him go after that, and we curled our bodies up together and fell asleep. I slept heavily and well and woke up in the morning with his arm across my body and his knees pressed into the back of mine, his breath in my hair. I reached up with my left arm and touched his horns. He was still sleeping and didn't stir. There were seeds in the bed that had fallen out of my pockets when we undressed. I gathered them and slid out from under his arm and went to the bathroom. Peter had a free period first thing this morning, so he could lie in a bit longer than me.

I showered and dressed and went downstairs to make tea. Dad's shoes and coat were in the hall, but my mum's weren't, so I guessed she'd gone home. Nobody else was about. Mr Lion would be out with Beauty, as they always went out really early, even in winter when it was dark. I walked silently across the kitchen in my woolly socks and felt the tiles against my feet. I filled the kettle and the sound of the water was loud in the quiet kitchen. I got a cup from the cupboard, trying not to clink it, not to let the cupboard door bang. But when I opened the fridge it burst into life with a loud rumble, and pressure in the kettle built up until it began to sing. I could feel it in my head.

I poured water onto a teabag and stirred it, fished it out with a spoon and added milk. It was five minutes until the school bus.

Peter was sleeping. I put the cup on the chest of drawers next to my bed, leaned over and kissed his face.

'Peter.'

He reached out with one arm and grabbed me. He didn't open his eyes. He pulled me down to the bed, my face next to his, and nestled against me.

'Peter, I have to go to college.'

I drew away and he opened his eyes. He needed to shave.

'I've brought you some tea.'

'Thank you.' His voice was thick with sleep.

I kissed him again. 'Bye, see you later.'

'Bye.' He lifted his arm again and touched my face, and I left.

The kitchen was quiet again. I grabbed my bag from behind the door and let myself out of the house. The earth was nearly bare. If I wanted roots from the garden I'd have to dig them up.

When I turned the corner at the end of our road I saw Richard walking up ahead. I ran to catch up with him.

'Morning.'

He smiled. 'Morning Lauren.'

We walked along the street in step with each other. The sky was brightening into day, the sun just appearing over the horizon.

'I'm going to the library,' he said. 'Want to walk with me?'

'I'll be late.'

'Not much.'

'Oh, why not? It might wake me up.'

But I didn't need waking up. Red and yellow chrysanthemums were loud in window boxes and the trees rattled their remaining leaves. We walked down to the canal path. The new sun was sending shivers of light across the water and frost clung to the grass at the water's edge.

23. Ali

I hadn't spent any of the money. Hadn't had the chance to. First time in my life I'd cash to spend and I was hiding away in the hills, only going out at night when the shops were closed. I'd buried it under a loose tile in the corner of the cottage. Sometimes I wished I hadn't taken it, then I wouldn't need to hide. I wondered if Smith and Jeannie were still looking for me. It was a lot of money, but they would want to get back to Leeds. They wouldn't spend forever wandering the country. I'd been here for nearly a month – I could tell by the moon.

Some days I thought I was being stupid. They wouldn't still be in Hawden. I could just come out of hiding, walk down the street in daylight and see what happened. But it had become a habit. I'd got used to being nocturnal. The daylight seemed a bit crude and brash, especially when the sun was shining. I sometimes ventured out into the fields for a bit at dusk, but I felt very exposed. My eyes were adjusting to the dark and I could see much more than I used to at night. I was learning the subtleties of different degrees of grey, varying depths of blackness.

Maybe it was the moon, but I felt restless. I took out the roll of notes. It had a satisfying weight in my hand. I took one of the twenties from the outside and slipped it into the back pocket of my jeans, put the rest back under the tile. I hadn't any plan. I wasn't short of food and it was Friday, a day I never went into town. It was a long time since I'd had any human company. I'd been reading Hannah's notebooks but they weren't enough.

The moon was still low in the sky when I got to Hawden. I was used to it silent and empty – sometimes the odd straggler walking the night streets, but otherwise only cats, once a fox.

Tonight there were people standing smoking outside pubs and restaurants. Groups of drunk girls teetered down the middle of the road in fits of giggles and high heels. Lads shouted at them from the corners and couples scurried past hand in hand in their weekend clothes. I stopped in a shop doorway and looked down at my clothes. Jeans and t-shirt both filthy, jumper now an indeterminate colour with a hole beneath one arm, jacket carrying dust from nights on the cottage floor and newspaper blankets. I could see my reflection in the shop window and I was a fright. Hair sticking out anyhow and dirt on my face. I couldn't just walk into a pub like this – I'd be thrown out.

I'd walked most of the streets on my night visits by now. I knew how to get across the town using back alleys. I made my way to the back of my favourite charity shop, the one where they often put bags of stuff out the back – clothes that weren't good enough for them to sell. Luckily there were a couple of bags. I untied the first, rummaged about and found a black hoodie. It was a bit on the small side – probably a child's – and it had a mark on the bottom at the back as though someone had dropped bleach on it. But the zip up the front worked, and the arms were just long enough. I hid behind the bags, slipped off my jumper and t-shirt and put the hoodie on over my bra. It hugged quite tight. I stuffed my clothes and my jacket down by the wall. I hoped they would still be there later.

My jeans would have to do. I needed the pockets. I had the twenty, and also some bits of change from the last time I'd spent any money – that day back in the coffee shop when I arrived in Hawden.

I fished out a twenty pence piece. When no one was looking I dashed across the street and into the market square to the public toilets. They were individual self-contained cubicles opening onto the road. Inside was grey and smelled of piss and chemicals and on the wall above a tiny sink was a square of mirror. There was no soap.

I wet my hands and ran them through my hair, smoothing it out and flattening it down. I managed to get the worst of the dirt off my face and neck using water. I wished I had an eyeliner. I used to borrow stuff like that from Jeannie or one of the others back in the squat. I looked so young without it, but I would have to do. It was time to stop hiding.

I left and walked into the middle of the high street. I felt very aware of the way my legs moved, wasn't sure what to do with my arms. There were a couple of people up ahead, no one watching, but I felt as though I was walking a catwalk. Actually no, I can't even begin to imagine what that would be like. But I felt on display and as though I had to get the walk right – pass some sort of test which made me ordinary.

There were a few pubs and I wondered about going in, but couldn't quite push past the groups of smokers by the door. Outside the working men's club there were more people, dressed in short skirts and long skirts, garish make up, tight tops, jeans. Three girls came tumbling out of the door with drinks in their hands and sweat on their faces. From inside I could hear the thump of music. And someone nearby was smoking a spliff.

I slid through the door and up the stairs. The music got louder. On the right was a side bar full of people sitting and standing, shouting conversations over the music. I hesitated, but pushed forward, past the queue for the toilets, to the main part of the club. There was no one on the door, although there was a stamp on a table. I stamped my own hand and went in.

I was swallowed by a room packed with people dancing like a single moving organism. I let it draw me in between sweating bodies, avoiding flailing arms and stamping feet. I swayed a bit to the beat so I didn't stick out, looked around the room. It was draped with fabrics from ceiling to walls, drawing down the roof and bringing in the sides of the room, making it look like a Bedouin tent. The ceiling was strung with netting filled with enormous fake flowers and pieces of plastic fruit. Lights flashed on and off, red, yellow, green, casting strange masks on the faces of the dancers. This was anonymity. I let myself be carried along and the sweat beaded up underneath my stolen hoodie.

The music changed from a fast dance beat to reggae and the crowd changed tempo, became less frantic. I decided to spend some money and wove myself between bodies to the bar. The wait was two or three deep and I wormed myself forward, slid between larger, drunker bodies until there was only one person in front of me.

Someone touched my shoulder, shouted in my ear.

'Hello Ali.'

As I turned I registered the distance to the door on my left, the number of people blocking my way, the fact that this person was on the other side of me and wasn't blocking my exit. My feet were ready to run.

It was Richard.

'I went up to Old Barn to see you, but you'd gone.' He put his mouth right next to my ear to make himself heard.

I nodded.

Someone left the bar with two drinks in each hand, and Richard slid into the space he'd left.

'Drink?' he mouthed, miming tipping alcohol down his throat.

I nodded again and leaned forward to shout in his ear.

'Lager please.'

He bought two drinks, one for me and a vodka and Coke for someone else.

'I'm with Lauren,' he told me as we moved away from the bar. 'Do you know her?'

I shook my head. We made a path across the dance floor, Richard holding the drinks high, turning sideways as someone spun out in front of him. A girl was leaning against a table at the side of the room watching. She was blonde and pretty, wearing jeans and a silky silver top which clung to her skin. Richard handed her the vodka and spoke in her ear. She looked at me.

The look was quick and sharp, not the bored, appraising glance you might give someone you don't know and probably don't want to. My muscles tensed again. What did she know about me?

It was impossible to talk, though.

The lager was cold, and in that hot room it slid down as easily as water. A new DJ came on, a guy with a long black hair and a face like a cat. The music changed and Lauren shouted, 'Let's dance.' She grabbed Richard's hand and took him into the crowd. I stayed with the drinks.

They were both good dancers, despite there not being room to do anything much with the bodies hemming you in on every side. Lauren lifted her arms and used the space above as well as around her. It was old music, Motown or Northern Soul or something like that. Richard moved from the hips, in tune with the beat, following every nuance. I wasn't a dancer. I always felt conspicuous. I'd be ok in a crowd like this because you'd melt in and no one would notice you. But I'd never get up and dance unless there were already loads of people dancing.

After a couple of songs they came back and we all went outside for some air. Lauren kept giving me sideways glances. They asked me where I was living now and I mumbled something non-committal about staying with friends.

Richard said 'There were some people asking about you, that night of the party, remember?'

I looked at him and his face was bland, as though it were something inconsequential.

'Oh,' I said. I had a drag on the spliff someone handed me. 'Did you tell them where I was?'

'No. I remembered you'd said you weren't allowed visitors up there. I said I'd look out for you and let you know they were looking.'

'Thank you.'

'Did they find you?' asked Lauren. Her face was pinched with curiosity. She obviously knew more than she was letting on.

'No they didn't.'

We went in and danced some more, had another couple of drinks. When it was my turn to buy, Lauren offered to go for me and I handed her the twenty from my back pocket. I saw her at the bar studying it intently. When she came back with the drinks I shoved the change in my pocket and downed my lager quickly.

I leaned against Richard and lifted my mouth up to his ear. 'I'm going.'

He frowned. 'Wait, we'll come too.' He leaned over to Lauren and spoke to her and she nodded, knocked back her vodka and Coke in one swallow.

This wasn't really what I intended. Were they hoping to come back to mine?

Outside, Richard said 'Fancy coming up to Hough Dean?'

And suddenly I was sitting on my gran's lap in her big armchair wearing pyjamas and she was telling me a story before bedtime.

'Little Red Riding Hood went on her way through the forest, skipping in the sunshine and humming a little song, until she arrived at Hough Dean.'

'What's Hough Dean?' I asked.

'That's the name of Granny's house. Unbeknownst to Little Red Riding Hood, the Big Bad Wolf has got there first.' And I snuggle against Gran because I know this story, and I know that Gran tells it differently to the storybook in my classroom at school. I know that in her version the wolf gets away to live another day and all the woodcutter gets is a handful of fur and Red Riding Hood's eternal gratitude, which in time he turns to his advantage and makes her his child bride.

'What's Hough Dean?' I asked Richard.

'It's where I live,' he said and, despite Lauren's eager face which made me want to turn tail, curiosity got the better of me.

It was quite a walk. On the way Lauren told me that Richard wasn't her boyfriend. Her boyfriend was called Peter, but he had a chemistry exam next week and he was busy revising. She tried to ask me questions about myself but I fobbed her off.

The road took us out of town along the valley bottom and it was really dark. I'd got used to living in the night time, but my cottage was up high where you could make the most of any light from the stars and the sky. Down here we were shielded by trees and by the hills themselves, rising up black and solid on either side. After a mile or so we turned right onto a rough track.

We didn't talk much. The track wound uphill and we were walking at a fair pace. I could hear Lauren's breath catching and I could feel my own tightening my chest. Richard didn't seem to find it an effort and kept slowing down for us to catch up.

When we reached Hough Dean the lights were on and there was music. Richard opened the front door.

'Hiya, it's me,' he called out.

We walked into a wide, brightly lit entrance hall. The music, which I think was jazz, was coming from a room to our left. A woman walked through the door and turned to greet us. I gasped.

'Meg!'

She smiled her beautiful smile.

'Ali,' she said, 'I wondered when I was going to see you.'

Part Three

BLOOD

24. Peter

Peter lay on a bed of straw at the back of the cave. The place smelled of his dad, but Peter was alone. The night sky was lighter than the cave's interior and he could see the mouth quite clearly – a black shape filled with indigo, its edges jagged.

He wished his dad was there. Not that they tended to talk much, but he felt his dad understood the difficulties. Lauren acted as though it didn't matter, as though his difference in horn and foot could be accommodated as easily as different hair colour or longer-than-average legs. She said nobody cared, and that she loved him for who he was. His dad said there were different ways of looking at the world, and Peter had told him about the polarization of light: how because of the angle of vision, you could only see the light vibrating in a single horizontal plane, but that there are infinite planes if only you knew how to look. His dad had nodded and smiled.

Lauren wanted to go to parties, spend evenings dancing, dressing up, drinking and squealing with her friends. A couple of times he'd gone with her, but he'd felt awkward, didn't want to drink with those people just because they were the same age as him. They seemed barely out of childhood. He watched Lauren laughing, bright and brittle in the middle of a crowd, and felt like he didn't know her.

The last time he'd crept away, gone up to the cave where he'd found his dad half way down a bottle of whisky. They shared the rest of it and watched the sun come up. His dad said, 'You can't be everything in her life.' Peter, knocking back another whisky, felt his eyes prick with tears.

That was back in the spring. Now his dad was in Greece with the woman he loved. Peter rolled over to face the back wall of the cave so he could see nothing but blackness. Then he closed his eyes.

25. Ali

When I was little, Gran sometimes used to tell me stories about a friend of hers called Meg. She said she was different from other people. She'd been alive for two hundred years and she would never die. She had been all over the world and seen all sorts of things. She was alive at the same time as Florence Nightingale and Mary Seacole and all those other people you learn about at school. She was alive before the lightbulb was invented and when the first man landed on the moon. Though Gran was alive for that as well.

I asked my mum if she knew Meg, and Mum said Gran was making it up. Nobody lived that long, could you imagine how old and decrepit she would be?

But Gran said Meg never got any older. She stayed the same and she always would.

After a while I kind of came round to Mum's way of thinking. I didn't mind. I liked Gran's stories, and I thought she'd made Meg up for me, to make me interested in history and as something to share. So I always went along with her and pretended she really existed.

Then one day I walked into Gran's house and there was this woman standing in the kitchen leaning against the worktop. She was the most beautiful person I'd ever seen. She had blonde hair and she was smiling. She wasn't like anyone else and I knew straight away that she must be Meg. I couldn't stop staring at her.

Gran walked in from the other room and said, 'Oh, Ali, there you are.' But I didn't look at her and I didn't speak. It was like sipping at a drink of nectar, something perfect and sweet.

Meg laughed. 'I think she takes after you, Frances,' she said.

I could see Gran, from the corner of my eye, looking from one of us to the other.

'Ali,' she said quite sharply. Meg was wearing a cream coloured dress which had no sleeves and ended just above her knees. Her arms and legs were golden brown. Her eyes were clear and looking at them was like looking at a lake on a hot day. 'Ali!'

Reluctantly I pulled my gaze away and turned to my Gran.

'Ali, this is my friend, Meg. Meg, my granddaughter, Ali. Now Ali, how about you put the kettle on and make us a cup of tea?'

Meg was there for a week that time and I spent as much time as I could at Gran's house. I tried not to stare at her all the time. I did things for her instead. I made her drinks, which she mostly left, and brought her cushions and a stool for her feet, and sat near her waiting in case there was anything else she needed. She was very gracious and never acted as though she was irritated by me. When she was chatting with my Gran I watched her, looking at the curve of her cheek and the lines of her collar bone, but mostly at her eyes which sometimes looked grey or blue, and once even black.

They talked about the past and about people they both knew in Paris. I didn't know Gran had been to Paris, but apparently she had lived there for two years when she was younger and that's where she'd met Meg.

When she'd gone, I said to Gran, 'Meg is the loveliest person in the world.'

And Gran said 'She's the loveliest person in the world for me. She always will be. But there are others like her. Maybe you'll meet them one day.'

Now Meg was standing in front of me holding out her arms. I ran to her and threw myself into them.

Behind me I heard Richard saying 'You two know each other?'

Meg disentangled my limbs from her body. 'Do you remember Frances?' she said to him.

'Of course.'

'Well, Ali is her granddaughter.'

How could Richard have known my gran? He would have been a child like me when she died.

I realised I'd only ever seen him in the dark before and he stood out more than everyone else then. Now he had taken off his sunglasses and he was looking at me. The room was full of his light.

'You too!' I said.

'Hey, what's going on here?' said Lauren, and we all turned to her. For the first time I noticed the mark on her neck which had nearly healed, and I realised how pretty she was and then I could hear the blood pumping in her veins, faster than mine, faster than the beat of the jazz coming from the front room. I knew the others could hear it too.

'Mum, this is Lauren who I met at the library. I thought we'd grab some beers.'

'Lovely to meet you, Lauren. Make yourselves at home.'

I didn't want this. Watching these two like spiders and the girl, Lauren, a fly in their trap. Such beautiful spiders too – if I wasn't careful I might find myself ensnared. I'm not sure I'm as strong as Gran was.

'I might get off, actually,' I said.

'Oh, Ali, but you've only just arrived.'

'Please stay.'

I looked at Richard. Everything had changed now I knew what he was. I thought of that day in Gran's kitchen when I first saw Meg and I knew this moment was going to be etched into my memory with the same intensity.

'We need to talk to you,' Lauren said.

I wondered if I should warn her. She was looking at Richard excitedly and she nudged him with her elbow.

'Don't let her go, Richard.'

That was another reason. They might not have told Smith and Jeannie anything, but the less they knew about me the better.

'Another time,' I said. I walked out before anyone else could say anything.

As I walked across the yard the door was flung open.

'Ali!' It was Richard's voice, but I didn't turn. I pictured my gran in Paris, sitting on the train at the Gare du Nord waiting for the whistle to blow, for the train to move and carry her back to England. She's looking straight ahead, refusing to look out onto the platform where Meg is pleading with her to stay. If she looks she will crumple and give in, become what Meg wants her to.

'It wasn't that though, Ali, becoming the same as her. That's in my blood anyway. If we could have been together, the two of us, for eternity, I would have leapt at the chance. But Meg wasn't offering monogamy, she wanted me to be a part of her crowd. She has a lot of love to give and a great hunger with it. I wasn't enough to satisfy it on my own.'

'Ali, where can I find you?'

I knew he could see me. The light from the door continued to shine out, but I carried on walking and didn't turn. For a moment I thought he was going to run after me. But he had a fly waiting in his trap that needed attending to, and when I reached the bend in the lane I disappeared from his view.

Back at the cottage I waited impatiently for daylight. I looked on the shelf and found a pack of out-of-date cherry Bakewells. I opened them and ate one after another. They were too sweet and too dry and left a bitter taste in my mouth, but it was something to do. I tried to doze but when I closed my eyes I found myself replaying the scene at Hough Dean. I wanted to make it different, make it Lauren that had left, back safe to her boyfriend. But she was still there, smiling and lovely and unaware and I opened my eyes again to the cold stone walls.

Eventually enough grey light seeped in that if I sat by the doorway I could just read Hannah's writing. It was cold and I wrapped the blanket around me, glad I'd returned via the town last night to collect my jumper and jacket.

23/4/92

E dropped in today for coffee. (This was a recurrent theme. E was her friend and she mentioned her a lot). She says the owner of Hough Dean has returned, a woman apparently. E seemed pleased, excited. She said they knew each other when she was younger.

I turned the pages. Hannah had retired from the library and was having a particularly steamy time with Don. Their relationship had gone on for so long at such high levels of intensity I was beginning to wonder if he really existed.

3/5/ 92

I've been hearing rumours about E's friend. People say she's come to make more of her kind, to cause trouble. I'll ask E – she'll know about that sort of thing.

8/5/92

E was round today. She didn't seem quite herself, a bit distracted. I asked her about that woman and she'd heard the rumours too. I said, you have the power to banish her, why don't you do it before she causes any trouble. E just shrugged, said she didn't want to interfere.

Then nothing more until nearly the end of the notebook.

30/9/92

*Scene in the street today. E should have stepped
in before this. Sally from Old Barn screeching at
E, calling her a witch and all sorts. E said she'd go
and talk to her friend, but it's too late, she's gone,
leaving all this havoc in her wake. E's going to have
trouble living this down.*

I peered at the letters. Could that E actually be an F? It was
early in 1993 that Gran moved to Suffolk to live near to us.
Mum always said she wanted to be with her family, but maybe
life had been a bit too uncomfortable here. I grabbed the next
notebook from the pile. It was lighter outside now, although
it was still really cold. My fingers were stiff so I rubbed them
together and breathed on them. I took another cherry Bakewell
from the box and opened the first page of the notebook.

5/1/93

*E is going away. It's been awful the last few weeks.
People have been leaving things on her doorstep,
making crank calls, spreading rumours about her.
I think Sally Lumb is behind it all – but there are
others. I heard a couple of women in the library
yesterday, one of them telling the other about how
E kills chickens in her back yard and collects hairs
from the backs of bus seats so she can put them in
wax dolls for curses. The other woman said E only
helped out in the charity shop so she could collect
things which belonged to people and use them
against them. I told them it was rubbish, that E
is no more a witch than I am. They looked at me
as if to say, well you're her friend, you probably*

*are a witch. Amanda dropped in for tea yesterday
and she asked me if I thought I should carry on
being friends with E. I said for god's sake you don't
believe that nonsense do you? And she said well,
true or not, you'll be tarred with her brush.*

*Then E came round and said she'd had enough. She
said I was the only person who still spoke to her
and before long people would stop talking to me
too. She said she had a granddaughter who she'd
only met a few times, but she thought she might
have inherited the bloodline and she wanted to get
to know her, prepare her. She said there was no
place for her here any more.*

I'm going to miss her more than I can say.

That's me, the granddaughter. I have to think back. What did
Gran do to prepare me?

26. Meg

I like to keep all the people I've loved. The first was Daniel who I lost to Napoleon. I try to keep him in my mind, but it's been so long. One sweet year we were together, and so many years since. He was the first, the most intense of all my loves, but sometimes I struggle to remember the colour of his eyes or the feel of his kiss.

Charles is gone too, my son and Daniel's. My memories of him are clearer. He lived a full life and we became the best of friends. When he was fifteen years old I caught a chill which turned to pneumonia. I lay feverish and my boy sat beside my bed.

'Please don't die,' I heard him whisper, as though from another world.

'I can't die,' I told him. 'Death already owns my soul.'

He held my hand, and mumbled words of prayer.

When, a few hours later, my human life slipped away I could hear Charles sobbing. My new form was still evolving and I couldn't move to comfort him. It was a blessing that he didn't go straight for the doctor, but sat with me through the hours of night. No one else was witness to that transformation. In the first light of dawn, still immobile, I spoke to him and he stared at me with horror and delight.

Gradually he accepted the truth, but he was embarrassed by what I'd become and asked me to be discreet, especially around his friends from the Scientific Society. We bought the house at Hough Dean and moved down from the moor. Charles' friends came round sometimes for meetings. I would wear a cap and welcome them, provide them with tea and scones as a mother should, then make myself scarce. Once, dressed in a suit belonging to Charles, I joined some of them on a botanical ramble: Charles and his friend John Nowell and a young lad from the town called James. Charles was anxious the whole time, but the two of them were so caught up in the small green growths on rock, wall and boulder, that they didn't pass a second glance when Charles introduced me as a visiting cousin.

Eventually death took Charles, whose life I had bought at such a price, and I was bereft. In those dark days as I hid away at Hough Dean, leaving the house only to feed like the animal I was, I made a vow that Death would take no one else from me in this way. I had the power to keep my loved ones with me, to defeat Death and make more of my kind.

Which was why Frances was such a source of pain and grief to me.

And why Andy is breaking my heart.

There have been others, of course. Before Charles' death I had already turned a couple of young men, one in Paris and one in London, both of whom I still visit when I take the fancy. After Charles there was Richard, my second son, who has been with me much longer now than Charles was, and is thinking of leaving the nest. And there have been others. Each has been a great love affair while it lasted, eventually fading in intensity. Sometimes on a lonely night when Richard is away I list them in my head, like Charles going through his botanical specimens. Sometimes I visit them and we relive old memories. Even so, up until then, if I'd had to choose one to be my only companion, it would have been Daniel Crossley, my husband, whose name I carry and who was denied to me, as Andy now denies himself.

Frances came to Paris in 1960, looking for her father. She was nineteen years old, lithe and firm, with long, brown hair that carried the light of the moon. The moment I saw her I was entranced.

She carried the bloodline and her instincts took her straight to the dark heart of the city, where she could smell our kind.

Her father wasn't in Paris and no one really knew where he was, or even if he still existed. There are ways that we can be killed, and some thought that he had fallen foul of hunters in Eastern Europe. Whatever, he hadn't been seen in Paris for many a year. Frances heard these tales, but she didn't move on in her search. I invited her to be a guest in my house and she stayed. I like to think it was because of me.

I hadn't met anyone like her before. She smelled so sweet and the blood pounded through her the way it does in all young girls but, unlike them, she knew it. She could hear it and knew the effect she had on us. Sometimes she would keep out of the way, go off on her own to explore the city, only returning when we'd had time to feed. But other times she seemed to enjoy the power she had over us. She and I would talk for hours. She talked to me of Hawden, which I hadn't visited for many years at that time. She told me the town was empty and run down, likely to die away completely soon with the end of the industry that had built it. She talked of blackened houses with no sanitation, empty mills and an ageing population eking out the last of its days. Of young people leaving for the cities or pastures greener, herself included, here in Paris looking for what life might bring.

The sofa was draped with a Persian throw, and she sat on it wearing white cotton shorts and a red striped t-shirt, her long brown legs drawn up in front of her, fiddling with her toes as she spoke. I listened to her words and to the beat of her young heart and I wanted to keep her.

She liked to read and one day I invited her into my library. I've collected a lot of books over the years and most of them I keep at my house in Paris, in a room lined with mahogany bookshelves and carpeted deep red. The window is hung with velvet three shades darker. That day she was wearing a yellow mini dress which only just covered her bottom and, as she read the spines, I stood behind her and drew a finger up the inside of her thigh.

She shuddered but didn't turn. I lowered my face so she could feel my breath on her neck. Still she continued reading, but she inclined her head, just a fraction to the left, baring her neck to me and I took my first bite. She tasted salty and young. She stood still whilst I took my fill, then when I drew out my teeth she turned and we kissed for the first time.

The period after that while her wound healed was one of torment to me. She played with me mercilessly. Some evenings she gave me her body like a gift, lying on the sofa in her tiny skirts which hid nothing, allowing my hands, lips and tongue to travel where they would. My teeth throbbed at the nearness of her blood, a skin's depth, a membrane, between them and her infinite sweetness. But we had agreed that she was to join me and there was to be no biting until the skin on her neck had mended.

Other nights she would go out into the city, visiting the clubs and bars, not caring if I was with her or not, revelling in her youth and freedom. She would tumble home in the early mornings, sometimes alone, but often accompanied by crowds of loud drunk teenagers who would inhabit my kitchen making tea and toast and exclaiming at its Englishness.

I took the second bite just before Christmas. We were at a party. She had been drinking and dancing and she was flushed with sweat and excitement. She flirted with everyone, knowing that I was watching, and there were a few young men hanging around her, hoping she would choose them to take home at the end of the night. I wouldn't have put it past her. She had brought lovers back before, although she always kicked them out before they got what they wanted.

Just after midnight she stumbled out laughing onto the balcony where I was enjoying the night air and fell against me. She wasn't drunk, just tipsy and over-stimulated. She dropped her head forward to look at something going on down in the street and I saw that the wound had vanished. I bit her without warning, grabbing hold of her as I did so, and her body was immediately limp and unresisting.

She changed after that. She stopped going out. We stayed in together, reading, talking, making love. The days passed quietly. Her blood had changed. She was well on the way to the turn and she no longer carried the heady fresh aroma of youth which had driven me wild. Her blood no longer tempted me, and I could take what I wanted from her without the madness gathering behind my eyes. She was companion and lover and no longer a food source for me.

For her part she clung to me. We saw very few other people in those weeks, and I realise she must have thought that was how it would be, just the two of us forever. She was so young, nineteen years old, she had no concept of what forever might mean.

The second wound had nearly healed and our time was close when I asked her about her mother.

I asked how it was that a young woman from a Yorkshire mill town came to be in Paris. Frances said it was 1940 and wartime. War is a time of many things, many terrible things, but it also brings opportunities to people who would never have had them otherwise. Her mother trained as a nurse and was sent out to France to look after the wounded on the battlefields. And that was where she met Frances' father.

He was wearing the uniform of an officer and it was that which turned her head at first. Later, by the time she realised the uniform had been taken from a corpse, it was too late. She was both smitten and bitten. And he was obviously taken with her too, as he had stayed around for the first bite to heal and they were waiting for the skin to close for the second time so she could stay with him forever.

But war causes great tide changes and she must have been a very strong young woman, because during the nights at the hospital, tending to young men in pain and fear, away from home for the first time and longing for their mothers, something changed in her mind and she decided that she wanted a different kind of longevity. She wanted motherhood: she wanted to see her blood passed on to her children, to look for her features in their faces – and his too, her lover and soulmate. She wanted his child.

The arguments must have been fierce. The fact that she won shows, I think, that he must have had the weakness of vanity. He wanted to show that he could procreate in the human way as well as our own. It's never a good idea to mingle our blood with that of the living: disasters usually follow.

But here next to me was Frances, the result of their union, leaning her head against my shoulder, her legs folded up underneath her and her hair falling forward to cover her face.

'The wound is nearly healed, sweetie,' I said to her. 'It will only be a day or two.'

She didn't look at me and after a moment I noticed a tear splash on to the skin of her leg.

I put my arm round her.

'What's the matter?'

More tears fell before she spoke. 'Who is Cristo?'

'Cristo?' I sat up a bit straighter. This wasn't what I expected. 'He's an old friend of mine. He lives in Athens, but he is visiting Paris and catching up with his friends.'

'Did you turn him?'

'Yes...' I was tentative. 'A long, long time ago.'

'And he was your lover.'

'Frances, what are you thinking? That is all in the past. Cristo and I, we chat about old times, we share a glass of wine or tea. Soon he will be on his way again. You have no need to worry.'

'There must be many more like him. You've had many lovers.'

I put my hand on hers and squeezed it.

'Sweetie, I'm here with you. The past is that, the past. You are my present.'

She lifted her head at that and looked into my face, her eyes brimming with tears, her mouth twisted.

'And the future? Is your future filled with many lovers too? Will you discard me when you have had enough?'

'Darling, I never discard anyone.'

She dropped her head again and mumbled something I didn't catch.

'What did you say sweetie?'

'I want a child too,' she said clearly through her hair. 'Like my mother.'

'Frances...'

'I'm going back. I'm going back to England tomorrow.'

I tried to argue, but she was resolute. She had already booked her passage home and packed her bags. It seemed she had been planning it for a week or more. I couldn't let it happen. She was mine, I'd never had a lover like her before and we were nearly there. A few more skin cells to knot together and then the final bite to bind her to me.

'I will come too,' I said, 'Paris, Yorkshire, I will follow you wherever you go. We are so close. Our time is here and you belong to me.'

She stared at me then with eyes as cold as her father's.

She said. 'If I choose to banish you, you can never return.'

And that is the terrible truth. Although I had power over other creatures of the night, she had power over me. Her mixed blood gave her a human body, a human appetite and lifespan, a human life in all respects except this. Our kind cannot hide from her, she can always detect us, and she has the irrevocable power of banishment. If she so chose, she could close off parts of the planet to me and live in places I could never enter, even after she has gone from this life, as the banishment is permanent. It is a terrible power and the reason that we do not mix our blood. Frances was a rare creature.

She left. She wrote to me, letters filled with love and sweetness, telling me how she had borne the child she wanted, although she said nothing of the father. She told me they lived alone, her and the child, but they had many friends. The child, a girl called Marianne, grew up, and Frances wrote that she was bewildered by her. She was so different from herself. No trace of the bloodline. No shared interests. Teenage years filled with misunderstandings, disappointments, angry disagreements, and then the girl left home and Frances was alone once more.

The years in Paris had gone slowly. After she left, everything lost its shine, and although I dallied a little, travelled and visited the past, they were empty years. Richard didn't need me much in those days: he had his own life and his own friends. So when I suggested a trip to Yorkshire he declined, chose instead to visit the circus in Istanbul, to follow them into Russia, then across the seas to the States and down to Brazil. The circus had long been his passion.

It was the first time I'd been home for many years. The house was in a bit of a state, and the road up to it was falling into ruin. Driving up there the first night my car got stuck, a wheel sunk deep into a pot hole with the chassis resting on the road itself. When it comes to cars I'm a bit of a helpless woman. I climbed out and surveyed the road for anyone who could help me. It stretched empty and full of stones, winding around the hills and reappearing further down the valley.

I tried lifting the corner of the car. I am strong, but I hadn't fed for some days and I couldn't lift it enough to clear the pothole.

That was when he appeared, my knight in shining Lycra, running around the bend in his fell shoes, his legs bulging with muscles and bespattered with mud from the hills. His blond hair was wet, his face fresh and glowing from exercise. Andy, my rock, my joy, my true love.

'Do you need some help?' he asked.

I smiled at him, hiding my hunger. Life flooded with colour. Here was a reason to come home, a reason to start living again.

'Oh, yes please. I don't know what to do.' I calmed my voice. I could hear the pounding of his heart from his run in the hills, his blood like a wild sea on the shore. He smelled of salt and sweat. 'I'm so glad you came.'

27. Cassie

It lasted for two months. We were happy for two months.

You and Andy were my whole life and it seemed life could not be sweeter. The tiredness and soreness after childbirth seemed a small price to pay, and I was happy to pay it for the life we had. Those first weeks, when Andy was off work and you were tiny and new, were like a tender dream. We woke in the early mornings and you were there, sleeping with your eyelashes resting against the transparent skin of your cheeks. We watched you and held hands, unable to believe our luck. Your little chest was rising and falling under the soft fabric of your babygrow.

You grew quickly. The more you fed from me the more milk came. It would well up and overflow. I slept with towels underneath me and woke in the night to find them sopping wet. I would look at your sleeping form and be tempted to wake you. But I never did: I let you sleep. And when you woke an hour or two later, hungry, the force of the milk would sometimes choke you. My clothes were constantly sodden. We lived those weeks in a bath of growth and happiness. When you drank from one breast the milk would shoot out of the other, sometimes hitting the wall on the other side of the room. Andy and I would laugh until the tears came.

Soon you filled your babygrows and Andy had to go back to work. We spent long lazy days together after he'd gone. We would laze in bed in the morning, enjoying the luxury of no responsibilities. Eventually we would rouse ourselves and potter in the kitchen making breakfast, chatting to each other. I knew that reality would kick in at some point, but for the time being I wallowed in the small milk-bound world we lived in.

Sally came to visit. She wasn't a baby person. She looked at you and said you looked fat.

'It's just her cheeks,' I said. 'Do you want to hold her?'

'Don't disturb her,' she said, moving away from your crib.

I laughed and put the kettle on. Sally had brought eggs from the farm and homemade biscuits.

'How's Terry?' I asked.

'He's fine. Not too much work recently.'

'Have you been feeding him?'

She grinned. 'You know he loves my food.'

I spooned coffee into the cafetière and was glad my husband was not like Terry. Andy was solidly human and at night he slept.

Sally rummaged in her bag looking for something. 'What about Andy?' she said, into its depths.

'Andy's ok. Why?'

'No reason,' she said.

'Sally, don't do that.'

She found a packet of tissues and removed one, blew her nose.

'I just heard he was up at Hough Dean a lot recently.'

'Hough Dean?'

'Yes, she's home at the moment. In residence, so to speak. Andy's been going up there in the evenings.'

'Don't be silly.'

'Just thought I'd mention it.'

'Well stop thinking. It doesn't suit you.'

I poured the coffee and you started crying, so I picked you up and fed you and Sally tried hard not to look as she dunked her biscuit and talked about the weather. We've never been the sort of sisters to have girlie chats. She only stayed for half an hour.

On the doorstep she said 'You could visit Frances Greenwood.'

'What for?'

'She's one of them. A half-breed.'

'So I've heard.'

'Well, she could banish her. Out of Andy's way.'

'Sally! I don't need to. Everything's fine.'

She stared at me with her blue eyes and didn't say anything. Then she walked off and you and I stood on the step watching her go.

I couldn't settle. When you went to sleep in your Moses basket I was restless, moving about the house. I washed up the coffee things, dried them and put them away. I trusted Andy. In the three years we'd been together there had never been anyone else for either of us. Now we had you and we were knotted together more tightly than ever.

I started to rearrange the cups in the front of the cupboard, then I got all the crockery out and put it on the table. I cleaned the shelves with anti-bacterial spray and wiped them dry with a clean cloth. Andy had been out in the evenings a lot recently. He went running. There were meetings at school. He belonged to the gym. He met up with Mr Lion for a pint sometimes. I was busy feeding you, changing and bathing you, singing songs in the hope that you'd go back to sleep. I didn't always ask Andy where he was going, and he was usually back by nine or ten.

By the time he got home from school that day I had washed all the crockery and put it back in the cupboards. I'd sorted through the cutlery drawers, cleaned them and lined them with waxed paper. I was looking in the food cupboard, wondering how many half-used packets were past their sell-by date when he opened the front door. The noise woke you and I lifted you out of your basket. We watched Andy walk into the kitchen.

Meg Crossley wasn't just anyone. I'd heard the stories.

He smiled. 'Hello you two, is everything ok?'

'Sally's been round.'

He put his bag down and hung his jacket on the back of a chair. He kissed me on the forehead.

'How's Sally?'

'Sally's ok.'

He must have heard something in my voice. He looked at me sharply, then sighed. 'Ok, what is it this time? What did she say to upset you?'

'She says you've been visiting Hough Dean.'

He kissed you on one cheek and then the other and you dimpled at him. He met my eyes.

'Cass, you know Sally. She likes to stir things.'

'Is it true?'

He put his hand on my arm.

'Yes. I've been to Hough Dean. I took Meg some lightbulbs she needed and we played chess.'

'Chess?'

'She's pretty good.'

'Oh.' I sat down and you nuzzled against me looking for milk. I undid my shirt and you latched on.

He knelt in front of us and looked in my face. 'I have you two. I don't need anything else.'

We ordered a takeaway that evening and snuggled up on the sofa in front of a film.

Two weeks went by and neither Andy nor I mentioned Meg. You fed and grew. I found that you loved going out into the garden. You looked at the flowers and the leaves on the trees and made little noises. Your first smile was when I showed you some yellow pansies.

Andy went out sometimes in the evenings, and now I noticed when he didn't say where he was going. In the second week I decided to follow him.

He went on his bike. I hadn't been out on the bike with you in the sling yet, and I didn't feel ready to try. I watched out of the window to see which direction Andy was headed and saw he had some pink roses wrapped in paper from the florist. Half an hour later I strapped you into your car seat and drove up to Hough Dean. I parked a little way down the lane, so we wouldn't be seen or heard. I carried you to where the trees stopped and the house came into sight. Andy's bike was in the yard leaning against a tree.

I'd asked him once, early on when we were just getting to know each other, if he played chess.

'Not any more,' he said. 'I got bored.'

'I came second one year in the school championship,' I said. 'Try and beat me.'

He laughed and kissed me. 'How about Monopoly?' he said.

At Hough Dean the windows were open at the front but I couldn't see anyone inside. I drove you home, put you to bed and cleaned the kitchen floor.

28. Peter

He couldn't sleep. He came out of the cave, sat on the ground, and watched the sky. The light from the crescent moon was diffuse, creating white surfaces, separated by deep shadows where anything was possible. He needed to run. He needed to stretch his limbs and burn up the energy spinning round his brain, build some distance. The hills stretched away to the north; Hawden nestled in the valley to the south. He breathed the night air into his lungs, turned his back to the moon and followed the pull of the pole.

29. Lauren

I'd been at a party, but it was pretty boring and I left to go and find Peter. He must have gone off somewhere because there was no trace of him. I met Richard on his way to the club and he asked me if I wanted to go with him. Mr Lion was dj-ing that night and I thought why the hell not.

That was when the girl, Ali, turned up, and we all went up to Hough Dean. It was strange. I mean, where had she been hiding all those weeks? I wanted to tell her about the money, find out if she still had the note with the code on it. But it would have seemed too weird to just come out and ask her when we'd never even met before. So I was glad we were all going to Hough Dean because after we'd all been together for a bit and had a couple of beers it might be ok to ask her.

But when we got to Richard's everything got really odd. For a start Richard's mum and Ali knew each other. And then Ali freaked and left and Richard chased after her, and I was left standing in the hallway with Meg and she was looking at me, up and down, like she was checking me out. I coughed and looked away. She must have been like a teenager or something when she had Richard. She'd got her hair tied up on the back of her head and she was wearing a black top and black trousers and she looked like she was out of a Bond movie – the glamorous spy relaxing at home.

She said 'How's your father?'

Her eyes were like Richard's: pale and a bit bloodshot. I guessed she must have the same eye condition.

'You know my Dad?'

'Andy and I used to be good friends.'

'Oh, he never said.' Then I remembered that day when me and Peter had come up here and seen them moving in, and how Dad had gone really still and whispered her name. I thought he was angry she was back, but maybe it was something else.

'Well, send him my love. Tell him I think of him often.'

Richard came back in on his own.

'Don't worry,' his mum said. 'I'm sure she'll be back.'

Richard's eyes had gone the same way, milky and unreadable. I looked at the clock.

'I hadn't realised it was so late. I think I should be getting back.'

'I'll walk you.'

'It's ok.'

I turned back to him, and his eyes were grey and clear. I was wrong. They were lovely eyes and he was smiling at me.

'I would like to walk you home,' he said. 'Please.'

I smiled back at him and agreed.

Walking down the lane, he took my arm and I leaned into him. It was nice to be close to another body. I wondered where Peter was and when he'd be back.

The next morning when I got up Cassie was there. This was new. It was too early for her to have just come round. She was wearing the same clothes as the day before at teatime. When she went up to the loo I asked Dad about it.

'Did Cassie stay over?'

'Yes, she did.' Dad was washing up, but he turned round and looked at me, his hands dripping with water and soap suds.

I took a bite of my toast. 'Does Mr Lion mind?'

He looked surprised. 'No, Mr Lion doesn't mind. Why should he?'

'He was dj-ing at the club last night.'

'I know...'

'Well, you two seem to have taken over his house and he has to go out all the time, tiptoe around when he gets back from a night. He probably feels like an unwanted extra.'

Dad sighed and grabbed a towel to dry his hands. 'Is that how you feel?'

'What?'

'Like an unwanted extra. Because it isn't true. Your mother really wants to get to know you.'

I took another big bite of toast and chewed it noisily. Dad waited.

'Well I don't understand,' I said, 'what the big deal is with now. Why does she want to get to know me now, when she hasn't given a fuck for the last seventeen-and-a-half years? Why should I care?'

'Give her a chance, Lauren. It's not easy for her.'

I spluttered toast crumbs.

'For her? What about me? And Mr Lion? Every time we turn around you two are gazing at each other, then she wants to take me into some corner and talk to me about when I was a baby. You're always singing. It's like living in a nut house. No wonder Peter never comes round any more.'

I started crying. Dad put his arms around me and I wailed into his shoulder. He smelled just the same as he always had and his arms were the same arms that had always held me and, although I was crying, for a moment everything seemed all right.

Then I noticed her. She'd come back from the loo and she was hovering in the doorway not sure what to do. I broke out of Dad's arms and ran upstairs to my room.

Peter's gone right into himself. Obviously A-levels are coming up and he wants to do well, but he's turned into some sort of recluse. Even more of a recluse than before.

Everyone's having parties for their eighteenth birthdays and, although we all have loads of work, there's fun to be had. Peter used to come to parties sometimes, even if he didn't stay long.

But since his horns have come through he's not really wanted to go. He doesn't seem bothered by them or embarrassed. He doesn't try and hide them like he always did his hooves. It's like he's just stopped trying to blend in. He doesn't want to go to parties so he doesn't go to parties. Not even for me. He says, you go, you'll have a good time.

So I go and I try to have a good time. If I turn off all this stuff, don't think about it, and just live in the moment, then I can. Sometimes after a party I go to the woods and find Peter and curl up next to him. He puts his arm over me and I try to sleep, but then I get too cold. I can't cope with the winter nights like he can. I stay for a while, but I have to creep home to my bed to get the warmth back into my blood.

30. Peter

Peter was asleep, curled up at the back of the cave, his child legs tucked underneath him, his chin touching his knees. His dad crouched beside him and smoothed the hair back from his face. Peter moved his shoulder and twitched a cheek muscle. His face was streaked with tears. His dad covered him with a blanket, then set about building up the fire. He put a pan of stew on the stove. When it was bubbling and the savoury herb smells wafted through the cave, Peter woke and came and sat by the fire, the blanket still around his shoulders. His dad gave him a bowl of stew and a hunk of Mr Lion's caraway bread. They ate in silence and watched the flames.

Peter was hungry. He wiped the bowl clean with the last crust of bread and leaned against his dad.

'All right, son?'

'Ok,' he said quietly.

'Things getting to you?'

'Hmm.'

His dad put his arm round him and poked at the fire with his hoof. Sparks flew up and landed in their coats.

'Why are we like this?' Peter said.

'Like this?' His dad crushed a spark that had begun to smoulder.

'Yes. And why do we live in a cave? And why don't we feel cold like other people? And why do you have horns on your head? And why haven't I?'

He was defiant and angry and his eyes shone in the firelight. His dad touched the hair on his head.

'You will have horns one day, when you're older.'

'Like yours?'

'Yes like mine.'

'And will I be able to run like you?'

'Yes, we can run together.'

He nodded and sat quiet.

'More stew?'

Peter shook his head. 'But Dad, people laugh at me. Why can't I be like everyone else?'

'Who do you want to be like? Like Mr Lion? Like Jimmy who can eat fire? Like Lauren who can hear the plants talking?'

'Just normal.'

'Like Joel Wetherby? Like the other boys at school? Is that what you want? Do you want to live in a house with doors and a television?'

Peter looked up at the sky. The first star had just appeared. 'Venus,' he whispered.

They sat and watched her and she winked at them.

31. Richard

I dreamed of my first girlfriend, Laura, that night. We were walking together through the town but everything had changed. It was like it is now, with all the green trees and the clean stone of the buildings. The sun was shining and we came to the canal.

Laura said 'This is all wrong. Why are there geese on the water?'

'It's different now,' I said, 'The soot has gone. The mills have gone. It's a clean place.'

She grabbed hold of my arm.

'Look!' she said. 'Look at that tree.'

There was a mature ash tree growing not far from the water. It was in full leaf and its trunk was covered in a pattern of greens and greys, liverworts and lichens.

'The forest is creeping into the town,' Laura said. 'It's taking over. Soon everything will be green.'

I turned around and saw that it was true. Moss was growing across the streets, spreading up walls and over cars. Ferns were growing in the mortar of buildings, from wheel arches, and lampposts; trees were bursting through where windows should have been; people were slowing down, coming to a stop as the moss grew up their legs and torsos and fixed them where they stood.

Laura beside me was shaking with fear.

'It's ok,' I said. 'It's beautiful. It can't touch us.'

A mountain stream was bubbling and leaping down the main road over mossy boulders. I turned to her and her hair had become green fronds. There was a bird inside her clothes and when I looked she was hollow. The bird was nesting in her ribcage. Her face was decaying before my eyes, her cheeks sinking in and blackening so her eyeballs protruded.

'Sorry Richard, this is not my time,' she said, and her voice slowed, deepened as though it were being played at the wrong speed.

'No Laura, don't go.' I grabbed at her, but there was no flesh, only clothes over bone. 'I've come back for you. We can be together.'

She shook her head. Her cheekbones were visible.

'Don't you remember Richard? I left you. I married Jack and we had children, goats, chickens. I'm dead now.'

She vanished then, and when I looked around there was no sign of the town. I was standing on a wooded slope next to a stream and a small group of deer were upwind of me, eyeing me nervously. I ran at them shouting my frustration.

Then I woke and found I was thinking of the girl, Ali.

She was obviously hiding from those two, Smith and Jeannie, and until that business was sorted there was no way I'd be able to talk to her out in the open or get to know her. I'd never met anyone like her before. Her grandmother, Frances, the half-blood girl in Paris, was Meg's obsession. I didn't pay much attention then, or to Meg's despair when she died. The blood was thinned in Ali, but apparently it shows more in some than in others.

I reckoned Smith and Jeannie would have gone back to Leeds, maybe leaving some scouts on the lookout, so that's where I went. It wasn't that difficult to find them. I asked a few druggies on the street corners where I could go to score, and gradually spiralled inwards through the city's networks until by the evening I found myself at a club in a basement waiting for the pair of them to turn up.

They arrived around midnight with a group of friends and colonised a corner table which was kept empty for them, even though the place was busy. This was obviously their space. I was in a dark corner on the other side of the club. There was no table service, but the barman came over with their drinks. Smith was cutting up lines of coke on the table. I remembered him and Jeannie standing nervously by the bridge at the canal party in Hawden, out of their comfort zone, and I'd wondered why Ali was so scared. He snorted the first line, then made a joke and everyone at the table laughed. I was getting the picture. He might not be that big a fish, but this was his pond.

I didn't stay. Although they had been friendly enough before, this wasn't the ground to meet them on. I needed to find Ali. It was time she knew the score.

I asked Meg if she had any ideas where Ali might be living. Was there an old family home or something? But she said Frances had sold everything when she moved away. There were other people living in the house now, offcomers. She said she'd only been there once anyway, last time she was here. Frances had refused to see her.

'She was angry with me because of Andy,' she said.

'You should learn to control your appetites.'

'Yes, son, I should.' She ruffled my hair. 'And what about yours? Andy's daughter is sweet. Has the first bite healed yet?'

'Nearly.'

'No boyfriend problems?'

'The goat boy? I don't know. She's very attached to him, but the second bite should deal with that.'

'Be careful. I've never turned anyone without their consent. I know it's done, but it's not always successful. She might turn against you.'

'She likes me. I can tell that.'

We sat quietly for a moment.

'And Ali?' I said, 'Is there any way I can find her? Her blood means we can't hide from her, but can she hide from us?'

'That only works one way, I'm afraid. I could tell you how to find any supernatural beings within a twenty mile radius of here, but half-blood smells just like human blood. You'll have to do some detective work.'

I walked into town and went for a pint at the White Horse. It was a quiet evening and I sat at a table with my beer and thought about where to start. After a while I'd tied my head in knots, but I thought I might go back up to Old Barn and see if I could talk to Sally. She might have some clues, something Ali had said or left behind.

I let my mind wander and found I was thinking about stonemasons, something I'd not given a moment's thought to for decades. I only worked with Mr S for a few years, but I think if a chisel were put into my hand right now I'd know what to do with it. I walked past the stonemason's yard the other day with Lauren and stopped to look at the blocks and slabs piled up in the yard. I touched the nearest stone and its surface beneath my fingers made my palms itch. I thought I might come back on my own and talk to the masons, ask if I could have a go. I remembered the hours it took to make that hole in the monument platform, chipping and scraping in the hot sun, day after day, and the sound it made and the grit that got in with my bread and cheese.

'We weren't employed to do that, lad, so we can't take it out of their time,' Mr S said to me 'That would be theft. Thou shalt not steal, that's what the Lord said, lad.'

'Well if we weren't employed to do it, should we be doing it at all?'

He looked a bit shifty at that.

'Well, it's the people's monument, and we're some of the people. You were right, lad, about the stairs being too dark, and if it encourages them strange goings on...'

As a fully paid up member of the Baptist church, Mr S found masonic ceremonies quite scandalous.

'Sit, Beauty, settle down.'

I looked up and saw Mr Lion leaning at the bar, his little white dog at his feet.

'She's a bit excitable today,' he told the barman, 'doesn't take anything to set her off. And she's got a thing about that old ruined cottage up above the woods at Hawtenstall. I can't walk past there without her barking fit to raise the dead.'

Beauty slumped down heavily and put her chin on Mr Lion's feet, her eyes closed.

'That's it, girl,' he said to her, and she opened one eye to look at him.

Sometimes I've wondered if I would like to get a dog, but their lives are over so quickly.

The next day I walked up to Old Barn and this time it was Sally herself who answered the door. She was smiling as she opened it, but when she saw me standing on the doorstep her smile faded.

'What do you want?' she hissed.

'I just wanted to ask you some questions. Can I come in?'

She took a step forward and put her hands on the doorposts blocking the way.

'*Can I come in?* Do you think I'm stupid? I'm not going to fall for a trick like that. You can stay right where you are. What questions?'

I took a breath before I spoke, relaxed my face muscles to keep from grinning.

'About Ali, the girl who was staying here. I want to find her.'

'She's not here.'

'I know she's not. I just wondered if she said where she was going, if she said anything.'

She stared at me and said nothing. I said nothing either and the moment stretched out. I could hear the birds in the trees and the sound of someone humming to themselves in the house. I remembered the man who opened the door to us last time.

'She was Frances Greenwood's granddaughter,' she said at last, spitting out the name.

'Yes.'

'Frances was one of your kind. A half blood. She should have banished you from this place, you and your mother. She ruined our lives, mine and my sister's, made us hate each other. You should go away from this place, we don't want your sort.'

'I just wanted to find Ali, I have something important to tell her.'

'She's a half-blood too, my husband could tell immediately.'

As if on cue he appeared behind her, his figure like before, both bulky and insubstantial as though he were made of shadows.

'Everything ok, Salgirl?'

She turned to him, keeping her hands firmly on the doorpost. When she smiled at him her face transformed.

'Yes, Terry. I haven't invited him in. He's looking for the Greenwood girl.'

'He came looking for her before. That time he had your niece with him.'

She peered back at me, her eyes full of suspicion and hate.

'Don't you think your lot have done enough to my family? Leave us alone. Stick to your own kind.'

She took a leap back from the door and closed it in my face. I stood staring at it stupidly for a moment or two before turning and walking back to the lane.

I walked over to Hawtenstall by the straightest route, down into the valley then up the other side. I hadn't been this way since we'd been back and it was a different place to the one I used to know. In the valley bottom I looked for landmarks, but there was only a chimney where the silk mill used to be. It was in the middle of woodland now, some of the trees reaching up half its height. I followed a footpath along the river from the bridge and the water was clear. The trees were nearly bare and the ground was covered with the brown mulch of fallen leaves. I found the mill, a few remaining walls tracing its shape, hinting at its size. I thought of my mother and sisters trudging up here day after day with their snap bags under their arms. What would they think if they saw it now? Would they miss the smoke that filled their lungs and caused their early deaths?

I followed the track up to Hawtenstall. Half way up, the woods stopped and the view opened onto fields, portioned out by stone walls. This was familiar enough, but when I looked back I still expected to see an industrial valley: Silk Mill, Lumb Mill and Crossley Mill following one on the tail of the other, the length of the valley marked by the thick slug of smoke that hung above them, held in place by the valley sides. Now so verdant.

Hawtenstall was unchanged, though of course cleaner. I wandered down the cobbled streets, not sure really what I was looking for. I went into the library and looked at the leaflets on display, the local history board, the healthy young girl behind the counter, and went out again. I was hungry. In the post office-cum-corner shop I bought a can of Coke. I followed the route out of the village past the Methodist chapel and down the sloping footpath into the next valley. It was all very pleasant, but I didn't feel any nearer to finding Ali.

I went to Lauren's house. Nobody answered but the door was open so I went in and called up the stairs.

'Lauren, are you there?'

She appeared on the landing. She was wearing a baggy white t-shirt and grey leggings and her hair was mussed up. She'd obviously been crying.

'Oh,' she said, 'it's you.'

Her voice was flat.

'Can I come up?'

She shrugged and went back into her room.

I bounded up the stairs and followed her in. She was standing by the bed looking out of the window, her body slumped with dejection. A faint aroma of sickness came off her and her clothes smelled as though she'd been sleeping in them.

I stood behind her and lifted her hair away from her neck. The wound had completely healed and her skin was glistening, covered with a slight slick of sweat. The smell of her blood filled my mouth and nose.

'Richard, what do you want?'

'Right now I'm hungry.'

'The plants have died back. Only stalks and roots.'

'I don't like eating plants.'

'Seeds. Bulbs. They'll all grow again next year.'

'I can't wait until next year.'

She breathed out a puff of air and slumped against me. There was a faint sound as my teeth broke through her skin and the blood began to flow.

32. Meg

My husband, Daniel, taught me to play chess, but we only played a few times. Once I'd grasped the rules I won every game and it stopped being fun. It wasn't until Charles grew to be a teenager that I found a worthy opponent. When he died, I think I missed the chess games more than almost anything else. There was no one else, you see, and never has been. A few people have claimed to be talented players, but when it came to the test they couldn't beat me. Richard has never been interested.

That evening I opened the front door and there was Andy, wearing jeans and a green t-shirt that was stained on the shoulder with what might have been baby sick. His hair was clean and soft. He held out a carrier bag.

'Here, I promised I'd bring these.'

'Thank you.' I didn't take them and after a moment he dropped his arm.

'Did you manage to get the electricity going?'

'Yes, I switched it on at the mains and it's fine.'

'Excellent,' he held the bag up again. 'Well, I'd best be going. You'll want to get these in before dark.'

'I'm not sure I can reach,' I said. 'The ceilings are very high. I don't suppose you...'

It was his skin I was most aware of. It smelled salty, but undercut with something sharp, some type of soap, a surface smell which covered him, keeping what was inside in, outside out. I felt a tingling in my dogteeth.

'Well... Cassie will be expecting me...'

'It would be kind of you. You've been so helpful.'

'Maybe...'

'I'll put the kettle on.'

'I suppose...'

I walked into the house and he followed me inside, staring anxiously into the dark, dusty corners. I could hear the blood in his veins, the stretch of his muscles. He didn't know his power.

'Amazingly after all these years the bulb in the kitchen still works,' I said. 'You could start in the lounge.'

I decided against the kettle. I found a dusty bottle of red wine and two glasses, poured some before he could refuse.

'It's my first day in the house,' I told him. 'I have to have someone to celebrate with.'

'The place could do with a spring clean,' he said, looking at the dust marks on my clothes.

The wine glowed in his glass. He tipped it to his mouth and a red stain appeared on his lips.

'Do you play chess?' I asked him.

33. Cassie

That night the bedroom was different. I moved around in it trying to see what it was. I sat on the bed. I drew back the curtains and looked into the night before closing them again. Then I saw that the mirrored wardrobe door was slightly ajar, so it reflected a different part of the room. By then, unease had settled in my stomach like a bad meal.

I stood by the cot where you were sleeping. I put my finger on your cheek and felt the tiny movements of your breath. You smelled of milk, and you were so tiny that my middle fingers and thumbs met at the front and back of your body. I let you sleep, despite the tingling in my breasts. Even the thought of feeding you could bring the needle hot rush of milk, the spreading dampness.

I got into bed, lay down, and adjusted the towels beneath me. Andy was in the bathroom cleaning his teeth. He'd been out again earlier. I was washing the curtains when he got back, scrubbing the dust and stains into the kitchen sink. He seemed a bit agitated. He put the kettle on to make tea, then changed his mind and poured a whisky. He offered to pour one for me.

The toilet flushed and he came into the room, got into bed wearing just his shorts, and turned to me. He ran his finger in a line from my forehead to my lips.

'Cass, I'm not going anywhere,' he said. 'I'm here to stay.'

I smiled.

He kissed me on the lips and then turned to switch off the light. In seconds we were both asleep. Afterwards I wished I'd stayed awake, watched the shape of him sleeping and listened to him breathe. But I went straight to sleep even as the milk oozed up, beading on my nipples and dripping onto the towels.

I awoke with a weight on my chest. I was lying on my back and something was pinning me to the bed. I lay still for a moment. Was something wrong with my body? No, it was a solid weight and it was cold. I opened my eyes.

'Hello sugar.'

I gasped and tried to twist, to throw him off, but he was too heavy.

'I'm your nightmare,' he said.

'Terry, get off of me.'

I glanced sideways to where Andy was sleeping, his back to me.

'He won't wake up,' Terry said. 'That's the way it is with nightmares.'

'Go home,' I said, more loudly this time. 'Leave me alone.'

'I can't. You've been cursed.'

He bent forward and kissed my lips. His breath smelled of onions and I turned my face away. He nuzzled my neck.

'Terry, stop it! Sally...'

He took my head in his hands, turned it, and pushed his tongue into my mouth where it thrashed like an eel. I couldn't move. His stubble rubbed on my face, and his teeth knocked mine. His saliva tasted metallic.

'Sorry Cass, I've been sent and there's nothing you or I can do about it. I'd rather be at home with Sal, but I'm not. So lie still like a good girl and make the most of it.'

I found that was all I could do. Since he'd moved my head I was paralysed. He was kissing me again, moving his head slowly down from my face to my neck and my chest.

He took my nipple in his mouth and began to suck.

'No Terry, not that.'

But he took no notice, and my body betrayed me. The milk flowed and he swallowed. Milk dribbled from the corner of his mouth, and his fat cheeks went in and out the way yours did. I could feel his bristles on my breast.

That was the worst thing, him drinking my milk. Lying there unable to move, with you so near in your cot, while Terry stole what was yours. That was the most terrible night of my life.

He didn't stop at that of course and it seemed to go on for hours. Andy didn't move, he slept through it all. I remembered Sally giggling once, telling me that one of the benefits of marrying Terry was that he was indefatigable.

'Even when I'm limp as a rag, he still wants more,' she'd said, and I'd tried not to think about it. The idea of a naked, lustful, overweight Terry was utterly repulsive.

'Sal's not going to like it,' he said when he had finally finished. 'I'd better warn you. She's going to go ballistic.'

'Will you tell her?'

He was putting his clothes back on at the side of the bed. Andy was snoring.

'I've no choice,' he said. 'This isn't a one night job you know. We're stuck with each other, us two.'

'But...'

'Tomorrow night,' he said, and kissed me on the top of my head. 'It won't be so bad if you're awake.'

I lay still in the bed after he'd gone. You were beginning to stir in your cot. I could hear the rustling of the blankets, then you thrust your arm against the bars and I heard the tiny hiccough of a cry.

I didn't let it get any louder. I slid out of bed and held you in my arms.

'Lauren,' I whispered.

Later in the day I stood at the kitchen window, watching the play of sunlight in the yard as it danced through leaves. You were sleeping and Andy had gone off to work after waking late and rushing breakfast. The house was full of quiet. I walked softly from the kitchen through to the living room. There were photos on the shelf, rows of books, a jumper of Andy's thrown carelessly over the back of a chair. I breathed it in, staring at the stripes of the book spines, the colours of wool in the upholstery. Then I lay down on the carpet and curled into a ball, looking right into the weave and spotting specks of dust that the Hoover hadn't wanted.

Terry kept his promise and came back again that night, but this time I was awake. I went to bed after Andy. I pretended I wanted to finish a book first, waited until he had fallen asleep, then lay in the dark next to his sleeping bulk, trying not to listen to my thoughts. And in the tender hours he came.

I felt his weight on my chest, crushing my lungs and heart, annihilating my heartstrings. But this time it lifted. When I looked he was standing at the side of my bed fully clothed. He pulled up a chair and sat down.

'Good girl,' he said. 'Nightmares only come to the sleeping.'

I lay awake until light began to creep into the room and he didn't move. I saw you lying in your cot and your eyes were open. I blinked and you were sleeping. Terry had gone.

The next day I spoke to Andy at breakfast.

'Do you think it's time to move Lauren into her own room?'

Andy looked up from his muesli. 'Already?'

'She keeps me awake at night. I hear her every time she moves. I lie there listening to her breathing just in case she stops.'

'Her room isn't quite ready. We still need to finish painting the woodwork.'

'Please Andy, I'm so tired.'

He looked at me and he seemed to be studying my face.

'Ok, maybe we could sort it at the weekend,' he said.

'No Andy, today. We could move her cot in there today. I can do it.'

He stared at me, then he put his hand over mine.

'Are you all right Cass?' he asked.

'Just tired.'

The next night after Terry had gone I crept through to the nursery and sat in the corner with my chin on my knees, listening to the sound of your breathing.

In the morning I answered the door bell and there was Sally, her face red raw from crying.

'Hi Sal,' I said, and opened the door wider for her to come in.

She didn't move. 'Why?' she said.

'Sal...'

'Just because that woman's trying to steal Andy, you didn't have to take my man'

'Has he... left you?' I asked.

'You know bloody well that he's left me, you cow. You couldn't make do with one husband, you had to have two.' She turned and walked away. I ran after her and grabbed at her arm.

'Sal, it's not like that, I...'

She shook me off and shouted into my face. 'I never want to see you again.'

I watched her disappear then went back into the house. You were crying. You weren't taking to the bottle since my milk had gone and you were hungry. You seemed to like it better when Andy fed you. I looked about me. I wondered how much there was in the house that I actually needed.

We'd been sisters all our lives and then, for seventeen years, nothing.

I walked up the hill to Old Barn. The trees had grown taller and the valley was greener.

The door knocker was the same, a brass circle to be lifted and rapped. When we were kids, Sal and I would knock, then hide behind the barn door to watch, wait until our old aunt came to the door and peered out and said in her creaky voice 'Who's there?' We would grasp each other's arms and stifle our giggles.

We never did it when Mother was at home because she would cotton on straight away and there would be Trouble.

The door opened. Sally was wearing an apron and she had smears of flour on her face and in her hair, which was streaked with grey.

'Cassie!' she said.

The clouds were racing across the sun making fast moving shadows.

She lifted her hands. 'I'm making bread.'

I couldn't speak.

'You know me, I've always been a messy cook.'

She looked up again and our eyes met and held. The space between us filled with all the things we needed to say. There were so many that the space bulged and ballooned until we could barely see each other for words. I almost ran away. But then the words vanished, because there was only one thing to say, and we fell into each others arms and hugged each other tightly like we'd done so many times before, and we spoke the word into each other's hair.

'Sorry.'

'Sorry.'

'Sorry.'

34. Lauren

I dreamed of Peter and woke full of happiness because we were going out for the day together, walking in the hills. I leapt out of bed, but halfway to the bathroom I stopped. A stillness came over me and I remembered. We had argued, Peter and I. It was Richard who was taking me out. I breathed in and out, counting. In for eight, out for eight. Six times. I felt the oxygen racing though my blood.

Richard and I were going to spend the day together, walking in the hills. I went to the window and flung back the curtains. The trees had lost their leaves but the sun was shining. It was going to be a beautiful day. I smiled and went into the bathroom singing.

Richard turned up while I was eating breakfast and prowled around the kitchen waiting for me. He was wearing jeans and the leather jacket.

'What if it rains?' I asked.

He shrugged.

'It's only water,' he said. 'People managed before Gore-Tex.'

'You smell nice,' I said.

'Do I?'

He grinned and nuzzled his face into my neck.

'You smell good enough to eat,' he murmured.

I laid my spoon on the table and felt his breath slide behind my ear. I felt the flick of his tongue and the hairs on my neck rose up to meet it. I dropped my shoulders and inclined my neck.

But there was just coldness. Richard was on the other side of the room and he hadn't spoken.

'Eat up,' he said. 'Let's make the most of the daylight hours.'

I blinked. I could still feel the rush of blood in my neck and my heart was racing. He was leaning against the worktop studying a map. I slid my hand inside my pocket and it was empty.

'I'll run up and fetch my head torch,' I said. 'Just in case.'

Dad would have had a fit if he saw me going upstairs in walking boots, but he wasn't in. Mr Lion was out with Beauty.

I went into my room. Peter was sitting on the bed holding a bunch of rosemary.

'What are you doing?' he said.

'I'm just getting my head torch. In case we overshoot and get caught in the dark.'

'That's not what I meant.'

I walked to my desk and opened a drawer. The head torch was in there, some dried roots, a bag of tiny brown seeds. I smiled at Peter.

'We're going for a walk, up in the hills. Richard's going to show me his favourite place.'

'Is he your boyfriend now?'

Peter's voice had gone strange. His horns were growing and stretching out to the sides. There were more than two of them and they were moving, blinking at me with slow moving eyes. He was surrounded by yellow light. The rosemary rattled and hissed.

'Peter... snakes...'

'Do you love him?' His voice was stretched full of holes.

'No, Peter!' I covered my eyes with my hands and breathed. I couldn't count. In, out, in, out, in, out. I moved my hands.

There was nobody there. The bed was ruffled from when I'd got out, the duvet thrown to one side. The curtain was moving slightly in the wind. I closed the window.

We walked up through the Craggs and on to the top road. There had been a frost and mud crunched beneath our feet.

'Where are we going?' I asked.

'Satan's Rock. Do you know it?'

'No.'

'It's near High Dene Reservoir. Round the other side of the hill.'

'Does the path go that way?' I'd walked this way before, but I didn't remember Satan's Rock.

'No, the path runs along the reservoir. But it's easy enough to scramble up.'

It was cold even in the sun and I could feel the tips of my ears going numb. A hawthorn tree shook its empty branches and the grass rattled, but I turned away. I lifted my head and took a deep gulp of air. It was good to be moving and to be getting up high out of the valley, where the vegetation was sparse.

Richard took my hand.

His palm against mine was cool and dry. I tried to concentrate on the scenery. The sheep in the fields, caked with December mud, and the brown-red swathe of trees filling up the valley, out of earshot below us, But my mind kept slipping down my arm to those hands, to the place where our bodies touched. So different from Peter.

Peter came round to see me two nights ago, the first time I'd seen him in ages.

He said, 'Lauren, you're being selfish and stubborn. Let her tell you what happened.'

He said, 'She's your mother. Give her a chance.'

He said, 'You're behaving like a child.'

That's how you're supposed to behave with your parents. I'm just making up for lost time.

We argued and he left. We didn't even kiss. I'd felt like I was reading from a script and the words didn't mean anything. I was angry and shouting at Peter. But I was thinking about Richard and how it felt that night in my room when he kissed me, how our mouths didn't quite fit together and we had to adjust the angle of our heads to get it right. I knew I had to stop shouting and kiss Peter, make everything fall back into place again. But that wasn't in the script I was following, and I watched Peter leave my room and slam the door, heard his footsteps on the stairs, the front door closing behind him.

We left the road to cross a stile and the path took us along a stone wall, edged with paving slabs to keep feet from the worst of the mud. We had to walk in single file and Richard was in front of me. We weren't holding hands any more.

A few fields later the path split into two: the path we were following going up, and another down into Rose Dean Clough.

Richard marched on ahead, but I caught hold of his arm.

'Can we go down there?'

'That's not the way.'

'Just for a few minutes. It's one of my favourite places. I want to show you.'

He hesitated and frowned.

'We haven't much time. It's dark by four.'

'Not for long. Just into the clough.'

He shrugged.

The path drops down steeply and it was slippery with mud; we had to walk with our feet angled out to the sides. Then it got steeper and there were rough stone steps made of boulders leading down to a footbridge. There was a lot of water in the stream and it roared over the rocks. I could hear the trees further down the valley.

On the other side of the bridge Richard stopped.

'Does this lead down to Rose Mill?'

'Yes.' I leaned against him and slipped my arm inside his jacket.

'Lauren, I'd rather not go this way.'

I nuzzled against his neck and kissed his hair.

'But it's where we first kissed. It's a lovely place.'

He held my face in his hands.

'Lauren, look at me.'

I looked at him. He had those sunglasses on and I couldn't see his eyes.

'I'm Richard, not Peter. You're getting mixed up.'

I remembered the kiss. We were sitting on the old wall of the mill, high up, way above the water, our legs dangling. I was scared and he was laughing at me.

'Why would you fall? You're sitting. You don't fall off chairs when you sit on them.'

'I don't get vertigo on chairs.'

'You don't have vertigo, you're just scared. I'll catch you if you fall.'

He grabbed out and caught me and my heart leaped in my body and I leaned back away from the drop so I was pressing against him, and when I turned my head his face was right up close and I didn't say anything. We stayed like that, millimetres apart, eyes open, our faces blurred, and I forgot about the looming death beneath my feet. We both moved at the same time and our lips came together and I wasn't scared any more.

'Come on, I'll race you.'

I pulled away from Richard and ran off into the clough. It was a narrow path that wound its way along the steep banks. I didn't get far before Richard caught up with me, put his hand on my shoulder.

'Please Lauren, stop.'

I shook him off and ran on.

The mill was just round the next bend, what was left of it. The chimney had fallen at some point and the half that was left didn't even reach the level of the trees. One of the walls was still standing, but trees pushed their branches against it and shoved them through the window holes. Down near the water moss grew over the stone and, higher up, lichens.

I stopped running. Richard hadn't run after me this time, but after a moment he appeared, walking slowly.

'Don't you love it here?' I said. 'The way the mill is being absorbed back into the land. Listen, can you hear a humming noise? The trees, the moss, that's them growing. In another hundred years you won't be able to tell the mill was ever here.'

I looked at him and he was crying.

I blinked and looked back at the mill. The stone walls stood grey against a blue sky, the same colour as the branches of the winter trees. How could he be crying? He had sunglasses on, I couldn't see his eyes, I must be wrong.

'Do you remember?' I asked. 'After we kissed I jumped off the wall and ran down the path and you chased me all the way to the stone bridge at the bottom.'

'Lauren!'

His voice sounded strange and tight. I looked at him but his eyes were still hidden.

'Lauren we haven't been here before. Not together.'

Where had his horns gone? They'd been growing quite nicely but I couldn't see them now. I reached over to him and touched his head with my hands. His hair was glossy and thick, softer than I remembered. Definitely no horns. I felt a bit sick and I swallowed. I wanted this day to be perfect. At the stone bridge we'd kissed again, and that time it had gone on for longer and our bodies had joined in a million places.

I leaned forward and kissed him on the lips. He didn't move, so I pushed myself against him and tried again, teasing his mouth open with mine, pushing with my tongue.

Our teeth knocked together and I tasted something salty. I moved away and looked. He was definitely crying. There were tears. There were no horns because he was Richard and this was not where I was meant to be. The sick feeling rose up again and my throat tightened. I turned and ran, but this time I didn't stop. Down to the stone bridge, over it and along the path through the clough to the valley below. I ran down the road past the church and the houses and across the main road on to the canal, all the way back into town.

When I reached home I stopped. There were voices inside the house and one of them was female. I really didn't want to see my mother just now. I turned quietly and walked away, hoping no one had noticed me.

I went to Jimmy's house. Jimmy would tell me what to do. He knew about everything: Peter, Richard, my mum. He knew what it was like to love someone and still be attracted to someone else. He knew about confusion.

It was Suky who opened the door. Her face was swollen and her eyes were red. She smiled a watery smile.

'Come in, Lauren,' she said.

I followed her into the kitchen and she put the kettle on the stove.

'Peppermint tea?'

I nodded and she got a box from the cupboard, mugs from the shelf.

'I've seen him,' she said.

'Who?' Richard hadn't run after me and couldn't have got here that quickly anyway. It must be Peter.

'Jimmy. I've seen him with that woman.'

Oh god!

'He wasn't back from the pub and I could tell it was happening again. I didn't want to lie there in bed, worrying and helpless. So I got up and dressed and went down there. I thought I'd find him.'

'Was he in the pub?'

'He was just leaving. With her. He was talking and she was laughing.'

'Maybe they'd just been drinking together in the pub. It might not have been anything.'

'I followed them to her car.'

'Car?'

'They both got in it and she drove off. I was standing there on the pavement under a tree watching. They would have seen me if they'd looked.'

I tried to remember ever seeing her driving.

'What sort of car has she got?'

Suky frowned at me. 'I don't know. Something sporty, expensive looking. Black. She patted him on the bum while she was unlocking it and he grinned at her.'

That was not Steph. What the hell was Jimmy getting into?

'Did he come back?'

'Eventually. He was gone for three hours. I pretended to be asleep and in the morning he acted like everything was fine. Like he'd just been to the pub. Same as he always does.'

'Have you said anything to him?'

'Lauren, I don't know what to do. I love him.'

'He loves you as well Suky, you know that. It's probably nothing.'

'He had a mark on his neck. It looked like a lovebite. I don't think he knew it was there.'

I put my hand on my own neck and rubbed. I could only think of one woman round here with an expensive, black sports car.

'She must be ten years older than him.' The kettle on the stove whistled and she stood up. 'Shall we have vodka instead?'

I looked at the clock. It was only just past midday. 'Why the hell not!'

I wondered, briefly, what Richard was doing now.

35. Peter

Lauren had told him not to eat the berries, but he thought he knew best. She lived in a house in the town, he was the one who knew the outdoors. She'd told him the plants spoke to her, but that was nonsense. She was making it up, the same as she made up stories to tell him about wood nymphs, wily foxes and old grizzled witches. None of it was true.

So he ate the berries and, later, after she had gone home for tea, he'd crept up to the cave and was sick. So sick it felt as though everything inside him was being forced out. The front of his body pulled hard against his spine, his pelvis jerked upwards. He bent over and the hot bile rushed out of him, over and over. His dad stroked his hair, wiped his forehead with damp moss.

Later he was empty. He lay in the cave and heard whispering coming from the woods. He saw stars through the cave mouth, shooting across the sky with tails of red and green. He turned his back and the cave tipped sideways. He slept, then woke again.

Someone was arguing with his dad outside.

'You can't have him. You can't ever have him.'

'It's too late, he has my mark.'

'Fuck your mark. You're not having him. Go!'

Peter curled into a ball. There was a tussle at the cave mouth. Someone was trying to get in, but his dad was fighting them. They were both shouting and Peter covered his ears.

He opened his eyes just a crack and peeped. His dad was standing over the other person. He looked huge, much bigger than he normally did. The other figure was cowering, retreating.

'You know you can never beat me,' his dad shouted, 'I don't know why you keep trying.'

The figure hissed. Gradually it faded, disappeared into the dark of night. The hiss became words which hung in the air after the figure had gone. 'One day. One day.'

Peter's dad stood silhouetted at the mouth of the cave, watching until the night settled. A sheep called on the hills and its lamb answered. An owl flew over, and the stars were still in the sky. Peter felt the tension leave his limbs and sleep came to cover him like a warm blanket.

His father came into the cave and crouched next to him. He felt Peter's forehead, then lifted his wrist and felt his pulse. Peter's eyes fluttered, struggling to stay open.

'Am I going to die, Dad?' he said sleepily.

'No Peter. No, you're not going to die.'

36. Richard

We were just an ordinary family.

I started working at Rose Mill when I was eleven and I was put to work tying ends. I worked there three days a week and on the other three I went to school. My father had worked at the Mill for many years and was well respected. We would set off together from home at five in the morning and walk up through the valley, past Silk Mill where my mother and sisters worked, past Banksfoot, Eaves and Jumble Mills all the way to the top of the clough to Rose Mill. It was the highest mill in the valley. The stream tumbled downhill and the light grew as we walked up the track, me and my father side by side. We didn't speak much. We were two men on our way to work.

That day there was a sudden stillness in the main hall. The machines didn't stop working, but it was as though all the workers in the room collectively held their breath. Three men stood in the doorway on the river side, one holding my dad's feet and two others supporting his shoulders. He carried no weight himself. He was limp and lifeless. I watched like everyone else as they carried him through the hall and out of the main doorway into the yard.

All eyes followed the body, but as soon as he passed out of sight the eyes turned to look at me, the dead man's son.

'Back to work,' snapped the foreman, and the breathing began again, the hum of industry.

I didn't move though. I stared at the door where they had gone. Then I saw the foreman walking towards me and I leapt to my feet and flew down the hall and into the yard.

He had slipped and been crushed by the stone wheels as they turned. Two of his workmates had leaped after him and pulled him free before the wheels had gripped him completely and pulverised his body, but they were too late to save him from having the life squeezed out of his chest.

I stared down at my father. He looked strangely loose and flat beneath his work clothes and there was a trickle of blood from the corner of his mouth. His eyes were closed as though he were sleeping. The men were silent. Behind us was the noise of the mill, the noise of the wheels as they kept turning.

'Mother,' I gasped suddenly. I took to my heels and ran down the valley in the direction of Silk Mill.

Lauren's feet flashed along the path as she ran, but she was soon obscured by trees. Trees that weren't there the day my father died. My vision blurred and I sat down on a rock. I didn't cry that day, but it was the beginning of everything. The first crack in my childhood, which soon broke into piles of dust.

I didn't work at Rose Mill again. I did a spell for Mr Gibson, but he couldn't get me to work inside, only on the pond. In the end I went to Mr S the stonemason and asked to be taken on as an apprentice. He asked why he should take me and I said that I wanted to learn to master the stone which had taken my father's life. He must have liked my answer because he agreed and I never went back to Rose Mill again. Until today.

There were birds singing.

I shook myself and got up, walked back up the valley to the top of the clough and into the fields. I didn't want to go on to Satan's Rock now that Lauren had gone. I turned in the other direction and took the path which led over towards Hawtenstall.

Mr Lion was walking along the path towards me. He stopped and called to his dog who'd run off. As I drew level with him I stopped and nodded good morning. There was a stone cottage which had fallen into ruins in the next field, and the little white dog was standing on its back legs, paws on the wall, barking.

'Come Beauty, come!' called Mr Lion.

The dog turned its head towards us, gave one last bark, and then raced back over the field to its master.

'Good girl, Beauty,' he said, and to me, 'Nice day for it.'

I agreed, and we continued our separate ways. Once he was out of sight I stopped and doubled back, vaulted over the wall and crossed the field into the next. I walked round to the front of the cottage.

One half had caved in completely and a tree was growing up through the hole where the roof had been. It reminded me of the ruins of Rose Mill and I shuddered. The other half was more or less intact and the doorway gaped like an open mouth. Inside seemed pitch black compared to the bright sunny day.

'Ali,' I called.

There was no answer but I didn't expect one.

'Ali, I know you're there. Can we talk?'

I took a step inside. The window was boarded up and lines of light showed between the boards. I could see food packaging piled on the window ledge in front of them. Further back was gloomier, but there were shapes. One of them was larger than the others.

'Ali, I'm your friend.' I took another step.

She must have realised I wasn't going to give up and go away because she coughed then.

'Hello Richard,' she said. She came out of the shadows. Her eyes shone in the darkness. 'I can't offer you tea, but I have cake.' She took one of the boxes off the window ledge. 'Past its sell-by date, I'm afraid.'

'How long have you been living here?'

'A while.' She shoved the cake box at me and I shook my head.

'It must be freezing at night.'

'I'm ok. I've got some insulation.'

She pointed to the corner. She had made herself a kind of nest out of newspapers and blankets. The papers were piled up, masses of them, with a shape in the middle just big enough for her body. She could slot into it, pull more papers over the top and cover herself with blankets.

'It's quite cosy actually.'

'But why are you hiding?'

She replaced the cake box on the shelf. 'Not everyone is my friend,' she said.

She had a red blanket wrapped around her body. She looked like someone who'd been at an all night party. Her face was pale from lack of sunlight, her hair unkempt.

'You need vitamin D,' I said, and she shot me a glance.

We stood for a few moments looking out at the field and the woods below.

'Is it Smith and Jeannie?'

She looked at me for a moment and then said 'Yes.'

'I have information,' I said. I told her about the conversation we'd had with them, Lauren and I, and how one of the notes had a code written on it. 'If it's still there then you could give it back. That's all they want.'

'Oh yeah, like they'll just say thank you and let me walk away?'

'I think so. Smith is more mad at Jeannie for taking your ring. They just want the code.'

She went back into the cottage and moved things about in the dark and came back with a wedge of money. She split it in two and gave half to me.

'Let's hope I haven't already spent it.'

We looked through the notes carefully, scanning each side for any signs of writing, but when she found the note there was no missing it.

St. Ann's 143. Ca66age in thick black felt pen.

'St Ann's?' I was puzzled.

'Cabbage? That might be a code.'

'Or a password.'

She ran her finger along the words. 'It might be to open a locker door.'

'If you know where the locker is.'

She looked at me then. 'But we don't need to know where it is. It doesn't matter if we're just going to hand this over to Smith and Jeannie.'

'No, it doesn't.'

We looked at the note. The writing was round and childish and went right across. Ali gathered the rest of the money and slipped it into her pocket. She held the message with the fingers of both hands and peered at it as though it might give her more clues.

'St. Ann's,' she said again. Do you know anywhere in Leeds called St. Ann's?'

'It could be a school.'

'Or a hospital.'

'We could google it.'

'I don't have a computer,' she said.

'You look lovely when you do that.'

'What?'

'Smile. I haven't seen you smile before.'

She grinned and turned her face away, self conscious.

'I have a computer,' I said

'Could we...?' Her face was animated again.

'Yes. Come on, let's go.'

On the way she said 'Where's Lauren anyway? I thought she was your girlfriend.'

'No, she's just a friend.'

'But you're trying to turn her into something else.'

She looked at me sharply and I remembered her grandmother.

'Well...'

'Does she know?'

I sighed. 'No she doesn't. And it's not really working. She reminded me of someone else, someone I knew a long time ago. But she's not really like her at all.'

'You could stop.'

'I suppose I could.'

'You don't sound convinced.'

'I don't know. She likes me, and she's beautiful. It might work out in the end.'

'Hmm.'

There were a couple of hits for St Anne's, Leeds. One of them was the cathedral.

Ali looked at the note again. 'There's definitely no e.'

We tried other combinations, without Leeds, spelling saint out in full, but there wasn't really anything – or rather, there was masses of stuff but none of it was relevant.

'We could try the phone book,' I suggested.

Ali looked doubtful. She lived in the internet age and distrusted paper. But I found the yellow pages and the regular directory and handed one to her. She turned the pages slowly, looking at them suspiciously.

'I don't know what I'm looking for,' she said.

'Anything really, that could give us a clue.'

It took quite a while, aimlessly looking through the pages for anything that caught the eye. We chatted while we looked. Or she did. She talked about living in the cottage, about finding food at night, about some notebooks she'd found that belonged to a dead woman. She talked and talked. I suppose having been alone for so long she had a lot of unspoken words. I glanced up at her every now and then. Her face was relaxed as she turned the yellow pages. Her eyes were an amazing shade of green.

My finger trailing down the columns came to a stop.

'What about this?'

'What? Have you found it?'

'It's a list of post offices. This one is on St Ann's Road.'

'A post office?'

'A box. A post office box. That must be what it is.'

'Do you think so? Is that how they work?'

'I don't know.'

'Well we haven't found anything else. Shall we google it, find out where it is in Leeds?'

I thought about mentioning the A-Z on the shelf but decided against it. Soon we were looking at Google Maps. St Ann's Road was fairly central, a fifteen minute walk from the station. It wasn't an area I knew.

'Ali.'

'Yes.'

'Why are we doing this?'

'Hm?'

'We don't need to know this. I know how to find Smith and Jeannie. I'm sure you do too. We could just go and find them and hand them the note and they could work this stuff out.'

'We could.'

'Or...?'

'Well the way I see it,' she said, 'the power is all in our hands at the moment. We could bargain with them. If we know what it is we're bargaining with.'

I nodded slowly and she smiled her smile again.

'That could be quite dangerous,' I said.

'It's better than sitting in the dark day after day in that cottage waiting for them to find me.'

'It was me that found you.'

'Hm, you're quite dangerous too.'

Our eyes met.

'So,' I said. 'It's a trip to Leeds is it?'

Her smile broadened and I could feel my own responding.

We decided to go the day after next. I was meant to be helping out in the college library, but I could easily skip. Meg would phone in and say I wasn't well, that my eyes were bothering me.

'You can move out of that cottage now,' I said.

'Where to?'

I shrugged. 'Here?'

She looked thoughtful.

'No,' she said eventually. 'I don't think that would work.'

'Why? There's plenty of room.'

'Maybe. But you and your mum take up quite a lot of it.'

I didn't really know what she meant, but she looked determined so I didn't push it.

'I might go and visit Sally again at Old Barn. See how she's getting on with her husband now he's back.'

'Terry?'

'I don't know his name.'

'Did you know he's an incubus?'

'God, that must be a nightmare.'

I laughed. 'Do you want to stay for a bit? I could cook some pasta.'

But she was putting her jacket on.

'Tuesday,' she said. 'I'll come round at nine.'

And she left.

My phone went off and I looked at the screen. A text from Lauren.

Richard I'm sorry I ran away. So sorry. I need to see you. Please can I see you now. I need you. Where are you?

I sighed. Life was getting a bit too complicated.

37. Lauren

Suky had drunk a lot more of the vodka than I had. At three o'clock she stood up shakily and announced she was going for a lie down. I was still sitting at her kitchen table when Richard found me. He knocked at the door and walked in. I threw myself into his arms.

'Richard, I'm sorry, I'm sorry.'

He stroked my hair and it felt nice.

'It's ok, Laura'

I looked up. 'Lauren. Not Laura.'

'That's what I said.' He smiled at me.

I hugged him tight again. 'I'm sorry I ran away and we didn't get to see the big rock thing. I missed you. I really want you to kiss me. Please.'

I lifted my face but he didn't kiss me, he stroked my cheek. Then he removed my arms from around him and went over to the table.

'Any of this left?' he asked, picking up the vodka bottle. There was a bit and he poured a slug into Suky's empty glass.

'Richard!' I went up to him again and pressed against him.

He put his arm round my shoulders.

'Lauren, what's the matter?'

'Everything. Everything is wrong. Peter's gone and my mother's turned up and she wants me to like her. And I want you, but only sometimes, and when I do I want you so badly that it's like hunger, an empty craving feeling. But it feels wrong. And I wish Peter were here and my mother would go away and you would stop confusing me and I don't know what to do.'

The last part of this speech rose to a wail. I could hear it even while it was coming from my mouth.

Richard kissed me then, on the forehead. 'Calm down,' he said. 'You're letting everything get on top of you.'

I wailed again, this time without words.

'How about you deal with one thing at a time?'

'Richard, kiss me.'

He pushed me away gently. 'How about your mother?'

I turned away in disgust. 'She wants to tell me stuff. She wants to tell me what happened, why she left us, me and Dad, when I was a baby. She thinks if she tells me then that will make it ok.'

'Maybe you should listen to her?'

'Maybe I shouldn't. Maybe there are some things that can't be put right, like abandoning your child and never contacting them for all of their life. Then suddenly turning up and expecting everyone to forgive you. Why should I listen to her?'

'She's your mother.'

'And?'

'She's alive and she wants to know you. You're lucky. My mother died when I was twelve years old.'

I frowned. 'Meg is your mother.'

'No, she adopted me. My mother died when I was twelve and my sisters too the year after. I was alone then.'

'What did they die of?'

'TB. Their lungs were weakened from working in the mills. All the fibre in the air.'

I tried to fit it into what I knew of him, but my mind was muddled.

'But she didn't leave you on purpose, your mother.'

'Maybe yours didn't either. You'd find out if you listened to her.'

I sat down at the table and rested my head on my arms.

'It would make things easier,' he carried on. 'If you sort things with your mother, then you can think about Peter next.'

'What about you?'

'Don't worry about me. I'm big and ugly enough to look after myself.'

I went home and Dad was in on his own. I asked him where Cassie was and he said she'd gone to see her sister.

'I thought they didn't speak to each other.'

'They made up.'

It was dark, but that didn't bother me. I was restless and wanted to act straight away. The lane up to Old Barn was easy enough and I still had my head torch in my bag. I told Dad I was going for a walk.

'Will you be back for tea?'

'I don't know.'

He frowned at that, but I left before he could say anything else.

By the time I came out of the top of the woods at Old Barn I had sobered up a bit and I could feel the cold night air racing through my lungs. I didn't want to lose courage. I went straight up to the front door and knocked.

Sally answered, and before she could say anything I said 'Is my mum here?'

She opened the door wider and I walked through to the kitchen.

The huge wooden table had a teapot and cups and a plate with scones on it. Cassie was there and so was Ali.

'Oh!' I said.

'Hello Lauren.' My mum smiled.

'Hi,' I said to her. Then I looked at Ali. 'What are you doing here?'

She raised her eyebrows. I suppose I was a bit rude.

'I'm staying here for a while,' she said.

'But I thought you'd left. You were hiding and Richard didn't know where you were. He wanted to find you because of the money. One of the—'

'I know. One of the notes has a code on it. He told me.'

'Richard found you?' Why hadn't he told me? Looking for the girl, Ali, was something we'd been doing together. 'Did you find the note?'

'Yes.'

'And?'

'Would you like some tea Lauren?' my mum asked, and I turned to look at her. She was still smiling.

'Yeah, ok,' I said. She poured a cup and pushed it over to me. I sat down at the table.

'What are you going to do with the note?' I asked Ali.

She gave a kind of shrug.

Then Sally called from the doorway, 'Ali, can you come and give me a hand?'

Ali got up quickly and left the room, and I was left alone with my mother.

Neither of us said anything for a few moments. I sipped at the tea which was strong and lukewarm.

'People keep telling me to give you a chance,' I said after a while.

She said nothing.

'They say I should listen to you.'

'What do you think?'

I looked at her. She was holding her cup near her face.

'I dunno. I think we've been fine for all these years, me and Dad and Mr Lion, so why do we need you to come along and upset everything? I don't know why I suddenly need a mother when I've been ok without one for nearly eighteen years.'

'Maybe you don't.'

'Everyone is telling me I do.'

'They can only speak from what they know about themselves. They're imagining being without their mothers.'

'Well what do you want then? I thought you wanted to be my mother.'

'I'd like us to get to know each other.'

'What about you and Dad?'

She looked away. 'I don't know. It's been a long time and he...'

'It's a bit weird if you want to know. He's started singing.'

She looked like she wanted to laugh. Her mouth made a wonky line as she tried to control it.

'I'm not sure that's because of...'

'It would be all right if he could sing in tune.'

She lifted her eyes and they were full of laughter. Her mouth wasn't behaving either: it turned upwards at the corners. I found my own responding and suddenly we were grinning at each other.

'I hope at least we can all be friends,' she said.

We lapsed into silence again. She lifted the lid of the teapot and looked in, but it was empty. She got up, refilled the kettle and put it on the stove.

'When you were born he was always singing. Lullabies he said. I said he was more likely to keep you awake and crying.'

'I don't remember. He must have stopped when you left.'

She collected the cups from the table and took them to the sink to rinse.

'Did he seem unhappy?'

'Not to me. But then he wouldn't, would he?'

'No, I suppose not.'

'I sometimes caught him looking at your photo. I think he missed you.'

She smiled and emptied the teapot into the compost bin.

'I missed him as well, you know,' she said. 'I always have – loved – both of you.'

I knew this was a cue. This was where I should say, well why did you go away then?

I jumped up. 'I told Dad I'd be back for tea. I'd better run.'

'I'm making a fresh pot, won't you stay?'

'Better not. They hate it when I'm late for a meal.'

I grabbed my coat and left the room before she could say anything else.

Ali and Sally were in the front of the barn moving something.

'See ya,' I called.

As I ran down the lane I remembered I wanted to know about Ali's money and the code on the note. I would probably see Richard soon, though, and he could tell me.

I was just in time for tea. Dad looked at me while we were eating.

'Where have you been?'

'You know where I've been.'

'How...?'

'Come on, don't be an idiot. Cassie texted you and told you I went up there.'

He looked at me for a moment then carried on eating.

'She says you ran off.'

'I had to get back.'

'We wouldn't have minded.'

'That would have been a first.'

Mr Lion had just finished his food. He put his knife and fork next to each other in the middle of his plate.

'Why don't you tell her, Andy?' he said.

We both looked at him.

'What do you mean?' Dad said.

'If the lass finds it difficult to hear the story from her mother, maybe you should tell her yourself. She might hear it from you.'

Me and Dad looked at each other. He'd spent years not telling me that story.

'Would you like me to?' he asked.

I shrugged. 'If you like.'

We finished eating and washed up, and then we took coffee into the front room. Mr Lion and Beauty went off to the pub leaving the two of us together. Mum's picture was still on the mantelpiece.

We sat down in opposite chairs and my Dad didn't say anything. When my coffee was half gone I said 'Well? Are you going to tell me?'

He grunted and sat forward in his chair. 'It's difficult,' he said.

'Tell me about it!'

He looked at me properly then and smiled.

'What happened?' I said. 'You were the perfect happy family and then what?'

'Well,' he said. 'It was the woman up at Hough Dean.'

'Meg?'

'Yes. She arrived back from God knows where. She'd been away for years.'

'She must have been really young.'

'She was just the same, she always is.'

'What do you mean?'

'They don't age. Not her sort. She'll always be the same as she was when she turned.'

I didn't understand.

'Anyway, I met her when I was out running one day. She'd got her car stuck in a pothole. She has a thing about sports cars – totally impractical up there.' He smiled.

'Was Richard with her?'

'No, I think she'd left him in Paris.'

I remembered Richard saying he'd been adopted. I was even more confused.

'I helped her with her car, and some stuff in the house. And we played chess.'

'Chess? I didn't know you played chess.'

He got out of his chair and poked the fire, mumbled something.

'What was that?'

'I was quite good,' he said. 'I played in tournaments when I was at school. I went to Germany.'

'Wow!'

'I never lost a game.'

'Ok, so you're a chess whizz. You've been hiding that one. What about Meg? Did you beat her?'

'Not the first time.'

'The first time?' Dad's ears had gone red. 'So you played a lot of chess with her?'

'Well, I'd not played someone like her before. She was amazing. And it got me out of the house.'

'I was in the house, your new baby. Didn't you want to be there?'

'Yes I did. It was lovely being with you and Cass. I just needed a break.'

'How much chess did you play?'

'Quite a few games, but then Meg...'

'Meg what?'

He sighed. 'Well, when she wants someone, she decides she must have them. She doesn't like people to get in her way.'

'So Meg wanted you – what? As her boyfriend?'

'I guess.' He shuffled in his seat, leaned forward and put his coffee cup on the floor.

'And what did you think?'

'I had you and your mum.'

'And you didn't want Meg?'

He sighed. 'I had a family.'

'Well?' I said. He picked his cup up again. 'What happened?'

'There were a few... incidents... where she tried to get close to me. She's very good at that sort of thing. She casts a spell. She's a beautiful woman and I...'

'Not too much detail Dad.'

'Well, lets say it was a close shave. We had a fight. She nearly bit me.'

'Bit you?'

'Yes.' Dad looked at me and must have seen the confusion on my face. 'You don't know what she is, do you?'

I slowly shook my head, but the truth was dawning, and when he told me everything started falling into place.

'And Richard?'

'Him too.'

I put my hand on my neck and rubbed it gently.

'So you resisted her?' I asked Dad.

He nodded. 'I could only do it by thinking of you.'

'What did she do?'

'She went back to Paris. But she'd put a curse on your mother, an incubus.' The fire flared and I watched him gazing into the firelight. 'I didn't know. Cassie was having these visitations, nightmares, and it was sending her out of her mind, but she wanted to protect me and the baby – you – so she didn't let on. She moved into the spare room.'

'Did you talk to her?'

'I tried, but she was very closed. Her milk stopped and she cried a lot. Said she couldn't cope. Then she left one day when I was at work. She phoned from a phone box along the road from the school, spoke to the secretary and said I had to come urgently. When I got there she'd gone and left you alone in your baby seat with a note pinned to the blanket.

'God!'

Dad lifted his coffee cup, but it was empty.

'I think I'll have a whisky. Do you want one?'

I remembered the vodka and shook my head. There was a lot of information I had to process and I wanted to keep my head clear.

Sometimes I have an intense urge to eat something, like oranges or garlic, lemon balm or dandelion. It could be my body telling me what I need or it might be the plants themselves calling out to me. The messages can get mixed up, especially when there are strong emotions involved.

My guts were aching and something was telling me it would go away if I could find Richard, but I didn't want to be with

Richard. I thought I might go and find Jimmy and talk to him, and then I remembered what Suky had said earlier.

'Oh my god!' I said, and Dad looked at me. 'It's happening again. This time Meg's after Jimmy.'

38. Lauren

We went straight round to Jimmy's house and hammered on the door, but there was no reply. Suky was probably fast asleep after all that vodka, and Jimmy wasn't in. I suggested we go up to Hough Dean to see if he was there. We had to find him and warn him. When it comes to resisting feminine wiles, Jimmy's not in the same league as my dad and if Meg had decided to get her teeth into him he wouldn't stand a chance. I mean, he really loves Suky, really and truly. But he's never had to deal with someone like Meg before.

My legs ached as we walked up the lane and I realised I'd walked a lot that day. With Richard in the morning up to Rose Clough, to Old Barn in the afternoon, and now to Hough Dean. It was strange walking with my dad. I hadn't been walking with him for ages. We used to walk all the time when I was younger, but not any more. I wondered if he missed it.

When we got there the lights were all on and there was music. It took a long time for anyone to come to the door – so long that we were about to knock again, when it opened and Richard was there.

'Lauren, Andy,' he said, smiling broadly.

'We were looking for Jimmy,' Dad said. 'Is he here?'

'I believe he is. Come in.'

I stepped into the hall but Dad didn't.

'I'll wait here if you don't mind. Please could you tell him he's needed?'

'Alright.'

Richard grabbed my hand and pulled me with him as he walked across the hall. I looked back at Dad and he frowned.

Meg and Jimmy were sitting on separate sofas on either side of the room. They both had drinks in their hands and they were laughing at something when we walked in. The music was Sarah Vaughan – I recognised it because Mr Lion has a CD he plays sometimes. Jimmy was wearing a shiny rust-coloured smoking jacket.

'Andy's here,' Richard said.

They both stopped laughing.

'Andy?' said Meg. She half got to her feet, then she sat down again. 'It's not me he wants, is it?' she said.

'He's here for Jimmy. Says he's needed.'

Jimmy was up immediately. 'Has something happened to Suky?'

He rushed out of the room without waiting for an answer, then came back in, pulling off the smoking jacket.

'You can keep it, Jimmy,' said Meg.

But he slung it on the sofa and left. We all followed him. Dad was still on the step with the door wide open and the hall was getting freezing.

'I've got the van,' Jimmy shouted as he ran past, 'but I've been drinking.'

Meg was staring at my dad. 'Hello Andy,' she said quietly.

He held her gaze for a moment, then turned to Richard. 'It seems you've become quite familiar with my daughter.'

Richard put his arm round my shoulder and pulled me to him.

'We're good friends' he said. 'Aren't we Lauren?'

Dad glared at him. 'Just stay away. You've caused enough trouble already, both of you.' He turned to include Meg, who looked like she might cry. 'Come on, Lauren.'

He followed Jimmy into the yard.

'Sorry...' I said.

Richard shrugged and kissed me on the cheek, and for a moment I thought about staying, but I didn't. The others were waiting for me in the van with the engine running. It was dark and cold, and our breath steamed up the windows.

'It's my fault,' Dad said as he drove down the lane, 'I should have warned you.'

'What's happened? Is Suky all right?' Jimmy asked.

'Suky's worried,' Dad said. 'Lauren, how far has it gone? Has he...?'

'We're just friends,' I said.

'Worried?' said Jimmy.

I put my fingers on my cheek where Richard had kissed it. It was red hot.

As a child I was hardly ever ill. When I was, I refused to take medicine from the doctors. As soon as I could get up from my bed I went out to the garden. The grass was cool against fevered skin. The scent of the flowers was soothing and I listened to what they had to say.

'Well just keep away from him. He's dangerous.'

Dad parked the van at Jimmy's and we all got out. I realised I was completely knackered.

'I'm going home to bed,' I told them.

They both kissed me and went into Jimmy's house. I felt relieved. Dad would sort Jimmy out, tell him what's what. Maybe he could even sort out the Steph situation as well. I walked home and put my aching limbs to bed and slept.

The next day was Monday, a school day. My first lesson was biology, the only subject that I had in common with Peter. We weren't in the same group, but Monday morning was practical, and his group and mine joined up. It was the only lesson all week we did together, and right from the start we'd shared a bench. This morning he wasn't there.

I tried to concentrate. I looked down the microscope at a group of cells and drew them in my book. I started to label features, and then I put my pen down.

'Can I be excused, sir?' I asked. The teacher looked a bit embarrassed and said ok without asking why. Probably thought it was a girl thing.

I walked out of the room and down the corridor, and then I started to run. I ran out the back way from college, across the playing fields and into the woods. I ran along the back of the sewage works and up the hill where I'd met Richard that day, and I didn't stop running until I ran out of breath and had to stop and bend over with my hands on my legs. After a few minutes I started again. I ran more slowly, but I didn't stop until I reached our woods and the rock where I waited for Peter. I collapsed onto it in a heap and buried my face in my arms.

I realised that I was crying, and that annoyed me, so I tried to stop. I was being quite noisy, gasping and choking, and I suppose being out of breath from the running didn't help. I relaxed my shoulders and tried to steady my breathing. In and out slowly until I was calm.

I put my fingers in my mouth and took a sharp breath in to whistle, but I choked on it. I tried twice more, and eventually succeeded in blowing the three sharp blasts that were our signal. If Peter was within hearing distance he would come. I hoped. It used to be something I could rely on, but I wasn't sure if I could rely on anything any more, even myself, even Peter.

I curled up as tightly as I could against the cold, hugging my knees and cramming my face into them. I might have to wait for a while. I felt like going to sleep again, but I was too cold. I ate some seeds. I tried not to think, to let my mind be a blank.

After what seemed an age, I looked at my phone and it had been half an hour. My hands and feet were numb. I thought about Peter sleeping out in the open. He had his goat hair of course, which made a difference, but even he must protect himself against the cold. The trees were keening in the wind and there was a whisper of discontent in the undergrowth. On one side a bramble patch was baring its spikes, but on the other was a lot of dead bracken. I gathered an enormous armful and curled up again on the stone with the bracken heaped on top of me. I was surprised at the difference it made. I wasn't cold any more.

It wasn't long before I was asleep. Something strange must have been going on in my body because I slept all day. Peter was too far away to hear my signal and he didn't come, at least not straight away. Something made him come this way eventually, but by then it was dark and had been dark for many hours. I was still snuggled like an animal beneath the vegetation.

I woke to hear him saying my name.

'Lauren, wake up.'

I could smell the woods and his animal hair, familiar smells which I loved, and I thought I might be sick.

'What are you doing?' he said. 'You have seeds on your face.' He brushed at my lips with his fingers.

I was freezing. I sat up and hugged myself.

'Waiting for you.'

'I've been running with Dad. We went up to the fells near Clitheroe. How long have you been here?'

I shrugged. 'Since the morning.'

'It's the morning now, nearly.'

I wanted him to hold me, warm me, but when I leaned towards him the world tipped and I was washed through with nausea. He glowed with blue and yellow light.

I closed my eyes and opened them and he looked normal again.

'I wanted to see you but you weren't here.'

'I'm here now.'

He put his arm round me and I shrank into myself.

'Look Lauren, you haven't exactly been seeking out my company recently.'

'I've been here for nearly a day.'

'Is something wrong?' he asked. 'I mean, it's not normal to sleep like that, especially when it's cold.'

'You're a fine one to talk about normal.'

He looked at me and, although it was dark and I couldn't see his face properly, his eyes reflected the moonlight and I realised that he'd changed. What I'd just said was petty and spiteful, and once it would have hurt him. But what I could see was bafflement and concern.

'Shall I take you home?' he asked.

'Why? Don't you want me here?'

He put both his arms around me and drew me close. I relaxed against his warmth and lay my head on his shoulder, feeling safe for the first time in ages.

'Of course I want you, Lauren. I was just worrying about you being cold.'

'I'm warm like this,' I said.

And we sat there for a long time, watching the sky change as morning got closer.

The steep valleys mean that it gets light here long before there is any sighting of the sun. I don't know what counts as sunrise, but it was probably around the time that the sky became pearlescent grey and I bent over with stomach cramps that left me breathless.

'Lauren, what's the matter?' Peter asked.

I was gasping with pain. He leaned over me and his smell filled my nostrils.

'Don't touch me,' I said.

'What? What's happening, Lauren?'

'I have to go.'

'Are you ill?'

'I need Richard. I need to find Richard.'

I could feel the removal of his warmth. He only leaned an inch back from me, but it was like a barrier had come between us and it hurt even more than the pain in my guts. He was surrounded by a halo of blue light.

'Don't let me get in your way,' he said, and his voice was cold.

'Peter, it's not like that. Richard's not what you think.'

'I'm sure. You'd know, after all.'

I was caught by another wave of pain and I groaned out loud.

'I have to find him,' I gasped. 'Will you be here?'

'I shouldn't think so.'

'Peter, I love you.'

'You've a strange way of showing it.'

'I'm sorry. I have to go.'

And then I ran. I needed Richard and the pain wasn't going to go away until I found him. I hoped he was at home. I didn't seem to be getting out of breath and my legs felt strong. As I got nearer to Hough Dean the pain became less, and I could straighten up.

On the lane I met the postman and he gave me a lift the rest of the way in his van. It was lighter still now, and the trees were displaying their branches in the new day.

There was a light on at Hough Dean. For the second time in thirty six hours I hammered on the door and it was Richard who opened it. He looked surprised to see me.

'Lauren!' he said.

The pain had gone.

'Hi Richard.'

He peered closer, staring at my eyes.

'You'd better come in,' he said.

The hall smelled of toast.

He took me into the kitchen, and Ali was there, sitting at the table and munching.

'We're going to Leeds,' he told me.

'I'm coming too,' I said.

Ali frowned, and looked as though she might say something, but Richard nodded.

'It might be best,' he said.

Ali glared at him. 'Do you know what you're doing?' she said.

'I can't leave her. Look at her.'

'Exactly.'

'You think I shouldn't continue?'

'Yes, that's what I think.'

'Well, I haven't made that decision. Yet. I might not.'

They stared at each other. She had toast crumbs by her mouth.

'Look, I don't know what you two are on about,' I said, 'but you're not going anywhere without me. I'm part of this too, you know. I was there when Smith and Jeannie told us about the code.'

They didn't look at me, but Ali dropped her gaze first. She put more butter on her toast.

'Whatever,' she said. 'Just don't blame me when everything goes wrong.'

I sat down at the table.

'Can I have some toast too, please? I'm ravenous.'

39. Peter

He rarely travelled by train, didn't often go to places he couldn't run to. This could be a day that changed his life. He'd thought long and hard about what to wear, whether to try and blend in or just to be who he was. He'd have liked to talk to Lauren about it, but she'd made it clear who she wanted and where she wanted to be. She hadn't time for him any more. He hadn't even had a chance to tell her about the interview.

In the end he'd phoned Greece and spoken to his mum. She said, 'Peter, you have a brilliant mind. You will be an asset to the University and they won't care how much hair grows on your legs, or about the shape of your feet.'

He knew people would stare. They would stare on the train, they would stare on the streets of Cambridge, they would stare in the cloisters of the university. And even though the professors would be interested in his work, his knowledge, his intuition, he knew they would double-take at the first sight of him, before swallowing their human curiosity, giving rein instead to shared scientific enthusiasm. It wasn't going to be easy.

He'd been back to the tailors. Smart trousers, shirt and tie, jacket. He knew he looked gauche and ill at ease. But so would any other teenage geek on the way to his first interview. That's what he would look like, horns and hooves aside.

Part Four

EARTHQUAKE

40. Cassie

When I left, I moved to a new city, one I'd never been to before, and I found work in a florists shop. I liked handling the plants. I felt as though they brought me closer to you. I kept your photographs in a carrier bag under my bed. I moved quietly and attracted no attention.

Terry came every night. He was meant to be sucking the soul from me, but he'd taken most of it that first night along with my milk, and the rest was stuck fast. He might have managed if he'd persevered. If he'd continued to rape me every night, perhaps I'd have been reduced to a husk, a papery shell that would have eventually blown away on the wind. But he had no desire. Maybe it was because of Sally that he couldn't do it. Apart from a few occasions early on when I fell asleep by accident, he left me alone.

He became thin as the years went by – not in girth but in substance. He needed my sister's food and probably her love too. I had none to give him. Eventually, he faded away entirely except between the hours of midnight and five when he would sit by my window and look out at the city while I sat on my bed reading library books.

I fully expected that this would continue to be my life. But one day at work I looked up to see a woman looking at the roses.

'Can I help you?' I said.

She picked out a stem – a pink rose just beginning to open – and turned towards me. 'I'd like a dozen of these please,' she said.

I'd never spoken to her before. I'd only ever seen her at a distance, but I knew her immediately.

'You!'

I could tell that my boss was watching. Meg's blonde bob was immaculate, her smile sweet as violets, her nails on the stem of the rose perfectly manicured.

'I want to apologise.'

'For...?'

'It wasn't a fair fight. I shouldn't have used my power to involve outside agencies; it should have just been you and me.'

'You mean Terry...?'

'He can go – has gone already, I expect. You're free.'

'So...'

'May the best woman win,' she smiled. 'Can I have them wrapped and tied with a bow?'

I looked at my boss, but she didn't seem to have heard except for the last part, because she handed me the tray of ribbons. After Meg had gone my boss commented on what an elegant lady she was, and said nothing about our strange conversation.

I went back to my room that evening and slept for thirty-two hours without moving. The next day I resigned from my job and caught the next train back to Hawden.

41. Peter

He was wrong: they didn't politely ignore his feet. They made a point of discussing them.

'It won't be easy,' they said, 'fitting in. You will meet some who think you shouldn't be here. How do you think you will cope?'

'I don't know,' he'd replied. 'I'm learning not to hide, not to pretend, but it's hard. I hope I will be able to focus on my work, to make friends, to ignore the others.'

They had nodded and handed him a leaflet about student wellbeing.

And although they wouldn't let him know, officially, for a week or ten days, they had made it plain they would welcome him in. All three professors shook his hand, said they very much looked forward to working with him and were excited to meet such a promising student.

It seemed a done deal. His dad would be delighted. His mum would be proud. He should phone them. He walked up and down the station platform, past the racks of bikes, the coffee kiosk, his phone in his hand, his fingers still.

What he wanted was to phone Lauren, to tell her his news. They had discussed it, before, when he was still undecided.

'Of course you should go,' she'd said.

And when he'd talked about how he would miss her, miss the hills, the woods, she'd poked him in the side and laughed.

'Do you think there's no countryside in Cambridgeshire?' she said. 'You can become a fen runner. The hills will still be here when you come home.'

'I suppose.'

'And besides, I won't be here either. Who knows what part of the country I'll be in?'

She'd got her UCAS form in early. She'd applied to London, Bristol, Durham and York. He could imagine her as a student, carrying piles of books into lecture theatres, wearing long knitted scarves, feeding the ducks in the park. She'd been part of his life for so long. If he closed his eyes he could smell her hair. His fingers hovered over the keys.

Then he heard her voice in the woods that morning. 'I need Richard. I need to find Richard.'

He shoved the phone into his coat pocket. Whatever she was doing right now it didn't involve him. She wouldn't welcome an interruption. And he didn't want to speak to his mum or dad. He wasn't ready to speak to anyone. He wasn't even ready to go home. He went into the ticket office and bought a one-way ticket to Kendal. He could get out from there into the Dales. He'd leave his suit folded behind a rock where he could return for it. He needed to run; he needed to get up high on the hills. He needed to run all night.

42. Ali

I was pissed off when Lauren turned up. Everything had been going pretty well. I was back at Sally's up at Old Barn, and she and her old man, Terry, were loved-up and as happy as anything. Sally's cooking, which had been amazing anyway, stepped up a gear when he came back. She didn't just make soups and stews now, she made chilli bread and chicken satay and key lime pie. It was even better than Gran's. Gran never made exotic things like that.

What Richard and I were planning was dangerous. I mean, Smith may have been cool about the wad of dosh in his shoe, but he wouldn't be if we took his whole livelihood. But I didn't feel nervous, just excited really. When I was with Richard things seemed a bit more... possible.

I didn't have any problem with Lauren herself: I didn't know her. I didn't like what Richard was doing to her and didn't want to have her white face and bloodshot eyes with us all day reminding me. She looked like she'd had a particularly heavy night and was suffering big time. But there was no point in arguing. And anyway, I felt a bit sorry for her and bad about saying in front of her face that I didn't want her to come. Her eyes followed Richard around the room and she had an inane smile on her face, like she was on drugs.

We got the nine o'clock train to Leeds and arrived after the worst of the rush hour. Richard had a map with him and knew where he was going. We walked from the station, under the arches past the Cockpit, along the main road. Then he took us along a side street, and another, and before long I was hopelessly lost. I was beginning to wonder if Richard knew where he was going, when suddenly, there it was: St Ann's Street. It was a short road, joining up two others. It had nothing particular to recommend it. There were a couple of trees growing each side on the pavement, and at the far end, through a gap between two buildings on the adjoining street, you could catch a glint of water, which I guessed was the river.

The buildings on one side were student housing, set back from the road behind rectangular patches of grass and fag butts. The other side had a taller, smarter block of flats, a garage and work yard, and at the far end a small row of shops.

We made for the shops, and sure enough, the furthest away was a newsagent and post office. It wasn't very big. The post office part was just a hatch at one side of the shop and there was a queue of about five people who took up most of the space. We looked in, but the three of us would have made the place positively crowded.

'I'll wait out here with Laura,' Richard said.

She elbowed him in the ribs. 'It's Lauren,' she said.

By the time I got to the front of the queue I'd the read the front page stories on all of the newspapers and could list the lead items in the latest issues of Country Life and Runners World. There was an old lady two ahead of me who was both deaf and stupid, and there was a problem with her pension. The shop sold white, pink and yellow bonbons, and also midget gems, mint imperials, chewing nuts, and a mix of sweets which was called Yorkshire mixtures. These were all in jars behind the other counter where no one was queueing.

By the time I'd learned all the varieties of crisp available I was at the front, and a middle aged lady sat the other side of the glass in a white blouse with glasses on a chain. She had a short grey hair and a look of efficiency I thought might be fake considering the snail pace of the queue.

'Yes?' she said, glaring at me.

'I wanted to ask about post office boxes,' I said.

She shook her head. 'You'll need to go to the main post office for that.'

'No, it's here,' I protested. I pulled out a scrap of paper which I'd copied the code onto and showed it to her. 'This is the number. See, it says St. Ann's.'

She glanced at it, then back at me.

'That's not a post office box number,' she said.

'It's not?'

'No, they only have numbers, not letters. It must be something else.'

I looked at the number, as though I didn't know it off by heart.

'What is it then?' I said.

She shrugged. 'An address?'

She gave a look behind me to where the queue had grown to the door, and I realised I wasn't going to get any further.

'Well, thanks then,' I said, and left.

Richard and Lauren were sitting on the wall in front of the student housing. She was leaning against him, her head on his shoulder, and he had his arm around her. They looked like a couple, like he was looking after his girlfriend who was feeling a bit worse for wear. I waited for some cars to pass and realised I'd twisted the piece of paper into a knot.

I shook my head as I crossed over to them.

'No good?' Richard asked.

'It's not a post office box number.'

'What are we going to do then?' asked Lauren.

'The woman said it might be an address.'

'Let me see.'

She held out her hand and I gave her the twisted paper. She unfolded it gingerly and looked at the code.

St Ann's 143 ca66ages.

'Was there a gap between the numbers?' she asked.

Richard and I looked each other.

'I don't think so,' I said.

'I've got it in my wallet.' He took his wallet out of his coat and removed the twenty pound note with the black writing. We all looked at it.

'Yes, look,' said Lauren. 'The one is slightly apart from the four and three. It's not St Ann's 143, it's St Ann's 1 43.'

'It could be,' I said. 'But how does that help?'

'The student houses are numbered, look. We're outside number five, and the next one is number four. Number one must be at the other end. We need to go in and find room number 43, or a locker or something.'

'You could be right,' Richard was looking at her admiringly.

'I guess,' I said.

'Well done Lauren.'

She stood up. 'Let's go then.'

Walking along the street Lauren and Richard held hands. I walked on the other side of Richard, and when he smiled at me I increased the space between us.

Lauren was looking a bit better. She stayed close to Richard, leaning towards him so not only their hands touched but also their arms, and sometimes their shoulders. It made her look a bit drunk and unsteady, but her face had more colour in it.

Student house number one was just the same as the others: painted a weird beige colour, a rectangular block twice as long as it was tall. There were steps up to a front door, which was locked, with a number key pad to the side.

'We don't have the code,' said Lauren, deflated.

'We must have. It must be on here.' Richard took out the note again and we all peered at it.

'The only numbers on it are 1 43 and 66 in the middle of cabbages,' I said. 'We could try the 66.'

Richard pressed in the numbers and tried the door, but it stayed fast. He tried 43 and various other combinations, but nothing worked.

'Maybe it's not the house after all,' I said.

'I don't know. It seemed like a pretty good idea.'

Lauren smiled at him and he smiled back. I turned away.

'Maybe it's some sort of ingenuity test,' said Richard. 'First get into the building.'

'We're meant to break in?' I asked.

'Well,' Richard began, but then the door opened and a boy came out with a folder and three books in one arm.

'Hi,' he said, holding the door open for us.

'Hiya,' we replied, and walked in.

The heavy door closed behind us. We were at the end of a corridor painted off-white. There was a sign on the wall saying 1-15. To our left, behind a fire door, was a flight of stairs with another sign, First Floor 16-30, Second Floor 31-45, Third Floor 46-60.

'That was easy,' I said.

'I guess they knew that sooner or later you'd get in,' said Richard.

'As long as we can get out again.' Lauren giggled.

The walls of the stairwell were painted the same colour and the stairs were made of stone. The place smelled of burnt toast and piss.

On the first floor there was a fire door through to a corridor, and the same on the second floor. We went through and walked along looking at the room numbers. Half way along was a kitchen. I wondered how we'd explain our presence if we met any of the students who lived on the floor, but the kitchen was empty. There were dirty mugs next to the sink and an empty pizza box on the table. Photos of grinning people were attached to the fridge with magnets. Room 43 was further on, two from the end.

It had an ordinary door with a keyhole. No keypad. Nowhere to enter a code.

'Shall I knock?' Richard asked.

I nodded and Lauren agreed. Richard rapped on the door three times.

Nothing happened.

I tried the handle and the door opened. We peered in. The room had a bed in it, a wardrobe and chest of drawers, and a desk with a chair. That was all. There were no clothes or sheets or posters on the wall. Room 43 was uninhabited.

'You moving in?'

A Japanese girl was standing in the corridor.

'I am,' I said. 'Or I might be. I was having a look.'

'It's nice here. Ok. Students are fun, and sometimes drinking, late at night in kitchen.' She smiled at me. 'Pizza too.'

'Thanks,' I said.

'You're welcome,' she said, smiling. 'I am Kiki. I am living next door.'

'Alicia,' I said.

'I have lecture now.'

'Ok.'

'See you again.' She smiled and shook my hand.

After she was gone we went in, closed the door behind us and searched the room. We looked in every corner, underneath the carpet, behind the bed. We took out each drawer and turned it over. But Room 43 was just an empty room. There was nothing in it except cheap furniture.

'There's nothing here,' said Richard.

'No,' I agreed.

We walked back along the corridor and down the stairs. The front door let us back out onto the steps and patchy grass.

'What now?' asked Lauren.

'We're missing something.' I said. 'We're really close. What can it be?'

Two girls came along the path wheeling bicycles and Richard had to move out of their way.

'Let's walk round the building,' he said.

At the far end were the bike racks, a long line of them, and quite a few bikes fastened with brightly coloured sausage-shaped locks. We walked by slowly, looking at them. Richard stood up straight, his face bright.

'They're numbered,' he said. 'There's a place for each room.'

Sure enough, each parking place had a room number on it. We counted along to number 43, and this time it wasn't empty. There was a neon green mountain bike fastened with an elaborate lock.

The lock had seven rings to line up, each marked with the numbers one to nine and the letters a to e. Richard started twisting them into place.

'There's no g,' he said.

We looked at the note again.

'Try a nine,' suggested Lauren. 'ca66a9e.'

He twisted the rest of the rings into place and the lock opened.

'It's a bike,' I said. 'What the fuck would Smith and Jeannie want with a bike?'

'I don't know,' said Richard. 'But we're not going to find out here. Let's take it and go.'

No one looked as we walked off with the bike. We walked quickly away from the student area towards the station and caught the next train back to Hawden.

43. Ali

The train wasn't very crowded. We put the bike in the space at the end of the carriage near the door and stayed with it on the flip-down seats opposite. Lauren sat in between us and leaned her head against Richard. She was quite rosy now, and smiling. She still looked like she was on drugs.

'Have you spoken to your mum?'

Lauren and I both looked at Richard.

'Yes I have,' said Lauren

'Is it ok?'

'My dad told me what happened. Your mum wanted to turn him.'

Richard looked surprised. 'I didn't know you...'

'You were in Paris.'

I met Richard's eyes above Lauren's head. Suddenly we were together and I felt responsible for Lauren, like he did.

'Your mum must be angry,' Richard said.

But Lauren had fallen asleep.

Richard met my eyes again.

'She's pretty far gone,' I said.

'Yes.'

'What are you going to do?'

'I don't know. I thought I could go back to how things were before, but I was wrong. Everything's different.'

'If you leave her alone, what will happen? Will she get better?'

'Yes, once this has healed.'

He pulled back the hair from her neck and showed the remains of a wound, a small dark piece of scab.

'That will be gone soon,' I said.

'A few days. But she's going to get worse, and she'll be hard to resist.'

'Keep away from her.'

'Then she'll be in pain.'

'Idiot!'

'I know. I should have waited.'

I looked away this time. I didn't ask him what he should have waited for.

When we arrived at Hawden we woke Lauren, but it was like trying to walk with a really drunk person. It was a mile up to Hough Dean. We managed to get her through the town, but once we got onto the lane Richard carried her on his back while I pushed the bike. She fell asleep again like a dead weight, her head dropped forward over his shoulder and her hair falling down the front of his jacket.

He took her straight upstairs and put her to bed in the attic room at the back of the house. When he came back we looked at the bike.

'Heavy duty,' he said. 'Look at the tread on those tyres.'

I never had a bike when I was a child. Emma did. She had a white bike with pink flowers painted on near the handlebars. She thought it was the coolest thing ever.

'Aleesha, would you like a ride on my bike?'

'No thanks.'

'Why not?'

'I don't like it.'

She pulled a face then, raising her eyebrows and smirking a bit, a face which said: I know you're lying, how could you not like this bike? You're just jealous.

'It's ugly. It looks like Barbie's bike.'

Emma loved Barbie. She had lots of them in her room. She smiled at me.

'Maybe Mum and Dad will buy you a bike when you're older. You could have a brown one.'

She was wearing shorts and white sandals and her legs were tanned. She swung onto the bike and rode off down our road. She wasn't very good on it yet and she wobbled, but when she stopped at the end and got off to turn it round she looked as pleased as anything, like she knew she was a princess and I was a worm.

A year or so after that, Gran offered to get me a bike but I said I didn't want one. Emma and her friends all had bikes and rode them up and down the street, and leaned them against walls whilst they chatted and admired their nails. I knew what she would say – or if she didn't say it, what she would think. She'd think I wanted to be like her but that I just couldn't get it right. That I was failing to keep up with her.

I said, 'I don't think bikes are my thing.'

And Gran gave me a look, trying to work out what I was thinking. I smiled at her.

'You could get me some books instead. You could buy a lot of books for the price of a bike.'

'I can't ride a bike,' I said.

Richard looked at me in surprise. 'I'll teach you.'

'When?'

'No time like the present. Get on.'

I hesitated, but he stood there holding the handlebars like the reins of a horse, waiting for me to mount. I laughed and lifted my leg over so I was straddling the bike.

'Sit on the seat, feet on the pedals.'

I glanced at him anxiously and he grinned.

'It's ok, I've got it steady.'

I leaned forward and put my hands on the handlebars next to his, shuffled back so my bum was in contact with the leather seat, then gingerly lifted one foot and put it on the pedal.

'And the other one.'

I lifted it and put it back on the ground. The bike wobbled.
'Again.'

I tried again and this time managed to get my foot onto the pedal. I was completely off the ground.

I grinned. 'What now?'

'You have to push with your feet.'

'Then the bike will go forward.'

'Yes, that's the point.'

'But you're standing in front of it. I'll run you over.'

He laughed. 'I see you've spotted the flaw in my teaching method.'

I put my feet back on the ground and he went to the back of the bike.

'Ok, let's try again.'

This time it was even harder without Richard to look at, but I managed to push off and move the bike a few feet, before I panicked, wobbled, and put both feet back on the ground.

'What did you do that for? You were flying.'

'Hardly,' I said, but I was grinning.

Richard was very patient and, after an hour or so and a lot of laughing, I rode around the yard with Richard hanging on to the bike behind me.

'My turn now,' Richard said.

I was still sitting on the bike and he swung himself in front of me.

'Tuck your legs in and hold on,' he said.

He stood on the pedals and we were moving, speeding down the lane. I held on to his jacket, but my hands slipped on the leather, and after a moment I put my hands inside. He pedalled hard as the lane rose and I could feel the tightness in his stomach muscles. We crested the hill and freewheeled the rest of the way down to the bottom, both of us whooping in exhilaration. One circuit of the Craggs car park and we were back on the uphill slope.

'Lean forward,' he called out.

My face was against his back and I could smell the leather of his jacket, could smell his hair, his skin.

When we were back on the level we heard a vehicle behind us. I looked behind and there was a red van.

'We'll beat him,' shouted Richard.

We raced in front all the way to Hough Dean, curving in through the gate and coming to a stop in the middle of the yard as the van came in behind us. We fell off the bike laughing. A man got out of the van.

'Hi Jimmy,' Richard called to him.

Jimmy eyed Richard with something which wasn't friendliness. 'I've come to get my tools.'

'Why, have you finished?'

'I've finished with you lot. You'll have to find someone else to finish the work.'

Richard looked surprised.

'Does Mum know?'

'I don't want anything else to do with your mother,' Jimmy said.

He went into the barn and came out with a bag of tools, then some sacks of sand and plaster, a couple of buckets. He loaded them into his van.

'Had your mum got her teeth into him?' I asked Richard.

'She'd taken a shine.'

'But he's not succumbed?'

'She'd only got to first bite. His friends have warned him. And he has a girlfriend.'

'Don't you check out that sort of thing first?'

'Usually. We've not been very clever this time. Either of us.'

The laughter had stopped. I thought of Lauren lying asleep in the bedroom upstairs and felt as though I'd swallowed something very heavy.

Jimmy put the last of his things into his van, got in and drove away.

'Bye Jimmy,' Richard called out to the van as it disappeared through the gate. We watched it go. 'I liked Jimmy,' Richard said.

'What about this bike?'

'You're doing ok for the first time.'

'That's not what I meant. I mean, a bike. Smith isn't a bike dealer you know. That's not what the police are after.'

'No.'

We stood and looked at it leaning against the side of the barn. It was neon green with big wheels, an aluminium frame.

'It's very heavy,' Richard said.

'Heavier than it ought to be?'

'Yes. When I lifted it on to the train it was hard work. It shouldn't be, not really.'

'What about riding it uphill? With me on it, too.'

'Yeah, I guess.'

I looked at him. 'For an ordinary person it would be hard work.'

He shrugged.

He started fiddling with the bike, trying to get the seat off. I looked at the handlebars. At each end there was a black plastic stopper, and after a few moments I managed to get one of them out. It was hollow and I put my fingers inside and touched plastic.

'There's something in here,' I said.

Richard had succeeded in getting the seat off and was looking inside the frame.

'Here too.'

We looked at each other. He had his shades on and I could see myself reflected in them.

'Let's take it into the barn. In case anyone comes.'

I nodded and we wheeled the bike inside. Richard switched on the light, a bare bulb hanging from a string, illuminating the big empty barn. He took off his shades and his eyes were shining.

He grabbed my hand and squeezed it. 'What shall we do?'

'Let's see what we've got first.'

My fingers could just reach the plastic inside the handlebars. I slid it out. A polythene tube, filled with tiny white pills. Hundreds of them, thousands even.

Richard was trying to get the packet out from the frame beneath the seat.

'We need something to grab it with,' I said.

'Tongs,' he said, and ran off to the house.

While he was gone I picked up the seat and looked at it. The top was brown leather, but underneath it was covered in black plastic. Where the plastic reached the edges it was joined with a rough line of glue. I pulled at it, but it was stuck fast.

Richard reappeared with a pair of tongs.

'Have you got a knife?' I asked him.

He fished a penknife out of his pocket and handed it to me. I cut the black plastic, carefully with the tip of the knife. Underneath, packed in tightly, was a bag of white powder. Richard had just fished another out of the hollow tube of the frame.

'Heroin?' I asked.

Richard opened the end of one of the bags with the knife. He licked his finger and got a few grains of the powder which he put in his mouth.

He shook his head. 'Cocaine. It's pretty good.'

'Not cut with anything?'

'Not yet.'

We looked at the two bags of powder, the bag of pills.

'We should use the twenty pound note,' I said. 'The one with the code on. It would be appropriate.'

He laughed. 'Not much though. It's strong stuff.'

He went back to the house again to find something to cut it on. I walked around the bike. I lifted it a couple of inches off the ground. It still seemed heavy. I didn't know anything about bikes, but I could imagine it would be difficult to ride it up a hill.

Richard came back with a hand mirror and used his penknife to cut a couple of small lines.

'I think there's more,' I said.

He looked at the bike. 'In the frame?'

'I don't think so. It would be too difficult to get to; we'd have to take the bike apart.'

'The wheels?

I nodded. 'I think those tyres are packed with the stuff.'

He squeezed one of them.

'Could be.'

He found the twenty with the code on and rolled it up tightly. He handed it to me and I snorted one of the lines, watching the white grains disappear from the mirror, feeling the hit on the back of my nose. I blinked. I'd never had stuff like this before, unadulterated. I could feel it rushing into my bloodstream.

Richard took the rolled note from me and hoovered up his line. He looked up. Our faces were inches apart and I could smell him. I could hear blood thudding in my ears.

I rested my fingers lightly on his knee.

'Shall we have a look?'

'Let's.'

Richard had changed the tyres on a bike before and knew what he was doing. The first one was off in a few minutes. A long plastic sausage was wrapped around the wheel, covering the inner tube and packed with more of the white powder. I whooped and danced around the bike while Richard laughed.

'Can I do the next one?'

I crouched at the side of the bike and Richard knelt behind me, showing me what to do. I could feel him at my back, his breath in my ear.

His hands and mine moved on the wheel, eased the tyre away from the frame, revealing another sausage. I lifted it from the bike and laid it next to the rest of the hoard on the barn floor. The tubes from the tyres were over six feet long.

Richard stood next to me and I took his hand.

'That's a fuck of a lot of drugs,' I said.

'A fuck of a lot of money,' he said.

'No wonder Smith and Jeannie wanted to find me.'

'What are you going to do now?'

We turned and looked at each other. We were really close, almost touching.

'I don't know,' I whispered.

We moved closer. My blood was racing now, and it felt so good I could hardly bear it. Our noses bumped against each other and we moved them, him one way, me the other.

'Richard!' Meg yelled across the yard, tearing in between us so we stepped back from each other.

'Richard! Are you there?'

He walked to the barn door.

'What is it?'

'I want to talk to you,' she called. 'Can you come in?'

'Five minutes,' he said.

I stashed the drugs in a cardboard box in the corner of the barn and covered it with some empty sacks that Jimmy had left behind. Richard put the tyres back on the bike. We replaced the stoppers in the handlebars, the seat. It took fifteen minutes to put the bike back together.

Meg was calling from the door of the house again. 'Richard, are you coming?'

'I'd better go,' I said to Richard.

But he grabbed my hand. 'You're coming with me,' he said.

44. Meg

The window to my room has a wide ledge, low enough to use as a seat. I've put cushions on it, a blanket. From here I can watch all the comings and goings at the front of the house. No one notices me. Even if they were to look up they wouldn't see me, as I sit slightly back from the window, in shadow.

That afternoon I was rereading *Against Nature* by Huysman, but his clever decadence was not holding me. My eyes slid from the page and I found myself looking down at the yard, watching.

Richard arrived with Andy's girl on his back, slumped as though she were half dead. I heard him come up the stairs to the room at the back of the house. Frances's granddaughter was with them and she waited in the yard with her bike while Richard brought the sick girl in. Ali's hair had grown and she had colour in her cheeks. There was a bit of Frances about her in the way she held her limbs, loosely, completely confident in her ownership of them. She was growing into herself. Even in the week or so since I'd seen her, she looked more at ease.

Richard came back out of the house and she lit up. I sighed. That poor limp girl sleeping in the back room, she was taking it badly. She must have a very strong link to life for her body to react in this way. If only Richard could have waited a while and found out a bit more about her before he started down this path. If he had told me she was Andy's daughter I would have warned him to back off.

In the yard Richard and Ali were laughing. The sound rang through the air and out onto the moors where it was answered by the calls of sheep and crows. They didn't notice, intent on each other and the game they were playing.

When Jimmy turned up I put my book down. No point in pretending to read any more. I felt my gaze harden with self-pity. Not an emotion I often play host to. You win some, some you lose, and the game goes on. No point in dwelling on what might have been. But here, this place, it seems to keep giving me the losing but never the winning.

First I lost Daniel, my husband and my first love. Then Charles my son and my friend, who taught me more than I taught him, whose brain and body have long rotted in the grave. Then I lost Frances. I followed her here but it wasn't the same as in Paris. The years had passed and she had grown old, created a life for herself with her daughter and her friends. I suppose I wrecked that life for her, but that wasn't my intention. It was then that I met Andy, who could be my greatest love of all. He could outshine even Daniel. If he stopped clinging to life that decays, love which can only shrivel, if he gave himself to me we could shine like twin stars.

I nearly had him. One day he came to my house to play chess, and after the game, which I won, I asked him to look at the car. He lifted the bonnet and looked inside the engine. I stood very near to him so that when he straightened up our bodies were as close as lovers'. He turned and we breathed each other's breath.

I stood still and waited. He lifted his hand and touched my ear.

He said my name, and his voice was rough.

I closed my eyes.

It was a mistake. He stepped back and the world swung around. When I opened my eyes the air was crystal cold, my breath forming small clouds. He was walking over to his car.

'I can't see anything the matter,' he called over his shoulder. 'If it happens again you'd better call the garage.'

I should have just bitten him there and then. But then maybe he'd have reacted the same way as Lauren: she is his daughter, after all.

He won the last game of chess we played. The roses he'd brought were in water on the window ledge and their smell hung in the air. He called checkmate and looked at me with such glee that I laughed out loud.

'Andy,' I said, 'stay with me for ever.'

His grin faded. I grabbed his hands in mine.

'Let me turn you.' He tried to pull away but I held him tight. 'Don't pretend you don't feel this.'

He stood up and yanked his hands from my grasp.

'I shouldn't be here,' he said.

He walked out of the room, out of the house. I followed, pulling at his clothes, shouting his name. He pushed me away and climbed into his car.

'Andy, tell me you don't love me. Tell me that and I'll leave you alone.'

'Meg, I have a wife and a newborn baby.'

'Tell me you don't love me.'

Key in the ignition, he said 'Let go of the door. I'm going to drive away and I will run you over. '

'You can't protect them,' I yelled into his face. 'Wait and see. You can't protect them against me.'

He turned on the engine, gave me a great shove and drove away, while I lay in the dirt screaming.

He never said it. He couldn't say he didn't love me because it wasn't true. I'd hoped Jimmy would make him sit up and notice, that jealousy would force him to acknowledge his feelings, but I always underestimate his goodness. Jimmy had been fun. He made me laugh and he'd fallen quite easily. I could have taken him back to Paris. He'd have liked it there, the clubs and the nightlife. With his fire-eating and his gift of the gab he'd have been a hit. We could have run together for a while. I watched him climb into his van and drive away.

Richard and Ali wheeled the bike into the barn and disappeared from my view. I swung my legs off the window seat and walked across the room to the landing. I took a long breath. I could smell the girl.

I wondered if Richard might have locked her in, but the door to her room opened easily. Considering her state, locking it might have been safer.

She was lying on the bed, sleeping softly, one arm stretched out with her head resting on it. Her blonde hair lay coiled on the pillow behind her. Her skin was paper white and there were dark shadows beneath her eyes.

I sat on the bed beside her and she didn't stir. I watched her chest rise and fall as she breathed, almost imperceptibly lifting her white shirt on the in-breath, revealing a millimetre or two more of her flesh where the shirt opened over her breasts. I leaned forward and gently opened another button so the shirt gaped wider. She was wearing a low-cut white bra which shone against her skin. I slid a finger under the edge of the fabric.

She parted her lips and let out a puff of air.

I ran my fingers lightly down her chest, over her breasts and stomach, down to the waistband of her jeans. Her breathing calmed again. I smiled. She was Andy's girl and he would want to be where she was. I would talk to Richard. I stood up, bent and kissed her lightly on the forehead, then left the room. I locked the door behind me.

I think of Richard as my son. I have seen mothers with their teenage boys, the bickering and the indulgence. They spoil them, do everything for them and in return hope for a little respect and unconditional love. They watch their girlfriends jealously, anxious that they will turn the son against the mother, that the mother will be found wanting. Richard is related to me only by blood and he was fully grown when I found him, but we have been together for many years now, and the relationship has never been anything but filial. I have taught him about our kind, helped him onto his two feet where he now stands so confidently.

So when I call him I expect him to come. Five minutes, he said. What were they doing in that barn? When he'd come to the door he was fully clothed. I was tempted to march over and find out what was going on, but instead I walked into the kitchen. For want of anything better to do I put the kettle on, paced while it came to the boil.

I went to the front door and called again, and this time they both appeared. He was pulling her by the hand. She glanced at the open gate, but she followed.

'Tea?' I said when they came into the hall.

'Yes please,' she said, and he nodded.

They leaned against the work surface, standing next to each other, not touching but undoubtedly a team. I handed them the hot mugs. He put his on the surface behind him; she held hers in her hands.

'Well?' I said.

He raised his eyebrows.

'You know what. That girl upstairs. What are you doing with her?'

'Isn't that obvious?'

'But are you going to finish the job?'

Richard looked down at his shoes. He looked sheepish.

'The second bite is nearly healed,' I said. 'Only a day, maybe hours. Then it will be time to turn her and she'll be new and bewildered. It's a full-time job looking after someone newly turned. Have you thought about that?'

Definitely sheepish. He rubbed his toe against the floor as though trying to move something with it.

Then he coughed and mumbled something.

'I can't hear you,' I said.

'I've changed my mind,' he said clearly.

Ali and I were looking at him.

'I thought she was the one, but she's not. She's actually in love with someone else.'

'So what are you planning to do with her?'

He looked at me helplessly and lifted his shoulders. 'Let her go?'

'She's in quite a state.'

'She says she's in pain when she's away from me. She sleeps for days at a time.'

'It's because she doesn't want to turn. The changes are happening in her body, but her mind won't accept it.'

'Won't that stop when the wound heals?'

'It will start to reverse itself. It will take time and she will need care.'

Richard picked up his tea. He looked at Ali. 'We have to go to Leeds tomorrow,' he said. 'I don't really want to take her.'

They were both smiling, sharing some secret between themselves.

'Do you want me to take care of her?'

He looked back at me. 'Tomorrow?'

'And after. You can leave her to me if you want.'

'Would you do that? That would be fantastic.'

'Well, what are mothers for? It won't be the first time I've got you out of a scrape.'

He grinned, and relief spread across his features. 'I'm not sure I'd call this a scrape,' he said. 'A stupid mistake.'

'Reckless carelessness with someone else's life and happiness,' said Ali.

I stared at her, but she didn't flinch. Richard was smiling.

'In time,' I said, 'when everything's fallen back into place, it won't seem so bad as that.'

'I hope so,' said Richard. 'Thanks, Meg. You'll be better with her anyway. You'll know what to do.'

'I think I will,' I said.

Later, when Richard and Ali had disappeared again, plotting and scheming together, I went back up to Lauren's room. She was still sleeping, but she had turned onto her side and her open shirt had fallen across her breasts and covered them.

I knelt at the side of the bed and smoothed the hair from her face. She sighed and pouted. I kissed her and her lips were warm, her breath slightly sour.

'You're mine now,' I said to her. 'I have something of Andy's after all.'

She murmured in her sleep and I stroked her hair. 'He'll come looking for you.'

I kissed her lips again, a lingering kiss, and her eyes opened and looked into mine.

'You and me,' I whispered. The words slipped inside her mouth and mingled with her saliva before she swallowed them.

45. Ali

'Of course they seemed nice,' I said. 'They wanted information. They wanted to know if you'd seen me. They weren't going to say 'if we find her we're going to break her legs and remove her face with a meat cleaver'. You might not have told them anything then.'

Richard had been around for a long time and he knew a lot more about the world than me. But where Smith and Jeannie were concerned he seemed a bit naïve.

We were on the train to Leeds again, and on the floor between my feet was a Tesco's bag-for-life rammed full of drugs.

'If you remember, Jeannie and I had a fight and I won. She's not going to let that go, I promise you. She's a hard bitch. I lived with them; I know them better than you do.'

I'd spoken to Smith last night. I phoned the club and asked for him. I told him I had what he wanted and I was prepared to exchange it for ten grand. We'd agreed to meet at ten o'clock tonight. He'd sounded wary, not unfriendly. I knew better.

When we got to Leeds we put the carrier bag in one of the station lockers. The day stretched ahead of us like an empty page, with just one appointment at the bottom that we had to work towards.

'What first?' Richard asked.

'Haircut,' I said.

Richard, it turned out, was loaded. Meg too. In fact most vampires are, except for the really new ones. If they've lived long enough, and are canny enough, they manage to accumulate. Richard had offered to take me shopping and, seeing as I was going to have money of my own soon, I'd accepted. I was still sporting the homeless-girl-dressed-from-a-skip look, although I was a lot cleaner now that I was living in a house with a bathroom and washing machine. It seemed like time to move on.

I normally cut my own hair with whatever scissors I could find. The hairdresser lifted the strands incredulously.

'It's called The Chop,' I said. 'Very fashionable on the streets.'

I asked for something funky, easy to manage. I asked her to dye it a bright colour.

When Richard came back two hours later he did a double take. My hair was copper coloured, short, uneven and stylish. They had a beautician at the salon and I'd asked them to do my face too. I was wearing dark smoky make up, kohl and lipstick.

'We need to get you some clothes to go with that,' he said.

He knew which were the best shops and had a knack of finding the back streets and the flights of stairs that led to the offbeat and the unusual. He seemed to know what I liked, which was impressive as I was only just discovering that myself. Up to now I had worn what I could find.

We went for lunch in a pizza place, where I had an enormous pepperoni pizza and a Coke. Richard had coffee.

Late afternoon, laden with bags, we booked into a hotel. I hadn't been sure about this. I knew we had money, but a hotel seemed such an extravagance. And this wasn't just any hotel: it was the best hotel in Leeds. I'd have gone for something simpler, but Richard insisted.

'Why have anything less?' he said.

We walked through the doors into another world. It was hushed and still, hung with chandeliers, a kind of peace covering everything like a layer of ash. I stood and looked around while Richard went up to the reception desk. There were a couple of people sitting in armchairs reading newspapers. A boy in a ridiculous uniform stood near the lifts. I realised what it was that was thickening the air and sliding down the thick wallpaper. It was safety. The people who came here could be sure that everyone else had money too. They wouldn't be offended by the sight of poverty or need. They could hide out here and pretend the rest of the world was like this.

Richard seemed to know what he was doing. He joked with the receptionist, stood tall as though he had a right to be here. I caught the eye of the boy by the lifts and grinned at him. He looked ridiculous in that hat, those gold ropey things on his shoulders. He almost grinned back, but he plastered the mask back on like a soldier.

Richard came over waving a plastic card. 'I've got us a suite,' he said.

The boy took us up in the lift, which was as big as a room and had flowers in it. I tried to catch his eye but he wouldn't look at me, although he smiled obsequiously at Richard. On the fourth floor he walked us down a corridor and opened the door to the room for us. I touched the gold ropes when I passed him.

'What are those for?' I asked.

'They're meant to look smart,' he said.

'They look stupid,' I said, and he did grin then, although he tried to cover it up.

Richard gave him some money and he left. I turned my attention to the room, which wasn't just a room, of course, but an apartment big enough to house the Queen. Richard took me on a tour. The living room with enormous sofas and a drinks cabinet. The bedroom with velvet curtains that were too long and draped across the floor, and a bed wide enough that it could sleep all the people who lived in our squat and still have room to toss and turn in the night. And the bathroom.

The bathroom stunned me. The shine on the taps, the expanse of white, the towels piled up in towers, the soaps and shampoos, new bottles of everything.

'This is just for us?'

He touched the back of my neck. 'Why don't you have a bath? Enjoy it. We've plenty of time.

'But my hair, my make up. I don't think I'll be able to do them like this again.'

'I'll do them for you,' he said.

First we opened a bottle of champagne and made a toast to ourselves. Then I took my second glass into the bathroom and soaked in the deepest bath I'd ever had, with bubbles up to my ears. I felt like Cleopatra.

'She bathed in milk,' Richard said, when I called this through to him.

'Same difference.'

There were so many towels that I could wrap myself up like a mummy. Then I found a robe in the bedroom which I put on and, after we'd finished off the champagne, Richard did my hair and my face.

It was the second time that day someone had put make-up on for me, the first being the first time in my life. It was very different when Richard did it. I could feel his fingers every time he touched me, and he was so close. I'm sure the hairdresser wasn't that close to me.

When he did my eyeliner he held the back of my head with one hand and drew it on with the other, his face close to mine and concentrating. I didn't breathe.

We went out at nine thirty.

I was wearing black jeans and a hoodie and Converse. Richard was wearing his leather jacket. We stood next to each other in the white bathroom and looked in the mirror. We looked too solid for the shiny room, too matt. We laughed, then Richard cut a couple of lines on the side of the bath and we had those. We tumbled out of the lift into the foyer giggling and the receptionist looked in our direction.

'Shhhh!' I said to Richard. 'It's the money church. Be quiet.'

We held each other's arms and walked across the reception area pretending to be sedate. When we got into the street we couldn't hold it any longer and we ran, holding hands and laughing, to the other end of the street.

We went for a drink in a bar and after about half an hour we calmed down. It was getting close to the meeting with Smith and Jeannie and there was no saying how that would go.

I went in on my own. It was early and the club was pretty quiet. Smith would never normally be there at this time. He likes to make his entrance when everything is already buzzing. He was here tonight though. Him and one other guy I vaguely recognised, who used to hang around the squat sometimes. No sign of Jeannie.

Smith and the other guy were sitting in their normal corner. I sat down next to them.

'Hi Ali,' Smith said, and he smiled at me as though we were friends. 'You're looking good.'

'Thanks. You're not so bad yourself.' Which was true. Smith always looked good, good enough to eat if that was your thing. He was wearing a blue retro Clash t-shirt and ripped faded jeans. He needed a shave and his silver earrings were shining.

'You look older,' he said, looking me up and down.

'I am.'

The other guy moved on his seat.

'This is Dave,' Smith said, but he didn't take his eyes off me.

'Hi Dave,' I said. I didn't look at him either.

'Can I get you a drink?' Smith said.

I shook my head. 'I'm not staying.'

'Shame.' He looked me over again and I could feel myself heating up. In the past, if Smith had ever looked at me like this I would have been very happy. I would have risked Jeannie's wrath and followed it wherever it went. But he didn't look at me at all then, and now it was different.

'Have you got it?' I said.

Smith nodded.

'Dave?' he held his hand out, and Dave handed him a bag. It was retro too, one of those rectangular Adidas sports bags.

'Nice bag,' I said.

He put it on the table. I unzipped it and peered inside. It was empty.

'In the bottom,' said Dave.

The bottom of the bag was stiffened with a piece of black plasticated card. I lifted it and underneath I could see a layer of wads of twenties. I felt a bit disappointed. I knew ten grand wasn't that much, but seen like this it was pathetic. I wondered if I should have asked for more.

I zipped the bag back up and put my hands on the handles. Smith put a hand on top of mine.

'And you?' he asked, his face so close I could feel his breath.

I extracted a hand and fished in my jeans pocket for the twenty with the code on it. I lay it on the table and smoothed it flat with my fingers.

Smith picked it up, and for the first time his gaze left my face.

'St Ann's 143 cabbages?'

'You'll work it out.'

But when they got there they wouldn't find a bike stuffed full of drugs. Instead there would be just the lock wrapped around the post. When they entered the combination it would release the key for a locker at the railway station. By then we should be well away.

'I'd best be going,' I said.

Smith looked back at me.

'Who'd have thought you'd turn out to be so beautiful?' he said.

I smiled, and because I could, and because I'd never see him again, I leaned forward and kissed him on the lips.

'Bye Smith. Say hi to Jeannie for me. Bye Dave.'

I slung the Adidas bag over my shoulder and left the bar.

That was when I got nervous and wished I'd had more coke. The club wasn't in the worst part of town, but you had to walk up an alleyway to get to it. We'd wondered, when making our plan, whether to meet Smith somewhere else, somewhere neutral and on a main street. But we'd decided it showed more faith to go to his home turf.

I was halfway up the alley when Jeannie shot out of a doorway and punched me in the face. I fell backwards against a lamppost and she made a grab for the bag. I clung on and she started kicking me. We pulled the bag between us. I could see the anger in her face and after a few moments she gave up on the bag and just laid into me. She was wearing rings and I felt a spurt of blood as one of them cut me under my eye.

She was screaming at me, 'Bitch. You fucking bitch!'

I was vaguely aware that Smith and Dave were in the alley watching.

I curled myself into a ball around the bag and covered my face with my hands.

'Fight me,' Jeannie yelled. She grabbed at my hair and pulled, trying to get my head up. It hurt like hell. She was kicking me all the time with her sharp boots. I wondered if Smith would join in.

Then suddenly she stopped and there was a strange noise, a bit like a cricket ball hitting a bat. Jeannie was flying through the air. She landed on Dave, knocking him over. Smith looked perturbed for the first time that night.

Richard was standing next to me.

'Good punch,' I said.

He grinned. 'Are you ok?'

I stood up, which wasn't that easy. I could feel blood on my face from the cut, and my thighs and hips felt bruised and sore from Jeannie's boots. 'I'm fine,' I said.

'Let's go then.'

I held on to the bag and we started walking away up the alley.

We'd gone about twenty feet when there were running footsteps behind us. Richard swung round and hit out, and Smith went flying back down the alley, landing in a doorway near the other two.

'Fuck!' he said loudly.

Jeannie was holding her arm and I wondered if she'd broken it. Dave looked from her to Smith who was rubbing his head. He looked scared, but he obviously decided that as the last man standing he'd have to come after us. He ran down the alley with a determined look on his face.

As he got close Richard seemed to grow a foot taller. He stood up on his toes and took his shades off and bared his teeth. His eyes were milky and veined with red. It wasn't much, but it was effective. Dave stopped in his tracks and screamed, then turned and ran back the other way.

Richard offered me his arm. 'Let's get out of here,' he said.

Back at the hotel Richard bathed my face and we popped some of the pills we'd siphoned off. My thighs and hips were starting to stiffen. I ran another bath and soaked in the hot water surrounded by mountains of bubbles while the drugs began to work their magic.

At some point Richard came into the bathroom. He was wearing jeans and a t-shirt and his feet were bare. He sat on the side of the bath.

'You're overdressed,' I said.

He held his hand out to me and I got out. He held a big towel and wrapped it around me, and then we kissed.

'Do you want to go out?' he asked. 'Go to a club or something.'

The room was shining like the inside of an alien spaceship. Up close I could see the stubble just breaking through his skin, tiny black bristles. There was a trace of saliva on his bottom lip. His hands were on my back pressing against the thickness of the towel.

'No. I think I'd like to stay in.'

He smiled and the spaceship went into overdrive. 'Me too,' he said.

46. Cassie

Andy was a fixer. A problem solver. He thought if something was broken he should mend it, get it working again. He'd spend time trying even if it was beyond repair.

I only stayed overnight once after I came back. It seemed to be going well. While I was with him I stayed focused, mostly. I remembered to laugh at his jokes. Long ago we used to share a bottle of wine in the kitchen and bitch about the other teachers in the staffroom. We were two amongst the many: us against the world. We used to go for long bike rides together, and sometimes I made jokes of my own. That seemed a long time ago.

I was getting up to find my coat when Andy grabbed my hand.

'You can stay if you want.'

I'd worked hard at invisibility in the intervening years. I wore cheap clothes in grey and beige. I scraped my hair off my face, highlighted nothing. Now back in my old life I had the wardrobe of a woman who wanted to be attractive. A lot of my make up was still usable and I'd started to play, to see if that woman still existed.

Andy used to fancy me.

I sat down again and he kissed me.

The first time we kissed was at a Year Eight disco. We were both on duty and we were sent to get back-up refreshments from the store cupboard. Standing amongst stacks of cola and catering sized tins of baked beans, it felt forbidden and exciting. When all the kids had gone home I took him back to my place and we went straight to the bedroom. Kissing Andy was familiar. My lips knew that story.

Upstairs we sat on the bed and looked at each other. Neither of us removed any clothes.

We sat for a long time.

'We can be friends,' I said eventually.

'But...'

'I've been offered a teaching job in Manchester. I'm probably going to take it.'

'But you've only just come back.'

'I won't stay away, not this time. And anyway, I'd be in your way here. You can't start something new with your ex hanging around.'

'What...?'

The front door opened and closed and we heard footsteps on the stairs.

'Lauren,' he said.

'I'll go home.'

'No, stay. We don't have to...'

'What would be the point?'

'We used to be a family.'

'Families change,' I said. But I stayed. We held each other on the bed, and slept fully clothed. At some point Andy pulled a blanket over us. In the morning you were in the kitchen and you hated me. I was happy to see that. Hate is a strong emotion akin to love. They can change easily from one to the other. But you can't make them out of nothing.

47. Lauren

When I woke there was a woman sitting on the edge of the bed. She smiled and stroked my face and I went back to sleep. When I woke again I was alone.

I sat up and looked around me. It wasn't my room. I didn't recognise this room. I remembered the woman and realised she was Meg. This was Meg's house and she had kissed me.

I swung my legs out of the bed and tried to stand, but I filled with sharp knives in every part of my body, and I cried out.

I called 'Richard!' very loudly.

I didn't want Richard, I wanted Peter. I wanted Peter to come and take me away from this place.

She came into the room and she was carrying Richard's big black coat.

'Put this on,' she said. 'It will make you feel better.'

I wasn't cold, but I did what she said, and she was right. The pain went away. Well, almost. I could still feel it tingling in my veins, trying to jab at me. But I could stand up and walk over to the window and look out at the daylight. The room must have been in the attic because I could see the roof sloping away from the window. I could see the tops of trees.

'What day is it?' I asked.

She smiled. 'All days are much the same.'

She stood behind me and touched my neck. She lifted my hair and twisted it into a rope and ran her fingers down from my ear to my shoulder. I could feel the line they left behind.

'I know what you are,' I said to her.

She kissed my neck on the spot I'd been keeping covered and placed her hands on my hips.

'Richard has gone away,' she said. 'There's only us.'

'I don't want to be one of you. I want to be with Peter.'

She turned me around and kissed me on the lips. 'I don't think you know what you want, Lauren,' she said.

When she left the room I heard the key turn in the lock. So that was it then. I was a prisoner. I looked out again. I could get out onto the roof, but there was no way down and the tiles looked slippery. If I fell, the best I could hope for would be broken bones.

I took off the coat and the knives started up again, turning and twisting in my veins. I hugged the sheet about me. I'd left the window open and the December air was slicing in, slashing at my bare skin. I listed plants in my head. Mullein, valerian, lungwort, black comfrey, coltsfoot. Coltsfoot. I saw the hoof of a young horse transmute gradually to a goat's, to Peter's, and I convulsed, close to vomiting. The pain was getting worse and I knew I'd have to put the coat back on.

I drew my thoughts back to flowers, to leaves, berries, stalks and seeds. I felt in the pocket of my jeans and smiled. The plants had always helped me.

Ivy, elder, rowan, hawthorn, yew.

I slid off the bed. I could barely stand up straight. Near the window I fell, but I put my hand on the sill and pulled myself up, levered with my elbows until I was kneeling and looking out across the tree-filled valley. The clouds had come untucked and were hanging down, touching the tops of the hills.

I put my fingers in my mouth and whistled three sharp blasts. Each one was like a punch in the guts and I nearly doubled over. After the third I felt sleep washing over me and pulling me down. I managed to close the window before I curled on the floor like a worm and let it take me into oblivion again.

Ramsons, horse chestnut, hedge mustard, lemon verbena, vervain.

When I woke I was on the bed with the coat laid over me like a blanket. The clouds had sunk lower and the house was wrapped in fog. I could see the white mist against the windows. Beyond there was nothing.

I shrugged myself into the coat and went back to the window which drew me. I opened it and the fog swirled in, touching my skin with damp skeins. I leaned on the sill and put my head through the opening, looking and looking. But the white was opaque and there was nothing to see.

I always loved it when the valley filled up like this.

It seemed like there was nowhere to go, that the clouds were fixing me in place, yet it wasn't true. I could move through it, slowly, unsure. If I went uphill, I might come out of the top and look down on the surface of the cloud, joining the sides of the valley like a damp soft flood.

I closed my eyes and Peter came to me.

He was with his father. They held out their hands and I took them and stepped out onto the roof. Their hooves were sure-footed on the tiles and when we reached the edge they leaped in a graceful arc, descending through the air, their feet landing softly on the grass. The fog billowed through my shirt and I was weightless.

They ran, and between them I ran too, faster than I ever had in my life. I no longer had the coat. That lay on the floor of the attic room. We moved through the white fog. I could see the ground under my feet, a circle of inches, but nothing beyond that. First we travelled along the rough potholed road which led to Hough Dean. Then the ground changed and we were racing over grass and heather, bounding up over boulders, gaining height all the time. I tried to work out our route, but the fog confused me.

Eventually we reached a plateau and they stopped running. Peter's dad let go of my hand and walked away into the fog. Peter and I were alone in the cloud. We held hands and stood close so our shoulders touched.

'Thank you,' I said to Peter.

'I brought these like you asked,' he said, handing me some pieces of root.

I frowned.

'Are you ok?' he said.

He shoved the root into my shirt pocket and I leaned against him.

We sat on a stone and wrapped our arms around each other, waiting for the fog to clear.

Plants all have their own characters and I don't understand how people can get them mixed up. Like basil and mint. Quite apart from the smell, they look completely different from each other. Basil is suave and smooth and sharply witty, whilst mint has a toughness about it, a gritty, beardy, grizzled freshness that takes no prisoners. And some of them have a sense of humour. Jack-in-the-hedge always makes me laugh; wood sorrel is shy and peeps at you when you've passed by and bindweed is so damn cheeky. All of them are stronger than they look.

Monkshood, *aconitum napellus,* also known as Tiger's Bane, Wolfsbane, the Queen of Poisons, is a perennial and dies back to the ground in winter. All parts of the plant are deadly poisonous, and it has been used by hunters and murderers and healers throughout time. A poison arrow tipped with aconite will instantly paralyse your prey. Taken internally it is a sedative, reducing fever, slowing circulation, dramatically reducing pulse and blood pressure. Too much and the heart goes into arrest. The tipping point is hard to find, a secret only known to the few. Its flowers are pretty, blue and bell-shaped. In the summer they nod wisely beneath the hawthorn in my garden. I feel that they have much they could tell me if they chose. At this time of year they are only root.

When I woke I was on the bed with the coat laid over me like a blanket. Outside night had fallen. I put the coat on and went over to the window. It was a clear night and the sky was full of stars.

I heard the key turn in the door and behind me Meg came into the room. I could smell her. She smelled of iron and salt and hunger.

'I don't want to become one of you,' I said.

'It's too late,' she said. 'You need us now.'

'Not you. I don't need you.'

'That will change with the third bite,' she said. 'That will bind you to me.'

'I won't let you bite me,' I said.

'Yes you will. When the time comes you will beg me to bite you.'

She didn't come near me. She had a tray of food which she put on the floor beside the bed, and then she left.

I looked at the food. Beef broth, liver, crispy bacon, slices of pork, raw eggs in a glass. I didn't want to eat her food. I ran my finger across the surface of the liver and licked it. Then I picked up and took a bite. I chewed it and swallowed and it became a part of my body. I wanted more. I wanted to eat it all.

I emptied my pockets out onto the tray, scattering the meat with seed and stalk and root.

Belladonna, papaver, datura, digitalis, mandragora, henbane, convallaria.

Monkshood.

I went back to the window. Where was Peter? Did he think I didn't love him?

When I woke it was morning and the tray by my bed was empty. I didn't remember eating any of the food, but I felt comfortable. The knives had stopped. I was heavy and couldn't move, but it was pleasant. I lay on the sheets and felt the weight of my limbs pinning me down. My skin felt like satin and I could feel the spaces between my toes and my fingers. My breath sounded like a distant sea.

Outside the sky got lighter. Clouds had come in during the night and they hung grey and still. There was no breeze. The trees were silent as winter. Nothing worried me. I put my fingers into the pocket of my shirt, but there was nothing there.

After a long time Meg came in. She looked at the empty tray and she looked at me lying on the bed and she smiled.

'I ate everything,' I whispered.

I turned my head away from her. It was all the movement I could manage.

She knelt beside me and touched the smooth skin of my neck.

'It's time,' she said.

She leaned forward, then stopped. I heard her swear but I couldn't respond. My blood had stopped moving and it was no good to her. I was immobile. The last sound I heard was her indrawn hiss.

48. Peter

That night there was cloud and then there were stars. Peter ran underneath them. His legs moved and his hooves bounced on the springy turf. Bounding over boulders and stone walls, he became the movement. The night breathed into him and filled him until the stars were his eyes, his skin and hair as inconsequential as the dead grass heads that moved in the breeze beside the path. He grew to fill the night and his body was nothing except movement and the passage of air.

North of Settle he headed for Ingleborough, springing up the hillside, desperate for the touch of the sky on his face, the glimpse of the moon reflected in the sea at Morecambe Bay. He reached the top, panting and sweaty, and ran on past the trig point and the shelter to the edge of the plateau.

There were so many stars, so bright, each one stamped into the darkness. In front of him the land unfolded in dark layers like a tumbled duvet; beyond, the smooth glimmer of the distant sea.

He stood still. Nothing changed, except that the sweat dried on his skin. Cold crept into his coat, making the hairs stand on end to trap the warmth from his run. The moon moved across the sky, and clouds gathered to the south with a whisper of warmer air. He curled in the lee of the shelter and fell asleep.

Half an hour would be enough to rest his limbs. Not proper sleep, not deep rejuvenating sleep, just a pick-me-up. The equivalent of an energy bar.

His heart slowed and his muscles softened. He dreamed of Lauren. She was standing at an open window and curtains were blowing about her as though there was a gale. She stood perfectly still although her hair whipped about her face. She was wearing a white dress or nightgown that billowed and flapped, but she didn't seem to notice any of that. Her face didn't move. Peter realised that she couldn't see because she had no eyes.

She lifted her hand and put two fingers into her mouth. She whistled, once, twice, three times. The wind grew more fierce and the curtains beat against her body. Her hand dropped back to her side.

Peter woke. It was no good, he couldn't stay away. She was the other half of the equation; he didn't make sense without her. He had to talk to her, at least. He drank some water and ate chocolate from his pack, then set off towards the south.

At Malham Tarn someone started running beside him. He turned and looked at the dark figure, the strong legs and worn hooves.

'Dad! I thought you were in Greece.'

'We have to get back quickly.'

'But how did you find me?'

'We need to hurry. Lauren is in danger.'

Peter sighed. 'She's left me. She's seeing Richard, the boy from Hough Dean.'

His dad snorted at that, and cold air streamed visibly from his nostrils. 'Has he bitten her?'

Peter looked sideways at his father. His hair had grown longer while he was in Greece. His skin glowed from the winter sun and the hairs curled on his chest. Peter decided to ignore his question.

'I got into Cambridge.'

His dad looked sideways at him, and nodded. 'That's great, son.'

'How's my mother?'

His dad snorted impatiently. 'Your mother's fine. Has Richard bitten her?'

'Dad, that's kind of weird.'

'You know what he is?'

'What he is? Smart, good looking.'

'No, Peter. He is a child of Death.'

Light glimmered on the horizon, and the broad back of the Pennines waited for the day to begin. As they ran, Peter's dad talked. He told Peter about Meg Crossley, who had made a pact in the dark of night, about Richard and his lost Laura, and the sad story of three drowned boys. He told him about Frances Greenwood and her ill-fated trip to Paris, the return visit when Meg met Andy who refused her, and the havoc that was left in its wake.

'I remember Laura, his first girl. She was a lovely lass who wanted a straightforward life. Even as a human Richard was too intense for her. Lauren has a passing resemblance to her, physically.'

'And you think he's bitten her?'

'It sounds that way. Does she have a mark on her neck?'

Peter shook his head. Then he remembered finding her asleep in the woods, her hair heavy on her neck. When she woke and sat up she held it close, not letting it fall back, as though shy of what it revealed. She'd played with her hair a lot recently, pulling it forward from her face in a new way. She wasn't normally self-conscious.

'I feel like an idiot.'

'I should have warned you.'

When they arrived at Hough Dean the morning was bright and cold. The windows of the house reflected the sun, making it look blind with fire.

The doors were locked. There was no noise.

'Do you think they've gone?' Peter said quietly.

His dad shook his head. 'Meg's car is at the front.'

'There's a window, next to the kitchen. We could get in that way.'

He remembered the awful smell which had come out of the darkness. He'd smelled it even before Lauren, before she'd shot back out choking.

The window was smaller than he remembered.

His dad gave him a leg up and he wriggled through. That day with Lauren they'd been filled with the fear of something unknown, of danger hidden in the darkness, discovery in trespass. Today his fear had a name and a face.

He slithered in across the work surface and onto the white tiled floor of the kitchen, and sat still in the crumpled heap where he'd landed. He'd made a lot of noise, but he waited and there was no sound.

Outside the sun rose red and bright in the winter sky. He unfolded his limbs and, trying not to let his hooves clatter on the kitchen tiles, he went into the hallway. Light from the leaded windows fell in patterns across the floor and there was no trace of the dead smell he remembered. A bowl of pink roses sat on a table next to the door and their scent was light in the air.

The door had two locks and a chain. He slid the chain across and tried the door. If the Chubb was locked he would have to find the key. But it opened, letting in a slice of cold air and the smell of winter leaves.

His dad was waiting on the doorstep. As Peter opened the door to let him in, there was a loud hissing noise behind them, followed by a deep growl.

Meg Crossley was standing at the bottom of the stairs wearing a silk robe. Her lips were drawn back, baring her teeth, and her eyes were wild and bloodshot. Her hair was dishevelled and there were streaks of blood on her robe. She looked like a wild animal cornered in its lair.

Peter froze. His dad very slowly took a step towards her. The movement was smooth, his right hoof sliding in front of his left. She was still growling, deep in her throat, and Peter's dad kept his eyes fixed on her face.

Peter saw what she had in her hand and shouted.

'Dad, watch out!

Before the words had left his mouth she had covered the distance. She raised her hand and plunged the knife straight into his father's heart.

He fell with the force of the blow and she collapsed into a heap near the doorway, crouching like a child, hugging her knees and looking out from beneath her hair.

Peter rushed to his father's side. The knife was sticking out of his chest and blood was spreading across his skin, blackening the hairs. There was no pulse. His eyes were closed and his heart had stopped beating.

'You've killed him!'

She rocked on her heels and made a low keening noise. She didn't look at Peter.

He pulled the knife out of his father's body and it made a sucking sound. It was smeared with his blood. The sharp smell filled Peter's nostrils, seeped into his brain, coloured his vision.

Anger made him stupid. He leapt to his feet but she was ready. She seemed both to grow bigger and to lose substance. Though he stabbed at her the knife met no resistance. She growled again and when he ran at her she lifted him bodily and threw him into the yard. The door slammed shut.

The force of the fall shook his spine, but he jumped up and ran at the door. It was locked fast.

He sprinted to the back of the house, but the kitchen window was closed now. He banged on it with his fists, then with a piece of stone, but it didn't shatter.

Lauren was inside as well as his dad.

He circled the house, trying all the windows, the back door, even the coal hole. Everything was barred, shut fast, impenetrable. He stood on the lawn at the back of the house and shouted.

'Lauren!'

But the only sounds were the bleating of distant sheep, the caw of a crow in the field.

He looked up at the house. A window right at the top was open. There was no ivy, no clematis; nothing to climb up. He clambered onto a window ledge and tried to get a toehold between the stones of the wall, but his hooves slipped and he lost his balance.

He returned to the lawn. There had to be a way.

The house sat quiet in the glow of the morning sun. Frost glistened on the roof and a pair of jackdaws hopped about on the chimney top. Peter realised what he needed. Who he needed.

In the front yard a bike leaned against the door of the barn. It was green and new. Peter leapt into the saddle and pedalled as fast as he could down the track into Hawden.

49. Suky

They were having breakfast in bed when Peter started banging on the door.

Jimmy had just kissed her and said 'I'm going to take special care of you now, my love.'

She was kissing him back, and the plate of toast was in danger of falling on the floor when the noise began. It was terrific, a rain of blows, and Peter shouting: 'Suky! Suky! I need you! Please come. Suky!'

And then more banging, loud enough to wake the dead.

They looked at each other, then, without speaking, got out of the bed and pulled on their clothes.

Peter was incoherent at first. 'Suky, bring the rope. Only you can save her now.'

She fetched a glass of water and made him sip it. He tried again.

'It's Lauren, she's trapped at Hough Dean. If she's still alive that is. If she's still human.'

And he told them what he needed them to do.

Jimmy ran to get Andy and Mr Lion, as he thought there might be value in numbers. Suky collected what she needed, and started up the van, with Peter in the passenger seat. Andy and Mr Lion were waiting with Jimmy outside their house. As they set off, they passed Cassie walking up the road, and they stopped for her too.

'Did you see?' she said when they opened the door. 'Someone's dug up Lauren's herb garden. It's a complete mess, all the roots dug up to the surface.'

Peter was panicking. 'Hurry, hurry. Get in. We may be too late.'

They filled Cassie in, and Suky drove as fast as she could, the van rattling and shaking on the bumpy track.

Hough Dean seemed peaceful. It was hard to believe Peter's tales were true. There was no wind and no one about. Just a few jackdaws cawing on the roof and the fence posts.

Suky thought: surely it's impossible for Peter's dad to die. He can't, because he is life.

They leapt out of the van and ran round to the back garden.

Peter pointed at a tree.

'That one. If you climb up, then throw the rope over to the chimney, you could walk across. Once you're on the roof you can get to the window.'

There was no point in thinking about safety nets, rotten branches, slippery tiles. Or even the fact that last night she and Jimmy had agreed that Suky wouldn't be walking the wire any more. Not for a few months, anyway.

Jimmy squeezed her hand. 'I'll help you,' he said.

He'd told her about Meg and her enchantments, and about Steph too, and although there had been some shouting and a lot of tears, they'd come through. They'd weathered the storm.

Jimmy went up first with the rope tied round his middle, leaning down every now again to pull her up to the next branch. It was a tall tree, but she needed to get right up near the top to be level with the roof of the house.

It was different from climbing the ladder in a big top. This was more solid, more organic, less predictable. She had to concentrate on where to put the next foot. When they were high enough, Jimmy unwound the rope and tied it to the trunk of the tree. It was not so thick here as further down, but it was still strong. Strong enough, she hoped.

The other end of the rope was shaped into a lasso. Neither of them were rope throwers. Catching the chimney with the end of the rope was the weakest part of the plan.

Suky's throw was hopeless. Jimmy had a go and although he hit the roof of the house in vaguely the right part, the rope flopped uselessly against the tiles and slid to the ground.

This wasn't going to work.

Jimmy pulled the rope back in and tried again. This time he touched the chimney.

He started to haul the rope in again, and as he did so the tree shook. Mr Lion was leaping from branch to branch like a cat and in a moment he was beside them.

He took the rope between his paws, looked at the house, blinked, tossed his hair out of his eyes and threw the rope. It landed neatly around the chimney.

After that it was business as usual. Jimmy pulled the rope taut and retied the end around the trunk. Suky stood on the branch and tested it with her foot.

'Ok?' Jimmy whispered.

'Ok.'

She shifted her weight forward.

'I love you,' said Jimmy.

She stepped out onto the wire.

She'd walked longer ropes before, and higher ones too, but this was different. The tree swayed and the rope moved. Twice she had to stop and regain balance. She could feel tension from the watchers below. They had faith that she could do this, but if she slipped and fell, they wouldn't be able to catch her. She closed her eyes for a second, reopened them, thought of Lauren in the house, and carried on.

She was nearly there when the rope slipped. The lasso hadn't caught right at the bottom of the chimney and as she approached, her weight pulled it the last few inches. It was more than a wobble. She lost her balance and fell.

Someone screamed and she grabbed out for whatever she could that would save her. She caught the rope with one hand. The wrench on her shoulder was excruciating.

'Suky, grab the rope,' she heard someone call. She raised her other arm, felt for the rope with her finger tips until she had purchase and pulled herself until she was hanging from both hands. She was five feet from the house.

'You can do it Suky.' She looked back to the tree and Jimmy was smiling at her from among the branches and the dead leaves. He looked like a monkey and she laughed.

Suky swung her body back up, using the strength in her shoulders, until her feet were on the rope again, and slowly straightened to standing. The rope was even slacker now, but she quickly walked the last stretch, stepped onto the roof and grabbed hold of the chimney stack. She shuffled to the left until she reached the open window, then, resisting the temptation to look back at the others, she slipped through and into the room.

It was freezing in there. Even colder than outside. The walls were white, but the sun was on the other side of the house. A narrow bed was pushed against one wall, and on it a body, its face covered with a white sheet.

'Lauren?' she whispered.

She pulled back the sheet. Lauren's face was as white as the room, her skin smooth and unbroken. Suky felt for a pulse but there was nothing.

She put her hand over her mouth and stifled a cry. 'Lauren,' she whispered again.

Then she remembered the others waiting in the garden, and rushed out of the room and down the stairs. She'd been here before with Jimmy, when he started working here, and knew where the back door was. She didn't see anyone, didn't stop to look. She dashed from the foot of the stairs to the back of the house, pulled back the bolts and opened the door. The others knew straight away that something was wrong.

'Where is she?' Peter demanded.

Suky pointed upwards. 'The attic.' It came out as a whisper.

Peter dashed past her and up the stairs with Andy and Cassie close behind him.

Jimmy and Mr Lion looked at Suky and she shook her head. 'Too late,' she said.

Jimmy opened his mouth to speak, but there was a loud crash from the hallway.

Suky took his hand and together they ran through to the hall.

Meg was sitting on the floor near the bottom of the stairs. She was hugging her knees and rocking back and forth. Scattered across the carpet were shards of glass and pink roses. Water pooled on the wooden table and dripped onto the floor beneath.

At first that was all they saw. Then they saw Peter's dad. Suky was right: he was far from dead. He was coming forward from the shadows. His chest was bare and she could see the wound, but already it was healing. He looked taller, angrier than she had ever seen him before. She held on to Jimmy's arm.

Peter's dad didn't seem to notice them. He was looking into the corner to the left of the front door. They followed his gaze and there was something moving in the darkness.

'How dare you!' he roared. 'How dare you say you have come for me? You will never take me. You have no business in this place.'

'Ok, you've made your point.'

The voice was smooth and a little scared. Suky peered, but couldn't make anything out, it was so dark. Darker than it should have been, considering the sun was shining through the stained glass windows on either side of the door.

'I'll just take what's mine and go.'

Peter's dad roared again. 'There is nothing here of yours. Except her.' He waved his arm angrily towards Meg, who was whimpering. 'Take her if you must, but get out of here.'

Peter appeared on the stairs carrying Lauren's body in his arms, with Andy and Cassie close behind him.

'That one is mine,' said the voice.

There was a whistling and a rushing noise, and a chasm opened up across the hall: a tunnel of darkness, separating

Jimmy, Mr Lion and Suky from the others. It was fantastically cold, and as they breathed out their breath caught in the air and hung in frozen clouds that obscured the view.

Mr Lion swiped a paw impatiently and the ice tinkled to the floor.

Something was trying to wrench Lauren's body from Peter's arms.

'Leave her and go!' Peter's dad's voice was louder than any sound Suky had heard. The walls of the house trembled and the chandelier fell to the floor with an enormous crash.

The figure was still trying to get hold of Lauren.

'It's too late,' it said. 'She's been playing with my toys; she's already mine. You can thank *her* for that.'

Something lashed out at Meg and she gasped in pain.

The darkness laughed. It gathered and condensed into a human shape. It shimmered and moved, its limbs and its face moving in and out of focus. It left Lauren and came to crouch next to Meg, its arm around her shoulders. Its lips brushed against the side of her face. 'You should have obeyed the rules, my angel.' It let out a slow hiss and licked Meg's cheek with a black tongue. She shuddered. Andy started forward on the stairs but stopped when the creature turned and stared at him. '*She* thinks she's in love. She thinks she can use the daughter as bait for the father. She should have known she couldn't finish off what someone else had started.'

Meg started to sob.

'Now give her to me!' The creature hissed and lunged again at Peter, reaching out for Lauren's body.

'NO!'

The walls shook and pictures fell to the floor. A mirror shattered. There was a roar from both sides of the hall as Peter and his dad lowered their heads and charged.

Meg wailed and there was a clash of horns, a scream of pain. The darkness seemed to grow, spreading into all the corners of the hall. The rushing noise they'd heard earlier came again and grew louder like a roaring river; a continuous rolling of thunder. The blackness touched Suky's face, licked at the sides of her mouth. Peter shouted again, 'No, she isn't dead' and the ground began to shake. Lightning flickered outside. Suky buried her face in Jimmy's chest and they hugged each other. She thought the earth was going to crack open and swallow them all. It was the loudest noise she'd ever heard, and she was sure it was the end.

Then the darkness vanished and all was quiet.

The sun shone into the room through the windows, catching on the pieces of broken chandelier and filling the air with stars. Peter's dad was lying on his front near the stairs, breathing heavily. Peter was sitting on the carpet amongst the broken roses with Lauren still in his arms. Her eyes were closed and her face was white as lilies. She sighed.

Meg leapt to her feet and ran out of the house. Andy ran after her, but they heard the sound of her car slicing through the winter's air as she drove away down the lane, leaving him shouting her name.

50. Ali

I was drinking coffee in a café outside the Gare de Lyon in Paris. There were tables out on the street with people sitting at them, but I'd opted to sit inside in the warm. I had a table by the window, and I'd ordered double espresso along with a glass of water. The coffee was thick and bitter, and I nibbled a croissant to neutralise the taste in my mouth. I was wearing a new coat that I'd bought in London, and a black hat which I kept taking off as it made me feel self-conscious. On the table were some orange gloves I'd crocheted before I left England. My rucksack leaned against my feet. It contained all my worldly possessions.

It was nine thirty in the morning and outside on the street was the tail of the rush hour, with all the accompanying noise of honking horns and rushing feet, a blur of coats, high heels, and briefcases. I was in no rush. I had all the time in the world.

I slipped my hand inside the pocket of my coat and touched the postcard. The day lay before me, empty of plans. I smiled and sipped my coffee. I knew Richard was here in this city. The streets smelled of him and his kind.

Two weeks ago I'd woken up with him in the hotel in Leeds, the bed vast with rumpled white sheets. The curtains weren't completely closed and the sun shone softly into the room. My body felt heavy and warm and I stretched, opening all my capillaries and letting the blood rush through.

Richard was standing in the doorway wearing his shades, holding two mugs of coffee.

I slid out from under the sheets and walked naked to the window to close out the morning sun. I could feel him watching

me. When I turned round he removed his glasses. His irises were cloudy, his look unreadable.

'Hungry?' I asked him.

He nodded.

'Shall we get breakfast, or do you fancy coming back to bed for a bit?'

He grinned. 'Breakfast can wait,' he said.

The coffee went cold too. I didn't remember it was there until later, and by then Richard had gone.

We were lying with our bodies entwined, the sweat drying on our skin, when Richard's phone went off.

'Stuff that,' he said. But it went off again a minute later, and then again. The fourth time it rang he groaned and pulled himself away from me.

'I suppose I better find out who it is.'

He answered it and walked through to the lounge. When he returned he was wearing a shirt, and had his shoes in his hand.

'It's Meg. She's on her way back to Paris. She needs me.'

I turned over onto my front.

'Can't she go by herself?'

'Something's happened. She's in a bit of a state. I'm sorry Ali.'

He pulled on his jeans and I sat up in the bed with the sheet wound around me and watched him. When he had his jacket on he came and sat next to me on the bed. He held me close and the leather was cold on my skin. We kissed and he pushed the sheet away with his hands, ran his fingers down my back.

'Ali, why don't you come too?' he said into my hair.

I felt the tingling of my blood rising to the surface, filling the tiny vessels in the skin of my neck where his lips brushed. I could feel the pulse of desire beating through my body. I slid my hands inside his jacket and held him tight.

'Maybe later,' I said. 'There's something I need to do first.'

The train journey was long and complicated, with three changes. By the time I arrived it was already seven in the evening. I

wondered about finding a hotel for the night, but I didn't want to lose the momentum that had carried me this far. In the morning I might be tempted to scurry away.

So when I got off the train I walked the familiar route home. Not much had changed. Some of the hedges had grown higher and the hill up to our street seemed like a gentle slope after the hills of West Yorkshire. But I could almost believe the intervening years hadn't happened.

Our house was different. The outside had been painted and the garden was as neat as a pin. Mum must have got a new gardener, I thought. The curtains pulled across the window hung heavy and let through only the thinnest of slivers of light from inside. Even the door had a new knocker.

I still had a house key. I wondered what they'd do if I just let myself in. Maybe they'd changed the locks. I decided not to find out and rang the bell.

It was Emma who came to the door. She had pins in her mouth and a thread of cotton stuck to her jeans. We stared at each other and neither of us spoke.

Mum called through from the front room, 'Who is it, Emma?'

Emma removed the pins and coughed.

'Are they collecting for something?' Mum called. 'There's some change in the tin in the kitchen.'

Emma didn't take her eyes off me. 'Mum, it's Ali,' she said loudly.

There was the noise of something being knocked over, the sound of footsteps, then Mum appeared in the hall. She grabbed my arm and pulled me into the light. She looked at my face.

'My God! Ali,' she said. 'You've changed.'

Emma was sticking the pins into the sleeve of her jumper but she didn't stop looking at me.

'It's been four years,' she said. 'People change a lot in four years.'

Mum was still staring. 'Emma, she looks like your dad. Don't you think she looks like your dad?'

'She always did. She was always going to be the pretty one.'

I frowned. Emma was wearing a brown jumper and jeans. Her blond hair was scraped off her face into a ponytail and she wasn't wearing any make up. But she was still beautiful.

'We're making curtains,' she said, explaining the pins and the thread. 'Would you like some tea?'

Emma took me through to the kitchen and made tea for us all.

Mum said, 'Ali, I can't believe it. I didn't think we'd ever see you again,' and when Emma handed her a mug of tea she looked at it and said, 'I don't think I can drink this.'

I still hadn't said anything. Even though it was me that had surprised them, the shock of seeing their faces felt like a punch in the guts.

Emma handed a mug to me. 'It's good to see you, Ali,' she said. There were tears in her eyes and I thought: bloody hell, she means it.

The first words I managed to say were 'Where's Dad?'

Mum snorted. 'Where he always is, I'd think. Propping up the bar in the Boatman.'

'Dad kind of fell to pieces after... well, after you left.'

'Did he?'

'He felt guilty,' Emma's voice was like Gran's. 'I'd never realised that before. 'We all felt guilty. And when the police didn't find you, he became convinced that you were dead. He left his job, said that if working hadn't kept him away from his family you might still be alive. He started drinking.'

The tea was hot in my hands. I wanted to put it down but the table was too far away.

Nobody said anything.

I thought about what I'd been planning to say. This wasn't what I expected. I thought they'd still be the same, like the streets outside, the hedges which were just a little taller, a little neater.

'I stole money from you, when I left,' I said to Mum. 'I wanted to pay it back.'

'Pfft!' she waived her arm at me. 'Give it to a charity for the homeless. I can't drink this, I'm going to have a G and T. Will you two join me?'

Later I walked down to the Boatman. Dad wasn't propping up the bar; he was at a table with some friends laughing and making jokes. He'd gone grey and was wearing jeans and a t-shirt. I only ever remembered seeing him in a suit. I stood at the bar and ordered a drink, and after a few minutes he saw me. He went very still.

His friends hadn't noticed and they carried on with their conversation. He excused himself and walked over to me at the bar. We stood facing each other.

'Ali?' he said.

'Dad.'

Then he hugged me and he smelled of beer and cigarettes, and his stubble was rough against my cheek and I could hardly breathe because my nose was squashed against his shoulder, but it was the best hug he'd given me since forever. We were both crying.

'Ali,' he said, over and over again.

I asked him if he'd come to Paris with me. All those years of being stuck in an office, and then in a bar, I said it was time to travel, to see the world. Emma and Mum had set up a business together as interior designers and it was thriving. They would be fine without him. They could come out and meet us for a holiday in Barcelona or Goa or Marrakesh. He squeezed my hand and said maybe.

I don't think he was ready to stand without the support of a bar.

I stayed with them for two weeks.

In the second week I got the postcard from Richard. He could have emailed. Or texted. But Richard is still attached to the old ways of doing things. The postcard had a picture of the Eiffel Tower on the front, and on the back a note: *Marriott, Champs-Élysées, I'll wait for you. Richard xx.*

I hadn't replied.

I put the black hat back on my head. I could smell his blood, and his nearness opened my pores, made me feel the life coursing through my body. I felt electric. I felt like singing.

I left the café and walked into the station. The departure board went on forever, listing trains to destinations whose names carried the taste of pistachios, the smell of frankincense, the slippery coolness of freshly caught fish and the heat of desert sand. I could go to any of these places. I could walk up to the kiosk right now and buy a ticket to wherever I liked.

I touched the card in my pocket again. The corners were soft from over-handling. I could go anywhere I liked, but I didn't have to go alone unless I wanted to.

51. Peter

Lauren was sleeping. She was as pale as milk, her lips almost as white as her face, but she was breathing and a vein throbbed blue in her temple. The mark on her neck looked like a bruise. She seemed very young. Cassie sat on a chair and Peter sat on the edge of the bed. There'd been so much poison in her blood they hadn't known if she would make it.

'You go and get a cup of tea,' Cassie said. 'You've been here all night. I'll watch for a while.'

In the kitchen Mr Lion had baked biscuits. He, Jimmy and Suky were eating them at the table and they pulled up a chair for Peter.

'You should get some rest,' said Suky.

There was nothing they could do now, except give her body time to recover. Andy and Peter had sat through the night, but Andy had gone to bed once the crisis was over. Peter was awake and edgy. He didn't want to sleep.

'Get some sugar in you, lad,' said Mr Lion. 'It'll do in lieu of sleep today.'

Jimmy said, 'I've got an appointment at the barbers. You want to come?'

Peter touched his head. His hair had grown long, covering his horns and ears. It was silky and soft and his skull itched.

'Why the hell not?' he said.

The barber trimmed Peter's hair so the horns showed and he cut round above his ears. When he left he could feel fresh air on his neck and cold touched the base of his horns.

'Looks cool,' said Jimmy.

Six months later

52. Mr Lion

Mr Lion swallowed and put the empty beer glass on the bar.

'Another?' asked the barmaid.

'Why not? One more, eh Beauty, then we'll go home and get some food.'

The barmaid pulled him a pint and he lifted it to his nose.

'Hello.' Steph was sitting on the next bar stool, three feet away.

He smiled. 'Hello.'

'I like your new hairdo. Very glam.'

Mr Lion put his hand up to his mane.

'This is how it goes if I don't straighten it. Lauren's taken her straighteners with her.'

'Has Andy gone too?'

'He's gone off travelling on his own. Lauren's gone to Greece with Peter and his dad.'

'It must be strange with them all away.'

'Just me and Beauty. It's lonely, after all these years being part of a family.'

'Oh Mr Lion.' Steph shuffled her stool nearer. 'They'll be back before you know it.'

Mr Lion sipped at his beer. 'I miss them. I even miss the things that annoy me. Lauren's used cotton wool pads left on the side of the sink. Milk left out of the fridge.'

'Everything's predictable when you live on your own.'

They lapsed into silence and drank their drinks: hers a pint of Guinness, his a Wily Badger Brown Ale.

'What about you?' she asked after a few minutes. 'Has there ever been anyone for you?'

'What, a girl?'

'Someone special.'

'No.' Mr Lion touched his hair, which was the colour of ripe plums. 'No, not really.'

'But almost.'

'Well, I thought so.'

'Tell me.'

Mr Lion coughed a little. 'You don't want to hear about all that. I was a fool.'

'Yes I do. I'll buy you a drink.'

Steph waved the barmaid over and ordered two more pints. They watched as she pulled them, the Guinness running slowly through the tap, the ale from the pump. She placed them on the bar and beer ran down the sides of the glasses.

'What happened? Who was she?'

'We met on the internet.'

'When?'

'Ten years ago. It wasn't the thing it is now, internet dating. We weren't even on a dating site. It was a site for cooks to get tips from one another, share advice and so on. My username was Goldenpaws. You could put up a picture of yourself.'

'Was she pretty?'

'She was gorgeous. Blonde and voluptuous. She didn't look like a cook.'

'What was her name?'

'Autumn.'

'Odd name.'

'She'd chosen it herself. I think she used it in real life, not just on the internet.'

'And you got on well?'

'Our conversations about griddle pans and kneading times got very flirtatious. And when we discovered the private messaging function, they got downright dirty.'

'Did you meet?'

'Eventually. The internet thing went on for a long time. We'd talk and talk, and sometimes we kind of acted, you know, imagining we were together. I thought about her all the time and she said the same.' Mr Lion pushed his mane back from his face. 'So we agreed to meet.'

'And...?'

'A disaster. She thought my picture was just for the internet. When she saw me she screamed. She had hysterics, called me a freak. She didn't want my kind of love.'

Steph touched him on the arm and he looked at her.

'Everyone's not like that,' she said. 'Some girls like something a bit different. Some even prefer it.'

'Really?'

She looked into his eyes. 'Yes, really.'

She turned back to her beer and he began to fiddle with his mane.

'You can borrow my straighteners if you want,' she said. 'I hardly ever use them.'

'Could I?'

'I'll pop them round later if you like. If you're in.'

'I'm going home after this one.' He looked across at her. She was draining her pint. 'I was going to make a bite to eat. It's a bit sad cooking for one, I don't suppose you'd like to...?'

Steph beamed. 'I'd love to.'

He finished his pint and stood up. 'Well, pop round when you're ready.'

'I'll just go home and get the straighteners.'

They parted outside the White Horse, touching hands briefly before going their separate ways.

'You have a lovely voice, Mr Lion,' she said.

Mr Lion's Playlist

1   Shy Guy – The Uptights
2   The Who Who Song – Jackie Wilson
3   Sally Go Round the Roses – Jaynetts
4   You've got Your Mind on Other Things – Beverly Ann
5   You Want to Change Me – Bobby Hebb
6   Foolish Me – Jo Ann Garrett
7   He's So Fine – The Chiffons
8   Stranger in My Arms – Lynn Randall
9   You've Been Gone Too Long – Ann Sexton
10 Don't You Leave Me Baby – Ray Gant
11 Hit and Run – Rose Batiste
12 Lonely Boy – Brenda Holloway
13 Don't Be Sore At Me – The Parliaments
14 Sweet Talkin' Guy – The Chiffons
15 Oh No Not My Baby – Maxine Brown
16 I Want To Give You Tomorrow – Benny Troy
17 Temptation is Calling My Name – Lee David
18 I'll Keep Holding On – The Marvelettes
19 Don't Pity Me – Sue Lynn
20 Mr Soul Satisfaction – Timmy Willis
21 There's a Ghost In My House – R. Dean Taylor
22 I Can't Help Myself – The Gems
23 I Go To Pieces – Gerri Granger
24 My Girl – The Temptations
25 There's a Pain In My Heart – The Poppies
26 I'm Gonna Run Away From You – Tami Lynn
27 He Was Really Saying Something – The Velvelettes
28 This Time I'm Loving You – Venicia Wilson
29 Nowhere To Run – Martha Reeves and the Vandellas

Acknowledgments

I would like to thank the fantastic team at Bluemoose: Hetha Duffy, Kevin Duffy, Janet Oosthuysen, Lin Webb and Diana Cooper Brady for their editorial skills and dedication. I would like to give a special thank you to Alison Taft, James Nash and Tom Palmer, who read this novel in stages at it was written – your feedback is always invaluable; to Helen Meller, Izzy Turner and Rachel Connor, who read early drafts and helped point me in the right direction; and to Poppy Turner for her eagle eyes. I would like to thank Charlotte Mellor Meecham and Megan Blunn for their wonderful cover design, and for trekking up a muddy clough in pouring rain in search of photos. Thank you to Henrietta Bond for coaching help after I'd dismantled the novel and didn't know how to put it back together; also to Andy Garner, Caroline Wright and Peter Baber for their feedback. Thank you to my son, Wilf, for putting up with a mother who, though present in body, is often in another world. And finally a huge thank you to my wonderful husband, Johnny Turner, for his support and encouragement, always.